THE
DOOR
OF THE *Heart*

Diana Finfrock Farrar

authorHOUSE®

AuthorHouse™
1663 Liberty Drive
Bloomington, IN 47403
www.authorhouse.com
Phone: 1-800-839-8640

Although based upon actual events and issues faced during 2012-2013, this is a work of fiction. Names, characters, places, and incidents are the products of the author's imagination or are used fictitiously. Any resemblance to persons, living or dead, is entirely coincidental.

Published by AuthorHouse 03/25/2014

ISBN: 978-1-4918-7124-9 (sc)
ISBN: 978-1-4918-7123-2 (hc)
ISBN: 978-1-4918-7122-5 (e)

Library of Congress Control Number: 2014904366

This book is printed on acid-free paper.

CONTENTS

ACKNOWLEDGMENTS

First and foremost, I must acknowledge my faith. For it has been through my Christian faith that I first heard God's call to make a difference. It was made clear to me, in numerous ways throughout the process of writing this work, that I had a story to tell and that He believed I must tell it.

I extend my deepest gratitude to Carol Toombs — my Collaborator, Big Sister and Bookend! Her guidance, both literary and spiritually, was an invaluable gift that I believe has helped make *The Door of the Heart* a work of significance.

I am also deeply indebted to Joyce Sáenz Harris, my editor, who worked quickly and deftly and still managed to respect my writer's voice. She *trimmed the fat without losing any flavor* and was instrumental in sharing the story with others.

I owe so much to my early readers who helped find my mishaps and straighten the bent places toward better understanding — Charlotte Moellering, Marilyn Stratmann, David Finfrock, Shari Finfrock, Jean Nash Johnson, Melanie Rogers and Rebecca Farrar.

I offer my profound appreciation to those whose insights helped me better understand and develop my characters as I was getting to know them myself: Robert Reed, David Miller, Kyle Farrar, Brett Farrar, Jayden Moellering, Jade Malay and Marci Stiles. I also extend an unexpected thank you to the numerous Dallas area writers of letters-to-the editor who helped provide much of the vitriol that I could not have created myself.

And I thank those who gave me permission to liberally sprinkle their own previously written words into the mouths of certain characters:

- *Gay Christian 101* by Rick Brentlinger @ www.gaychristian101.com
- *Lessons from a Gay Couple,* an article by Elizabeth Rose

But most assuredly, I reserve the greatest appreciation for my partner in love and in life — Charlotte Moellering. She was obliged to travel this year-long journey with me, like it or not. And it certainly didn't prove to be the type of travel that either of us is accustomed to! She accepted my periods of obsessiveness as well as absentmindedness, all with a grace, patience and love for which I am extremely grateful. You are my heart. I love you.

DEDICATIONS

To Charlotte Moellering — my partner in life and in love

And to my parents — Mama & Papa Frock,
who taught me there is never a wrong time to seek justice

Every time you stand up for an ideal, you send forth a tiny ripple of hope.
— Robert F. Kennedy

FOREWARD

Texas is a place rich in tradition, where long-standing values of family, faith, hospitality, and community run as deeply as the roots of the live oak boring into the clay soil. And that is where this story finds us, looking deep into the human heart and its capabilities for love, for hatred, and for change.

No one wants to suffer the penalties that come from living divided no more.
But there can be no greater suffering than living a life-long lie.
— Parker Palmer

Chapter 1

BOTH SIDES OF HUMANITY

They may as well have gunned him down. The pain he experienced as the crowd gathered round him was every bit as real as if they had shot him in the gut. Or in the heart. Actually, that would have been preferable to enduring this. They were pointing and laughing. They were calling him terrible names. And it was only the third day of school.

Dr. Price had gotten there quickly and Jamie had held it together until the door had closed behind them and Dr. Price had rested his arm gently on his shoulder. But with that touch, so full of compassion, and within the safety of the principal's office, he had fallen apart. Words left unspoken for so long had tumbled out amidst his tears.

"You'd think I'd be used to it by now ..." He was angry. Angry about what those guys had done, angry at the crowd's reaction, but most of all, angry at himself for letting it get to him.

"But they just won't leave me alone. They've been doing this for a long time and I'm tired of it. I'm tired of being teased, and threatened, and shoved into walls — or toilet seats." He had to pause to choke back the sobs that threatened to engulf him at that memory.

"They just can't stand that I'm different from them.

"Sometimes they push me so far I just want to slug 'em and call them names. You know? Become the bully myself." He doubled over and slugged his own thighs instead, then pressed his balled fists hard against his streaming eyes. But the tears came anyway and Dr. Price let them come.

"But I know I can never do that … because I know how it feels." He wiped his nose with the back of his hand, continuing to stare at his knees.

He wished with all his heart that he wouldn't feel anything anymore, but he did.

"Crazy, but the teachers all think these guys are my friends, when really, my only 'friends,' are probably the kids who don't want to be around me at all. But that's my fault, I guess, 'cause I've never told anyone about any of this before."

He had always thought he could protect his mom and dad, and his little sister, with his silence. He had never wanted them to be a part of this: his embarrassment; his shame; his self-hatred. It had always been his: his secret and his responsibility. Until today. He searched his principal's eyes, seeking their comfort — maybe even their protection — before he continued.

"They've threatened to kill me if I do. I don't think they'd really go that far, but I've never wanted to give 'em the chance.

He looked out the large window of Dr. Price's office, attempting to regain composure. "They're right about one thing, though. I don't belong here." Never had that felt so true as it did today. Jamie O'Dell wished with all his heart that he could be anywhere other than at Westmont High.

Today, they had taped a big "G" over the "R" on his Devil Rays ball cap, and someone had scrawled "is gay" in hot-pink puff paint just under his name on the back of his jersey. Both had been exhibited on a crude manikin — effeminate features drawn on a canvas face, head and jersey hung on a broomstick, sneakers dangling below the jersey from black net pantyhose. A baseball bat, placed just under the shoes, sported a sign, "FAG." And it had all been on display outside the gym for almost an hour before being found and immediately taken down by one of the coaches.

It was just too big. Now everybody knew, because they had all seen it. The damage had been done.

And this time he was talking.

Ed Sloan gripped his highball as if to squeeze the comfort he desired right out of the glass. He was incapable of relaxing despite the lavish comfort of the room. And his ruddy complexion was not due to the afternoon heat outside.

"That's the way I see it, Ed." Bill Pritchett swirled the amber liquid in his glass, careful not to meet the commissioner's eye. He was no match for the commanding personality sitting opposite him, especially when Ed Sloan was as enraged as he was this afternoon. Bill's level head and steady demeanor had been the perfect foil to Sloan's zeal over the years, and if their decades-old partnership had taught him anything, it had taught him that this was a time when he needed to exercise his diplomatic skills.

The incident had encroached on their perfect day — opening day of dove season — and they now sat, unable to shake the nagging tension that stalked them. It was palpable still.

"Well, I just can't accept that, Pritchett. I certainly don't intend to let my boy, or the others for that matter, take the fall for that O'Dell kid without a fight." And Commissioner Sloan knew how to fight. He was a proud and principled man whose steely gray eyes could garner the strength of an ally or pierce to the core a vulnerable opponent. His commanding baritone often overpowered even the most brilliant of colleagues, and he knew how to utilize his size and position to prove his point, make the sale, or get the vote. Standing nearly six foot four, he could tower over most adversaries, and when challenged he could intimidate with a lift of his arrogant brow or a thrust of his aggressive jaw.

"Well, the truth is, Ed," Bill persevered, "this is an uncommon situation. Even you can admit that, can't you?"

Sloan did not reply, but instead helped himself to another glass of whiskey while the portraits of former statesman, esteemed and otherwise, watched the two sparring friends from gilded frames hung high on the walls that surrounded them.

"Bella McLoughlin from News 25 wants another interview and I got a call yesterday from the people at *Daybreak Austin*. They want you to appear on their local morning show. Ed, times are changing and this may be a time where you can't just dig in your heels and try to bellow louder than everyone else to make this go away. You've got to show some compassion here, friend."

Ed took another swig, the thought of more negative media attention burning his insides as much as the stout liquor in his gut. *How dare they turn on him like this!*

He was admired by his public. They listened to what he had to say. They followed his lead. They looked up to him. His message hadn't changed. So why had they? Ed was incensed at the betrayal. He had basked in the respect that his office and the media attention had brought him, and he had preened in the adoring spotlight, spreading his feathers frequently and without restraint at every opportunity. He took pride in the fact that his admirers saw in him a morally right compass and followed his trumpeting call to righteousness, unquestioningly. But now his feathers were being tarred.

"I know you don't want to see your kid punished like this, but you've got to think about how this incident is playing out in the public eye." As Sloan's campaign manager, Bill Pritchett thought about public perception a lot.

"Times may be changing, dammit, but I don't intend to." Ed set the decanter down with a force that commanded Bill's attention. "All I can say is that the O'Dell boy asked for it. He's a fucking pervert. And Michael was just protecting himself from that kind of behavior. Hell, the whole school ought to be grateful to Michael for standing up for Christian principles!"

It was quiet in the room now, save for the ticking of the pendulum housed in the great grandfather clock and the tinkling of ice in the men's glasses.

"Okay, Ed, let's go over the details again. Give me everything exactly as it happened. Maybe I can think of something to do." Pritchett hoped this tactic would defuse the negative energy fueling his friend's resistance to reason.

Coverage of the incident was still going strong in the local paper, but now there was increasing interest in this story from surrounding towns. The worship of Texas high school football and its standout players began early, and Michael Sloan was a promising young sophomore quarterback and kicker, the pride and joy of his powerful father. His popularity as a talented player, coupled with his father's prestigious position, made Michael's suspension from the team an issue the media had pounced upon, as much as, so it seemed, the initial reason for the suspension.

While rushing to put its own stamp on the issue, the media was running the story ad nauseum, creating a sideshow of polarization. It began as the *Temple Daily Telegram*, the *Killeen Daily Herald* and the *Waco Tribune-Herald* blamed the potential downfall of the Devil Rays football season on the unfair punishment of those rightly wanting to defend traditional morality and then editorialized on the obvious dangers that homosexuality in a community's midst can bring. That caught the attention of the more progressive urban communities, like Austin, which countered with their own headlines: "BIGOTRY DOES NOT BELONG!" "COMMISSIONER ATTACKS GAY TEEN!" and "WHOSE SIDE IS GOD ON?" In pandering to their audience's prevailing views, both sides obviously pushed their own agendas.

Pritchett certainly didn't relish seeing Ed's head placed upon this media circus platter, but the Land Commissioner's rigidity was making that inevitability difficult to avoid. Continuing to dodge the stream of inquiries and interview requests from reporters was just as damaging as encouraging Ed to continue speaking publicly. His raw emotions had gotten the better of him in his last encounter with a camera, and the media had run with it.

"The best players should be allowed to play the game, period," Ed had declared. "Our schools and communities deserve that. If every red-blooded American man, woman and child does not stand up and shout the gays back down into their place right now, then none of us will be able to avoid the depravity they will bring on us all! It has already begun with these unjust suspensions right here, and now is the time to take charge."

Energized and emboldened by the roar of his approving constituents, the Commissioner crossed the line.

"We got Osama for cryin' out loud. Surely we can contain this threat which is every bit as serious to the continuation of American culture as we know it!"

The sound bite had gone viral. And the next morning's headlines had read, "TEXAS COMMISSIONER EQUATES HOMOSEXUALITY WITH TERRORIST THREAT."

And if this wave continued building strength, it had the potential to wipe out Ed's reputation and possibly even his career. Pritchett grimaced when remembering Clayton Williams' comment, made decades ago, equating cold wet weather having spoiled a scheduled campaign event to being raped. The Texas gubernatorial candidate had stated that "if it is inevitable, just relax and enjoy it." That one thoughtless statement had taken off like wildfire across the dry Texas prairie and Williams had been reduced to political ash — an idiot, a caricature of chauvinism. He had been destroyed in the polls. Ed's recent declarations resounded in Pritchett's head, bringing back the memory of news programs from his youth: grainy black-and-white visions of fire hoses trained on Negroes in Selma and Montgomery.

The stately clock chimed the quarter hour. "I've told you before, Pritchett, but I'm happy to oblige if it amuses you," said Sloan, as he pushed himself back into the chair even further, more than ready to embark on this story of injustice yet again.

Pritchett knew the details. Ed had needed to vent about them all morning long. Pritchett had actually encouraged Ed to talk, hoping it would cool his emotions, which were still as hot as this summer afternoon. They had perched upon faded green stools, squinted into the early morning sun, and pondered their options. "Gay people are part of the fabric of our society," he had told Ed. "You're gonna have to come out and say something like that to diffuse your earlier comments." Sloan's response had not been positive. "I refuse to be a political and religious boomerang changing direction on the whims of public opinion. I've got principles, dammit!" He had sprung from his stool, turning it over, and had begun pacing the riverbank, his long strides resembling the rhythmic pounding of a hammer driving in a nail.

Pritchett had decided to bide his time. And the scotch was now mellowing Ed's temper.

"So, I get a call from the school principal. And he says I have to get up there right away, that Michael had gotten into a little trouble. I asked, 'What kind of trouble?' I was already on the road to Austin and had a shitload of work to do for the Land Commission. 'Well,' he says, 'seems Michael had played a prank on another kid'..."

"Ed, a prank? Really? I doubt that's what Price called it. Those boys did something that could be considered a hate crime these days." *That's the trouble with this world today*, thought Bill. *Too many people confuse pranks with abuse. Pranks are done in innocent fun and no one is hurt. But these boys intended to hurt.*

Sloan's son and several of the other athletes had done a masterful job of humiliating Jamie O'Dell in front of the whole school. And those who had seen it, almost the entire student body, became unrelenting in their baiting. Seemingly, the effigy had given everyone permission to be cruel. Even those who had never before had a disparaging thought about Jamie, much less a derogatory remark, now joined in the "fun."

"A hate crime? Come on, Bill, all they did was make a dummy with his jersey number on it and put it in front of the school." Then chuckling to himself, Sloan continued, "Honestly, I think it was pretty clever. Devil Gays instead of Devil Rays? And the eyelashes and lipstick were nice touches, too."

"I can see it now," said Bill gesturing with his hands as if reading a headline. "Texas Land Commissioner Tarred and Feathered." He leaned forward, looking directly at his friend, and punctuated every phrase with a nod of his head. "By his constituents — in front of the Capitol building — but members of the Human Rights Campaign call it just a 'prank.'"

Sloan eyed his friend from over the rim of his glass. He had gotten the point. He dismissed the sarcastic tone of his campaign manager with a wave of his hand, and sighed. "It was only up there for less than an hour, Pritchett."

"Ed, this is serious stuff!" Bill leaned in even further to press the point. "What they did was more than just inappropriate. It was purposefully done to hurt and shame — clearly to punish Jamie. How do you consider we get everyone to buy into this 'self-defense of morality' route that you are suggesting? Jamie didn't do anything. Help me out, here."

Sloan's expression turned grave. Determined to drive his point home, he squared his shoulders and began in his deepest, most resonant voice of authority.

"Bill, homosexuality is not the way God planned it!" He raised his arms dramatically to the sky, in an effort to enlist heaven's help for his cause. "We responsible adults, particularly those of us who honor God through our public service, should not allow boys like that to interact with other kids. It just isn't safe. If we give in now, what is next? Condoning pornography at school? Asking us to be tolerant and understanding of campus pedophiles? Most of them don't even shave yet, for God's sake."

Ed dropped his bravado momentarily, "Kids are impressionable at that age. Don't want them getting the wrong ideas, you know." He took another mouthful of scotch to fortify himself and held it in his bulging cheeks before swallowing with a frown. "Hell, even the Boy Scouts are being called to compromise their morals on this one. A good scout pledges to keep himself morally straight, but does anyone else besides me see the irony in a gay kid attempting that same oath?" Ed laughed loudly at his own joke.

"Okay." Bill reversed his tactics. "I'm the first to admit that I don't know much about homosexuality, but I don't think it's reasonable to equate being gay to being a pedophile. If that were the case, we should both be considered rapists simply because we prefer women."

"Good God, Pritchett!"

"And I think you're reaching a little too far with the morally straight definition, too. I'm just asking you to think for a minute before you consider saying those kinds of things in a public forum."

"Bill, whose side are you on?"

"Look, Ed, I'm not 'on a side'. I'm just trying to help you get out of this mess with the least amount of damage. I can't promise 'a fix' when public opinion goes against you. And 'the public' is much larger than this little corner of Texas. You got crucified the last time you talked to a reporter, and we can't let that happen again or this will continue to dog you for the whole football season." Pritchett took a deep breath and exhaled slowly. "Maybe much longer. We have to use common sense on this and not resort to inflammatory language that will only make things worse. I understand you want to protect your son, but you have to be careful not to vilify the victim in your efforts. That's all I'm saying."

Ed let out an audible groan over this last statement. "The *victim*, Pritchett? Michael, Phillip and Denny are the only victims here, and that's only if you don't count the whole goddamn school and surrounding community, too. Everyone's being affected by this circus they call justice here except the initiator." He put his glass down on the chair-side table and studied it deeply, eager to describe the moral battle that was at hand. "Hell, they are the ones who got suspended from the football team and are being sent to the alternative school for the rest of the year, just for upholding their values — the values of all of us. While the O'Dell kid is still free to…"

"And they'll be damn lucky if Patrick O'Dell doesn't press charges, or they could be going somewhere else for even longer, Ed. I know you feel strongly about this, but we have to …"

At this, the door opened and Ed's wife entered the room.

"Wow, you boys really outdid yourselves this morning. I'll wrap your doves in bacon if you'll fire up the grill, Ed. And, Bill, would you like to call Ginny and have dinner with us? We'll have plenty."

Tammy Sloan's spritely build and energetic personality typically brought a graceful agility that complimented her role of politician's wife. But today, her energy was a well-practiced habit she had put on. Nothing about the past week had been ordinary. This crisis had taken a toll on the whole family, and her share of the burden had been extraordinary. Both the men in her life had been defamed, and the ramifications of that were infecting her entire family. How to be everything to everyone who needed her so?

Even so, she carried herself with an air of self-confidence. Raised in Highland Park, an old-money area of Dallas, Tammy had been perfectly prepared to catch the eye of an upwardly mobile young man. And Ed had sought her out immediately when they first met as freshmen at Southern Methodist University, charming her shamelessly to win her heart and then laying claim to her throughout their college careers. Her flowing locks of auburn hair and sunny disposition, her bright eyes and heavy lashes, had marked her out from the other girls — yet she had been refreshingly unaware of the magnetism she possessed. She was the beauty that complimented his brawn, the polish that gave his veneer a shine.

But underneath her vivacious, agreeable personality lay inner strengths, as yet untested and even unimagined. An unexpected resilience had allowed her to bend over the years, not only under the pressures of a public life, but also within her own marriage. She had learned how not to break — a necessary trait to contend with her formidable husband of almost twenty-two years.

"Thanks, Tam, but I think we'll have to pass this time." Pritchett was ready to leave Ed and his misery behind for the evening. "Would you mind sending her your recipe, though? She doesn't quite know what to do when I bring home a bunch of wild game."

"No problem, I'll send her an email." She moved her husband's feet and sat down on the ottoman with a sigh. "So are you helping him sort this whole thing out, Bill?"

"What he is trying to do is talk me into compromising my integrity, is more like it," Ed said, as he settled back in his comfortable chair.

"Oh Ed," she sighed. She shook her head and affectionately patted Ed's leg.

"Tam, you've got to get him to understand the difference between affirming homosexuality and upholding basic human rights. There really is a difference if you're willing to look at it that way."

"I think you have a better chance of convincing him of that than I do. How do you think our marriage has made it this long?" And she gave a little laugh.

"We have to do this, Ed." Bill pursued. "Think of your reputation and how your re-election could be affected. He turned to include Tammy in appreciation of her pain. "I know you're both upset about the punishment that Dr. Price handed down on the boys. But ..." now he addressed Ed directly, "You have to acknowledge your hurt, accept it and move on. You can't continue to blame Jamie for something the other kids did."

"That's about enough, Pritchett," rumbled Sloan.

Tammy recognized the edge in his voice and what it presaged. In this mood, Ed would brook no contradiction. Yet she had strong feelings of her own. "Ed, you're not going to want to hear this, but

I think Bill may be right. The truth is, Michael did do something wrong, and we all have to accept the consequences that come with that. Otherwise, he will never learn accountability. And worst of all, he will believe that we condone such cruelty."

Sloan's eyes widened, "Condone? Tam, I *support* what he did. What Michael did was virtuous! He was standing up for his beliefs — just like we taught him."

Tammy felt the familiar knot in her stomach. He could squelch her with a look. Or a word. And he had done both so many times in the last few years. Ed hadn't always been so domineering, so hard. How had it come to this?

"How can you agree with punishing that?" Ed bored into her open, trusting eyes with his own squinting malevolence. "If that gay kid would have just stayed locked up in his damn closet, we wouldn't be going through any of this right now! Those kinds of people have a place they belong, and it isn't with the rest of us God-fearing Christians." He continued muttering to himself as he settled back down into his chair and threw back the last of the whiskey in his glass.

"I agree that standing up for your beliefs is a good thing, Ed, but Michael and his friends crossed a line."

"Crossed a line?" Ed sputtered and hurled himself forward, planting his hands on the ottoman where she sat.

"Oh Ed, try to calm down," she said. "You know I hurt for Michael as much as you do, and I hate to see him in so much pain. He loves football, and his buddies on the team mean so much to him." She shook her head, attempting to erase the memory of Michael's stricken face when told he would be suspended, and therefore considered ineligible for football, as well as any other extracurricular activities for the remainder of the school year. "And then there's the embarrassment caused by the press. They've turned him into some kind of a monster, forgetting that he, too, is nothing but a child. But even so, as much as I hate saying it about our own son, Michael and the others were wrong."

"What? Et tu, Brute?" Ed addressed his wife, dismissing her with his snarly sarcasm.

Yes … me, too, Ed, I'm afraid. She knew better than to share those thoughts out loud. Instead, she tuned out his rampaging, and followed her own thoughts. She thought first of Jamie, and how terribly he must be hurting, and then she thought of his mother. She saw Marcie O'Dell's face. She saw it every morning when she dropped Kelly off at school. Mrs. O'Dell was there, without fail, every day dropping her own son off. Tammy tried to imagine how hard that would be for a mother, letting her son out of her protective circle, when she knew what he would face that day at school. And her heart went out to her. She reached toward the lamp table and plucked a tissue out of the bronze plated holder. Her eyes began to fill with tears as she reflected on Mrs. O'Dell's pain, and on her own pain — on every mother's pain for that matter — when they are forced to become helpless witnesses to the suffering of their children.

As a volunteer at the hospital, she had seen the face of a mother whose child had received a deadly diagnosis. Unfortunately, she was much too familiar with that expression, and it was exactly the face she saw each time she encountered Marcie O'Dell. It made her think. *What diagnosis had the community given Jamie?* Abomination! — they had called him 'abomination'! *What a terrible thing to call a child!* She reflected on this new insight and what such judgment inevitably brings: the slow death of a human heart as it withers in the white heat of hatred. And then she caught herself. *They… if I'm really honest, I have to say, we.* And that hurt. How had she participated in this collaborative judgment? Who was really guilty? The one who received mistreatment, as Ed would want her to believe? The one who inflicted the injury? Or the one who observed abuse, but did nothing in response? And then it came to her.

And so, she spoke up again, just as Ed had proclaimed, "… and that's all there is to it."

"No, Ed, that is not all. There is much, much more. I've been thinking." Her voice was surprisingly strong. "You are both parents, and so am I. So which one of us could stand to witness our own children being treated like we've been treating Jamie? Could you stand to have Greg treated this way, Bill? Ed, can you feel, even for a moment, what Michael must be feeling? Without allowing his pain to be your own? Just think of Michael for a minute. He has lost his dreams … and he must be humiliated being stuck there in the alternative center … and having to read what's being written about him. I'm his mother, and I can't stand it. And I can't imagine what Marcie O'Dell is going through watching her son suffer. These are children, Ed... Bill..." And she looked each man in the eye. "So, tell me, how does a mother reconcile herself with that?"

"For God's sake, Tammy, what has all that got to do with the price of tea in China?" Ed looked over at Bill and shook his head conspiratorially. "Women!"

But Tammy went on. "I just want you to see that Jamie is a person, a child really, and not just a stereotype. And as such, he deserves compassion and, yes, even protection. That's what a community is supposed to do for its children."

"You're preaching to the choir now, Tam. That's exactly what I have been doing. Protecting our children!" Ed bellowed.

"But not this child, Ed." Tammy spoke gently, compassionately, and then confessionally. "But then, neither have I. I have done nothing more than stand idly by, not speaking up when I have heard slurs disguised as jokes over the years. Or when I've heard others preach hatred rather than love. So now, I have to live with myself for allowing such animosity into my own home. Michael wouldn't have done what he did if I had taught him that compassion for the person comes first, even if you don't understand his ways."

"Compassion my ass."

Tammy held her ground even as she placed a conciliatory hand on her husband's knee. "Ed, hon, if this kind of behavior, masked as fun, isn't stopped, it will only escalate, and I shudder to think what the *next prank* will be. I just can't allow hurtful words or actions in my presence any longer. And I hope more than anything that I can somehow make it up to the O'Dell family." And with that, she pecked him on the cheek, stood up, and left the room.

Sloan watched her go, stunned into momentary self-doubt before he shook off that unfamiliar, disturbing, lapse and grabbed instead for his comfortable old shoe of self-righteousness. He wrapped his anger around himself like a blanket, secure in his knowledge of right and wrong, and prepared to do what he must to prevail.

But his bravado had been shaken by her speech, leaving a fissure in what had previously been an immaculate prejudice. The sharpened blade that had cleft it was nothing more than words spoken from the heart of someone he loved and knew so well — but obviously not so well as he had thought.

Cautiously, Pritchett posed the question, "Well?"

Sloan simply shook his head, knowing that in addition to the possible political fallout he was facing, he now had a new burden to carry — possibly the heaviest load of all given the opposition he now knew existed in his very own home — his wife.

Tammy had let that kind of talk from Ed slide for years, but now she felt herself flung from her old pattern of compliance as if from a car wreck. She walked away from the study as if in a dream — only in this moment beginning to understand the magnitude of what had just occurred. She could hear the kids playing a video game in the den and she went in to look at them, as if needing to count heads to prove that all was still right in her world.

She had heard other voices too, and followed them, only to find Michael sitting in front of the television alone. He was on the couch with the controller, and the conversation she had overheard was Michael and the voices of the computer generated soldiers in his game. She stood behind him for a few minutes and watched as he played what she knew was his favorite game. *Call of Duty* places the player in control of an infantry soldier who makes use of various authentic World War II firearms using simulations of actual battlefields. She watched as his soldier — this time it was Sergeant Jack Evans of the United Kingdom — took part in the securing of a pivotal bridge following the landing at Normandy. She had seen him play this game before, but hadn't noticed the focus of the game was more than just shooting at the German forces. Michael actually moved in conjunction with other allied soldiers rather than alone, and it appeared to place a heavy emphasis on the usage of cover — behind walls and barricades — and the protection and rescue of fellow countrymen.

"I'm glad to see that this is more than just shooting people."

"Geez, Mom." He didn't turn away from the flat screen in front of him. "Can you give it a rest?"

"Hey. Watch the attitude, mister." Tammy moved between Michael and the TV. "I don't think you heard what I said. I said that I was relieved to see that the objectives seem to be more along the lines of teamwork rather than just killing the enemy."

"Sorry." He paused the game and removed his headset. "It's about war, Mom. And about getting back home. Sometimes you kill people. Sometimes you don't."

"You're exactly right. And I'm glad to see the picture of brotherhood being illustrated. That's all I was saying. It's a fact that even during times of war, compassion is still desired. And necessary."

Michael rolled his eyes and leaned his head against the back of the couch. "Okay. I knew you had to be headed there."

"What do you mean, honey?"

"I mean, can't I even sit here and play my game without getting a lecture? It's not like I've named all the Krauts 'Jamie' or anything."

Michael started to put the headset back on, but Tammy intervened. "Michael. You're turning everything I've said around. Listen to me for a minute. Please."

Michael put the headset back on his knees, but looked straight ahead instead of meeting his mother's eyes.

"Just so you know, I wasn't referring to any of that. But since you brought it up, I do believe that there is a good parallel there for you to remember. Concern, empathy, and kindness belong everywhere. Whether at Westmont High or the European front." Her voice cracked with emotion. "I know your heart, Michael Sloan, and it isn't one that feeds off meanness. And I think you'll begin to feel better when you can let go of your anger."

He continued to look straight ahead, avoiding his mother's eyes. He stared a hole into the paused image on the screen while she spoke.

"I know you're hurting. We all are." She squeezed in beside him on the couch and rested her hand on his leg. "But blaming me for your feelings won't get you anywhere, honey. Anger will only turn into resentment, and resentment will eat you up. As hard as it is, you have to face this and work through it. And we can do it together."

She looked at her son, his dark hair falling across his forehead, his squared jaw clenching. He was the image of his father.

Michael said nothing. Tammy drew him in her arms and kissed his cheek. "I love you, Michael. And I am here for you. Always."

His brooding posture and prolonged silence persisted, and Tammy decided to take her leave. As she walked out of the room she heard the game start up again, and the all-too-familiar constriction of her insides returned.

After dinner, Tammy sat down at her computer to compose the email to Ginny Pritchett with the recipe for the bacon-wrapped dove.

"Ed, how long did you grill that dove?" Her fingernails clicked against the keyboard. "I want to tell Ginny exactly what to do. Poor Bill, he brings home all that wonderful game and she doesn't know how to prepare any of it."

"Poor Bill? How about poor Ed?"

"What?"

"Where is all that compassion of yours now, Mrs. Sloan? I certainly didn't see any evidence of it in your performance in front of Pritchett earlier."

Her tapping stopped and she looked up at him, the clenching in her stomach threatening to return. She had wondered when this anticipated retaliatory blow might occur. "I'm sorry that you feel that way, because I'm trying to be nothing but compassionate with regard to this whole thing."

"It wasn't very compassionate when you contradicted me this afternoon right in front of Bill Pritchett. You're supposed to have my back. Talk about a slap in the face! And where did all that nonsense come from anyway, Tammy? I've never heard you talk like that before."

"Maybe I've never felt so strongly about something before, Ed. I know you're accustomed to my total support, but I just can't give it this time." She turned away from the monitor in order to face Ed. "Maybe

Jamie can't help it that he is that way. What if he can't help being who he is any more than we can help being who we are?"

Ed crossed his arms and shook his head in revulsion as Tammy spoke.

"No matter what we may have been taught to believe about homosexuality, I don't think it's up to us to judge and punish him. And as much as it hurts me to acknowledge it, that is exactly what Michael and his friends did and what you're doing now. And anyway, Bill asked me to talk to you." She pointed in the direction of Ed's study. "He sat right there and he asked me to help you understand."

"Well, I understand all right. You have made yourself perfectly clear."

And he left the room abruptly without answering her initial question about the doves. Ginny would have to figure out the grill time on her own.

The next morning, Ed left for Austin early. Tammy stood in the kitchen, sipping her coffee as she watched his black Escalade drive down the long gravel drive and out onto the blacktop beyond. He had to leave much earlier these days, in order to get Michael over to the Academy by 7:30. She had kissed them both goodbye. But they had left in sullen silence. She sighed, longing to release the sadness and fear she held within.

The heat of the September sun had not yet begun its daily broiling, and the pleasantness of the day along with the swing on the front porch beckoned her to join them, despite the troubles that drove away in Ed's SUV. There hadn't been much conversation last night after what Ed had called her "performance in front of Bill Pritchett." Ed was totally unaccustomed to having Tammy voice an opinion that was in opposition to his. Throughout their two decades of marriage, they had found little occasion to quarrel on anything of major consequence. She had been a consistent partner, a reliable ally, and a superb mediator when it came to compromise, whether in the political or personal arena. Ed could rely on Tammy to soften his coarseness and to articulate those emotions he found so difficult to express himself. Tammy helped Ed appear more human. They were a good team, and yesterday afternoon's conversation in the study had rattled them both.

She cupped the mug with both hands and held it close to her face, feeling the warmth between her fingers as she gently swayed. She loved this porch. There was something healing about it. It spoke of good books and sweet tea and friends gathering. It held summer smells, like freshly cut grass and late summer blooms. She settled more deeply into the soft, floral pillow that she kept there for times like this when she needed the solitude and solace that only her porch swing could provide. Instinctively, she looked to the magnificent oaks planted by Ed's forbears over a century ago. They had always provided her with great comfort. Sentinels from the past, they provided perspective, as well as the grounding and sense of belonging she was so desperate to recover this morning.

The air was delicious in the early morning hours. The grackles and mockingbirds vied for premier position in the branches of the great trees, while the rhythmic call of the doves countered with ostensible songs of peace. Squirrels skittered across the expansive lawn. The cicadas had not yet begun their incessant buzzing, but as the sun continued to rise, their songs of summer would soon begin. The small pond on the edge of their property hinted at unknown life under its surface with little concentric circles popping up here and there as turtles and fish kissed the still plane of the dark water, taking in tiny breaths only to continue their secretive swims.

So much of this simple journey called life was untouched, unchanged. Why, then, did she feel as though it had all just been turned on its head?

It had felt good to stand up to Ed last night. All she had done was speak up for what she believed. Such a small thing, unless you were married to Ed Sloan. Plenty of people did this every day, but it had been a big step for her. She could look her newfound strength in the eye and call it hope — or name it foolishness. But which was it? She marveled at how one little speck of confidence might outweigh the suffocating feelings of shame, even fear, that had constricted her breathing for so many years. But then her heart lurched as she once again realized the precariousness of her situation and the fragility of this newfound hope.

"I just can't go back to covering over my own thoughts and feelings with a sweet smile and a sympathetic nod," she told herself. "But ..." She couldn't, wouldn't finish that thought. *Damned if I do. Damned if I don't.* She felt mired in a pit of impossibility. She felt like jumping off that swing and just running – running hard and fast. But she resisted that impulse, breathing slowly and deeply instead.

The tightness in her chest had not dissipated since last week's meeting at the school, and she feared the ripples of unpleasant consequences had only just begun to spread. Her heart had been broken to find that her only son was capable of such a careless disregard for another. The devastation he had inflicted upon that boy and his family was incomprehensible.

They had also learned that this hadn't been the first incident. Dr. Price had interviewed Jamie and his parents, garnering information about past abuses. Apparently, Michael and his football buddies had repeatedly tormented Jamie. It had begun in their seventh-grade year with characteristic middle-school taunts and teasing. But over the past three years, the bullying had intensified, and Jamie had been persecuted numerous times. He rarely came home with a bloodied nose or black eye. His scars were more of the emotional kind. Once he had been wrestled to the ground while they scrawled HOMO, with eye black, across his face. He had also been forced into a "game" of bobbing-for-apples, but they had used hot dogs in a locker room toilet and had thrust his head into the bowl repeatedly. Out of fear, Jamie had never reported these events, nor had he identified the aggressors. And the only reason this latest incident had come to light was because of the number of students and faculty at Westmont High who had witnessed its occurrence. When pressed by Dr. Price, Michael had confessed his involvement through hot tears as he was forced to incriminate his friends.

And now, this additional media misstep by Ed, if you could call it that, had inflated an already painful incident into an even more agonizing experience. His protectiveness of Michael had prompted the "Osama" comment to the gal at News 25 the day after everything had happened at the school. It had been excruciating to endure. The piece had played incessantly for two days, with little clips before commercial breaks enticing viewers to stay tuned. Regrettably, most had indeed kept watching and had repeatedly heard Ed's encouragement of all Americans to "shout down the gays in support of justice for all," or something pugnacious like that.

When she had expressed her concern, Ed had defended his bellicose performance for the media by telling her, "Tam, where there is fear, there is no faith." Ed was anything but afraid, and as was his practice, he had immediately appealed to the faithful to strengthen his position. He had counted on Tammy's ironing out the situation, just as she had unquestioningly and willingly done in the past. But this time she did not rush to his aid. She realized now, that was her first step in finding her voice. *Interesting,* she thought. *My first step in finding my own voice was refraining from speaking.*

She felt sick just recalling the images of that day. Hastily putting down her coffee, she leaned her head against the back of the porch swing and closed her eyes. The girls would be up soon. She took a deep, cleansing breath, expanding her lungs to their fullest capacity before she slowly exhaled.

Whom had she let down? Ed? Michael? Their daughters? Herself? Realistically, her family could be ruined. She knew that was a risk. Yet she still felt pushed toward that perilous edge of self-truth. Hiding in the storm cellar might afford safety from the initial winds of the damaging storm, but was she prepared to live in the aftermath of the storm's fury once she emerged?

The thought of doing either gripped her with a paralyzing anxiety. She dug her thumbs into her temples, massaging them in rhythmic circles, hoping to calm her churning thoughts. She could claim that tightness in her chest and call it resolve, or she could give in completely and call it fear. "Please, God, help me," she whispered aloud, as she pinched the bridge of her nose and then moved her fingers down to her jawline, slowly tracing her face from ears to chin and back again. She felt as if she might be sick.

Was she throwing away her life as she knew it? Half the town would side with Ed, despite his outrageous comments of late. He had the ability to command unlimited agreement from those who revered him.

And she understood all too well the intricacies of maintaining small town relationships given the complexities of having to lead a public life.

The clenching in her stomach persisted, despite her best efforts to quell all disagreeable thoughts. She opened her eyes and blinked hard through her tears. The morning sun shot through the trees and swathed the unsuspecting world with glorious rays of brilliant light, turning the six stately columns that framed the porch into blindingly white pillars of fire. She blinked again to adjust to the overpowering brightness. The warm sunbeams caught the three-carat beauty on her left hand, and the stone seemed to dazzle as it had that day long ago, when Ed had first slipped it on her slender finger. They had been so in love. She turned her hand back and forth in order to better catch the glimmering rays, and she watched the many facets of the stone come to life. Sparks appeared to jump right out of the platinum setting, the diamond blazing with its own internal flame.

She really hadn't been unhappy. And she still loved Ed. They were fresh out of college when they had married and both their families had been exceedingly pleased with the match. He was loyal, a good and dependable provider for the family. He had been a good dad to the kids, and in the beginning it had been fun. He had eagerly shared with her his love of the outdoors — teaching her to camp, to canoe, and to hike his favorite places in the Texas Hill Country. She remembered camping on the Pedernales, sleeping outdoors, and watching fireflies and stars light up the sky. The solitude of nature had brought with it intimacy. And intimacy had brought love. She sighed.

Her life with Ed had been exhilarating, really. Campaigns and fundraiser dinners had afforded her much more excitement than the usual PTA elections and Junior League budget meetings that most women attended. But the births of their three children, the twins and then Hannah, had brought her more joy than anything else — each born with innocence and promise. Not a thing on God's earth had really changed since then, had it?

A small shift between cloud and sun altered the sunbeams again, and the whole landscape of the yard was transformed. Where there had been an almost overwhelming light, there was now only darkness, or so it seemed.

The sadness once again encompassed her like a gathering storm. She looked across the yard, then back at the pond, and took another slow, deep breath. The fish and turtles shared their habitat happily, it seemed. They were each equipped to breathe a different kind of oxygen, and neither expected the other to conform to their ways of survival. One could scratch his way out of the water, sunning on logs for a change of scenery, while the other was happily fated to an aquatic existence. Neither was right; neither was wrong. It was just the way it was. And look at how easily they shared space. The turtle and the fish didn't have to even think about acceptance. They just lived it.

If her own life could only be that simple.

Tell me and I forget. Teach me and I may remember. Involve me and I will learn.
— Benjamin Franklin

Chapter 2

FAMILY BUSINESS

"Kelly! Will you play that thing somewhere else! I'm trying to relax here." Ed was in his recliner with the remote in his hand. It had been a rough couple of weeks, to put it mildly. Not only was he juggling several big projects in the Land Office right now, but a steady stream of contentious email was hitting his inbox daily. Most of those weighing in had not been friendly, nor supportive, of what the press had labeled his HOMOS ARE TERRORISTS position.

Ed was no stranger to opposition, and in fact, he had always relished such polemics among his colleagues; but, a good number of these were his constituents, and that put his political radar on alert. He'd had no idea there would be so many. His muscles tensed, his temples throbbed, and his stomach refused to digest even the blandest of diets without grumbling. And his nights had been fitful too. His mind refused to turn off; and so, he was robbed of the much-needed respite from the day's stress that only a good night's sleep could bring. He was pretty sure his blood pressure was sky-high. All he wanted to do was come home from another long hard day and relax at home. But all this racket!

Kelly was working on her All Region Music and had been practicing a difficult four-measure run repeatedly. Auditions were just a few weeks away, and she was determined to make the top band. But she had stopped in the middle of the phrase when her father had raised his voice.

The hurt on his daughter's face was apparent, and Ed quickly softened his voice. "I just need a little quiet, darlin'. That's all." He had already flipped through two college football games and a documentary on sea life, when he had landed on his old standard: *The O'Reilly Factor.* He smiled at her reassuringly, then turned back toward the oversized screen on the wall.

"Sure, Dad. I'll go practice in my room." She waited, but received no response. She packed up her clarinet loudly and grabbed her stand, dropping her music all over the floor. "Argh!" she exclaimed in frustration as she marched herself out of her father's inner sanctum.

Agitated by yet another interruption, Ed barked. "Son, be a gentleman and help your sister take all her things up to her room. Now!"

Michael looked up from his iPad, but his father wasn't even looking at him. Ed was continuing to dictate from his position in his chair, totally engrossed with Bill O'Reilly's commentary. Kelly was already half way up the stairs when Michael began picking up the sheet music strewn across the floor.

Tammy peeked in from the kitchen where she and Hannah were frosting cupcakes. Everyone was walking on eggshells around Ed. And it was tiring. Each of them were dealing with emotions of their own and the additional burden of having to sidestep Ed and his irritation was getting to be too much to sustain.

"Hannah, honey. Do you think you can finish up the last few cupcakes and add the sprinkles to make them pretty while I go in to talk with Dad for a few minutes?"

"Uh-huh." Hannah licked each of her fingers. "I'll make them really yummy too, Mom."

Tammy handed her ten-year-old a damp wash rag, hoping to encourage a different kind of hand cleansing. "Now, as soon as you finish these, it will be time to get ready for bed, okay?"

Hannah issued a thumbs-up and Tammy left the kitchen. But before doing so, she picked up the little note addressed to Ed from their great-niece, Grace Keene. She was in kindergarten and the care she had taken to write out DEAR UNCLE ED on the outside of the envelope was obvious.

"Whoa!" Ed whooped. "Don'cha let her get away with that, O'Reilly." When Tammy entered the den, Ed was participating in the conversation with the right-wing political pundit and his guests as if he were a part of the panel himself. "That's not what we're doing at all! Tell her the way it is!"

"For heaven's sake. What are you watching?"

"Hold on a minute." Ed continued to give his full attention to the screen and held up his hand like a stop sign until the last guest had finished speaking.

Tammy sat in the chair next to his, waiting for his show to allow her an opportunity to speak.

"Okay. They're done." His hand finally came down. "The talking heads tonight were arguing about an alleged 'War on Women' by the GOP in general, but here in Texas, in particular. How absurd can you get? We conservatives are simply trying to protect life and the way to do that is to better regulate sex education, contraception, and abortion; but all the crazy liberals are crying foul and calling it a 'War on Women' instead. I just don't get it. Any reasonable person should be able to see this tighter regulation is a necessary improvement and will save lives all across the board. It's what Texas needs."

Tammy had always thought herself a reasonable person, but she was having trouble with Ed's reasoning. Legislating a woman's reproductive system would save lives? She had questions, but she knew now wasn't the time. "I forgot to give you this before dinner. It's from Gracie. Isn't it cute?"

"Humph." Ed reached for his readers and then tore off the end of the envelope, not taking the time to appreciate Gracie's careful penmanship. His mouth turned down into a frown as he read the typed letter from Gracie's teacher.

"What is it?" Tammy couldn't fathom what Gracie's teacher could have written that would disturb Ed so severely.

Ed tossed the letter onto the coffee table in front of him and removed his reading glasses, attempting to squeeze the pain out of his head with his large hands. "Oh, it's nothing. They want me to come up to the elementary school for State Fair Day or something. Seems they need a Big Tex and Gracie volunteered me."

"Oh, Ed. How fun!" Tammy clapped her hands together. "You'd be the perfect Big Tex. And you could use a little fun right now, couldn't you?"

"Fun? Tam, are you serious?" Ed's head swiveled and he pierced her with his eyes, willing her into silence. "You really think I have the time to deal with a bunch of little six-years-olds right now?"

Tammy broke his gaze and looked into her lap. Was it the pot roast or something else that made her suddenly feel sick to her stomach?

Ed tilted his head, first one way then the other, and his neck cracked loudly several times on each side. "There you go. That's what I've been needing."

Desiring to quell the sickness she felt inside, Tammy dared a sideways glance in his direction, hoping to smooth the evening's mood. "Are you not feeling well tonight? You hardly said a word at dinner." Maybe she could regain some normalcy. That might help.

"I've had a splitting headache all day." Ed clicked the TV off, put down the remote, and again squeezed his head, attempting to eradicate the pounding in his head from the relentless tension he was experiencing. "And I haven't slept in days. I'm wiped." He placed his hands on his knees with his elbows bent, readying himself to stand up; but instead he remained seated next to Tammy, looking down as he spoke. "I can't tell you the number of reporters I've had to dodge at work. And the emails I've been getting lately. It's ridiculous, Tam. I've been called everything from a Christian hero to a second Hitler. But the majority have labeled me as a 'backward-leaning idiot with my head up my ass.' Somebody actually said that!"

Tammy risked a show of affection and reached out to put her hand on his leg. Ed did not respond. "Ed, I'm worried about you and the way all of this is affecting you. Can I get you anything that would help you feel better?"

"How 'bout a shotgun?" Ed smiled at his joke. "There have been plenty of media hounds taking potshots at me lately." He held up an imaginary rifle, cocked it and then took several shots across the room. "Pow! Pow! Hell, I'd really like to take aim at a few of them myself!"

That was the main reason he hadn't tuned into FOX earlier in the evening. He was afraid he might see his own mug shot on the screen again. No matter the network, they were putting his face up there and letting the political spin doctors do their dirty work. Some made him out to be a country yahoo who didn't know shit from Shinola, and others were inviting him to speak at their church luncheons for so eloquently defending conservative Christian values in an all-too-secular world. He never knew what to expect. This instability was completely foreign to him and very disorienting — untethering even.

"That isn't funny, Ed. I'm serious. I'm worried about you."

"Well, sounds like you're not the only one. Pritchett's all worked up about this thing too. It just won't go away. Like it's gotten a life of its own or something." Ed leaned over and pulled off his boots, dropping them one at a time onto the floor next to him. "He came by my office this afternoon. Seems he wants me to read a scripted statement of some kind — hoping to somehow put all this to bed once and for all. Helluva lot a good that'll do!"

Tammy did not hesitate. "Do it, Ed. Please. For your health. For the kids' sakes. For all of us. Do it, sweetheart!"

Ed raised his eyebrows. Tammy's imploring tone had surprised him. "You mean give in? That's what he's wanting me to do, you know."

"I don't see it that way at all, Ed. I think Bill just wants to help you say that words can sometimes be hurtful and that you want to apologize for any hurt that you may have caused. I'm sure that's all there is to it."

Surprisingly, Ed did not respond.

"And acknowledging all that publicly can only help with your constituents." Tammy looked at him through her long lashes. "And maybe even your family?"

Ed looked into her beautiful eyes, noticed her full lips. Things had been strained lately. He knew that. Between him and Tammy, and even between him and the kids. Maybe she and Pritchett were right. An apology for hurt feelings wasn't the same as an apology for the underlying values he held so dear. Maybe he could win all the way around — with the media, with the voters, and with his family. "Is it that important to you, doll?"

"Yes, Ed. More than you know."

Ed had been fixated on the repercussions that all this outlandish media attention was having on his career, and it hadn't helped that Pritchett had been hounding him every day about trying to repair the damage already done. It honestly hadn't occurred to him that any of this might be affecting his wife, or his children. It wasn't that he didn't care. He simply hadn't thought about it at all. "Okay. I'll call him. I'll make it happen. For you and the kids." And he leaned in for a kiss.

"Mom! Dad! Who wants a cupcake?" Hannah appeared in front of them with a plate full of chocolate cupcakes decorated with white buttercream icing and topped with multi-colored sprinkles.

"Me! I want a cupcake!" Ed bellowed. That was his pet name for Hannah — his Cupcake. And he stood, gathering her up in his arms and lifting her high off the floor.

"Can I take some upstairs to Michael and Kelly?" Hannah looked down at her mother from on high, and vigilantly righted the plate of goodies, careful not to spill her delectable treasures.

"Sure, honey. But then off to bed for you."

Ed put her down and barely had time to grab a cupcake off her tray before she ran upstairs to find the others.

"I'll call him now, Tam." And Ed reached for his cell.

❧⟨♡⟩☙

"**Y**ou almost done?" Michael tossed his iPad on Kelly's bed; then, sat down beside it, facing his twin as she sat across from him. He unwrapped the cupcake Hannah had brought him and took a bite. "I need your help."

Taking her clarinet with her, Kelly had retreated to her room as she had been told to do earlier. Her cupcake remained untouched. She finished the last several measures before stopping. "What?" She looked up from the etude she was working on and rested her horn in her lap.

"I don't know what to do about Ashley." He pointed at the iPad then ran his fingers through his hair. He kept his head down, concentrating on picking the sprinkles off the frosting and eating them one at a time.

"Why do you think I would know anything about her? She has totally avoided me for the last couple of weeks, Michael. Like I've got some plague or something. She is, like, so shallow." Kelly brought the horn back up to her mouth, disappearing behind her stand.

"Come on, Kel. Listen to me for a minute, okay? That's part of the problem. Since I'm not allowed at any school functions, it's like she's ignoring me too. I can only really talk to her on Facebook these days.

And I can't take her to the homecoming dance or the game. Nothing."
He fell back onto the bed, staring up at the ceiling. "But she still wants
to go. Even if it isn't with me. And all of that means I'm screwed. What
do I do?"

"You want the truth?"

"Of course." He stayed flat on his back, but lifted his head to address
his sister. "That's why I'm talking to you."

"Forget about her. Ashley is shallow. She only thinks about herself
and you deserve better."

As twins, Michael and Kelly had shared that unique bond that
only twins can truly understand. When they were toddlers, they had
developed their own language. They had always finished each other's
sentences. They had been each other's best friend and confidant. Their
profound bond, mysterious and intriguing to others, was a way of life
for them. Twin, an ancient German word meaning "two-together,"
(they had actually Googled it), captured the true essence of Kelly and
Michael's relationship. "Two-together." Living as life-long companions.
Sharing secrets and laughing about things only they could understand.
Their connection was intense, and they felt one another's physical and
emotional freight even when parted. This bond they shared was so
strong that no outside influence could break it. They were born that way.

So Michael instinctively turned to his sister. He really didn't know
who else he could trust these days. His social life had been turned upside
down since his suspension, and he felt as if he were now on an island.

"C'mon, Kel, I can't do that. My popularity is tanking right now," he
told Kelly. While still staring at nothing in particular, he continued, "A lot
of my friends have disappeared. I mean, they've actually unfriended me
on Facebook and everything. And I don't know why they've hung me out
to dry. Nobody is talking, and I'm not about to ask them. I mean, what
do I do, call 'em up and say 'Hey, why aren't you my friend anymore?'"

"Well, I don't know about everybody else, but I can guess about
Ashley. I think she only liked you 'cause you were the new quarterback.
But now you're not. You know, she can't afford to like you anymore.
You may not be popular enough for her now."

"Well thanks for that load of crap. You didn't have to be *that*
honest, Kel."

Kelly dodged the stuffed horse he threw at her. "Well, I think it's the truth, Michael. That's how she is. The cheerleader and the quarterback are like Barbie and Ken or something. The perfect couple. You know."

Yes, he knew. Michael had to admit that he had enjoyed having one of the cheerleaders as his girlfriend too — and a junior to boot! It looked good. She looked good. It was all about building social capital in high school. Like so many other teens, he had gone along with peer pressure to maintain his popularity. But now, he was feeling the sting of rejection as those upperclassmen and their friends blacklisted him for identifying them as co-conspirators in the whole Jamie thing.

He lifted his head again to look at Kelly while resting on his elbows. "Maybe I can fix it. I've still got time. What if she just doesn't like what the others guys and I did to Jamie? Or maybe she's ticked because I had to tell on the other guys. Either way, maybe I can just tell her I'm sorry and that will fix everything."

"But are you really sorry?"

Michael had to think before answering. Of course he was sorry. Sorry he had to go to the Miles Academy. Sorry he couldn't play football this season. Sorry he was losing his friends. But was he really sorry for what he had done to Jamie O'Dell? He took the last bite of Hannah's cupcake and wiped his mouth with the back of his hand.

But he had waited too long to respond, and Kelly continued. "Don't be a jerk, Michael. Maybe being gay isn't the worst thing in the world. But being a jerk is."

Michael couldn't look at her. The truth hurt. "Great! Now you're sounding just like Mom. That's all I need. If I'd wanted another lecture, I'd of gone to her!"

She peered over her stand at her brother sprawled out on her bed, his face turned upwards and his eyes open, but seeing nothing. "Hey, you came to me and asked me to be honest with you. That's all I'm doing, Michael. I've told you before. I think what y'all did was wrong. And that's the truth."

"So you think people are avoiding me because of what I did to Jamie? Or because I had to finger the other guys? Or because I'm just not the quarterback of the team anymore?"

"Prob'ly all of the above, Michael. But I really don't care. I just care about you. And that's why I'm being honest with you now. 'Cause I don't think anyone else is."

That was exactly why Michael had sought her out. He always did when he was troubled about something, whether big or little. He knew he could always count on Kelly. But it didn't mean that he liked hearing what she had to say.

"It's happening to me, too, you know." She waited for him to turn his head and look at her before she went on. "Some of the guys at lunch the other day started giving me a hard time. They were asking whose side I was on — the football team or the fairies?" She shook her head and made a face as she thought about the boy who had instigated the interrogation. She had liked Ryan. He was cute and she had thought he was nice — until then. Kelly understood all too well the feelings one experiences when falling in love for the first time. And her compassionate heart stirred as she followed her own thoughts. *I can't imagine being someone like Jamie and what he must feel like when he likes someone. It's hard enough for me. I can't imagine being gay and going through all that.*

She shook her head again and looked toward her brother as she spoke. "Look. I'm going through everything just like you are, Michael. Only I'm still at school and have to face them every day. You don't. So don't expect me to feel, like, all sorry for you and your girlfriend, okay?"

"Who said that to you?" Michael sat up, agitated.

"It doesn't matter. People are gonna think what they're gonna think. What matters is that we stick together on this. Okay?" She could see the color rising in Michael's face. But whether from anger or shame she couldn't tell. "You and me are what matters here, Michael. I love you. Whether you're the football star or not. That doesn't matter to me. What matters to me is that you get back to being who I know you really are."

They sat facing each other. Michael on the bed, Kelly still behind her music stand. For them, silence was a form of communication in itself. Nothing more needed to be said.

I have decided to stick with love. Hate is too great a burden to bear.
— *Martin Luther King, Jr.*

Chapter 3

HOMECOMING MUMS

Just two days later, Tammy was standing in the kitchen, cleaning up after a hurried breakfast when the doorbell rang. It was Bill Pritchett.

"Morning, Tam. Is he ready?" He peered through the open door, looking for Ed.

"He just went up to put on his tie. Come on in, Bill."

"We haven't got much time. He'll have to go over it on the drive down to Austin. Can he read in the car?"

"That's not a problem for him at all. Back in the day, in our 'Pre-Pritchett Era,' I used to drive him to stump meetings where he would practice his speech in between stops. It was kind of fun, actually." Tammy enjoyed the memories of those early days together, watching Ed woo the crowds with his good looks and style. "Don't worry. He's a pro at that. But how in the world did you get all this set up on such short notice? And on a Saturday morning, even?" Tammy still held a dishtowel in her hand. They had only just finished breakfast, and the kids were all still asleep.

"You have no idea, Tam. I've been preparing for this all week, hoping he would soften enough to make this statement. Whatever you did to change his mind, I thank you." Bill bent from the waist, bowing to her as if she were royalty.

Tammy playfully popped him with the towel. "Oh stop it. I didn't do a thing, I assure you."

"Well, maybe now, at least we'll all have a chance for employment after the next election!"

Ed must have heard the bell ring, for soon his footfalls could be heard tapping out a quick staccato beat down the stairs. He was definitely in a hurry and carried his jacket on one arm. "Let's go, Pritchett. There's no time like the present." He gave Tammy a quick kiss, and they were out the door.

Tammy didn't have the nerve to watch the thing live, but about an hour after the press conference was scheduled to occur, she turned on Fox News, just in time to hear Alisyn Camerota questioning whether Ed had defected from his conservative base. This was exactly what Ed had feared. She then flipped over to ABC and caught the tail end of *Good Morning America Weekend Edition*. Dan and Bianna had obviously been discussing Ed's apology and had found his sincerity lacking. They were bandying about a phrase the field correspondent had coined: "The Commissioner's Empathy Deficit."

She shook her head, "Poor Ed!" These reviews were definitely mixed, just as all Ed's recent encounters with the press had been.

Well, at least it was a start.

Just then, Kelly lumbered down the stairs and sleepily appeared in the kitchen, "Hey, Mom," she yawned.

"Well good morning yourself, sleepyhead!" Tammy quickly turned off the television. The kids had been through enough and Kelly didn't need to see this. She wanted to protect her children, if it were possible, from the continuing barrage of negative press aimed at their father.

"Breakfast?"

"I'm not hungry yet, Mom." She plopped down at the table, then got up and went into the utility room, returning with two bulging bags from Hobby Lobby.

"Sophie and I combined all our stuff and I'm gonna start. Wanna help?" And Kelly emptied the two bags of goodies onto the table.

"I'd love to, but Homecoming is weeks away. Why the rush?"

"Mom, you have to get all your stuff early, or there'll be nothing left." Homecoming season was on the horizon, and young girls all over Texas were preparing to gladly yoke themselves to gaudy blooms that would reach the floor and weigh more than a Thanksgiving turkey. The prospect of mammoth, over-the-top displays of silk chrysanthemums, festooned with flowing ribbons, plush animals and an array of colorful trinkets, spawned competition among girls and their mothers to see who could make the biggest — and therefore, the best. The whole thing had morphed into a tradition of gargantuan proportions that, Tammy thought, just went to prove everything really is bigger in Texas.

"Soph is coming over later on, but I want to get started on mine now."

"Okay, but not until after you've eaten some breakfast."

"Aw, Mom." Kelly grudgingly walked over to the pantry and grabbed a box of strawberry Pop Tarts. She ate one without even warming it in the toaster.

"There."

Tammy sighed. Raising teenagers was a whole different ballgame, but if this little mutiny was Kelly's attempt at rebellion ... she smiled her gratitude that Kelly was such a level-headed child.

"So, what all do you have there?" Tammy gestured to the table replete with Kelly's riches. "Boy, homecoming mums have certainly come a long way since I was in high school. Back then it was a real flower, given by a boy to his date. There were a few ribbons on them, but it was basically a flower. A modest corsage that you actually pinned on your dress or blouse."

Kelly had already perfected the teenage eye-roll. "Oh, Mom, that is so old-fashioned. Nobody, like, waits for a date to give them a mum anymore."

"I just don't understand why girls today don't want to wait until a boy gives them one."

"Mom, it's not about the boyfriend."

Tammy pulled out a chair and sat at the table, sifting through the ribbons and baubles that soon would become part of Kelly's pride and joy. There would certainly be nothing modest or unassuming about the homecoming decoration her daughter would fashion for herself, thought Tammy. For what sophomore girl could risk having such an important status symbol as this being constructed inadequately?

Tammy had to smile to herself. She had dealt with much the same thing in her public life with Ed: What she wore, what she said, and who she was seen with — they were always scrutinized by others — oftentimes played a role, however small, in her husband's success. And truth be told, she had enjoyed playing to the crowd. *My own concerns about 'status' aren't much different than Kelly's mum issue*, she mused. But at least Kelly had an excuse. She was a teenager, and at that age, so much importance is placed on what other people think of you. In fact, your whole self-worth is at their mercy, if you let it be. Tammy's thoughts instantly shot to Michael, as well as to Jamie O'Dell and the other boys.

"Mom, let's put the teddy bears right in the middle of each one. And I can glue these little megaphones onto their hands, like they did in this picture. What do you think?" She reached across the table for the hot-glue gun. Kelly had harvested decorating ideas from Pinterest and wanted to replicate an example she and Sophie had found there. Aside from Michael, Sophie Campbell was Kelly's best friend.

"I think it's going to be fabulous, just like you." Tammy smiled at her older daughter. *Where did the time go?* Her little-girl looks had gradually given way to the advent of womanhood. Her wavy dark hair framed her face and cascaded over her shoulders. And over the past year or so her body had developed curves — in all the right places. *She didn't know what a beauty she was.*

"Oh, m'gosh. Look at this, Mom." And Kelly read from the web page. "A front-and-back-mum sandwiches her body and is attached to a dog harness for strength and comfort." She turned her iPad around for Tammy to see. "Check it out!"

Tammy scrolled down and read the description under the next picture: "Technology has even made it possible for mums to be outfitted with colorful LED lights and connections for iPods or CD players, adding splash with audio and visual capabilities." Tammy was dumbfounded. *Who had engineered such outlandish extravagances?* She couldn't help herself, "As if a mum sandwich isn't enough, they have to add lights and music, too?" It was just too outrageous. She turned the screen back toward her daughter. "Do people even care what's on the inside of anyone anymore?"

"Of course they do, Mom! See, the girl *is* the insides of a mum like this one." Kelly picked up the two empty shopping bags and held one under her chin as she dangled the other down her back, parading around like a runway model — flipping her hair this way and that while holding her nose high in the hair. "This girl is gonna be cared about a *lot!*" And she fell back into the chair laughing.

Tammy enjoyed seeing this playfulness in her daughter and joined in her laughter. She grabbed one of the paper shopping bags and dunked it over Kelly's head, covering her well past the shoulders. So much had robbed them of carefree fun and enjoyment lately. It felt good to laugh.

Kelly removed the bag from her head, folded it, and placed both bags in the chair next to her.

Still holding several strands of two-inch ribbons in one hand, Tammy reached over to push Kelly's hair out of her face and back behind her ear. "But seriously, sweetie, do kids at school look at anything besides popularity these days?"

"Some do." Kelly tilted her head to one side but continued sorting little plastic footballs, helmets, and megaphones by color and size. "But a lot of people only want to be your friend, if, like, you're popular. You know."

Tammy began spelling out HOMECOMING 2012 and KELLY with the large glittered letters that would soon be glued onto the widest gold ribbons hanging from the mum. These days, some mums could weigh as much as twenty pounds. Some of the heavier versions actually had a sturdy polyurethane base attached to a cord that would hang around the girl's neck, but Tammy had insisted that Kelly's be one of the smaller versions that only required the standard cardboard backing.

"Do you have to deal with that a lot with your friends?"

Kelly stopped and looked up at her mother. Her big brown eyes, punctuated by her raised dark eyebrows, answered the question her mother had just asked. It was not unusual for their banter to be interspersed with more meaty topics. .

"I'm not one of those snooty girls, Mom. You know me." She reached over to collect the small pile of musical notes that would go under her name. "Yeah, I like to make new friends." She looked up at Tammy now. "But I'm not like that. Neither is Soph."

"I know, sweetheart, there's always been more to you than that. I guess I was just wondering if it has gotten any harder for you.

"Since the whole Michael and Jamie thing, you mean?"

"Yes, darling. How has all that played out between you and your friends?"

"Well, a lot of the kids thought it was all pretty funny at first, you know, like with the dummy and everything. But there were some who got kind of spooked by the whole thing. Nobody wants to get sucked into something that might hurt their reputation."

"What do you mean, 'spooked by the whole thing'?"

"Well, speaking out, like, puts you on one side or the other, Mom, and at first everyone was waiting to chime in until they heard what the really popular kids were saying. No one wanted to be caught on the wrong side of this thing. And then, when word got out that Michael and them would have to go to the Miles Academy for the rest of the year, everybody got really mad at Jamie. I mean, the football team just lost three of its top players. I've heard a lot of kids say some really mean things about Jamie and sometimes they say it right to his face." She paused and then continued more hesitantly, "And well, there are some other kids who don't want to have anything to do with Michael anymore either, since he's been suspended and there's been all that ..." She trailed off as she thought of what the media had done to her brother, and instead gestured with her hand as though shaking off the negative publicity like so much muck stuck to her fingers.

"What are some of the things you've heard kids say?" Tammy braced herself. She had expected this, but it was still going to be hard to hear. "About Michael? And about Jamie, of course?"

"Oh lots of stuff, mom. Once the media said those things about Michael, it made him a fair target too. There's been some teasing and name calling from people who find it cool to take down the football quarterback, but I really don't want to talk about that." Again, she paused. "But, about Jamie ... I've heard lots of kids say it's just wrong to be gay, but I don't know if that's what I believe."

"So, what do you believe, sweetie?"

"I mean, God created him too, right?" She looked imploringly at her mother. "But they say Jamie deserved what happened to him and, like, he should be the one to have to go away. That's just wrong. He didn't do anything." Her searching eyes studied her mother, wishing that her words about her friends' actions weren't really the truth. "It's almost like everybody wants to wreck somebody else so they won't take a hit themselves. And I hate that!" Kelly shook her head and picked up her glue gun. "Let's just say that it has become very unpopular to have anything to do with any of those guys these days."

Tammy watched her daughter retreat into her work and decided to give her some space. *Kids, not unlike their parents, seem to go with the prevailing winds*, reflected Tammy. Everyone wants to be on the winning team — to be inside the fold rather than out. They disregard issues that don't impact them personally and argue vehemently against any that might cause discomfort or make them deal with the unfamiliar. *I guess that's human nature*, she told herself. *But was life really that shallow?*

Just then, Ed's face popped into her consciousness, and she smiled. He was, to use his own words, certainly no "boomerang." He held true to his convictions despite the cost, and that was always something she had admired in him. And it looked like Kelly had inherited his same courage and strength of conviction. Tammy just wished Ed could let his heart be open to new truths, as Kelly seemed to be doing. *If he could only allow his trumpet to sound on the side of justice and mercy, and not just judgment.*

Tammy felt that familiar pang in her stomach. Just then, Kelly put down her glue gun and leaned back, gathering her thick dark hair into a ponytail. She began tying several of the thin navy and gold ribbons around it.

"Mom, I just feel sorry for Jamie. Not because he's gay, but because of what Michael and his friends did to him." She divided her ponytail in two and gave both sides a quick yank. Then she shook her head, allowing her ponytail and the ribbons to flip back and forth in a satisfying way. Leaning forward on her folded arms, she fastened a level gaze on her mother's face. "I wouldn't want somebody to do that to me. How embarrassing and humiliating. Jamie's a nice guy, and he didn't do anything wrong. Nobody deserves that kind of treatment."

Tammy grabbed Kelly and hugged her fiercely. "You have such a beautiful heart, Kel, and I'm so glad you're my daughter."

Kelly teared up on hearing her mother's affirmation. "I don't understand why Michael and his friends always pick on Jamie. That's just not who Michael is. Usually he's a really nice guy, mom. I don't understand why he lets his *friends* talk him into all this. Like, he's just a different person when he's with them." She stopped for a moment, looking down at the ribbons in her hands as she gently pulled them through her fingers. "I'm just tired of it all, and I wish it would go away."

"Have you talked with Michael about any of this?"

"Yeah, we've talked." She put down the little megaphone she was about to attach to the center of the mum and put her elbows on the table, resting her chin on clasped hands. "We both thought that Miles was only for kids who did really bad things — like bringing drugs to school or something like that. But when I told him I thought what he did WAS a really bad thing — that it was bullying really — it really ticked him off and we didn't talk for almost three days. But he's coming around now."

Tammy admired her daughter's ability to confront the issue head-on with the person who mattered the most to her. Michael confided so much more in his sister than he did in Tammy. Each time Tammy had approached Michael, he had been very detached and almost defiant. She was so grateful that they had each other, that Kelly had found the courage to speak her truth, and that Michael was able to receive it. It had to have been hard for both of them. They had been tested, and their intimate bond had held up.

"Coming around, how?"

Kelly absentmindedly flicked through various screens on her iPad, occasionally pausing to look at some special embellishments, outlandish or not. "Well, I told him I was really proud of him becoming the quarterback and all, but when he did what he did to Jamie, I couldn't be proud anymore. I told him he was still my brother and that I loved him, but I was really kind of ashamed that he had acted that way. And I said that I wasn't comfortable talking about him anymore with my friends, 'cause when I speak up I get picked on like Jamie."

Tammy opened her mouth to speak, horrified at the prospect of Kelly becoming yet another victim of bullying, but Kelly interrupted.

"Don't worry, Mom. Nothing's gonna happen. That was a while ago when I told him all that. Michael started feeling really bad when he saw how all this was coming down on me. So we've been talking again, Michael and me."

"Good. He hasn't shared with me. Is he really doing okay?"

"Yeah, Mom. He's starting to get it, I think. He knows what he did wasn't him. And I think he's figuring out being popular isn't the most important thing."

"I'm so glad to hear that. We both know his heart. But Kelly, what about you, honey. You mentioned being picked on."

"Well, sometimes, but when it comes up, I say what I think. I mean, I know Jamie, and I've always thought he was a pretty nice guy. He's been a good friend to me. And Mo-m, she drawled this out into two full syllables, somebody just put the whole thing up on YouTube. They've turned it into some kind of joke about homecoming now. 'Take me to the Dance.' I haven't looked it up, but Soph told me you can see what it says on his cap and jersey, the fishnet hose, everything. It's out there for everyone to see. Poor Jamie. They just won't quit."

"My heart breaks for him, too, Kelly. No one, and particularly not a child, should be treated so badly." She suddenly thought of all the recent news stories about young people who had been pushed into taking their own lives by actions such as these. Their sense of helplessness in the midst of such degradation had gotten the better of them. *Oh surely, he wouldn't* ... Her heart leapt to her mouth and she reassured herself as she said a little prayer for Jamie and all the others like him suffering so. But it seemed such a small thing to do in light of her daughter's mature and brave actions.

Hannah bounced into the room then and immediately began wreaking havoc with Kelly's artistic inventory, as only a ten-year-old could.

"Ooh, I want to make one, too!"

"Not on your life, midget!" Kelly playfully snarled as she aimed the glue gun point-blank at her little sister's face, prompting an eye-roll from Hannah. She then turned her attention to the miniature cowbells that would hang from the longest, widest ribbons and began attaching them one by one.

Kelly was finished talking. Tammy could tell. She watched as Hannah monitored Kelly's creation. It was obvious the adoration Hannah held for her older sister. And of Marcie O'Dell again. The Odells also had a daughter — just a little younger than Hannah. *What on earth had they told her?* Her heart sank. It had become painfully obvious to Tammy. They were all victims.

Just then, the doorbell rang. That would be Sophie. But before Tammy could get up from her chair, Hannah went running. "I'll get it!"

It had taken nearly all day for Sophie and Kelly to complete their masterpieces, and now the girls were clearing the table while Tammy finished preparing dinner. She called out to them over the sizzle of the frying pan.

"Sophie? Can you stay for dinner tonight?"

"No, Mrs. Sloan. Thank you, but I have to be at the choir spaghetti dinner. We're already trying to raise money for our spring trip."

"That'll be fun. We'll have you over another time then. How about that?"

"Sure! And thanks." And Sophie was out the door.

Glad it's not me, Tammy thought. Amazing how she had already adjusted to a schedule freed from so many extracurricular obligations. An unexpected benefit of Michael's suspension had been all the extra time they could now share as a family. And Tammy loved their new dinner routine. Instead of the quick meals she had become accustomed to preparing with everyone eating on the fly, she could now take the time to make some of their favorites. Luckily, she thought, Kelly's band obligations had not yet reached a critical point. But for Michael, football had become king, and it had ruled their family schedule for the past several years. And it had proven to be even more of a time tyrant after Michael made the varsity team. The early-morning and late-afternoon drills, in addition to all the social opportunities that football brought, had robbed them of precious family time such as this.

"Mmm. Mmm!" Hannah dipped her fried chicken strips into the cream gravy her mother had made. "This is my favorite in the world!"

"What do you know about the world, pipsqueak?" Michael helped himself to another serving of mashed potatoes.

"I know a lot about the world, Michael. I know what Ms. Randolph told us in school today. It's our question of the week: Pollution and Our World. We learned about how our trash and stuff heats up the earth, then all that mucks up the sky, and then all of it together makes lots of animals die. That's why we need to recycle everything and not use paper bags and stuff for our lunches. So there!"

"Well then, Michael. It seems that you stand corrected." Tammy smiled at Michael and passed the creamed corn over to her husband. "Doesn't it, Ed?" Tammy tried to engage Ed in the banter. "It seems our Hannah is actually quite worldly."

"Hmm?" Ed looked up impatiently, his tone indicating that he hadn't been present for this conversation at all and didn't appreciate the intrusion now. He had been brooding and closed off like this since coming home from the press conference this afternoon, ever since the incident really, and it was getting wearing. She stifled her resentment. Although it wasn't exactly a scene out of an Ozzie and Harriet episode, it still warmed Tammy's heart to hear the good-humored interaction around their dinner table, and she didn't want Ed's mood to dampen theirs. She turned to Hannah to speak, but it was Kelly who piped up.

"Yep. Sounds like you'll have to start carrying a lunchbox to school now, Michael. No more sack lunches for you! Like, you wouldn't want something to happen to Spock, would you?" Spock was their orange cat. He spent as much time outside under the big front porch as he did indoors. "You know, you've got to do your part and everything."

Michael squinted his eyes and turned down one corner of his mouth as he countered, "Hey fish-face, you better look out 'cause they say it's the aquatic animals that take the first hit. Now, pass me the paper towels while I go get a plastic cup!"

Michael got up from the table to retrieve a red Solo cup from the cupboard to make his droll point. He needed a moment to regroup. What he didn't want to divulge was that it was actually his sack lunch which had caused a problem for him just yesterday. One of the upperclassmen at the Miles Academy had snatched it out of his hands and then three others had appeared alongside him. Each had demanded a dollar from Michael to buy it back. He had initially responded by grabbing one of the culprits and insisting they return his lunch, but a school administrator had witnessed Michael's "infraction" and ordered him to eat at a table by himself. Before following the administrator to his lunchtime lockup, his eyes met with those of the hostage-takers. *So this is how it felt*, he thought. He winced as he remembered how he and his friends had harassed Jamie just like this several times last year. *To go hungry or pay the bribe?* Michael had pulled a five from his pocket, which the 'goons' had happily accepted. When he finally began eating his lunch, however, it was only to find that his chips and Little Debbie were missing.

"Meh." Kelly dismissed Michael's last remark with a classic eye-roll and a swish of her long hair.

"Michael! Kelly! Don't make fun. This is for real. Ms. Randolph says so." Hannah's round eyes implored understanding from her two older siblings.

Ed continued leaning over his plate, mechanically shoveling food into his mouth, as if engrossed in a gripping book that he could not put down until it was finished.

"Hannah, honey, I agree with you one hundred percent." Tammy looked around the table to draw everyone in. "I think we should come up with ways we can be more environmentally responsible as a family." Michael returned to the table as Tammy continued to speak. "Okay. Thinking caps, everyone. What can we do to help make our footprints on the environment smaller?"

Hannah practically bounced out of her chair. "No more plastic!"

"That's an en excellent start, Hannah. What else?" Tammy looked toward the others.

"Um." Kelley looked into the next room at the bags full of decorations for her mum. "I know. Let's use reusable bags instead of getting paper or plastic."

Trying not to look too eager to give his two cents, Michael finally spoke. "Okay. I'll start buying my lunch instead of taking it from now on." *This was sweet.* He got out of having to explain the real reason behind his desire to quit taking a lunch to school. The only thing worse than having been bullied like that would have been telling his mom about it.

Tammy held up a paper napkin in her hand for all to see. "How about if we start using my linen napkins instead of paper from now on?

Not only will it reduce our waste, but it will make every mealtime special, too."

"I can't wait to tell Ms. Randolph all about this tomorrow!" Hannah wiggled in her chair as she used a piece of bread to wipe up the last bit of gravy on her plate.

"Ed, sweetie? What about you? Can you add anything to our ideas?"

"Umh?" Ed wiped the corner of his mouth. He had sacrificed enough already. Look at what he was going through, after all. This morning's press conference was a disaster. How could his family expect him to forfeit anything else in his life right now?

"Sure." There was no missing his frustration. "You kids can walk everywhere. That way I won't have to drive y'all so many places. That's a way I could save gallons of gas and loads of money."

"Daddy." Hannah pleaded with her father for a better idea, but *Wheel of Fortune* came on, grabbing the attention of everyone around the table, and put a stop to all other discussions.

As she sat at her dressing table that night, applying her cold cream, Tammy reflected on the day. It had been, in general, an agreeable one; it was, nevertheless, rampant with contradicting emotions. Having dinner with the family had been enjoyable, despite Ed's brooding detachment, and helping Kelly with the mums had been fun too. But there was something about her conversation with Kelly that haunted her. She couldn't remember exactly what it was, but she remembered the constriction in her stomach and the uneasiness that still remained. Despite the pleasurable evening they had spent together, there was still something lurking in her mind — a dark cloud that was actually inside her, not just hanging overhead.

Looking into the mirror, Tammy continued preparing for bed. She noticed the fine lines around her eyes. She could no longer just call them laugh lines. She also noticed the puffy skin above her eyelids. *This was age.* The very lines of living drawn out on her face for all to see. She turned her head from side to side, looking at herself from every angle and thought of her circle of friends. *Maybe I should also think about calling a plastic surgeon. Just for an opinion. But how would I keep people from finding out?*

And that was when Tammy connected herself to this whole awful thing. It was in the disquiet she had felt when Ed blurted out those preposterous statements to the press. She had felt it when talking with Ed and Bill Pritchett a few weeks ago. And she felt it again today, when talking with Kelly.

When did I stop being true to myself? she asked the face in the mirror. *When did I begin letting others' opinions determine my own? When did I choose silence and speaking for Ed, rather than speaking for myself?*

She looked deeply into the eyes she saw staring back at her. *I have become dependent on others for my self-worth. And even for my thoughts and beliefs.* And it had taken Jamie O'Dell, and all that had happened to him to finally get her thinking for herself for the first time.

Why do I need others to validate my worth? She addressed her question to the face in the mirror. *And if they are validating a mask that isn't really me, does that even count? I become a cipher — someone's perception of me — I only exist in someone else's mind.*

Looking at herself with her hair pulled back and all make-up removed allowed her to see all her natural blemishes. The real Tammy. And she was beautiful. And then she knew: She could no longer cave. That familiar 'caving in' feeling was what she had felt so frequently in her life. And she wanted it to stop. She knew what she must do, and although it still frightened her, she felt affirmed in some way by having finally recognized that part of her that had hidden just under the surface for so long.

Tammy looked at herself again, newly appreciating the woman she had found there. *Who knows how many young people like Jamie have been driven underground or forced into a closet by attitudes such as mine?* She wiped a tear from the corner of her eye. *Good grief. I've put my own self in a closet with my silent acquiescence.*

In bed, with Ed snoring beside her, Tammy lay awake for some time. *I will not be a victim of my fears. That is not what I want to model for my children.* She watched the shadows of the trees dance across their bedroom walls. As a child, shadows such as these used to cause her to cower in fear. She understood now. Fear causes people to hold back — whether withholding support where support was needed, or living a lie, even to yourself. All for fear of retaliation of some kind. Like Kelly, Tammy had begun to feel a compulsion that would no longer allow her to remain silent. For silence she now realized, was compliance. It would take courage to speak up in her social circles, much more than she had demonstrated when talking with Ed and Bill Pritchett a few weeks ago. She laughed silently at herself. *And I gained the necessary fortitude I've lacked from a fifteen-year-old with glue sticks!*

She resolved to call Marcie O'Dell tomorrow. In spite of her apprehensions, she smiled and turned over to fall asleep.

If you are neutral in situations of injustice, you have chosen the side of the oppressor. If an elephant has its foot on the tail of a mouse, and you say that you are neutral, the mouse will not appreciate your neutrality.
— Desmond Tutu

Chapter 4

COFFEE SHOP

Marcie O'Dell sat alone waiting in the little coffee shop on the corner. What could Tammy Sloan possibly want to talk with her about? Circumstances being what they were, it had been very uncomfortable being around her since they had last been together in Dr. Price's office with all the others. She had noticed Tammy Sloan watching her and Jamie as she dropped him off at school every morning, and that made her uncomfortable. In fact, she had found herself averting her eyes and even sitting far forward in her seat, turning her body just so, so as to shield Jamie from Mrs. Sloan's curious gaze. *Was there malice in those eyes?* Honestly, she couldn't say. She had never managed to look over in her direction, much less return her gaze. So why had she agreed to meet her here today? Some things were just too painful to continue reliving, and she certainly did not want to invite yet another traumatic encounter.

Had she really sensed empathy in the voice over the phone yesterday, or was it just her own attempt to seek, and usually find, the good in everyone? "I'm the eternal optimist all right," she admitted half aloud to herself. Yet it just didn't seem right to dismiss the possibility that Tammy Sloan's overture could indeed be genuine. "One could only hope," she murmured as she took the first sip of her chai latte. *But even hoping for hope does not come without a certain amount of risk*, she reminded herself.

Tammy walked into the coffee shop and went up to place her order before sitting down. The girls behind the counter had engaged her with small talk while preparing her coffee, but exchanged quizzical looks when she left to join Mrs. O'Dell. The town was small enough that both women were easily recognizable and the girls were well versed in what had happened at the school, thanks to the non-stop coverage and the attention it had brought to their town. Their curiosity was aroused by this pending encounter. With raised eyebrows and attentive ears, they buzzed with false activity, scuttling around the shop in order to gain a vantage point for the conflict that was sure to follow.

As Tammy approached the table, she extended her hand before sitting down. "Marcie, thank you for agreeing to meet with me like this. I can only imagine the courage it's taking to face me, of all people."

Marcie smiled and nodded her appreciation of Tammy's sensitivity. "I must admit that I was very surprised to hear from you."

Their initial discomfort was considerable, each fumbling to find appropriate words. They had been long-time acquaintances, but never friends, and it took a moment before Tammy could find her own courage to begin. She breathed deeply.

"And for that, and for everything really, I am so very sorry," Tammy looked into her latte for the right words. "For whatever it's worth, I am sorry to have played a part in your family's pain."

Before Marcie could find the words to register her surprise at this unexpected confession, Tammy went on, "I realize now that I remained silent when I needed to be involved. And my silence has allowed these terrible things to happen to Jamie. I should have put my foot down when I first heard the boys saying unkind things about him. So many people have been hurt, most especially, you and Jamie — but my family too, and others. Marcie, I am simply heartbroken for Jamie — and for you."

Marcie felt tears welling up in her eyes. She had never expected such compassion from Tammy Sloan.

"How I wish everything could just go back to normal. Whatever that means now." Tammy took a sip, enjoying the heady scent of hazelnut, and then realized with a start that Jamie's "normal" wouldn't give the O'Dell family much of a reprieve. She chanced making eye contact with Marcie. "I am so sorry. That was very insensitive of me. I was going to say that if I could turn back the clock … but that wouldn't … I'm sure going back to normal isn't exactly …" Her eyes dropped to her hands and the cup they were cradling.

"That's all right. I understand what you're trying to say, Mrs. Sloan. I …"

"Oh, please call me Tammy."

"You can't imagine how good it feels to have someone see Jamie as just another boy who's hurting. It's been such a long time since anyone's been able to see him in that way." Marcie choked on a sob.

And with that, the ice was broken.

Tammy paused to take another sip, letting the hot liquid loosen the tightness in her own throat, before continuing. "That's why I'm here today, Marcie. I don't want it to seem that I condone Michael's behavior in any way, but I don't know how to offer the comfort and support your family deserves without abandoning my own. If I try to accept your family's alternative values, I run the risk of alienating my family. Ed and Michael may just never understand, and that frightens me."

Marcie smiled at the unintended judgment in Tammy's words. She could see that Tammy was trying. "Of course it does. It would frighten anybody. Family is a wife and mother's first priority, and I can see how holding the views you've just shared with me would make it very difficult for you at home, given your husband's …" She paused searching for the kindest way to say this. "Assertive stance," she finished.

"That's a very kind way of putting it. You know I'm here not just because of what Michael did, but I am also very embarrassed by the things Ed's been saying. I want you to know that I think very differently than he does on this. I don't really understand homosexuality, but as my fifteen-year-old daughter says, I know God created the homosexual too. And I believe everyone who God created is a neighbor whom Jesus asks us to love and care for."

Marcie reached out and placed her hand on Tammy's arm, but did not speak. The bustle inside the shop had picked up. No anticipated discord had ensued; and therefore, no one seemed to take notice of the budding intimacy between these two near-strangers, perceived by so many as potential adversaries.

"I appreciate your sentiments more than you know," said Marcie. "There's a lot of misunderstanding in our society about sexuality. Particularly about same-sex relationships."

"I hate to admit it, but I think I'm part of that society which doesn't really understand." Tammy paused. "Truthfully, I've never even thought much about gay issues because I didn't think they involved me. And I just didn't want to get embroiled in all the conflict that surrounds the whole thing these days." That was true on so many levels, but if she was making a confession, she needed to go all the way. "Huh, just saying that, I've realized I've never taken the time to educate myself about the issues — or even to work out my own inner conflicts about homosexuality, for that matter." She looked deeply into Marcie's eyes. "But now I know someone who is gay and I see how they're hurting, and that makes all the difference. I just don't know what to do."

"Oh, but Tammy, you're doing it. You're taking the first step by coming here and risking conversation on the subject. You're being honest with me and with yourself. And it sounds like you're willing to listen with the possibility of changing your mind."

"It seems so small, but you're right. That's what's missing in our world today. All the political harangue from both sides keeps conversations like this from happening. Oh, how I wish that Ed would find a different way to express his convictions. Something that actually invited dialogue for a change." She became lost in the swirling foam that topped her coffee, studying it with a thoughtful gaze as she thought of the many ways that Ed had short-circuited her attempts at conversation, not just on this subject, but on so many things over the years. "I'm sure it's no news to you to hear that Ed is still very angry. He doesn't give much consideration to alternative lifestyles. He's all about family values."

"You know, Tammy, my family doesn't feel that there is anything 'alternative' about our family values at all. My guess is that we share many of the same ideals, standards, hopes, and dreams that you do — for ourselves, and for our children and future grandchildren."

"Oh I didn't mean to imply ..." Tammy began and then stopped, flustered. "Of course we do. I hope I didn't offend you."

"You didn't, Tammy. Not to worry. We share another thing too, you know — a mother's heart. I think that is what allows us to empathize so strongly with one another." Marcie smiled at Tammy. "We are both mothers, and we understand the love a mother has for her child."

"Yes," agreed Tammy. "And we can also understand the hurt that we feel when our children hurt, or when they inflict hurt in others."

"Exactly. So may I use that connection to show you something?" Tammy nodded her acquiescence.

"So tell me, Tammy, when Michael was born, did you choose to receive him and love him based upon his looks — or maybe his temperament — or perhaps on his cognitive abilities?"

"Of course not, you know better than that." Tammy answered with a sideways glance, not knowing where Marcie was going with her statement.

"And now that he has gotten into some trouble, causing considerable grief to your family and your husband's career, do you love him any less — either of you?"

Tammy Sloan's expression was suddenly full of comprehension. She had been hurt by Michael's choices and she had also hurt for him, knowing the consequences he must now face, but her love for her son had never wavered.

"Well, in the same way, I don't place qualifications on my love and acceptance of Jamie. His sexuality is just part of who he is."

"So, you and your husband are in full acceptance of Jamie's ... being so open, I mean?" she asked.

"If by 'being open' you mean simply being honest about who he is, yes, we are fine with it. Jamie has always had a sweet and gentle spirit about him, Tammy. When he was in preschool his teacher described him as 'everybody's friend.' She told me once that another boy had dropped his cookie on the floor and it had to be thrown away, which sent the poor child into tears. But instead of continuing to eat his own, Jamie broke it in two and offered half to his friend. I also remember a time when a little girl in the neighborhood was being picked on and Jamie had been recruited to join in. Not only did he refuse, but he received a black eye for his efforts to stand up for her."

Tammy listened attentively.

"But then, as early as kindergarten, he already felt different from the others somehow. He has said he didn't know what was different at the time, but just that he knew he was different. He felt it. He had already learned — before leaving kindergarten, Tammy — not to be honest about who he was, with himself or with others, for fear of retribution.

"Pat and I thought he was being picked on because of his softness of spirit, for he was often called names and even ostracized, especially by the other boys. Somehow, even at that young age, they were able to sense his differences too. Of course Pat and I never suspected the real reasons for the bullying. I guess those who are the closest are frequently the most blind."

This statement resonated with Tammy, but for completely different reasons. She hadn't seen how Michael was changing. She had been blind to Jamie's predicament. *Heavens*, she realized, by thinking gays and their treatment by others was irrelevant to her life, she had allowed herself to overlook their very existence.

"It isn't that we didn't want to see our son as gay. It was more that it didn't occur to us because we had never known him to be any other way. Jamie, the way he was and the way he is, is all we have ever known and loved."

While in a recent counseling session, Jamie had confessed to both parents, "I wish it *was* a choice, 'cause if it was, I'd have chosen *anything* but this." Marcie paled as she shared the story with Tammy.

"Tammy, he actually told me that he used to wonder a lot, and sometimes still does, what bad thing he had to have done to be born this way — to feel this way? My beautiful, good-hearted son, having to wrestle with such a question. It breaks my heart." She had to pause and regroup before she could go on. "Imagine having to question the basic goodness of your very being. To have to question your self-worth to that degree at any age would be horrible, but to have to do it at the age of fifteen, or even worse, at the age of five?" She fought hard not to succumb to the despair that threatened to engulf her.

"Especially when those questions are fueled by another's lack of sensitivity and sometimes outright cruelty," Tammy offered gently. She understood.

"You know, someone once said that we can't be human without each other. It's through the eyes of others that we learn who we are. My poor sweet Jamie. Imagine the image of himself that he has received from the outside world and he kept all that from us for so long. That's why Patrick and I work so hard now to create a safe and loving place for Jamie at home. We hope, that in some way, our love and total acceptance can make up for the negatives he's received everywhere else."

Tammy nodded her encouragement.

"Can you imagine the hurt and guilt I've felt," Marcie continued, "after finding that my son felt so alone for so long and was afraid to talk — even to us — the two people who love him most in the world?"

Tammy didn't have to imagine it. The pain was written all over Marcie's lovely face.

"And my guilt stems from thoughts that I may have contributed in some way to that negative self-imaging." Tammy absentmindedly stirred her coffee. "I was vaguely aware of the other boys having teased him in the past, and I never did anything about it, other than to offer a rote 'Be kind to others' sort of response. I knew what I had been taught, and I wasn't sure of what I felt about the whole issue, so I chose not to see it. It just wasn't personal … yet."

Marcie's expression was now one of appreciation, if not a little admiration. Although it hurt to hear these confessions of intolerance and indifference, it was indeed a victory for Jamie.

Their coffees now long gone, the women began to gather their things. But before separating into the parking lot outside, Tammy took hold of Marcie's hand and held her gaze.

"It was good talking about things that really matter. I'd really like to do this again."

"Me too." Marcie smiled as she placed her free hand over Tammy's. "I could use a friend."

Tammy and Marcie took one another in with new appreciation. They saw in each other not only a new friend, but a much desired and heartily appreciated ally, one who symbolized for them the courage they each needed to face their respective situations.

She got the call on the way home and had turned around immediately to go back into town. And now they had ridden in an uncomfortable silence for most of the drive home from the Miles Academy. It was a stark contrast to the wonderful conversation she had just shared with Marcie a few hours earlier. Michael's lip was swollen and his cheekbone was already beginning to purple. He would have a full-blown black eye by morning. He was reticent to share any details, but when Tammy looked over to see his hand pressing into his side and his face etched into a grimace, she became really concerned.

"Michael, do we need to go straight to the doctor?"

He took a few measured breaths as he sat up a little straighter, adjusting the seat belt for comfort.

"No, it's nothing really. I'm fine, Mom."

"It's not nothing, Michael. You look like you're in pain."

Michael felt the burn in his eyes and he tried to avoid his mother's gaze by turning to stare fixedly out the passenger window. He didn't want her pity, and he knew he needed to hide what he was feeling or he'd have to suffer sympathy — which could be his undoing. The truth was he felt terrible. But it wasn't anything that any doctor could treat. There was no bandage that would help him today. He had been hurt worse than this after some of his football games, but the injuries today had brought him no glory. Just shame. And that was what he didn't want his mother to see.

Tammy reached over and touched Michael on the arm, lightly caressing him through the fabric of his white shirt, part of the "uniform" he was required to wear every day. She could feel the tension in the strong, young muscles under her hand and hoped that her touch would help him relax. When he made no attempt to move from her ministrations, she was encouraged; and so, continuing to drive with one hand on the steering wheel, Tammy began lightly massaging his left shoulder and then the base of his neck.

"Thanks, Mom," she heard him mumble appreciatively.

"I'm glad it helps." She couldn't see Michael's face. He was still looking out the window, but he nodded. "I think you'll feel better if you talk about it, honey. Want me to stop the car?"

He shook his head emphatically. "No. Just keep driving."

"Okay, but only if you'll tell me what happened."

Michael slowly turned in his seat to look at his mother, and he let out an audible sigh. "Oh, Mom, I don't want to talk about it." Tammy put on her blinker and started to pull over to the shoulder of the road. "Oh, all right. Geez, Mom!"

Tammy pulled back onto the road and kept driving, but now with both hands on the wheel and eyes focused straight ahead as Michael began his story.

"Apparently Phillip and Denny told some of the other guys at Miles that I squealed on them about the Jamie thing. They said they wouldn't have gotten suspended if it wasn't for me. So now everybody there thinks I'm a rat."

"And are you?"

"No, Mom. I'm no rat. I would never have given up their names on my own, but when Price said he'd heard they were involved and asked me point-blank if that was true, I couldn't bald-face lie to him — not with you and Dad sitting right there. Geez!"

Tammy let some time pass before she gently queried, "So, then what happened?"

"So, I got beat up!"

"But what happened, Michael? Aren't there teachers there who constantly monitor everything y'all do? How did you get hurt?"

"Yeah, it's like friggin' kindergarten, Mom," Michael shrugged. "They walk us to classes. They walk us to lunch. They even walk us to the bathroom. That's where it happened."

"In the bathroom?"

"Yeah." Michael looked out the window again. "They escort you to the door, but they don't actually walk in with you. I guess they think we're trustworthy enough to pee without their help. Wrong."

"So what happened, honey?"

Michael watched the trees pass by as they sped down the road toward their house. A Williamson County worker was on a tractor up ahead, probably mowing the grass alongside the roadway for the last time this season.

"Michael?"

"It's really no big deal, Mom." He turned and actually looked at her. "Really. It's just embarrassing, that's all." But it had been more than embarrassing. It had been humiliating. Only a few boys were allowed in the bathrooms together at one time, and Michael had felt self-conscious the moment he walked in. There were only two urinals, and a senior was already in place in front of one of them; both stalls had also been occupied, so Michael had no choice but to use the urinal next to the twelfth-grader.

"What's wrong, dickhead? You *pee shy* today?" Michael had stared straight ahead, ignoring the taunt and willing his bladder to work. It was then that a toilet flushed and another senior pushed open the door to his stall. "Nah, Derek. He's not shy. He talks all the time. He rats out his friends. Makes 'em take the fall with him."

That's when Michael felt the blow to the back of his head, forcing him into the metal pipes rising out of the top of the porcelain basin. Holding a hand over his eye, he turned, with his fly still down, only to receive another blow, this time to his jaw. They kicked him behind his knees, causing him to crumple to the ground, chuckling as they left him there in the bathroom.

"Michael?"

"Okay. There were a couple of guys — one at the urinal and one in the stalls. The guy next to me called me some names. I told him to shut up and then the other guy came out of the stall and decked me." He shrugged his shoulders. "That's about it." He looked out the window again.

"Michael, I don't think the school knows all these details. We need to report this!"

Michael answered quickly this time. "No, Mom. Please, no." He swallowed hard. "Somebody else already did." The last thing he wanted was for his parents to get involved and blow this up like they did the other one.

"Who?" Did the other boy turn in his friend?" She was glad he was starting to open up and wanted to keep him talking.

"No. They came after me because they think I'm a rat. They were just making sure I know what happens when someone rats out someone else around there."

Michael rubbed the back of his right hand. She turned away from the highway just long enough to catch a quick look and saw the abrasions on his knuckles. Tammy wondered if Michael had also struck one of his attackers. She knew the zero tolerance stance they had for fighting at the Miles Academy. She couldn't imagine what further trouble he might find himself in if he were caught. *But he hadn't done anything! They had attacked him!* Her son was being beaten at school and there was nothing she could do about it. Why should he have to face further punishment for simply defending himself? She almost said it aloud. *Now I really know how Marcie has felt!* But Michael's voice interrupted her thoughts.

"There was also a guy in one of the other stalls. I guess they didn't know he was there. Or they didn't care. But after they left, he came out and saw me on the floor. He asked if I was okay. Duh! I told him to just go away and leave me alone. But he wouldn't." Once again, Michael looked over at his mother and she could see the puzzlement in his eyes. "He just stood there, leaning against the stall with his arms crossed, watching me. He wouldn't leave."

"Who was it, honey?"

Michael looked straight ahead as they turned into the gravel drive to the house. "I don't know. Some guy. I've seen him around. He's in one of those classes for the special-ed kids, so I never see him except at lunch."

Tammy turned off the ignition and looked at Michael as he talked. She knew that children with special needs were protected from certain disciplinary actions — like being sent to places like Miles. Ed's sister, Edith, was a teacher. Tammy had heard her rant about kids with disabilities who couldn't be punished for their actions. Apparently, they were protected from school placement changes unless a committee deemed the behavior not a "manifestation" of his disability. The only exceptions involved drugs or weapons. Good grief! Who was this kid who had come to Michael's rescue?

"Anyway, after a few minutes, he got me some wet paper towels and helped me wipe the blood off my mouth. Then he asked me where it hurt and should I go to the nurse. When I said I didn't want to go to the nurse, he pulled me up and told me that we needed to go tell the principal — but that he had a plan. He said my teacher would notice I'd been hurt and would send me there anyway. If he went with me, then he could be my witness and it wouldn't be like I was ratting or anything.

And so, that's what we did. He walked into Mrs. Redrow's office with me and really, he told most of the story himself. I don't get it. Why would he do all that for me? I mean, he just saw how I got beat up, so why would he risk that same thing? We don't even know each other."

Why indeed, she thought. But she was so very grateful. There is no way to know what lies underneath appearances, she reminded herself, or beneath the stereotypes that set our expectations so low for one another. She never would have guessed that someone with a drugs or weapons offense in his background would have shown such compassion. But he had.

"Michael, that's compassion in its truest form. When we offer assistance to those in need and seek justice for them — especially when we do it at some risk to ourselves — that's loving our neighbor, my friend." She took his hand in hers and gave it a gentle squeeze. "You met a Samaritan in the flesh today, it would seem."

Michael was quiet for a long time before he volunteered, "You know, it felt really good having someone care like that."

His mother smiled over at him, "Yes. I'm sure it did." Michael continued looking straight ahead, but he gave her a little half-smile back.

"And what you do with what you received today is very important."

He nodded. She could tell she had definitely gotten through to him, but as he un-clicked his seat belt, he turned toward her grinning and pointed at his blackening eye. "You mean this beauty?"

"Careful you, or I'll be tempted to make them match!" Tammy swatted him playfully on the backside as he pushed open the car door to make his exit.

She didn't know what had prompted such openness. She would have preferred the kind of face-to-face, heart-to-heart talks she had with Kelly, but it was apparently easier for Michael to talk this way — in the car, with both of them looking out different windows. *Well, whatever it takes*, she thought.

Michael hadn't opened up to her like this in over a year. Maybe even longer. How could she feel almost giddy, when she was watching her son limp up the steps to the house, having just been beaten up at school? It was a little confusing, but she didn't care. She guessed there wouldn't be much more conversation. Maybe there didn't need to be. But she felt that she had glimpsed a side of her son that she hadn't seen in quite some time.

Welcome back, Michael, she thought.

Kelly was sitting on the couch, with feet perched upon the coffee table, painting her nails.

"So what happened to YOU?" She held the brush in mid-air, the bottle of *Bikini So Teeny* on the table in front of her.

"Somebody asked me to the prom. What do you think happened to me?" Michael kept walking.

"Michael. Seriously. What happened?" She screwed the top back onto her neon polish and followed him up the stairs.

She tapped the closed door, but didn't wait for a response. She walked right in and found him lying on the bed, flat on his back. "Tell me."

"It's just more bullshit to add to my bullshit life! I got beat up in the bathroom today. There you go."

"That's all you're gonna tell me?"

"There's really not a whole lot to it, Kel. Some guys think I'm a rat, so they pummeled me in the john. But the weird thing is that some other guy that was in there offered to help me out. I still don't get it."

"So do you know these guys?"

"The guys who decked me? Yeah. I know 'em. But the kid who stepped up to make sure I was okay? I don't know him at all." He propped himself up on his elbow to look at this sister. "Isn't that weird?"

"Not really. Sounds like it was just someone being nice, to me. Trying to help you out, you know?"

"Kel, this is Miles we're talking about. People don't just go around 'being nice.' It's survival I'm talking about. You've got to act tough."

"To keep from getting beat up, you mean? So how's that working for ya these days?"

Michael dropped back onto his back. He didn't answer.

"I think you should just be thankful that someone stepped up for you. You know, had your back." She shoved his backpack off the chair so she could sit down. "Just 'cause there aren't many guys there brave enough to be kind doesn't make it weird."

Michael still lay in silence, looking up at the ceiling of his room.

"It sounds like it's easier for you to accept that someone beat you up than it is to accept the fact that this one guy was nice to you."

Kelly put her feet on the chair, her knees bent just under her chin, so she could blow the polish dry. She waited him out. She knew he would eventually talk.

"Well, maybe it is." He sat up, punched his pillow and then leaned against the headboard.

"How come?"

"I don't know."

"Come on. Talk."

"No, really, I don't know."

She rolled her eyes in exasperation. She didn't believe him.

"I guess it's just different with guys, Kel. You want everyone to think you're tough. You know. 'There's no cryin' in baseball.'" That sort of thing." *A League of Their Own* had always been a family favorite on movie nights. "It's an unspoken rule that if you show a weakness, you're fair game."

"So have you shown them your weakness?"

Michael's head snapped to attention. "No! What do you mean?"

"Well, they beat you up, so they must think you're weak. You just said it yourself."

Michael reached for his phone. Kelly heard the familiar tones of the *Words with Friends* app, but she wouldn't let him off this easy.

"I know your weakness, Michael." She could hear the ascending 'plop, plop, plops' of the letters being arranged for his game. "You're not really like them. And maybe they know it."

Michael continued playing. He did not respond.

"Well, looks like we're done here." She got up and walked toward the door. "I'll send Mom up with a steak for your eye. You're gonna need it."

Kelly had barely closed the door shut when he flung his phone to the foot of his bed. She knew him better than he knew himself. But what had made him more upset? The fact that she had pegged him? Or the fact that she was right? Maybe he needed to call her back in there to help him figure that one out too! *God!* He hated this.

And it was then that it came to him. He remembered a time when Jamie O'Dell had been the one on the bathroom floor. And Michael had been one of those laughing that day. He cringed, now knowing just what he had done.

Since Ed had to stay in Austin overnight, Tammy decided to indulge herself with a little TV in bed. She had always enjoyed propping up the pillows, snuggling under the covers, and watching a good movie, usually with something comforting to drink and a good nibble or two close at hand. Tonight she had poured herself a glass of cab and had brought her favorite dark chocolate and sea-salt candy bar to bed with her. Comfort food par excellence! It was too late to catch a movie, so she started flipping channels, looking for something entertaining, when she landed on a rerun of *Law & Order SVU*. Well, a good drama would be okay too. She watched for a while before she caught the gist of the story.

Detectives Stabler and Benson were investigating a crime where the alleged perpetrator was a prime suspect only because of the way he looked. There was no evidence against him. Nothing to authenticate suspicions. Just innuendo. The suspect had been labeled by neighbors, placed in a pigeonhole by a society that typecast him as a troublemaker. A young black man in his teens. A hoodie and baggy pants. It was enough for his neighbors to immediately assume he was a thug, and therefore, a viable person of interest. Tammy found herself comparing this alleged ruffian with Michael's savior from earlier that day. She hated to admit that she still felt surprise at the person who had helped. He had to be a real trouble-maker in order to be at Miles, and she just didn't expect someone there to abide by the golden rule.

Benson was now interviewing the young man's neighbors at the station, where they were making a spectacle of themselves with their prejudiced comments and presuppositions. Tammy couldn't take any more of this. She muted the sound on the TV. And only then did she see the flaw in her own thinking.

Wouldn't her own son be "just another trouble-maker" too, if she viewed him through the same lens that she so readily applied to the boy who had come to his aid? She was just as guilty of stereotyping as were those racist neighbors in this show. Funny how the universe conspired to keep sending you the same message until you finally got it. Her pastor had called this "synchronicity" and had suggested this was one way the Spirit spoke through the events of our lives. Well, she was getting this message loud and clear. And she had some work to do.

Marcie's words from that morning came back to her then. She had said something to Tammy about people not being able to see Jamie for who he really was. That he was just a boy who was hurting. Not a stereotype of their perceptions. This whole thing — with Jamie, with Michael, with the Samaritan — with Ed and herself. It was about much more than homosexuality. It was about basic humanity.

Be the living expression of God's kindness.
— Mother Teresa

Chapter 5

RECONCILIATION

S he wanted to steer her family toward something better than this. Earlier in the evening she had attended a Worship Committee meeting where plans for their World Communion service were being discussed. If she, Tammy Sloan, couldn't find reconciliation within her own home, how in the world could she be expected to participate in the planning of a service about exactly that? World Communion Sunday, held on the first Sunday of October every year, originated in the Shadyside Presbyterian Church in 1933; and since then, other denominations and numerous congregations had participated and promoted this service of Christian unity and ecumenical cooperation.

Since her show of courage in the study less than three weeks ago, she had felt neither unity nor cooperation with Ed on any level, and her conversation in the coffee shop with Marcie had only reinforced her desire to improve communication at home. She had left the planning meeting feeling bereft. She had not actively participated, offering no ideas, sharing no opinions. Witnessing tonight's plans for this special service had only emphasized the troubled waters she had been treading with Ed.

And the press conference had only accomplished so much. Ed's statement of regret had stimulated renewed interest in *the story*. It seemed the press was going to be unrelenting in their criticism, regardless of what he had to say. His motives and integrity had been questioned by progressive opponents while he was also being criticized by his own conservative political base for flip-flopping on his previous statements.

Ed had done the right thing. But he, and all those around him, had not felt much better because of it. Tammy reflected on her own difficult decision to do what she felt had been right by speaking her mind. *Well, I don't feel a whole lot better myself,* she thought.

She stepped out of her house shoes and pulled back the covers. Ed's silence had been as damaging as any hurtful words he could have said. After their decades together she was used to his moods, but this was becoming a way of life.

She watched Ed peruse the headlines that were highlighted in the Flipboard app on his iPad. He was taking everything in, working up to whatever it was that his opinion would be. Compromise and listening to understand an opponent's view would never be Ed's strong suits, no matter what the issue. And now, more than ever, he saw negotiation as a form of concession — unconscionable and, therefore, an impossible option for him.

As she watched him scanning the daily news, she could no more discern whether he was reading an article about breaches in national security or school lunch menus. But whatever the current topic, and despite his current mood, she knew that she had to bring up their ongoing detachment — just another subject he might balk at or attack her for bringing up. But she had to try. She owed it to the both of them — and to the kids.

She had brought a cup of tea to bed with her. "Would you like me to get you something, hon?"

"Um." He swiped the screen to advance to the next page. "No. But thanks." He continued reading.

"Let me know when you're finished reading. I'd like to talk to you about something." She blew on her cup.

Ed kept flipping through articles, finally closing the cover of his iPad almost ten minutes after Tammy had requested his attention. "Well at least they're just running the same stories about me now. I didn't see anything new out there today."

"Well, I think we should take that as good news, then. Don't you?"

He put his iPad on the nightstand, took off his readers, and placed them on top. "I'll take what I can get these days."

"You know, these days we might just have to work a little harder to find the good."

Ed gave her a deadpan look as if to say, "Duh!"

"And I think we can do it." She attempted another sip of tea. "Mmm. Just right." She knew she had to bring it up. It was now or never. She couldn't keep living like this. "Do you remember Jack and Donna Reynolds?" She brought the cup to her mouth again.

"Who?"

"You know, Jack and Donna. From Michael's Cub Scouts when he was in about third grade."

"Oh, yeah. How could I forget that guy?" Ed had met Jack when helping Michael, a Wolf Cub at the time, with his Pinewood Derby. Or was he a Bear? Anyway, each scout was given a block of wood, four plastic wheels, and four nails. A finished car must use all nine pieces and not exceed a certain weight or length, and it must fit on the track used by the entire pack. The idea behind the Pinewood Derby was for a parent, usually the father, to spend time helping his son design, carve, paint, and add weights — fine-tuning the final car and preparing for competition.

Ed had devised the plan, sketched it out, and then had carved Michael's pine block himself with his band saw. Reynolds had accused Ed of taking over the construction of Michael's car, thus violating the spirit of the event. He had pushed to have Michael disqualified from the race, and he had almost won. Yes. Ed remembered Jack Reynolds, all right.

"I just don't want us to end up like them, that's all." Tammy's plea was sincere. "We could all see the way they lived separate lives, remember? There didn't seem to be much in the way of 'family' going on there at all. They were just not a part of each other's lives, emotionally or physically."

But Ed could not recall what Donna Reynolds looked like. He looked toward the ceiling, trying to bring her face into recollection. But all he could remember was Jack Reynolds and his fat little kid with the red hair and freckles.

Tammy turned to face Ed, her tired eyes searching his face for a reaction. "I don't know if they were always like that or not, but, I don't want that to be us, Ed. I meant it when I said, 'I do.'"

"And I did, too." He quit searching for the enigmatic countenance of Donna Reynolds and turned instead to face his wife, the partner he had chosen so long ago. "I'm sorry for the way I've been acting lately, Tam." He rested his hand on her supple thigh. "You know I love you."

She patted the large paw resting on her leg. "Yes, sweetie, I know." And her heart swelled. "I've got an idea. Let's leave all of this behind us." She put her tea cup on the nightstand. "Even if it's just for a little while. I think we could both use a little change of scenery."

"Ed bristled. "Dammit, Tammy, you know I can't be leaving town right now. I don't think you understand how ..."

She waved her arms wildly, as if to stop traffic, and interrupted him. "Oh no, Ed. That's not what I meant." And she turned her whole body toward him, sitting on her feet now and leaning in. "Let's just go on a date. A night on the town — down in Austin — that's all. Just to get away from everything. And to give us a chance to reconnect too."

Ed's expression had gone through a veritable smorgasbord of emotions as his features registered, first, the agitation with which he had met her every comment these last few weeks, and then his characteristic exasperation. But then something miraculous happened. His visage softened and a tentative smile began to creep across his face before it transformed his whole countenance into an all-out grin of anticipation. His expressive journey was as easy for Tammy to follow as a trail of breadcrumbs. She beamed.

"And I know just the place," he said.

The Oasis was known by Hill Country locals as the Sunset Capital of Texas. And over the years, Ed and Tammy had celebrated many happy occasions under the brightly colored umbrella tables on its multi-level decks. It was nothing fancy, but it was Texas at its finest: You could listen to live music featuring local bands nearly every night and choose from a menu that boasted a variety of Texas specialties. Ed always went for the Hatch Green Chile Burgers, while Tammy varied her experience a bit by alternating between the Grilled Chicken with Roasted Tomatillo and Poblano Rajas and the Grilled Red Fish with Cilantro Lime Butter. Depending on the time of year and the temperature outside, they washed down every meal with a glass of wine or a cold Shiner. Tonight

Tammy was in "vacation mode" and chose the fish to summon up delicious memories of their last trip to Vieques Island together, while Ed ordered a bottle of Geyser Peak, their favorite Sauvignon Blanc, to complement the festivity of the occasion.

Ed had connections, and he had arranged for one of their finest tables next to the ledge. They had a fabulous view of Lake Travis and the evening sun, which was just beginning to set over the water as the Sloans toasted to a new beginning.

"I'm so glad you suggested coming here, hon. It's always been such a special place for me." She closed her eyes, taking in the warmth of the evening sun's golden rays as they danced across her face.

"Anything for you, doll." He kissed her cheek tenderly.

Unaccustomed to any kind of public display of affection in her marriage, it thrilled her that he had let his feelings for her escape his insistence on propriety and the constrictive box he had formed around his heart. The late September breeze whispered to her heart, imploring it to stop its steady beat. Their glasses clinked, bringing a much-welcomed merriment to the table.

Their feelings of shared happiness, of intimacy and togetherness, had been missing from their relationship for some time. Tammy tried to pin point exactly when things had begun to change for them, but it was impossible to do so. It had been a gradual process. *Like the proverbial frog in a pot*, she told herself. If dropped into boiling water, the poor little fellow would frantically try to climb out. But if the water was temperate, and the heat was increased very slowly, the frog was lulled into a stupor and didn't realize what was happening until it was too late. *If we can just acknowledge how we've both changed in unintentional ways,* she thought, *and then work toward making any necessary adjustments together, we'll be fine again.* She had a good feeling about everything. This place had a way of doing that to her.

As the sun cast its orange haze over the rippling waters of the lake, Tammy felt all her recent tensions evaporating. She entered into the serene beauty in front of her and let her soul rest in those waters, luxuriating in their support. She was weightless, expansive, a part of the whole. Her thoughts drifted, first, to the lake and to all the life teeming there, and, then, to their own little pond. And she remembered her reverie of a few weeks ago. "A little bit ago," she told Ed, "I was on the front porch, watching our pond. All the turtles and fish in there together. And it made me think of something. Of you and me, actually. We aren't so unlike them, you know."

Ed's mouth was full. He had gotten an especially hot jalapeño in that last bite and his eyes had begun to water. He couldn't talk just then, so he nodded at Tammy, encouraging her to continue with her thoughts.

"I watched them and thought about how different they are. One can climb out onto land and uses lungs to breathe, and one keeps to the water and uses gills, but neither one tries to get the other to live or breathe their way. They simply co-exist. They live and let live — and swim side by side. They ..."

Ed gulped his ice water and interrupted. "Tammy. Turtles are carnivores. They *eat* fish!" He shook his head in amusement and reached for another chip.

Now it was Tammy's turn to be exasperated. "You're completely missing my point, Ed! I'm just using the way they live together in our pond as an example of how I hope we can bridge our differences." She leaned in toward Ed and placed her hand on his forearm. "So we can accept and respect — and enjoy — one another again, Ed." She looked deep into his eyes as she said this last: "It's a fact that we don't see eye to eye, but we can still live in peace and harmony. It just takes tolerance — like the turtles and the fish. Acceptance of one another just the way they are. And it's all there, right in our own front yard."

Ed mumbled under his breath, but was loud enough for Tammy to hear. "Not in our house, though."

"Exactly!" Tammy breathed a sigh of relief and leaned back in her chair. This was going to be easier than she had imagined.

"So, Mrs. Sloan, what happened to your tolerating and accepting me and Michael instead of trying to change us?" He scooped up a generous serving of guacamole with his chip and popped the whole thing into his mouth, crunching loudly, as he attempted to stare her down.

"What?" She was blindsided. "How long are you going to hold it against me that I don't agree with Michael's past decisions or your insensitive words? Just because I can't defend you on this doesn't mean you need to question my love or support!"

"If we had it your way," and he spread his hands wide, completely ignoring her question, "we would turn our entire value system on its head."

Tammy just stared at him. Had he really just said that? She gripped the stem of her glass to keep it from slipping between her fingers.

"And that, my dear, is exactly why we need more people like me and Michael. Believers who are willing to stand up to all these attacks on traditional morality. I'm tired of all this bullshit propaganda being promoted by liberals with progressive agendas! Don't you see? Our individual freedoms would become license if not constrained by Christian morality and individual responsibility. The future of our 'one nation under God' depends on people like us. Because if we don't do it, who will? I refuse to aid in the demise of society as we know it, Tammy. I just won't do it!" Ed punctuated his speech with a deep breath and shake of his head. He turned away from his wife, looking beyond their table to survey the crowd for approval of his assertions.

The sun fell into the water and disappeared, along with its warmth and its shine.

"So you're saying my being supportive of you means that I have to agree with you on everything? And not have my own opinions?" *If that were the case, Ed might as well get a mirror to sleep with every night.* "Really, Ed? Are you saying that is who I have to be? Who I am to you?"

"Tammy, for Christ's sake, do you have to make everything so hard?"

Their server, Catrin, a perky UT student, suddenly appeared with two large plates: Tammy's grilled red fish and Ed's burger. Oblivious to the large portion of consternation already present at the table, she asked if there was anything else they would need.

Tammy looked up at Catrin and smiled. "No, thank you. We've got more than we can handle here already."

"I'm just asking for one simple thing." Ed looked around at the other tables now to make sure no one was watching their date-turned-argument, and then he practically hissed at her. "For you to support me. Like you always have." He picked up the bottle of wine and then, in what would otherwise have been a gallant gesture, he refilled her glass, then, his own.

Was she being selfish to want to be her own person? No. She didn't think so. But of course he would see it that way. They faced each other, but it was Ed who waited for Tammy's response this time.

"I'm afraid your 'one simple thing' isn't all that simple, Ed."

He looked at her, uncomprehending, and Tammy sighed.

How do two people BOTH lose an argument?

If you are always trying to be normal, you will never know how amazing you can be.
— *Maya Angelou*

Chapter 6

AS IN UNCLE TOM'S CLOSET

E d Sloan had held the office of Texas Land Commissioner for twelve years now, and in all that time, he had never become inured to the sense of history and the thrill of power he experienced upon entering the General Land Office's suite each morning.

Established in 1836, his position was the oldest continuously elected executive office in Texas history, predating that of even the governor.[1] He took pride in being one in the line of this venerable succession, men who had steered the GLO over the years and, therefore, had had such a strong impact on the whole State of Texas. On entering his own spacious office each morning, he would nod his respect to his predecessors whose portraits lined the walls. Then, before settling in to whatever was on his agenda for the day, he would read once again the framed GLO mission statement he kept on his desk, thus recommitting himself to his responsibility: "to serve the schoolchildren, veterans, and all people of Texas by preserving their history, protecting their environment, expanding economic opportunity, and maximizing state revenue through innovative administration and prudent stewardship of state lands and resources."

It was a tall order, but one Ed felt uniquely qualified to carry out. He saw himself as the protector of the entire state and worked diligently to defend its citizens and its land from anything that he deemed threatening. No wonder the Commissioner had such a high opinion of himself.

71

He sat at his impressive desk, rifling through the stack of reports that his top assistant, Holly Anderson, had placed there.

"Thanks, Holly. I'll get back with you in a bit, after I've looked over everything."

"Okay, let me know. I'll just keep working with Trey on the Resource Management Codes until lunchtime." Dismissing herself by patting the top of his desk with her well-manicured hand, she turned to leave. "And don't forget that after next Friday, I'll be gone for two weeks."

Peering over the top of his readers, he watched her leave his office. *She certainly was a looker.* Ed's standards would never allow him to be unfaithful, but Holly's trim hourglass figure could tempt even the most moralistic of devoted husbands. She was pleasing to the eyes; and therefore, in an effort to draw desired attention to them, he sometimes made hers the public face on the more unremarkable matters that crossed his desk. He also found her attractiveness and charm great assets in bridging the inevitable divides the Land Office encountered when navigating between opposing positions, which was the case on most of the issues they faced.

She had been a real find, all right. Tall for a woman, she was able to look many men straight in the eye, yet, she remained appealingly feminine, thus garnering the respect of her predominantly male counterparts without seeming to threaten them. She had a gift for smoothing robust egos and strong emotions, and her striking appearance could bring attention to the GLO's position in a way that he certainly could not.

Besides all that, Ed admired her strength of character. Holly's husband had been a local hero, a firefighter killed in the line of duty years ago. In saving a seven-year-old girl from a three-alarm fire in a neighboring town, Bruce Anderson had himself sustained multiple injuries and had died two weeks later from complications. It had been a terrible tragedy, and Ed remembered how the whole town had rallied around the young family — flag protocol and all. They had flown their flags at half-staff all across town in memory of Captain Anderson. He would never forget the emotions that Bruce's death and funeral had evoked in their small community. Even Ed had been touched. Allegiance!

Valor! Sacrifice! What more could anyone ask of a young man? And, despite overwhelming heartbreak and the difficulties of raising two young children on her own, his young widow had exemplified many of those same inspiring traits. She had remained faithful to his memory and dedicated to her children, seemingly to the point of sacrificing a personal life.

Ed didn't remember ever seeing a boyfriend escort her to any of the staff Christmas parties or fundraising dinners over the years. She had stayed true to her lost hero. An admirable woman, indeed. And upon further reflection, Ed realized that he had benefited from Holly's virtues himself. Had she actually been attached to a man, she probably wouldn't carry that wonderful mystique that worked so effectively for her, and subsequently for him. *No need to fix what doesn't need fixing.* He left the questions of Holly's love life behind and returned to the stacks of paper on his desk.

The first thing he saw was a report from the latest DART (Dallas Area Rapid Transit) executive session. He received their meeting minutes due to the energy agreement they held with the state, which created additional revenue for the Permanent School Fund. Apparently, the panel had just approved a plan to extend employee health benefits to domestic partners, including gay and lesbian couples and their children.

"Good God!" exclaimed Sloan. "It's everywhere!" He disgustedly read on and was glad to discover that the plan would still have to receive final approval by the full board in a vote next month. *Those damn fools better come to their senses. Looks like a call in to Bates and Robertson encouraging them to put a stop to this would be in order.* And he set the entire folder of correspondence in the three-tiered tray to his left, indicating immediate action.

He briefly glanced at, and then pushed aside, the report on the Border Energy Forum and guest-worker program. The Border Energy Forum was a collaborative effort among the ten border states along the U.S.-Mexico border, four from the States and six from Mexico. The original idea was to exchange information about the best ways to produce and consume energy and to enforce environmental protections in those fast growing regions, but because of the efforts of Ed's nephew, Henry Keene, even more conversations were being had now with regard to potential partnerships for economic development by means of the undocumented worker. It was all about disparity of opportunity and protection. This was going to look good come election time, and Henry had this one all wrapped up.

Ed smiled. He felt a second father to his sister's son, and Henry sure had been a much desired bright spot for Ed lately. Edith's husband had died when Henry was very young and from that day on, Ed and Tammy had been very involved in Henry's upbringing, and in helping Edith as much as they could. Thankfully, he had his talented nephew to count on these days. He saw no need to bother himself further with this file right now, and he happily moved on to the next stack.

"Damn liberals." he muttered to himself as he waded through dozens of letters regarding gun control. Conservative Tea Party members and left-wing Democrats were both weighing in with verbose entreaties, but they all boiled down to "Change the law" or "Not!" It was all just a waste of time and energy as far as Ed was concerned. This was Texas, for God's sake, and Texans were going to keep their guns. And he pushed a large stack of unread missives aside, never intending to look at them again.

Oh, good! Here was the invitation to the 27th Annual Abraham Lincoln Birthday Celebration organized by the El Paso County Republican Party. *It may be the armpit of Texas,* he thought, but he would definitely attend. The chairman of the Veterans Land Board was scheduled to speak, so Sloan would arrange for a photo op. He needed to kick-start his campaign earlier than usual to make up for all the bad publicity he had received over the O'Dell kid. It was a damn shame too, for he had lost some good momentum with folks on both sides of the aisle over that whole debacle. Now he would have to take every opportunity to get his face in the papers, or on the six o'clock news, in order to show that everything was getting back to normal. He needed to turn the tide with the media, and this might just do the trick. *You couldn't lose with Abe Lincoln.* That invitation went into the all-important three-tiered tray for Holly, as well. He would have her begin on his speech right away, before she left on vacation.

Lastly, he shoveled a few more thick files and reports aside in order to see the latest on the Boy Scouts' current problem. He opened this file slowly and carefully, reading each article that offered both encouraging and discouraging updates on the matter.

He kept abreast of this issue, not because he had any real direct power to assist the scouts in their desires to stay "morally straight," but because he knew that when he spoke, his voice was heard by a large audience. And Ed was an Eagle Scout. He wanted to preserve the integrity of the organization that had meant so much to him in his formative years.

The Scouts' home office was in Irving, set between Dallas and Fort Worth, but even so, his opinions and influence could make a difference up there. He would continue speaking out against immorality and depravity and offering protection to the children of Texas whenever and wherever he could. Besides all that, it wouldn't hurt to secure another firm block of votes for next October, especially with that young Bush kid recently throwing his hat into the ring. Ed knew George P. Bush wanted to use this little-known but powerful post to continue his family's political dynasty, and this newest Bush was fluent in Spanish and considered a rising star among conservative Hispanics.

Pritchett wanted Ed to lay low on this whole topic of gays and scouts. He thought Ed had said more than enough about homosexuality already, but they both knew he had to draw his conservative base in tighter, now more than ever. Sloan didn't like gays, and he *did* like winning elections. This could be a double-whammy win if he played his cards right.

"Commissioner, your nephew is here," his secretary, Mary Anne, beeped in.

"Let him in, of course," Ed responded, and he began clearing his desk of the disorder before him.

"Good morning, Uncle!" boomed Henry Keene as he came through the door separating Ed's inner sanctum from the rest of the office staff. He looked so much like his late father, having missed out on the height and dark coloring of the Sloan lineage. At only five-foot-eight, he had dark blonde hair and brilliant blue eyes that often twinkled with laughter. Henry's disposition was perpetually cheerful, and everybody liked him. He was an anomaly within the political machine in which he worked, and yet he thrived there. People on both sides of the aisle counted him as friend.

"Good morning, boy! I was just reviewing your report on the guest worker plan. Looks like you've got it all under control."

"Yeah, it's looking good, I think," said Henry, as he sat down opposite his uncle in one of the big wingbacks. "Representative Kline is willing to carve out a sliver of middle ground in the debates. It appears that he is more than receptive to our offering up the possibility of a guest-worker program as a trial case for how Texas will handle both legal and illegal immigration reform."

He continued to talk, while simultaneously scrolling through emails on his phone.

"And at a House subcommittee hearing just yesterday, Buck Reeves said that he would support a measure that would offer at least temporary legalization for illegal immigrants who are currently working in the state. Pretty good coming from the chairman of the full committee. It's all coming down to approved occupations and time frames, though."

"Actually, son, as in all things, it is coming down to old-fashioned political posturing," Ed assured him. "Both sides have wanted to act on this, but they have been unwilling to work together until you got them talking to each other." This last comment was made with a fatherly pride that didn't go unnoticed by his nephew.

"Well, one can only hope," Henry smiled a little self-consciously as he continued to catch up on numerous unopened emails.

Ed nodded, leaned back in his chair, and folded his hands behind his head. "Well, it appears to me that their hardline stances on immigration overhaul are a thing of the past. Looks like they'll soften at least enough to find some kind of middle ground between deportation and full citizenship. Then we just have to hope the damn Mexicans will buy into it." Unable to conceal his pejorative attitude, this last comment exposed his exasperation with Texas' southern neighbor. "Good work, though, son!"

A huge grin instantly spread across the face of Henry Keene, but it was not in response to the compliments he had just received from his powerful uncle.

"Look what Amber just sent me," he said proudly as he leaned over the enormous desk and thrust the phone toward his uncle. It was their one-year-old, sporting an infectious smile just like her father's.

"It's her third tooth!"

"Magnificent achievement for the little princess," said Ed in a kindly voice. He truly cared for his great-nieces, who were really more like grandchildren to him, but he couldn't get over how differently Henry approached fatherhood than he had when his kids were young. Whereas Ed had been happy to leave the lion's share of child rearing responsibilities in Tammy's capable hands, Henry was a doting father to little Savannah and five-year-old Grace. He was much more involved in the tedious demands of daily parenting than Ed had ever been, and far from feeling obliged, he seemed to revel in it.

Henry sat back down, still smiling, and continued clearing his inbox. "So how is Michael faring over at that Educational Center?" he asked.

"He's pretty miserable over there, honestly. He told me that he is not so much as to make eye contact with some of the guys in his class. They've threatened to beat him to a pulp if he does. Can you believe that? Those teachers over there are letting those hoodlums get away with that kind of thing every day!"

"Poor kid."

"Now I ask you, Henry, how is that justice?" Sloan began to finger an unlit cigar that he kept in a tray on his desk. "When I took my oath of office, like your grandfather did before me," he nodded toward the portrait hanging just to his left, "I pledged to do my best to preserve, protect, and defend the Constitution against all enemies, foreign and domestic. And my friend, I believe the homosexuals are the enemy right now! They're polluting everything that America — Americans — hold sacred. 'One Nation Under God.' That's what we call ourselves, but we sure aren't acting like it! Letting such perversion ..."

Sloan's face reddened as both his temper and voice rose, but it was Henry who now spoke.

"Uncle Ed, I know you're upset over this whole situation. You hate to see Michael over there getting bullied. But isn't that the precise reason he's there? Because he was doing the same thing to another innocent kid?"

Ed looked his nephew straight in the eye as he very deliberately chomped down on the tip of the cigar and chewed it almost threateningly.

Then, he removed it from his mouth and, using it as a teacher would a pointer to drive home his argument, he pronounced, "But Henry, the O'Dell kid provoked Michael."

"How so? Did he call him names or threaten him?"

Ed was fuming now. "No!" he finally admitted. "But what kind of examples do schools want to set for our kids these days? If they would only make people like that keep their shameful behavior behind closed doors and out of the lives of decent people like us."

Henry just smiled at his uncle and slowly shook his head. "You know, being true to who you are isn't really considered provocation." He opened his mouth to continue speaking, but Ed interrupted before he could resume.

"I know. Tam doesn't agree with me on this either," and he tossed the cigar back into the little ceramic tray in disgust. "She wants me to just let go of everything and not blame Jamie O'Dell for the punishment Michael got."

"Can you do that? Have you tried?"

"Honestly, I don't give a damn what those people do in private, Henry. Don't even want to know. But nowadays they feel all empowered to prance around with their rainbow flags shouting all that equal rights crap. It's just too much for me."

Ed had seen too much change. He had witnessed the Texas landscapes, both physical and psychological, being forced to adapt to ever increasing demands thanks to urban sprawl and all the newfangled, cosmopolitan ideas about diversity. And now, here they were — being forced to even consider same-sex marriage. *What a travesty! If God weren't immortal … He'd be turning over in His grave.* Ed preferred uniformity. Conformity. "One Nation under God" … It was what he was comfortable with. It was all he had known.

"But, if they were content to still live quietly in the closet that our society has created for them, you'd be okay with that?" Henry asked, knowing full well that he was guilty of provocation himself now.

Ed resumed playing with the moist-ended cigar, rolling it over and over in the tray.

"Is that the way you really want it?" Henry pressed. "Uncle Tom's Cabin now equipped with a closet?" He was one of only a few who could stand toe-to-toe with Ed Sloan.

"Hell, yes! That's where they belong — out of sight — out of mind." Ed practically jumped across the desk at Henry as he shot out of his chair and leaned all of his weight on the desktop, hands spread wide. "This all started when we threw away the whole 'don't ask/don't tell' thing in the military. And now we find ourselves in a landslide of immorality. Is this the kind of world you want Grace and Savannah growing up in?"

"Of course not." Henry remained calm as he leaned forward in his chair and rested his elbows on Ed's imposing desk, his hands clasped underneath his chin in a relaxed manner. "It's my hope," he nodded thoughtfully, "that their world will one day be much more inclusive — full of tolerance and acceptance and equal opportunity. That's why I'm working so hard on this immigrant worker program. It's all about equal opportunity and equal protection under the law. To offer a chance at happiness to those who can't find it in their home countries."

"But that's entirely different," scoffed Ed. "They aren't out there sinning for everyone to see."

"Of course they are. Just like you and me."

"Hell, Henry, you know what I mean. Flagrantly sinning."

"No," Henry answered, "I really don't. First of all, I don't agree that being gay defines a person as sinful. I know several same-sex couples, and they lead very respectable lives. And secondly, even if it was, I seem to remember a story about a teacher in sandals, a woman, and a circle of angry men with rocks." He smiled gently at his uncle and then continued, "But that's a conversation for another time." He then picked up his previous train of thought.

"What you said a minute ago is that you're fine with gay people living their own lives, but you just don't want them mingling with yours. And so, you want to relegate them to the fringes of society. Right? Wouldn't that be like your agreeing with reforming the current immigration system only if we put limits on the neighborhoods where those new citizens could live and the types of jobs they could get? In neither scenario does either group have access to the full liberties our constitution protects."

Henry could see how Ed was struggling with this. *It was paradoxical,* Henry thought, *how the wide-open spaces of Texas and the small world view of the good-old-boy-mentality could so easily co-exist within the same state — or within the same person.*

"Come on, Henry, you've blown this all out of proportion now," Ed walked around his desk to thump Henry's shoulder with his large hand.

Henry grabbed his uncle's hand in his own and replied, "I know it's hard for you, Uncle Ed, but the world has changed. America is no longer the Norman Rockwell portrait of your boyhood. We're not a homogenous population, sharing the same cultural and religious values any more. We are a polyglot, and a multi-cultural, interfaith nation. We have to learn to accept the differences we see, and sometimes fear, in one another. But even more important," and he stood now, in order to place the screen of his phone in Ed's direct line of vision, "we need to teach my girls and their friends to do the same." He clapped his uncle on the back and then drew him into a bear hug.

Ed was not comfortable showing tenderness. It was not natural for him at all, and he paused too long to respond to his nephew's generous attitude toward his apparent lack of compassion.

"You know I love you." Henry smiled and waited for a response. But receiving none, he winked at his uncle, gave him another one-armed hug, and walked out of the office whistling. "See ya, Mary Anne. I hope your husband gets better real quick. Hey Trey! Holly! I can't wait to see what you guys get going with the Desalination Project. Keep me in the loop, okay? Hey, Mac! I'm ready to come catch some more bass if you'll invite me back out to your lake."

Ed could hear his cheerful good-byes to all those in the outer offices as he left the building and, somehow, he felt left out. Something inside him ached. Why hadn't he told Henry he loved him, too?

But Ed had learned at a very early age that any show of tenderness — any whatsoever — was a sign of weakness that no man or boy should entertain. Toughness had been equated with manliness; manliness, with success. And success was the brass ring you reached for. "Eddie, you're not gonna go off cryin' like your sister, are ya?" How many times had he heard this from his grandfather? "Come on, man. Buck up!" "Don't be a wuss!" "Are you a li'l girly-girl, or what?" These were favorites he'd get from his father and uncles any time he had shown emotion. He had adored his mother, yet with the overbearing machismo with which they were surrounded — he as a child; she as the subservient wife — neither were allowed to show any of the affection they felt so deeply in their hearts. "A boy shouldn't be fussed over like that," meant that Sloan's young mother was denied a mother's passion to hold, cuddle, or comfort her child. And Eddie absorbed the intended message that real men didn't need all that. Thus, it was ingrained in him that 'feelings' were dangerous and that expressing any sensitive emotions brought with it consequences that would question his manhood.

That was the language of love that was spoken in his family of origin, the tradition in his household that exemplified status, stability and security — all things he learned to desire with all his heart. He had learned that being a male Sloan was a privileged position that demanded its own respect and he was practiced in seeing to it that that respect was offered him. But his early education hadn't prepared him for this touchy-feely world with its shape-shifting mores he now found himself in. A man had to have a place to stand.

Yes, his world was changing and it frightened him.

It's a matter of taking the side of the weak against the strong,
something the best people have always done.
— Harriet Beecher Stowe

Chapter 7

HENRY KEENE

As Henry Keene left the Land Commission office and began the fifty-minute drive home to Horseshoe Bay, he was aware of conflicting emotions. As excited as he was that this afternoon's meeting with two of the Immigration Committee members had been cancelled and that he now had this unexpected opportunity to surprise Amber with a mid-day rendezvous, he found he couldn't quite put aside his worry about his uncle. Despite their differing opinions regarding most social issues and theological interpretations, he loved his Uncle Ed deeply, and he could see that this thing with Michael and the fallout from his anti-gay remarks really had him by the balls. *Poor Uncle Ed.* If only he could see beyond the absolutism of his convictions. He's got a great heart and if he could let that lead him in social matters like it had in the family's tragedy ...

Henry was thrust back to that time when he was nine and his mom had knelt down so she could look him straight in the eyes. They were standing on the grate of the old floor heater in the living room and he was still holding his schoolbooks, having just come home from school. She'd come out of their bedroom when she'd heard the door open and him calling out in the musical way he'd always done, "I'm ho-ome!" So innocent. So happy still. He really hadn't ever understood what it meant having lymphoma, other than that his daddy was too sick to play "Batter Up" or even "Clue" anymore. She had held him by his upper arms — just above the elbows — and she had searched his eyes earnestly, taking in all the details of his face. He saw pain, and anguish, and bravery in hers. And then he had known. Even before she'd said it, he'd felt something crumple inside and he was already crying when she'd found the words, "Henry. Sweetheart. Your father has died." She'd gone on to say some other things about how and when and what was next, but he couldn't follow it. Everything had changed. And Ed had been there for him when he needed him most.

Henry reminisced on the many ways Ed had stepped in to fill the void his father had left. He'd taken him fishing, first in the creek, and later out on the lake. He'd taught him how to shoot a .22 and how to clean it properly after an afternoon of target practice. He'd taken him out to the deer lease, long before he was old enough to actually hunt, just to get him outside and to get his mind on something other than the grief that filled his home. And, while his mom had Tammy to sit with her and listen as she processed her grief, he had his Uncle Ed to sit on the front porch and spit watermelon seeds into the yard, or let peanut hulls pile up around their feet as they shot the breeze, or to simply sit, watching whatever or whoever passed by.

Looking back on all of that now, Henry had to smile. Those were all such "Ed" things — nothing even remotely touchy-feely, but sensitive to a young boy's needs nevertheless. And motivated by love. That he knew without a doubt.

Ed and Tammy had been faithful in their support too. Even with the birth of the twins and the simultaneous launching of his political career — with his first successful run to represent District 52 in the Texas House — Ed still took the mentoring of his nephew very seriously. While Henry was still in high school, Ed had encouraged him to follow in the Sloan family tradition of business, law, and eventual public service through elected office. And so, Henry had attained his undergraduate degree in business finance from Texas Christian University and his Juris Doctorate from Texas Wesleyan. Both schools were in Fort Worth, so Henry even credited his uncle, in a roundabout way, for being responsible for his present happiness since it was there that he had met Amber and married her. Best day of his life! Well, one of the three best days. The births of his daughters ranked right up there.

He picked up his cell phone and punched "home."

She answered breathlessly. She'd been out in the yard with Savannah when she'd heard the phone ring, and she'd had to run in to pick it up in time. With a twenty-eight-pound weight on your hip, that took a lot of wind. "Hi, hon. Whatcha know?"

"Well, I know I'm about four blocks from the house and I've come to escort you and the littlest princess to lunch."

"Really? What fun! How'd you manage that?"

He told her of the cancelled meeting that had freed up his afternoon. "And I decided there is nowhere I would rather be than with you. Think you can tear yourself away long enough to enjoy an almost tete-a-tete with your paramour and husband?"

"Oooh! Both of you? How nice! I'll just slip into something comfortable and I'll be waiting."

He hung up as he turned onto their street, and moments later, as he pulled into the driveway, Amber was already opening the front door with little Savannah in her arms. Both were waving.

Seeing them took his breath away. Dressed in faded jeans and a blousy white top, his wife was a vision to behold. Her shoulder length blonde hair perfectly framed her heart-shaped face and set off her bright smile and almond shaped eyes nicely. A natural beauty, she didn't wear much make-up. She didn't have to. And Henry Keene positively adored her playful spirit, and her authenticity. She was grounded and good and honest and kind. He could go on. But there was their precious, precocious Savannah, perched on her mother's hip. She smiled at her daddy with outstretched arms as he walked up the drive toward them both.

"Let me see that new tooth, my littlest peanut," he said, picking her up and feeling for the little "piece of rice" in her mouth. He breathed her in as he kissed the top of her little blonde head, her bouncy curls corralled into two yellow poufs of sunshine. It appeared that her eyes were going to be a lighter blue, just like Amber's.

He leaned in to kiss his wife. "I'm glad I could surprise my best girl for lunch." But what had been intended as a quick affectionate peck deepened into something more and he became lost in her essence. Only a few seconds passed, but his response was not lost on Amber. She smiled knowingly, her eyes twinkling with flirtation as he pretended to reel backwards.

"Whoa there, Mata Hari. I only promised lunch!" Just then, Savannah reached for his sunglasses, causing them both to laugh, which was just enough to break their spell. "Don't you think we should go celebrate this new tooth? What are we waiting for?" And he started to herd his girls toward the car.

"Oh darling, what fun! Let me go get Savannah's shoes." Amber dipped low and expertly extricated herself from under Henry's proprietary arm, handing off Savannah as she went. "And would you see to her car seat?" Before popping back into the house, she yelled back to him, "We have to be back by 1:30 for Gracie's school bus."

Their celebratory lunch date was at a burger joint because it had a playground that could entertain Savannah, giving them a chance to chat.

"So will you be in Austin very long this time?" she asked. They were only about an hour north of Austin, but Henry frequently chose to stay there overnight when late dinners were followed by early-morning meetings.

"Just one night this time," he replied as he watched his little girl squeal with delight as she crawled through the cornucopia of plastic balls in which he had set her. "I'll be meeting with Tim Kline tomorrow night, then on Wednesday morning at eight with Buck Reeves. I had hoped to get them both together, but for now, this is the best we can do."

"I hate it when you have to be away. The girls miss you ... and so do I. She said this last looking up at him through her thick lashes, a pretty, pretend pout on her face — until she dissolved in laughter. "I can't even be seductive any more. Too many years of being Mommy!"

"Oh, you do just fine, believe me." Henry reached out and took her hand in his, turning it over to tenderly kiss the inside of her wrist. "I hate being away from you, too, Amber. But hopefully I won't have to do this much longer." Many of Henry's overnighters had been occasioned by his need to get his name and face in front of those who could help him with his own political aspirations. Having already gained valuable experience during a clerkship with one of the Justices, he was now taking advantage of his work with the General Land Office to broaden his network across the state. Henry wanted to become a Judge, but not just any judge. Ultimately, he hoped to serve on the bench of the Supreme Court of Texas, but there were stepping stones he would need to cross first. They both believed that the time away from home now would be worth it one of these days.

"Yeah, I've heard that one before." Amber leaned against him and gave him a playful shove.

"I know it's tough now; and no, it probably won't get any easier for a while, but if I can get lucky enough to receive an appointment without having to face a general election first, that would make everything so much easier."

"Well, I'd appoint you. And I might even vote for you if you play your cards right."

"Well that is comforting to know, sweetie. And I'll send you a picture of me and the governor if you donate to my campaign." He flashed a grin as he ducked to avoid a plastic ball as it came straight towards them.

There were three other children playing in the balls with Savannah. Two little boys, who seemed to be brothers, were happily throwing balls at each other and laughing as they hit their marks. A little girl, perhaps a few months older than Savannah, stayed in one corner off to herself, avoiding interaction with the others. Then there was Savannah, who crawled between the brothers as they hurled colorful missiles at each other, who climbed out of the pit only to immediately climb back in, and who, when she approached the seemingly introverted girl only to be pushed away, happily accepted the redirection and started the cycle all over again.

Having an older sister had already taught her a great deal about social interaction, compelling her to join the play of older kids without reservation. Henry knew she would not be one easily tamed. But with all of her busy interest in everything going on around her, she was a happy child. And even at this tender age, she showed that spirit of life he found irresistible. In fact, as he watched the children play, he couldn't help but notice how well-formed each of their distinct personalities already were. And none of them could have been over four years old.

Amazing, he thought, the God-giveness of our nature. He related these observations to Amber, and for the next few minutes, they silently watched Savannah's joyous explorations, content to be in this moment of shared enjoyment of their child. And then, the familiar shadow fell over Henry's heart.

Lately, he had come to realize that whenever he was totally absorbed in enjoying his daughters like this, his thoughts would invariably turn to his father, as they did now. His dad had faced death knowing that he would leave behind a cherished wife and child. And, as their older daughter, Grace, now neared the age that he had been when his father had first become sick, Henry had discovered an unimaginable empathy for his father. He understood, as never before, the agony he must have endured as time had grown short with his family. Henry had always focused, as a child would, on his own hurt and loneliness, and only recently had made the emotional jump to this new perspective. He could hurt for his father now, in a way he could not before. Becoming a father himself had given him this wonderful gift of unconditional and immeasurable love for another human being.

"Ow," exclaimed Amber playfully, as another wayward throw by the two-year-old younger brother hit her on the arm.

Henry got up to retrieve the errant ball and tossed it back into the fray. "He's got quite an arm for a little guy!"

Amber was holding her drink and sipping through her straw when Henry returned.

"Do I tell you enough just how much I love you and our life together?" He sat down and slipped his arm around her, his brows knit with an uncharacteristic concern that was not congruent with the playfulness he had just been exhibiting.

She slowly lowered her Coke and looked at him with eyebrows raised. "Where did that come from?" His solemn expression prompted Amber to lean into him and rest her hand on his thigh.

"I just want to make sure that you know how much you mean to me," he said, and then tilting his head in the direction of where Savannah continued playing happily, he continued, "how much *all* my girls mean to me."

"Silly man," she said as she cupped his face in her hands and kissed him. "You show me every day, with everything you say and do. All you have to do is wake up in the morning and I know that you love me! I couldn't ask for anything more."

Henry's sunburst of a smile instantly returned, dispersing the gloom of his earlier thoughts in a flash of utter happiness.

The older boy now patrolled the perimeter of the ball enclosure like a robot, his back stiff and both his arms out straight in front of him, talking nonsense in a mechanical voice.

"Oh, I almost forgot to ask. Has Ed talked to you about receiving something from Gracie?"

"No, why?"

"Well, apparently Grandparent's Day was back in September. She sent an invitation to your mom, of course, but she said she also sent something to him. Their whole kindergarten class sent letters to their grandparents."

"Really?" Two more balls came lofting through the air toward them, and Henry returned them both.

The monotone voice of the older brother gave a play-by-play of Henry's ball retrieval. "Good throw. Watch out below."

"Yeah, I didn't know about it either, until she told me this morning that she hadn't heard back from him."

"Well, what did she say in her letter?"

"I'm not sure exactly. I'm guessing it was something the teacher had them copy from the board, but Gracie told me she had asked him if he would come be Big Tex at the school's State Fair Days. Isn't that cute? But apparently he never responded, and now they're over."

Henry's smile disappeared. "I'm sure it's all that business with Michael. Ed's been obsessed with trying to make the negative publicity disappear and still hold to his principles. It's eating him alive."

"That's what I figured, but I was just wondering if he had said anything to you about it."

Henry stared across the playground at nothing. "No. He didn't say a thing." He loved his uncle dearly, but did not understand Ed's preoccupation with how others lived their personal lives when he so easily dismissed a personal relationship within his own family.

"Hon, it's no big deal. Really. Grace didn't seem upset. She just told me that the State Fair Days at school were over and that Uncle Ed didn't get to be their Big Tex."

"Da Da Da!" shouted Savannah who had climbed over the rim of the corral, gotten her skirt stuck, and was hanging head first — not dangerously so, but definitely in a predicament all the same. The boy robot stood in front of Savannah as her blonde curls touched the floor. He waved his rigid arms and repeatedly shouted in his robot voice, "Danger, she's stuck!" until Henry could retrieve her. The other little girl watched everything from the safety of her corner.

Their celebratory lunch date now over, they gathered their things — Savannah's shoes, a single sock, a sippy cup, and her special "Roo" — and then headed back home together. Gracie's school bus would be delivering her soon.

"**D**addy! Today was Library Day!" Gracie came running, having seized several new books from the stacks scattered across the coffee table. "See what I got!" She held them up for Henry to see as she danced around him where he stood in the kitchen having just entered from the garage. She was eager to begin.

"My favorite day of the week!" Henry laid his briefcase on the kitchen table and lifted Gracie high into the air. "And it looks like you picked some swell books for us to read this week, snugglebunny." He put her down and then had to laugh. Savannah had come toddling up, too, over laden with her picks.

"Mine!" she declared, before dropping them all to the floor and raising her arms up in a plea to be lifted on high like her big sister.

Henry obliged by tossing her up high overhead before setting her back down on terra firma. "There you go, peanut. Looks like you made some very wise choices yourself."

Savannah was a mass of giggles as she raised her arms up once again.

"Not on your life, button nose. You girls are gonna wear me out. Now git outta here so I can say hello to your sweet mama." And he morphed into their favorite "Daddy Monster" and chased them squealing and giggling out of the room.

Amber took the girls to the library every Friday, after Gracie got out of school. They always got to choose seven books apiece, one for each night of the week, and she let them take their time, encouraging each girl to choose bedtime treasures they most wanted to discover with their Daddy in the coming week. Every Friday they left the library with armfuls of promises — places to explore, characters to meet, dreams to dream, and wonderful things to learn. The girls thought this was the best possible thing in the world, but Henry knew he was really the lucky one. Bedtime story time was fast becoming his favorite part of the day. First, though, there would have to be dinnertime and then bath time. He pulled Amber to him and gave her a warm kiss hello.

"Gracie," he called, "how about taking these books back to the living room? And then, maybe you can come back in and help Mommy and me get the table set for dinner?"

Savannah fell asleep at the dinner table, her head nodding low to rest on the tray of her high chair. But she and Gracie had played too hard all day to skip their baths. So while Amber gave the girls a quick bath, Henry finished cleaning up the kitchen. He met Amber in the bathroom as they were finishing up and held out the towels for them, scooping a worn-out Savannah into his arms. As he slipped a Dora the Explorer nightgown over her head, he called out to Gracie, "Meet us on the couch as soon as you're dressed!"

Their hair was still damp and the smell of baby shampoo was intoxicating to him as they scrambled over each other, jockeying for their accustomed positions on the couch. Each was clutching the book they wanted their Daddy to read in one hand and their special "lovies" in the other. It was always the same. Gracie settled in on Henry's left, her little Bunny nestled in the crook of her arm, and Savannah perched in his nest with her little "Roo" pressed against her cheek as she contentedly sucked her thumb. Most daddys had a lap, but Gracie had dubbed Savannah's particular placement a "nest" long ago. And no deviation from this father-daughter ritual was ever entertained.

There was nothing better, Henry thought, *than this nighttime routine with his girls.* No day was ever too stressful and no other issue more pressing than this special time they shared together at the close of every day. The only time they ever missed was when he had to stay out of town overnight. And even then, Amber would pull out her iPad and the girls would Facetime with him, telling him about what they and Mommy had read that night and showing him the books they had already picked out for his return.

They had both chosen books about animals tonight, and since it was Savannah's turn to go first, they opened her book first — *Big Al*.[2] Big Al was a huge puffy fish, scary and fierce-looking, and he had no friends. Big Al was also very lonely and he cried big salty tears into the big salty sea. Henry made his voice sound like a giant, crying fish, and Savannah's lip immediately protruded. As Henry turned the pages, the girls grew quiet, their compassion growing for this oversized, ugly, but sweet and endearing fish. But the more Big Al tried to befriend the other little fish by playing games and being silly, the more they steered clear. Savannah clapped her hands with glee as the story progressed and Big Al saved all the smaller fish who had gotten trapped in the fishermen's netting. The net was strong, but Big Al proved to be even stronger. All the little fish were freed, and they realized their fears had been unfounded. In the end, that one huge, puffy, scary, fierce-looking fish ended up having more friends than anyone else in the sea. Savannah and Grace both cheered as Henry turned the final page. They counted all the colorful fish on the page to see just how many friends Big Al really had.

"I think Big Al has even more friends than Savannah does!"

"Well, I don't know about that, Gracie. I think she has a whole lot of friends too. Don't you, peanut?" Henry looked closely at the back cover of the book as he placed it down on the couch. The little fish trapped in the net had looks of terror on their faces. With eyes wide and gaping mouths, it seemed to Henry that they were recoiling from the big and different looking fish who had come to save them, as much as they were shrinking from the netting in which they were ensnared. He couldn't help but see the parallels between those skittish fish, who only felt safe in schools with others just like them, and people like his uncle. Hopefully, books like *Big Al* would help the next generation be more open to swimming in a bigger sea.

"Mine now." Gracie placed her book in her father's hands: *Old Turtle*.[3]

It started slowly, as far as children's books go, speaking of a time when all the animals and all the things of the world — the rocks, the winds and the waters — could speak and understand each other — and God. But then an argument began.

Henry read about how they hadn't noticed it happening at first: Breezes whispered that God was never at rest, he was like the wind;

rocks responded that He was strong as stone, like a great immovable rock. And the mountains rumbled that He was like a majestic, snowy peak, high above the clouds.

Savannah became restless without as many pictures as she was accustomed to, and she wanted Henry to quickly turn the page to get to the next picture. "Savannah, stop it! I want Daddy to read," Gracie said.

Several more pages outlined the differing ways that the creatures of the earth defined "their God." Each described God as they "saw" Him — in their own image — their definitions limited to their own likenesses and by their own understandings. Stars saw God as glimmering lights while the waterfall envisioned God as a flowing stream whose currents course through the very heart of everything.

Gracie, being just old enough to grasp an understanding of God herself, was fascinated by the personifications in the story. The traits and qualities that each inanimate object or animal applied to its understanding of just who God is made sense to her.

They obviously couldn't agree with each other's interpretations and their arguments grew in intensity and became louder. Henry let his voice grow bigger as the argument intensified, roaring out the last "L O U D E R" that was printed on the page just like a lion. Gracie put both hands over her ears, looking up at their dad with wide, expectant eyes.

That's when a new voice spoke up. The voice yelled, actually, "STOP!" It crashed like thunder and it whispered like a butterfly when it sneezes. Again Henry read with dramatization, sounding for all the world like rumbling thunder and then tiny, soft sneezes. He paused and looked over at Gracie, eyebrows raised, increasing the suspense with his silence.

"I bet it's gonna be Old Turtle, Daddy." Gracie could hardly contain herself as Savannah helped Henry turn the page which displayed the illustration of a very large and very old tortoise. "It is! It's Old Turtle!"

"I think you're right, angel."

"He looks very old."

"Gog!" Savannah touched the face of the enormous turtle.

"He's not a dog, Savannah. He's a turtle. That's Old Turtle, who the book is named for."

"Gog."

Gracie exhaled loudly, then whispered to herself. "It's not a dog."

Henry smiled, noting that their interpretations were based upon their own life experiences, as well. Gracie, at six years old, was much more worldly. Savannah, however, had never seen a turtle before and she was confident in her declaration: "Gog."

Henry read on. Old Turtle never said much, and certainly never argued, especially about God, but then she began to speak."

"She's a girl, Daddy! Old Turtle is a girl!" Gracie wriggled in her excitement.

Henry had assumed the turtle was a boy too. *Hmmm. Why do we think of some animals as female while others we immediately see as male?*

The wise old turtle then went into great detail stating her agreement with all the varying concepts that all the others had argued about. Her soliloquy covered almost two pages. Savannah yawned and placed the satin ears of her little Roo against her nose, snuggling deeper into her Daddy's nest.

God just *is*, the turtle summed up, and then she prophesied the coming of humans, saying that they will be reminders for us of all that God is and can be. But the story went on to illustrate that, just as in real life, the people lost sight of the fact that they were to be messengers of love. Instead, they injured one another, and the very earth itself, through their neglect, abuse and cruelty, causing irreparable damage and even death. They had completely lost sight of God, who He was, and who they were supposed to be.

"This is a sad book, Daddy." Gracie held her Bunny close to her chest. "It hurts my feelings."

"Yes, it's sad what they're doing to each other and all the beautiful things in the world, isn't it?"

"Mmm. Hmm." Gracie nodded her bowed head in agreement.

The simplicity of these stories, both of them so far, and the way they so accurately pegged our weaknesses as human beings was profound. And so very disheartening.

"Let's keep reading to see what happens next, okay?" Henry asked gently. Gracie nodded her tentative agreement and snuggled more closely into her daddy's side, only peeking out at the pictures once another great voice began telling of all the ways that *God is*. It apparently took a very long time, but finally the people really began to listen. Once they listened, they were able to hear … and that is when they were finally able to see God in one another.

"Did Old Turtle say all that to all the people? Or was it God?"

"I think it was God. But it could have been Old Turtle saying exactly what God had asked her to say. I'm not really sure. But either way, the people listened and made things right, didn't they?"

"Yeah. It's not so sad anymore. I'm glad everyone listened." Gracie reached up to turn the last page herself. "Look, Daddy," Gracie beamed, "Old Turtle's smiling now!"

"That she is, Gracie. And do you know who else is smiling?"

Gracie leaned across her daddy to read the word he was pointing to. "God!" she declared triumphantly. "God is smiling. And so are you, Daddy."

"Yes, little one, so am I." He looked down at his lap and over to his left side and then lifted his eyes to the armchair where Amber now sat. *So am I*, he thought.

Savannah's sleepy head lay against Henry's chest, her neck bending under its weight. Amber picked her up, careful not to forget Roo, and took her back to her room.

Henry tucked Gracie in and then headed back to the couch where the girls' library books still lay. "Hey Amber, have you read these books yet?"

Amber curled up next to him, tucking her feet under her bottom, just as Gracie had done only a little while ago. "I haven't actually read them, but I screen everything before we check them out. They really picked some powerful stories this time, didn't they?"

"I'd say. I mean, these are worthy of being Sunday school material. And I'm not talking about the children's classes."

Amber picked up *Old Turtle* and began reading.

"The way this story tells of nature, and then the people, arguing about their perception of God — creating God in their own images …"

"And they each think their way is the right way."

"And the only way." Henry tried to remember how many arguments he had heard, that day alone, where one group felt they had such a lock on the truth that they refused to dialogue with *the other side* at all.

Before he had finished brewing his morning coffee, he had already seen proponents on both sides of the gun control and abortion issues going after one another tooth and nail, and legislators so entrenched in their own ideologies, they couldn't come together even to efficiently fund relief for the desperate victims of Super Storm Sandy. Shouting one another down, discrediting and even vilifying the opposing view, was the *modus operandi* these days. There was no listening anymore. Certainly no listening with the possibility of changing one's mind. And nowhere was this attitude more painful to Henry's heart than where his Uncle Ed was concerned.

"Wish there was a way we could get Ed to read this book."

Amber put the book down and drew her husband close, "Darling, I don't think he'd even get it."

*Love takes off masks that we fear we cannot live without
and know we cannot live within.*
—*James Baldwin*

Chapter 8

SOMEDAY IS HERE

The leaves were late turning this year. Typically, the countryside this far north was already ablaze in an October brilliance. But New England's summer dry spell and mild temperatures in early fall had detained Mother Nature from her full palette of autumn splendor thus far. Nevertheless, here and there, glimpses of dazzling burgundy, vermilion, and gold flashed amid the varying shades of greyed-greens and soft yellows, heralding the promise of glory still to come.

Holly was driving at this point. They had been taking turns, cutting across the country on scenic highways and stopping along the way at points of interest which were steeped in history or graced with natural beauty. Their route had made for a splendid drive. They had driven over a thousand miles so far, and still their sense of adventure and excitement was sky high. Holly wasn't the least bit tired. Her heart was overflowing and was energizing her whole being. When she could, she would take her eyes off the winding road for as long as she dared, just to take in all this beauty.

"I'm so happy, my heart is about to burst!" she exclaimed. "There is just so much gorgeousness all around. I see something like that mountainside bursting with color over there and I think it just can't get any better than this. And then we turn a corner, and wow! The next vista is even more incredible than the last one."

She navigated another hairpin curve around a bend, and as the road straightened out a bit, chanced a quick glance over at the passenger seat.

"And the best part is I have you to share it with. It makes it all even grander, somehow, being able to share ..." Holly searched for the words that came closest to expressing all that was inside her, "my gladness — my deep gratitude for God's extravagant grace in creating all this. And then, knowing that you understand. That you feel it too. I do love you."

"I know. I love you too. God really did outdo Himself in this corner of the world, didn't He? Beauty upon beauty. Grace upon grace."

They drove along in silence for a while, each contemplating private gratitudes.

"You know, sometimes I just can't believe all that we have — all that He's given us. I mean, the fact that we found each other in the first place, then the way He opened our hearts when it was the last thing in the world either of us expected ..." Holly's voice trailed off as she sought the best way to describe the magnitude of her feelings. "But maybe more than anything else, I thank God for the way He's helped us really overcome, and not just survive, all that we've each had to face on our way to becoming 'us.'"

"Yeah. When you look back at all that's happened — that's still happening — it's impossible not to see that one set of footprints in the sand, carrying us."

They drove along the last stretch of highway content in their companionable silence, each of them following their own journey to this moment, knowing they were getting closer to their destination. Holly again glanced toward the passenger seat, this time to see a silent tear spilling down the face of her beloved.

"Honey?" questioned Holly. "Talk to me."

"Our someday is finally here, sweetheart." This was uttered in not much more than a choked whisper. "I only just realized it, just this minute. We've waited so long, but our someday is finally here."

Holly kept driving, but no longer saw the countryside before her.

Their someday! Yes, this time in their lives, these next few days in particular, had seemed such an impossibility — such an unreasonable dream even to hope for. They had almost begun to believe it could never happen for them. Amanda and Stephen, Holly's children, didn't even remember their father. He had died when Amanda was only three years old, and Steve was just a baby. She was devastated, but with two little ones, she didn't have the luxury of cocooning herself or her grief. Instead, the survivor in her was determined to go it alone and raise her kids without the complications of another relationship, and she had done just fine for many years, until …

"Darlin', you're losing your lane."

Holly just smiled at this statement that had snapped her back to the city street they now found themselves on. Those five little words said so much more to her than the concern for safety that would seem obvious to anyone else. Although their lane truly was merging with another due to some construction ahead, this was also their silly little way of telling each other that their happiness was spilling over, that they were in love.

As they pulled into the parking garage of the magnificent hotel which towered above them, they just looked at each other and smiled.

"Holly, I'll go inside while you wait on the bellman to get our bags." And then with a wink, "I want to make sure we get the upgraded room."

Nervousness blended with excitement as they made their way up to the 19th floor. Yes, they had been able to get the upgraded room! The hotel was on the Canadian side — a front row seat facing both raging torrents as they cascaded into the Niagara River far below. They rushed to the window of their suite and were dumbstruck with awe as they gazed upon the thundering falls, another sure manifestation of God's handiwork — this time expressed in the language of pure power and majesty. They stood silently, hand in hand, for quite some time.

The peaceful stillness inside their room that Sunday afternoon, juxtaposed with the fast-moving, roaring current of the Niagara just outside their window, provided sharp contrast. And Holly became pensive as she thought of the lives they had temporarily left behind in Texas. She reflected on how their quiet intimacy afforded a similar refuge of sorts from the unending balancing act of managing careers, friendships, and families. It was not at all unlike this serene setting, poised as it was over the turbulence below, providing safety from the water which was carrying everything in its path along with it at a furious pace.

"Isn't it funny," she mused, "but it seems to me that those rushing waters mirror our lives in a lot of ways."

"I know what you mean. I was just remembering how surprised I felt — now that is an understatement — when I was able to really acknowledge the feelings I was beginning to have for you. I was scared to death of losing our friendship. What if you didn't feel the same way? But my feelings were pulling me away from what I thought was safe and into the unknown."

"Like being on what you thought was a safe little boat," Holly said as she pointed upriver, "and then finding yourself being caught up in a current that was taking you straight over the falls."

"Well thanks a lot, Wife-To-Be! I hope you fare better tomorrow than Houdini did when he went over the falls."

And with that they dissolved into laughter, and laughed until they cried.

The couple had fallen in love and had come here, as many had before them, to be married. They had completed all the usual preparations, as typical lovers do — planning tomorrow's ceremony, buying the rings, and arranging a special post-service dinner and honeymoon trip. And each had gone to some pains to find a special gift for the other to serve as a permanent symbol of their love and commitment. Now these would be exchanged, along with the rings, in less than twenty-four hours.

Other than a few counseling sessions, Holly and Anne had never talked with anyone about their relationship before, so the conference call with Rev. Karen DeVita, that Thursday afternoon almost fifteen months ago, was an event that had caused both women great stress and anxiety. Having learned from society to hide their happiness and the love they felt so deeply for each other, they found it an almost insurmountable task even to send the initial email scheduling that call. But getting married in a church was so important to both women that they were willing to face colossal internal fears and risk even greater societal pressure.

"Okay, when she answers, you should be the one to talk first because I'm literally shaking so much that I'm afraid she'll hear it in my voice and then question my sincerity." This was Anne, gentle and full of compassion, who made decisions from her heart and felt all things deeply.

"And you don't think I'm just as nervous?" answered Holly, the more matter-of-fact of the two, who had the ability to compartmentalize and conduct business as usual even when her insides were in utter turmoil.

So when Rev. DeVita answered the phone, Holly took a deep breath and began telling their story.

Both women had been married before. Both also had children. And both had said to each other that their previous lives had been real and true — authentic expressions of their emotional and physical attraction to their mates, and not just lies attempting to hold at bay unwanted or unknown desires. They each had sincerely loved their husbands. And now, mystery of mysteries, they found that they sincerely loved one another. Holly explained that although she was naturally cautious about sharing her deepest emotions, and that intimacy had not come easily for her, she had adored Bruce and losing him in such a traumatic and untimely way had been excruciatingly painful. She had vowed that she would never again let herself hurt that way; and so, she hadn't allowed herself to get close to another man. Anne had snuck up on her: a good girlfriend, a safe harbor, a listening ear, a soul friend, and then — something more.

Her nerves now having settled down slightly, Anne was able to join in. She told how her husband of twenty-two years had left her for another woman. She had not seen it coming. They had one son together, and she had been a stay-at-home-mom until the divorce was nearly final. Then, she had jumped at the opportunity when an opening as a church secretary became available in Thorndale. She desperately needed something to do that was entirely her own, completely separate from her previous life, and she could think of nothing that she would enjoy more.

"I just realized something," Anne exclaimed. "After our marriages ended, we each went about becoming whole within ourselves. I, the stay-at-home-mom, sought completeness by starting a career; and Holly, the career woman, found her path in raising Amanda and Stephen. Funny, I never even saw that before."

Reverend DeVita asked several questions exploring the nature of their friendship and the relationship's transition into a desire to enter into marriage with each other. They took turns speaking as they built their story for her.

"We'd always been good friends, supporting each other through our shared life experiences: our children growing, our husbands leaving us ... parents dying."

"We found we could count on one another being there and giving us the perspective we needed." Anne's eyes filled with tears. "We seemed to balance one another out somehow."

Holly squeezed Anne's hand. "It took us quite some time to come to the full realization of what we were experiencing. And even longer to accept the truth of it — our truth."

"What gave me courage to go forward was remembering what my counselor told me: that the body is just a vessel, after all. And that the human soul, where our initial attraction began and then evolved, is what really matters."

"That comforted me too."

"So I guess ... love trumped." After listening for almost ten minutes straight, Karen had summed up their story in just two words.

"Yes, it most certainly did." Anne's initial fears that her vocal cords would seize up in paralysis had subsided, and she had been able to contribute to the conversation with surprising ease after all.

"So why do you want to travel all the way up here to get married? It isn't that I don't want to officiate for you, but can't you find someone closer to home who can help you?"

They answered in unison with a resounding "No." Texas, their state of residence, did not currently allow same-sex couples to marry.

"And neither do forty-one other states, either," Anne piped in. [4]

"And then there is the confusion in the churches these days. Some pastors and priests are willing to officiate at same-sex union ceremonies, but that is generally done without the sanction of the church, and we wanted to be legitimately married and to have that marriage blessed in Christ's church. Anything less feels demeaning. And we don't want what we feel for each other, or what we hope for our future together, to be belittled in any way."

"So there really aren't any other options for us. In order to be legally married, and to have that marriage blessed by the church, we have to travel from where we live, not far from Mexico, all the way to Canada."

"We have to cross a national border — simply to get legally married."

"We wish we didn't have to." Holly looked down at the phone as she spoke to Karen. "We actually looked into Massachusetts or

Vermont, but you have to be a resident there for one year before you're eligible to obtain a marriage license."

"Will your families, especially your children, be upset that they were not present for such an important event as this?"

"We haven't told our children. We haven't told anyone about our plans, to be honest." Holly had looked directly at Anne when answering that last question, and they each had held their breath.

"Actually, you are the first person we've ever talked to at all about us and our plans," interjected Anne. "But we know our kids. Well, they're all adults now, really. And we know our extended families. Whenever we do tell them, they will understand why we weren't ready to risk sharing this part of who we are right now, and we anticipate they'll be happy for us. Honestly, we're still trying to get used to it ourselves."

Holly felt the need to clarify for Karen, who had never experienced Bible-Belt America. "Karen, we live in Texas, not Ontario. Not everyone is understanding or accepting of couples like us. As a matter of fact, some can be downright cruel. That's why we feel such a need to protect ourselves and our relationship until we're strong enough inside ... to withstand whatever inevitable pressures will surely come from the outside ... once we begin to be more open."

"Holly's right about Texas, but I really think our kids will understand," said Anne. "They are good people, and they know their moms are good people, too. And that their *bonus-moms*, for that matter, are too. Yes, they will understand, if and when we tell them. That's one area where we don't feel we have to worry."

"So girls, how do you expect your relationship to change with marriage?" came the question from nearly two thousand miles away.

They looked at each other. How does one answer that question?

"I think it changes everything and nothing," Anne answered after only a brief moment of reflection. "Having the opportunity to profess our love for one another before God, in a church. That is everything we've wanted. But then, when we come back home to Texas, we'll continue to live our lives just as we always have — and there's the nothing part."

"Our marriage won't be recognized at home, but at least we'll know that it was, and always will be, recognized here," Holly added.

Karen filled the silence left on the line after this last assertion.

"There is one thing I want to make clear for you and I think it will help you now and in the future. God has already blessed your love for each other, or we wouldn't be having this conversation right now. He put that love in your hearts. And then He gave you the ability to be open to that miraculous gift. So rejoice in what He has already blessed."

Anne's eyes filled as she looked over at the woman who would be her wife. Holly was stunningly beautiful and she had certainly had her share of possible suitors over the years. She was tall, with delicate hands and a slender form. Her long, golden hair and graceful elegance routinely captured the attention of even the most casual of observers. Her smile was infectious; but, it was her eyes that were her most remarkable feature. They were so dark and engaging, and such a contrast to her much lighter hair. When peering into her eyes, one could sense the depth of her spirit and the inner strength that lay just below their protective surface.

"Don't feel the need to apologize for your love and certainly try not to take it personally when someone from the outside may question it — or you," Karen's voice counseled through the phone on the table. "You are both children of God, and all He asks of you is to love and cherish one another."

Holly's heart lurched for just a moment at the mention of outside questioning. Her mind jumped immediately to the reality of personal attacks. She knew she would have to be very careful in order to keep her position at the Land Commission. Ed's traditionalist stance was no secret, and, she had no desire to become a target of his contemptuous slander, or to have what she and Anne shared disparaged by him in any way.

Holly had never worked anywhere else, and with the toxic economic climate in their area, she couldn't afford to lose this job. Besides, she loved her work, and, despite his unwavering conservatism, Ed Sloan had succeeded in creating a friendly atmosphere within the agency. They were a team and she liked that; even if, at times, it was a fellowship that Holly felt she couldn't fully join. When the others would regale one another with stories from their family lives, it was a struggle for her not to share her own personal happiness. Instead, she had to be careful to steer all friendly inquiries as to her own life away from the relationship that she and Anne shared, and concentrate instead on what the kids were doing and the latest book she had read. *Thank you God — for the gift of compartmentalization.* It had gotten her this far safely and would continue to protect her, Holly predicted.

"And as far as legality goes, it is the Province of Ontario, the Canadian government itself, which will grant you the license you need for holy matrimony. Therein lies the confusion for most people. The government marries you, not the church. A member of clergy is no more than an appointed agent of the province, or the state, as in the case of the United States. The legal contract which binds you in marriage is granted by the government, not by the church. So no matter what words we say, or prayers we lift up, you will not be legally married until the proper governmental papers are signed immediately following the ceremony of blessing that I will perform. Simply put, marriage is a civil matter which frequently occurs in a house of worship.

"And throughout Canada, when any couple is married, whether a man and a woman, two men or two women, they are all equally recognized as partners, not husband and wife, etc., but partners, legally married and allowed all benefits afforded to them under the law."

The conversation had continued for at least another thirty minutes. Holly and Anne had specific scriptures they wanted read, and a poem they wished to have included. And there were questions: What about witnesses? And could special music be arranged?

But now, eight months later, here they were — so far away from home, sitting quietly together in a room overlooking this massive force of nature which was commanding its way into the dark pools below.

In a way, they were not unlike beads of water preparing to embark on a life-changing course that they now realized would change everything. There was no "nothing" in this equation after all. Were they ready to take on a new identity in the eyes of the world and experience being treated differently than they ever had been before? They weren't really sure, but they knew there was no going back. The currents underlying their change of course were just too strong to deny.

In a way, that had been the question that had propelled Anne Nelson into counseling several years earlier. Was she ready for this? Just acknowledging the reality of her new feelings for Holly had created seismic shifts in her own self-awareness and had threatened cataclysmic repercussions to her life as she knew it.

Her world view had been toppled once before when Sam had told her he was leaving, and Allyson Higgins had been wonderful in helping her rediscover her inner compass and regain equilibrium. So here she was again, sitting in Allyson's office. But this time, Anne felt surrounded by the unfamiliar. Well, truthfully, everything in the office was exactly as she remembered. It was what she had been feeling lately that was completely new, and frankly, quite frightening.

"So what am I supposed to do with these feelings?" she had asked, completely stunned to have just said all of this out loud to another person. Her heart was pounding, and it felt like it just might leap right out of her chest if she said another word.

"You are supposed to *feel* them, Anne." Allyson had been her counselor for more than a year after the divorce, but back then they had worked on dealing with the grief of a failed marriage, experiencing the death of common dreams, and learning how to establish her own separate identity. They knew each other very well, but this was completely new territory.

"Why are you so afraid of entering into this new relationship?" Allyson had asked with a friendly smile.

"Are you kidding me?" Anne answered with a laugh that belied her increasing tension. Her tightly clasped hands more aptly portrayed the nervousness she carried inside. "I've talked about Holly many times before, right here in this office. I've talked about our fifteen-year friendship. I've talked about how close we are. I've talked about how she has been a source of strength for me in times when I didn't have any myself. And now, after all these years, I find myself falling in love with my best friend!"

And then, with her eyes widening and fixed straight at Allyson, she said, "I can't believe I just said that out loud. I'm afraid of losing my best friend if she doesn't feel the same; but then if she does, I'm afraid of what all this will mean." She had spoken these last words while bringing her clasped hands to her breast, perhaps an unconscious movement to protect her heart from unknown dangers. She had been through enough heartache — they both had. So why risk everything? Weren't things fine just the way they were?

"Well, I think you already know the answer to your first fear — whether or not Holly shares these new feelings you are experiencing." She looked conspiratorially at Anne. "And I doubt that you would have brought this up if this was unrequited love — just something that you could let die, then bury and move on." Allyson smiled at Anne's resurrection of a favorite coping mechanism from her past, sweeping problems under the infamous rug of denial. "What I am hearing you say is that you are more afraid of what may come if Holly does indeed return your feelings, therefore redefining your relationship." She waited to allow this to sink in. "All of which I believe you feel has already happened."

"You know me well," said Anne softly, breaking the gaze she held on her lap. "So, by all social standards, this means that I'm gay. But I've never been attracted to other women. How can I *come out* if in fact I have never actually felt *kept in*?" The exasperation was easy to hear in her voice now. She was desperate for answers. "This is crazy!" She reached for her purse and pulled out a tissue, but then kept the purse in her lap, clutching it for reassurance.

Allyson gave her time to regroup and allowed the silence to fall gently around them before asking quietly, "Why is it so important to put yourself and the feelings you are now experiencing neatly in a box? Why must you own a label?"

Her voice was a soothing one, and usually ameliorated Anne's anxiety, but this time Anne was too overwrought to be able to benefit from the calming effects of her counselor's compassion.

"Because I need to know who I am! And I need to be able to tell others who I am!" Anne's exasperated reply almost exploded in the room.

"Is that your need, Anne? Or is it that of your community?"

After years of staying at home to raise her son, Mark, Anne had over-identified with her role of being wife and mother, quite losing her identity as Anne, the woman. She had worked very hard the last several years to regain a semblance of individuality, reacquainting herself with lost dreams and daring to hope for the possibility of new ones; and, like the proverbial caterpillar, had recently evolved from chrysalis to fly on untested wings. As she learned to tend her own soul, she had begun painting again, had discovered her voice, and most importantly, had deepened her relationship with God, attending to that relationship more carefully than ever before. If a metamorphosis such as this is indeed the nature of things, why then did this new life-change seem so absolutely foreign?

"Anne, I want you to know that your experience is much more common than you may believe. You are not crazy, and your feelings are not irrational. I understand your desire to define who and what you are because, in today's society, our need to label sexual orientation is very strong. But the world isn't divided into just cats and dogs. It's a fundamental of taxonomy that nature rarely deals with distinct categories. The living world is a continuum in each and every one of its aspects, including sexuality. You see, sexuality can be measured on a scale, emphasizing the gradations between exclusively heterosexual or exclusively homosexual histories. That being said, there is something called sexual fluidity — meaning that love and desire isn't rigidly heterosexual or homosexual, but fluid, oftentimes changing as a person moves through the many phases of his or her life."[5]

"So, are you saying that every person experiences life changes like this?" Anne was perplexed, and a little argumentative, but now also somewhat more hopeful to learn that she was not the only woman to have experienced such a divergence.

"Of course not," answered her counselor. "For some, their 'place on the scale' is one hundred percent one way or the other. But it *does* mean that there are women, and men, who are capable of falling in love with another person, regardless of gender."

"Really?" I've never heard of that before." Anne lessened the grip on her purse and was finally able to lean back into the deep plush chair and listen, without undo agitation, to the answers of questions previously unknown to her. But her heart still felt as if it might beat right out of her chest at any moment. *How in the world was she going to be able to explain all of this to Holly?* "By the way, I am in love with you, which means I'm a fluid person sexually." That made it sound as if she were some free spirit willing to jump into relationships —and the sack — on a whim. And with whomever was available.

"Remember, just because a phenomenon is not well known or understood, does not make it 'not so,'" said Allyson, as she reached for a book behind her desk and began thumbing through the pages. "Admittedly, it is more common for women to experience fluidity than men, and when they do, most of them just continue to quietly live their lives choosing not to talk about it. But examples are plentiful: co-workers finding a fulfillment in each other that the men in their dating pool weren't providing, single moms experiencing a deep-seated connection from the common bonds they share, or like you, a woman's twenty-year marriage ending in the comforting arms of a supportive female friend."

Observing a somewhat more relaxed visage in her client, Allyson continued. "Usually, these types of relationships are formed from the intimate emotional connections of a close friendship. As a result of these deepening emotional bonds, physical attraction sometimes follows, and the lines of traditional sexual orientations, as we have so carefully delineated them, begin to blur."

"But I've never been attracted to another woman before. Does this mean I'm bisexual?" And she again squeezed the purse in her lap, trying to hold on as the rollercoaster she felt she was on took another unexpected dip.

"No, not at all. Let me be clear. Fluidity is very different from bisexuality, which is a distinct, but not exclusive, sexual preference. With bisexuality, there can be varying degrees of attraction, but there is indeed attraction to both males and females."

"Allyson, all of this frightens me," Anne admitted as she removed her glasses and rubbed her eyes. "And it leaves me feeling all adrift. I'm just a small-town woman who fell in love, and I honestly don't feel any different than I ever have. But ..." She had to stop. There was no way she could put into words all the complexities she was feeling.

"I know. Assigning labels helps us feel part of a community, especially with regard to our sexual orientation. Labels help us make quick sense of our surroundings and can serve as helpful shortcuts in all our interpersonal relationships. Although they may seem comforting, they can also lead to exclusion and prejudice."

Anne was well acquainted with the sharp blade of discrimination. She had seen it stab the hearts of so many these days. There was that young man in the church where she worked whose family had kicked him out last year when he had come out to them. And she had just seen something on CNN last week about an effeminate middle-school kid from Oklahoma who had hanged himself in his bedroom closet after suffering intense bullying at school. In both those situations, the poor young fellows had gone to the "trusted adults in their lives," but to what avail? The parents she personally knew from church had turned their backs on their hurting son when he had gone to them with his truth. And in the case of the Oklahoma boy, his school counselor had insisted that he forgive his attackers; then the school had proceeded to punish him when he was hesitant to do so. In neither case did the bullies themselves receive any consequences for their actions.

"Fluidity, as I just described it, can be easily dismissed by both heterosexuals and homosexuals because of our tendency to be suspicious of, and to reject, experiences which don't match our own."

"Well, I certainly don't appear to match most people's experience," Anne laughed nervously, in order to keep from crying. "And although I understand what you're saying, Allyson, I have always believed that sexuality was determined at birth — that we were born one way or the other, and that it isn't a choice."

"For what it's worth, Anne, I don't believe you made a choice to love Holly any more than I chose to love my husband. Love happens. There is a reason we call it 'falling in love,' because we really have no control over it at all. We can't make someone love us, nor can we make our love for someone else disappear, just because it's inconvenient or uncomfortable. Perhaps you were born with the ability to be fluid in your sexuality, whereas others may have been born one way or the other."

"So what you're saying is that I should just accept who I am and what I'm feeling and not worry about trying to label what I'm doing or trying to defend myself?" Although Anne sat a little straighter than she had only an hour ago, this would be a daunting task. Was there enough bravery inside her — and Holly, too, for that matter — to carry this out?

"Absolutely," answered Allyson, seeing both resolve and renewed confidence beginning to stir within her client. "It can be difficult to accept such a lack of definition in our lives when our friends, family, churches, and governments tell us that our sexuality must be static, and preferably conventional, whatever that means. Embracing the complex is rarely easy. We don't like being encouraged to consider concepts we are uncomfortable with, or being asked to contemplate things we have never even thought of before."

As the two women rose and moved toward the office door, they hugged, and in that embrace, Anne felt unconditional acceptance. How freeing it was to know that someone could know her truth and still love and accept her for herself. It gave her hope and imparted courage. As she walked to the parking lot, she reminded the still tentative part of herself of Allyson's words. She was not the only person to experience this later-in-life-journey. She was not crazy, nor bisexual, nor gay, nor even straight — it didn't matter — and she didn't need to label herself or her feelings in any of these ways. Falling in love was not a choice, but a gift from God. Her spirit skipped ahead of her as she crossed the asphalt to her car. And as she pushed the ignition button of her Prius, her spirit soared. She could do this. And her thoughts turned to first steps she would take toward moving forward in her new life with her new love. She would go forward with joyful acceptance, not oppressive apprehension.

Chapter 9

TRUE LOVE IS WORTH THE WAIT

Now, feeling as though a million miles from that counseling session long ago, and not a mere two thousand, they hardly ate a bite at breakfast. They forced down a little coffee and a bite or two of fruit and scrambled eggs. It was such a beautiful array of food, but their insides were in knots. And it was raining.

"It rained on the day my parents were married," said Anne. "My grandmother told my mother it was good luck if it rained on your wedding day."

"Well, let's take it as a sign of good fortune, then, "replied Holly with a huge smile as she stepped into the car, making sure that her skirt wasn't caught in the door. As she fastened her seat belt, she looked over at Anne, hardly able to contain the love she felt in her heart. Anne's countenance reflected happiness, joy, and carefree fun. She soaked up life with great enthusiasm and was quick to share that enthusiasm in return. She could light up a room just by walking in; people liked her and were naturally drawn to her infectious personality. But today, Holly felt that she could practically swim in those sparkling sapphire eyes that had become so familiar to her. Anne was a beam of light breaking through this dreary looking day — so full of life and joy waiting to be shared. *Oh yes, this would be a very lucky day, indeed.*

"Even if we get slowed down by this weather, I think we'll have plenty of time," said Anne, as she checked the map on her phone.

"I'm not worried, I think everything will be just fine." Holly was still lost in Anne's eyes as well as her thoughts.

It would take them twenty minutes to get from downtown Niagara Falls to the little town of St. Catharine's where Karen DeVita's church was located. The United Church of Canada is the country's largest Protestant denomination and this particular congregation was an amalgamation of three downtown churches — Methodist, Presbyterian and Congregational — coming together to form a progressive, welcoming home in the small community they served. They had come to Sunday worship yesterday in order to time the drive, get a feel for the sanctuary, and meet Karen DeVita and the two witnesses who would make their wedding ceremony possible. The reality of it all was setting in. This was going to happen!

Karen DeVita had sent them an email about a month before the wedding: "I've found your witnesses. Fran and Tom Billings are the music ministers at White Spire, and at the last worship council meeting, when I brought up the need for witnesses for your ceremony, they both jumped at the opportunity." The pair had greeted the women with true affection after the worship service yesterday, hugging them both and telling them a little about their own roundabout story to love.

"It is so wonderful to meet you both," Fran grinned as she motioned for Tom to join them where they stood on the chancel steps after church.

"And we feel so honored, so blessed, to be able to participate with you tomorrow on your special day." Although she had spoken these words to Holly and Anne, afterwards, she looked up lovingly at her husband who had just arrived by her side, including him in her joy.

Holly and Anne shared wide smiles, and Anne reached to take Holly's hand in her own. "We can't begin to tell you what it means that you offered to help us."

Tom responded, "We understand finding new love later in life, and we remember what it feels like. So whenever we can help others sanctify their love and commitment though marriage, it renews ..." his eyes turned glassy, and he paused as his voice caught in his throat, "our own vows. So really ... we want to thank you two ,.. for allowing us to help in this way."

"Don't mind him, he's a crier," said Fran, as Tom reached inside his jacket pocket for a handkerchief to dab his eyes. "It's one of the things I love most about him," and she touched his arm affectionately.

"Well, I believe this one has just found a kindred spirit, then," said Holly as she put her arm around Anne, who was also in need of a tissue.

While Tom blew his nose, and Anne continued fumbling in her purse for a Kleenex, Fran and Holly shared a knowing expression of deep appreciation for their weepy better halves. And all this was occurring as other church members hugged each other, herded young children, and invited each other down to the basement for weekly fellowship time. There were singles, families, and couples — couples like Tom and Fran and couples like Holly and Anne — and everyone was accepting of everyone.

"You see," said Fran, "Tom and I have known each other for many years. We were each married to others back then. Our spouses were friends, and our children played together all the time. Then my husband got transferred to Toronto, and we had to move. We were there for six years when my husband suddenly died, but we'd created a life there by that time. I still had one child in high school, and we wanted to stay. We didn't want any more change, as you can understand.

"And while she was in Toronto," Tom joined in, "my wife got cancer. She was sick for some time."

Fran touched his arm again, an obvious attempt to help him stay composed.

"She would undergo treatments and get better for a while, just to have it all come back again. It was a physical and emotional drain on all of us. The kids were out on their own by that time, but they came back to help me as much as they could. It was a very sad and lonely time for me."

"Then one day many years later, we were both attending a music conference in Toronto," said Fran. Their conversation was not unlike a musical counterpoint where the relationship between voices is harmonically interdependent, but independent in their rhythm and contour. Fran would carry the melody for a few measures only to pass it off to Tom, until taking it back up again a few bars later.

It was Tom's turn now, "And I traveled up for the weekend, having totally lost touch with Fran and her family years before."

"So, I guess you can say it was music that brought us together again," Fran said. She took in the beauty of the sanctuary as she continued, "and then God created the opportunity for us to serve this wonderful church together, after the amalgamation almost seven years ago now."

"This is where we were married, and this is where we serve. I guess you noticed, she leads the choir, and I'm the accompanist. "Tom's eyes were still rimmed with tears as he reached over to the organ and picked up the music he had left there. "But we're co-music ministers and plan all the music for services and special events at the church together." He tucked the music under his arm and blew his nose heartily.

Fran punctuated this with a gentle smile and confirming nod of her head.

"What a beautiful story. Thank you for sharing your lives with us." Anne smiled. "Music has played a big part in our lives and our relationship too. That's why having you serve as our witnesses tomorrow is so perfect and will mean so much to us."

"Anne has a beautiful soprano voice, and I play the piano," Holly said. "Playing has been a safe way of expression for me for as long as I can remember. I rediscovered my music after many years of loneliness and pain."

Tom nodded in understanding.

"And I was inspired to find my voice for the first time after hearing her play!" added Anne proudly. "Now I sing in the choir every week."

Fran's expression was one of deep understanding. She could sense a deep connection between these two, and her broad smile spoke more than any words she could possibly share with these two lucky women who had found true love.

Holly and Anne had purposely not searched out Rev. DeVita right after church because they knew she would be busy greeting all those who had attended worship that morning. But she was now on her way to meet the visitors and was nearly halfway up the main aisle.

"Oh, Karen!" Fran called loudly in order to be heard over the scattered conversations still going on. Have you met our friends, Holly and Anne?"

"I wondered if that was you." Karen smiled, as she came up the chancel steps to hug them both.

They had actually found the church online, as they searched for a pastor whose congregation would allow them to marry two women from Texas with no witnesses of their own. But it was definitely a "God-thing" that they found Karen and the White Spire church. She was spiritually deep, irreverently funny, and so incredibly sincere. Her eyes twinkled when she spoke, hinting at an underlying mirth just begging to be released. But best of all, she was also 5'10" and could look both Holly and Anne in the eyes as she spoke. She was perfect.

"Oh, Karen, we are so happy to finally meet you. Holly and I loved the service, and we feel so at home here."

"I believe there is a reason your journey brought you to this place to begin your life together." And giving their hands a squeeze, she continued, "We may not always understand God's plan, but we can certainly feel it at times, can't we?"

At home, they certainly felt. For after worrying about ministers, witnesses, licenses, travel dates, keeping their dresses wrinkle-free for 1,600 miles, and a host of other details big and small, they finally stepped out of the car on that rainy Monday morning into the warmth and welcome of White Spire, a church they already felt a part of on this, their wedding day.

The church secretary had greeted them at the door, happy to finally meet the women she had spoken to over the phone. They had shed their coats in the hallway and gathered with the others before entering the sanctuary.

Karen was dressed in white robes, and she began the service with just the right words: "Let us pray."

The women clasped hands tightly.

"Gracious God, you are always faithful in your love for us. Look mercifully upon Holly and Anne who have come this day to seek your blessing ..."

Even with cloud filled skies, enough light spilled through the stained glass windows, which lined both sides of the entire Sanctuary, to illuminate the entirety of the room. It was magnificent.

"Holly and Anne, understanding that God has created, ordered, and blessed the covenant of marriage, do you affirm your desire and intention to enter this covenant?"

Their answers sounded so small in such a big sanctuary — the wedding party and all guests numbering only five. But had they shouted from the balconies in this great room, the volume of their voices would still be unable to match the conviction in both of their hearts. And they answered in unison, "I do."

"God of mercy, your faithfulness to your covenant frees us to live together in the security of your powerful love ..."

Tom had offered to play for them, and the organ gently intoned *Jesu, Joy of Man's Desiring.*

They had been seated while the music played, but now they stood, hand in hand, facing Fran. *How did they get there?* It was Fran's melodic voice heard reading the poem from the greeting card that Holly had given to Anne last Valentine's Day. "True love, when it comes, is always worth the wait. Sometimes I wish that we had met sooner, that the detours along the way could have been fewer. But then something tells me we found each other at just the right place in our lives."

They were both openly crying now, gentle tears spilling down each of their faces as they listened to their new friend read the poem which matched her own life as well as theirs. The two of them faced her now, listening ... hand in hand, heart in heart. Partaking in the beauty which surrounded them.

Fran continued, "Now here we are — right on time and so right together. And I want you to know I would have waited forever for this ... for you ... for the love of my life."

They hadn't been able to arrange for any flowers, but Karen had informed them, just as they were walking into the sanctuary, that an elderly gentlemen in the church had felt an unexpected calling to bring in a floral arrangement that very morning. He was a renowned master gardener in the community, and a more beautifully fragrant and meaningful display could not have been prearranged.

"Holly and Anne, since it is your intention to marry, join your right hands, and with your promises bind yourselves to each other as partners."

And as they looked into each other's eyes, they began reciting to one another.

"... to be my partner and life companion. With Divine assistance, I promise to cherish our union and strive to love you more each day than I did the day before ..."

"... I will trust you and respect you, laugh with you and cry with you, loving you faithfully through good times and bad ..."

"... I give you my hand, my heart, and my love, from this day forward and for as long as we both shall live."

Now moving even closer to the partners, Karen proceeded, "What do you bring as the sign of your promise?" The rings were produced and blessed, and they each placed one upon the finger of their beloved, saying, "This ring I give you as a sign of our constant faith and abiding love. In the name of the Father, and of the Son, and of the Holy Spirit."

Karen prayed, "May these rings be to Holly and Anne symbols of unending love and faithfulness, reminding them of the covenant they have made this day, through Jesus Christ our Lord, Amen."

And it was done.

In the end, we remember not the words of our enemies,
but the silence of our friends.
— Martin Luther King, Jr.

Chapter 10

TRICK-OR-TREAT

It had been two months since the town had been turned on its head. And it was now Halloween night in central Texas, where temperatures could range from 82 to 35 degrees. Tonight was the latter. It had been a crisp day, but after sundown the biting wind cut through every goblin and ghost, causing last-minute costume changes for many. Alex wouldn't like it, but Marcie would have to insist that she wear a heavy jacket over her pink leotard and tutu.

The phone rang, interrupting her thoughts, but before she could wipe the flour from her hands to answer it, Alex had come running. "I'll bet it's Daddy!" she shrieked as she raced over to check the caller ID. "Hey, Daddy!" she squealed as she lifted the receiver. "I'm already dressed, and Momma just pulled out my orange pumpkin to hold all the candy I'm gonna get!"

"Hi there, sugar. I bet you are the prettiest ballerina in town." And Alex happily turned back and forth, causing her dark curls to whip her cheeks and her tutu to swish in a most satisfactory sort of way. "But, honey, I'm sorry. It looks like I'm running a little late here at work, and I don't think I'm going to get home in time to take you out tonight."

"O-oh, Daddy." Her little head instantly drooped. The tutu stopped its swishing, and the phone now hung at her knees.

Marcie smothered a smile at the dramatic change in demeanor of her younger child and at the petulant, protruding lip that was now in full bloom across her face. It told her all she needed to know. "Here, sweetheart, give me the phone, and I'll talk to Daddy."

Alex gave up the phone and walked, flat-footed, out of the room.

"Hey hon, it's me," he said from the other end of the line. "I've gotten caught at work and won't be home in time to take Alex out tonight. I hardly got to talk with her, though. Is she okay?"

"Oh, she'll be fine. She's just disappointed right now, but as long as she still gets out tonight, she'll be okay." Her mother watched as the pathetic little ballerina plopped onto the couch in the next room, beside her big brother.

Jamie had just finished his homework and was watching television. "What's wrong with you? Did Mom say it's too cold to go out tonight or something?"

"No, Daddy just called and said he can't take me." Again the lip.

"Well, you'll still get to go trick-or-treating. Mom will take you." And he tossed one of the little sofa pillows over at her, hoping to start a volley which would lift her spirits.

She grabbed the pillow but held it tightly to her chest and looked up at him with pleading eyes. "Will you go with me, Jamie?" A brief pause. "Ple-e-e-ase." And there it was: the strategic, helpless pout. *Six years old*, thought Jamie, *and she already has the moves down. The little conniver!*

"You'll be able to walk faster than Momma can." And her eyes suddenly opened wider and shown brighter. "I'll get more candy if I go with you!" Eagerly now, "And besides, I'll even share."

Jamie didn't want to go. He didn't feel like leaving the house much these days. It was the only place where he felt safe. Just today there had been another incident. One of the coaches was holding the door for all the boys as they ran into the locker room from the track. He stood there with a towel, playfully swatting the backsides of each player as they sprinted by, but when Jamie came running up, he had held the towel in his hands and said, "Not you, son. Can't have anyone getting the wrong idea." Jamie had been mortified.

A number of the other boys heard what the coach had said outside, and they took the ribbing into the locker room. "Jamie, don't look at me while I get undressed. We can't have anyone getting the wrong idea." And the guys had howled with laughter.

Another, much larger boy, took a towel and wrapped it around his waist like a skirt and pranced around several others. "Please Coach Hendrick, I don't want you to get the wrong idea … I really AM a girl!" and they had collapsed in laughter again. Thankfully, his clothes had still been there this time when he had gotten out of the showers. He didn't know if he could endure having to walk naked through the locker room asking for his clothes again.

"Jamie, puleese!" He was onto her six-year-old wiles, but her smile was hard to resist with all its gaps that looked just like the face of the plastic jack-o-lantern she held in her lap. Still, he really didn't want to leave the house.

Marcie had been standing at the doorway with a mixing bowl in her hand, stirring something in preparation for dinner. "Jamie, it would be very nice of you to take your sister out tonight. That way, I could get the kitchen all cleaned up while I pass out candy."

"Aw, Mom!" He slunk lower into the couch. "I really don't feel like it."

"I think it might be good for you. You know, get you outside for a change." Her brows knit together with worry as she contemplated the sullen face of her son. "And this way, you won't have to keep getting up to answer the doorbell all night."

He had heard what she had not said. And maybe she was right. It was still hard for him to face friends and neighbors, and this way at least, he wouldn't have to open the door to any of those who had been so relentlessly cruel lately.

Jamie felt he was too old to go trick-or-treating, but he reluctantly agreed to take Alex out as soon as it was dark.

"You get the best candy when you go after dark," Alex had insisted.

The sun was just beginning its descent as they finished their evening meal.

"Finish up your peas, missy. If you want to go out," Marcie admonished her daughter, "You'll need to finish your dinner." Alex didn't much care for peas, but she knew she couldn't leave the table until she had made them disappear, so, she rolled them up in small balls, using bits of the Mrs. Baird's bread that remained on the table, and then obediently swallowed them whole — one by one. "There!" She triumphantly proclaimed.

Marcie sighed. She remembered giving similar Halloween instructions to an exuberant Jamie, eager himself to embark on one of his own candy expeditions. He had been a tiger that year, and she had made the costume herself. She had finished it weeks before, and Jamie excitedly wore his "tiger hoot" — it was so endearing how he couldn't properly pronounce the word "suit" — every day in anticipation of Halloween night and the treasures he would receive. His own dark hair peeked out from beneath his tiger head, perfectly matching the dark whiskers she had painted on with black eye liner. His long dark lashes had further emphasized his beautiful blue eyes …

The clink of a dropped fork brought Marcie back to tonight's dinner table, and she couldn't help but notice the contrast in Alex's buoyant smile, now engaging her dessert enthusiastically, and Jamie's leaden expression. There was no sparkle in his eyes this Halloween.

As soon as the plates were cleared from the table, Alex grabbed her plastic pumpkin and headed toward the door, pulling her coat on over the pink netting as she went. "Come on, Jamie. It's dark!" Jamie grabbed his heavy coat and they entered the bitter cold.

"Let's start over in the Blairs' neighborhood," she suggested as she skipped down the street. "I heard they give the best candy over there."

"Okay, sport, you're the boss tonight." The wind was at their back for now, but it would be a miserable walk back home later on. Alex, however, seemed to be oblivious to the cold. *Oblivious of everything, really,* Jamie thought. *Lucky Alex.* He wished he could be as unaware of things. Jamie dug his hands into his pockets as they walked the several blocks over to her chosen destination, and as Alex reached the first house, he continued stamping his feet to keep warm.

"Trick or treat!" she squealed, but too soon. The door had not yet even opened.

"Oh, and who are you, darlin'?" asked the lady as she unfastened the lock and opened the storm door.

"I'm a ballerina." Alex's curtsy seemed awkward under her big coat. "Trick or treat!" she repeated.

The lady smiled and dropped some licorice into her pumpkin. Since it was the first of the night, it resounded with a loud 'kerplunk'. She craned her neck looking out into the yard. "And where are your parents, my little ballerina?"

"Daddy's still at work and my Momma is passing out candy at home. But Jamie came with me tonight. He's my big brother." And she turned to point proudly in Jamie's direction. He had purposefully stood in the darkness hoping to go unnoticed.

"Do I know your parents, missy?" She continued to peer into the darkness wanting to catch a glimpse of the brother she could not see.

"I don't know." Alex could see the woman was reaching in for another piece of candy, so she continued. "My momma's name is Mrs. O'Dell."

The lady was about to drop another piece of candy into the plastic pumpkin, but hesitated. "Oh, is that your brother over there, I see?"

Alex turned in his direction and waved, causing Jamie to begin walking toward his sister. "Come get some candy, Jamie!"

And, as Jamie approached the front porch, a look of recognition crossed the homeowner's face. "Ah," she said lifting her chin to peer down at him through what had previously been wide and friendly eyes, but were now nothing more than slits. "So your brother is Jamie O'Dell." She squinted with repugnance at the boy who now stood before her.

"Yes ma'am, he is." Alex had said this with pride. She loved her big brother. Jamie was a good big brother. He teased her, but it was all in fun. And he spent time with her — playing pet shop, helping her draw, making up songs. Sometimes he even allowed her to play barbershop with his dark, wavy hair, even if he frequently ended up with headbands, barrettes or short pigtails which would cause her to shriek with delight.

Alex wanted to share her good fortune with him and innocently asked, "Can my brother have that one?" And she pointed to the Baby Ruth bite that was still in the woman's hand.

But the woman slowly pulled the extra candy back toward her body, taking a step backward into the house as she did so. "Oh my, it's getting cold out here. You'd better hurry along now." And she shooed them off the porch as if they were so many chickens.

"Come on, Alex." Jamie muttered as he put his hand on her shoulder and turned her toward the street. He could hear their muffled voices as the door closed behind them.

"I've heard it can run in families."

"Certainly don't need any of *that* around here."

"Tricks — one. Treats — zero." He murmured to himself, as he exited the porch.

"Huh?" asked Alex, as she hopped down the steps like a bunny. "Let's go to that house next." And she was off to the house next door before he could respond.

Yes, this was going to be a miserable walk back home tonight, and he turned to face the hostile wind which struck him with its biting cold.

Marcie knew immediately — as soon as they opened the door. Alex went bounding over to the dining room table to dump her pumpkin and squeal over the treasures she had collected, popping Sweet Tarts into her mouth, even as the counting and sorting began. But Jamie … He was even more withdrawn and despairing than when he had left a couple of hours before. Maybe it wasn't such a good idea after all, asking him to take his sister? Something had happened; of that she was sure. She was also sure that Alex would be no help at all in discovering what it was. And she doubted she could get it out of Jamie. He was so resistant to letting Patrick or her in on what was happening to him. So she would take a slant approach — give him some time, and then see if she could engage him in conversation. For now, she would simply welcome them home with the hot chocolate she had made and hope that it would warm his spirit as well as his chilled body.

Nothing in her own childhood had prepared her for this. The youngest of five children, Marcie Kidd O'Dell had been nurtured within a close-knit and loving family. She had not known unkindness, having been surrounded by affection her whole life long. She was petted, but not indulged; encouraged, but not given false praise. Hers was an upbringing that most could only dream about, a benevolent and gentle inheritance, bestowed on her and her siblings by their faithful and loving Mama and Papa. Annie and Joe Kidd had lived their faith in the everyday, and because of that, Marcie had grown up with a strong sense of safety and security. She knew she belonged. She knew she was loved. She didn't have to question her basic worthiness.

It had given her a great foundation, but, it had not given her experience in dealing with the ill will — no, call it like it is — the downright cruelty she now saw her own child experiencing. Thank goodness, little Alex had been oblivious to whatever had happened, or she would have had to amend that to "her own children." Alex thought Jamie hung the moon, and it would have broken her little heart if she had recognized any mistreatment of him. And she wouldn't have understood. Heck, Marcie herself couldn't understand. How could anyone be so unloving, so judgmental — and of a child? Sure, Jamie was almost fifteen now. But that was still just a child. Still unformed and being formed. And she didn't like the way his world was attempting to form him.

The hot chocolate seemed to be doing its work in reviving Jamie somewhat. She would bide her time a bit longer, and then see if she could get him to talk about tonight. She placed a saucer of cookies in front of him, and he immediately reached for one. She made herself a cup of tea, replenished his chocolate, and sat down across the table from him. She took a cookie herself, an oatmeal raisin, and dunked it in the steaming tea before taking a bite. Together, they sipped and dunked and chewed in companionable silence.

What doth the Lord require of thee, but to do justice, and to love kindness, and to walk humbly with thy God. Funny how that verse popped into her mind. It had been the guiding principle in her childhood home, and it guided her now.

"Jamie? ... Sweetheart?" As she broke the silence, she asked God to guide her words. Let her be kind and show mercy and not push him further than he wanted to go. Help her to listen without putting her own need to protect him above his need to retain dignity. *Give me wisdom, O God,* she prayed, *for I am unable to do this alone.*

Pat got home late. Alex, still excited from her evening of ringing doorbells and collecting goodies from the neighbors, had already gone to bed. He had slipped into her room, kissed the top of her head, and coaxed her into curtailing her candy sorting — by size and by flavor this time — until morning. Jamie was already in his room with the door closed, but Pat gently tapped on the door and wished him a good night.

He now leaned on the doorframe of the dressing room, watching his wife brush out her long brown hair. Pat winced at Marcie's haggard look and pale complexion, so different from the usual warmth and beauty reflected in her olive skin. Lately, she had been almost ashen. And tonight her green eyes were swollen and red rimmed, hardly recognizable as those "dazzling green emeralds" he knew so well, those beautiful windows into the very soul of the woman he loved so much.

"So what happened?"

"Oh Pat, as if Jamie didn't have enough pain already. And tonight I'm afraid I caused even more." She looked up at her husband's reflection in the mirror, but her brush became still. Clutched with both hands it now rested in her lap.

"I feel so bad. After you called, I asked him to take Alex out. He didn't want to go, but I suggested that it might beat the alternative of having to face everyone who would come here if I ended up taking her out. Anyway, Alex really wanted him to go with her, so he agreed. Reluctantly."

"Did he get hurt?"

"If you mean, did he come home bloodied, no. But apparently some woman a few blocks away recognized him. I don't know how. And, oh Pat, she made a snide remark and refused to give them candy."

"Are you serious? I can't believe a grown woman would stoop to such infantile …" He stopped himself. "You would think that an evening of trick-or-treating in your own neighborhood would be safe. It's been almost two months!"

"I feel like I set him up, Pat. I should have anticipated that something like this would happen."

"Damn!" Pat struck the doorframe with the heel of his hand.

It was uncharacteristic of him to react so aggressively and Marcie turned with a start.

But Pat was at a tipping point. "Bigotry is something no one should ever have to get used to," he said, nearly choking on words meant, not just for their fifteen-year old son, but for himself, as well. "They're trying to define him with their malice, and we can't let that happen. We need to stand up for who he really is."

"I know that, Pat. But it's different this time," she answered. "He's been hurt to the very core these last few months. That one hateful incident has given everyone, it seems, permission to join in in the cursing and the heckling."

"Is it really different, Marcie? Isn't it really just the same thing he has faced in the past, only this time they raised the stakes, so to speak? They had to make it more public — a thorough humiliation this time. They obviously hadn't gotten to him the way they wanted to before." He stood with his arms hugging himself, seeking comfort that was not there. "They haven't received the satisfaction they desire yet, or they wouldn't still be trying."

Through tears of anger and hurt, Marcie keened, "So what else could they possibly want from him?"

Pat was silent. The hurt was still fresh. *These had been friends who had done these things to Jamie. Friends!* Pat would never forget the brokenness he saw on his son's face when he walked into the principal's office that day. He had gotten to work early, jumping headlong into the brief that he had to finish by the one o'clock partner's meeting, when his secretary had beeped in the call.

"Pat, I'm sorry to bother you, but it's Marcie on one. She's at the school with Jamie, and she says she needs to talk to you right away."

He had known immediately that it must be bad. Things had been escalating since last year. *Damn it! They're only fifteen-year-old boys.* How could someone acquire a capacity, an affinity even, for so much hatred at such a young age?

They had to be taught, he answered himself. Just like that song in *South Pacific. How did it go again? 'You've got to be taught before it's too late, before you are six or seven or eight, to hate all the people your relatives hate.' Yep, you've got to be taught all that hate and fear. It doesn't come naturally. Think how the boys had enjoyed one another when they were younger.* These were the same guys who had earned merit badges with Jamie. They had gone to rifle ranges and on overnight camping trips together. They had played Little League together and celebrated wins with pizza parties — more than he could remember. They had attended Sunday school and family night suppers as families — together. Jamie had called them friends. *Hell, we had ALL called them friends. But some friends they turned out to be. 'It's got to be drummed in your dear little ear. You've got to be carefully taught.' Yep. That was it, all right.* And he thought of the woman tonight and her Halloween candy. They had all been carefully taught, without a doubt.

Pat looked steadfastly into the sorrow-filled eyes of his wife's reflection as she resumed brushing her hair, and he hesitated before responding. Since just before Labor Day, their lives had been so exhausting, both emotionally and physically, but he couldn't stop now, despite the fresh wounds and the great effort it would require of them both.

"They haven't been able to defeat him," he finally answered her. "So they will keep trying. And they'll keep bringing in bigger and bigger bats as long as they perceive him to be an easy target. So it's up to Jamie and us to disarm them."

He stepped toward her reflection, and she turned to face him as he continued.

"Don't you see, those kids have made a stand, and they have to win now in order to save face. They have to be proven right in order to feel okay about themselves and what they did. And that is where none of us can afford to help them out by remaining silent any longer."

He knelt in front of her now, and she ran her fingers through his wild, unruly hair, wanting to comfort the pain his husky voice betrayed.

"Silence can be a very effective way to communicate, especially when it's timed to let a speaker hear the import of his last words, or let others reflect on what they've just heard. Letting something sink in, you know? I use it in courtrooms all the time. But to remain silent in the face of injustice, of bigotry, of abuse — communicates what? Our agreement? Our shame? Our fear or vulnerability?"

As he spoke, Marcie remembered her mother and a time when she had not remained silent. An irate husband had been verbally assaulting his wife, who was easily seven months pregnant at the time, and he looked ready to strike her. Marcie's mother, standing only 5'2", had marched up to him and demanded, "Stop that right now, young man!" And the husband, so startled by this unexpected intrusion, had stopped. Before he could regather his anger, Marcie's Mama had confided that she understood the pending responsibilities and pressures of parenthood, and how tensions could mount. She had told him she believed he was a better man than his temper made him out to be that day. She was not judgmental. Instead, she encouraged him to find that better self and the better way. Looking back, Marcie realized this example of confronting injustice and extending compassion encapsulated the extraordinary parenting that had formed her. But back then, she had not understood the courage required of her tiny mother to make that challenge — to protect that young woman and her unborn child.

"You're right, Pat," she said, as she cradled her husband's face between her hands and looked into his impassioned eyes. "We've only wanted to protect him, but what kind of protection has our not speaking up really offered?"

She pulled his head to her breast and held him as she gently rocked back and forth. The only sound was that of their breath, ragged at first, but then slowly beginning to commingle into the same comfortable cadence as they rested in one another's arms.

After a few minutes, though, Pat lifted his head away from her embrace, revealing a new energy that had entered his eyes. "We need to change the way we think, that's all!" He took her hand in his. "What we need to do is focus on the protection we can give Jamie this moment. And it seems to me the first thing we need to do is examine ourselves to see if we are indeed feeling any shame? any fear? any vulnerability? Is there anything that is holding us back? And then, the next thing would be to work through those issues. I've heard of this group called PFLAG[6]. It's for family members of lesbians and gays, and if we decide we are harboring some of those responses, perhaps meeting with them can help us work through them. One of the partners at the firm told me it has helped him and his wife deal with their difficulties when their granddaughter came out. He said the funniest thing. He said, 'parents and grandparents have to come out, too.' But if you think about it, he's right. And there is no shame in admitting that we're having a difficult time." He squeezed her hand for emphasis.

"And finally, we need to speak our truth. Honestly and straightforwardly. And speak it without shame. Whenever we're in a situation where speaking up will make a difference, we have to be vocal in our support of Jamie. But even more important, we have to let him see us do it."

"That sounds so easy. But what do we say?"

"Well, what do you feel?"

And without hesitation, Marcie affirmed, "I feel love for my son and I'm proud of who he is as a person. And all I ask is for others to be kind to him and to give him the chance to let them know who he really is."

"Then say it."

"I can do that," she smiled.

Pat kissed her hands. "So can I."

Playing with the dark curls around his ears, she sighed. "We thought we were doing the right thing, but helping him hide, it seems, has only made things worse. I can see now that by being supportive of Jamie in every way that we can be here at home, but not saying or doing anything outside these walls to show him and others that he has our full love and support, we inadvertently ... "

Lifting his face toward her and speaking in an urgent whisper, she lamented, "Oh, darling, what has our silence taught Jamie? What has it said to others? And why haven't we seen this before?"

Placing his hands on hers, he answered confidently. "Who knows what anyone else has heard up until now; but, from this day forward, we must be sure there is no room for misunderstanding how we feel. We will speak the truth — out loud, and in love."

Hope stirred in her heart. Lately, it had felt as if the world were pressing down on them, and it had been hard even to breathe. *Was this what all people felt under the weight of oppression?* In the grip of the mounting injustice against Jamie, she and Pat had suffered a slow and torturous asphyxiation as they had tried to ensure their family's survival through silent love and private acceptance. The relentless viciousness of all the hate-filled attacks had slithered, python-like, around them, squeezing ever harder as they were perceived to be weakening. But after talking just now, Marcie no longer felt weak. And she could tell Pat didn't either. They gulped their lungs full of pure, cleansing air — the bonds of oppression broken. They headed to their bed, hand in hand, feeling as if they had just been released from the clutch of the ever-strengthening coils of impossibility and injustice.

Dignity means that what I have to say is important, and I will say it when it's important for me to say it. Dignity really means that I deserve the best treatment I can receive and that I have the responsibility to give the best treatment I can to other people.
— *Maya Angelou*

Chapter 11

FRIENDS AND FAMILY

"Tammy. It's Marcie. Have I caught you at a good time?"

Tammy held the phone in the crook of her neck as she finished blotting her forehead with a kitchen towel and tossed it onto the granite countertop. "Sure. I just finished my first Pilates video. Whew, what a workout! I was just about to get myself a cold drink. What's up?"

"Hold off on that drink, okay? Something happened last night and I really want to talk with you about it. We're even more alike than we knew, Tammy. Meet me at the coffee shop again?"

"Oh, Marcie, I'm a dreadful mess. I couldn't possibly go out anywhere like this and it would take a while for me to clean up."

"Then meet me at the Sonic. My treat. Happy hour starts in ten minutes and I have so much to tell you."

"Well, all right then. Sonic it is. Give me fifteen minutes, okay?"

"Sure. And Tammy ... thanks."

Tammy quickly threw on a clean shirt and jeans and gathered her damp hair into a loose ponytail. As she grabbed her purse and headed for the door, she noticed the bag of leftover candy from the night before. Best to get that out of the house or the Pilates would be all in vain.

Tammy was curious. What new connection had Marcie discovered? This would be the first time she'd seen Marcie since their initial meeting in the coffee shop, but she had thought of her often, replaying their conversation in detail and marveling at how close they had become so quickly. They had each emailed the other that first day to express their grateful appreciation for the understanding they had experienced in the other, but since then, they had even missed each other in the drop-off lane at school. It will be really nice, Tammy thought, if we can just pick up our friendship where we left off last week, but she couldn't help feeling just a bit nervous. It had been a long time since Tammy had made a new friend, not merely an acquaintance, and she was very aware that she was already placing expectations on the relationship. More than anything, she wanted the opportunity to deepen their fledgling intimacy with more meaningful conversations, but ... *Settle down*, she told herself, *and let it be what it will be.*

She focused instead on getting to the Sonic safely on this drizzly, gray day. The Halloween cold front had brought with it some much-needed showers, and Tammy didn't begrudge having to get out in the rain. The slap of the windshield wipers was keeping perfect time with the '60s classic on the radio. "Sweet Ca-ro-line ..." she sang along, drumming out the rhythm on the steering wheel with first one hand and then the other. She smiled to herself. *Kelly's music training is beginning to rub off on me.*

The song ended, and her thoughts turned to last night. As usual, Halloween at the Sloans' had been rather uneventful. Because they lived so far off the main road, kids rarely made it to their front door asking for candy, and Tammy had taken Hannah to a "Trick-or-Trunk" event at the church, as was their custom. The twins had stayed at home — Kelly practicing her clarinet, and Michael lost in a video game. And Ed hadn't made it home until late last night. He hadn't even gotten to see Hannah in her butterfly costume, and she had wanted her Daddy to see her diaphanous creation, all pink and purple Saran Wrap held together with bright green pipe cleaners. Kelly had helped her with quality control, ensuring that the pipe cleaners were twisted tightly enough to keep the wings from falling apart, and Michael had engineered a harness to hold the wings onto Hannah's slender, leotard-ed "butterfly body." Tammy's heart soared as she remembered the way the twins had pitched in to help their little sister. And how absolutely wonderful it was to see that Michael seemed to be coming out of his self-imposed isolation and re-engaging with the family.

"Thank you, God," she whispered aloud. "Thank you for your healing, restorative love."

Tammy pulled into the Sonic and drove around the lot looking for Marcie's car. Not seeing it, she pulled into one of the drive-up booths, turned off the engine, and waited. It was fun to receive a spontaneous invitation like this from a friend. Friend. That wasn't a word that Tammy used loosely, and it thrilled her that she already felt comfortable calling Marcie her friend.

She was parked under the protective awning of the building, but intermittent drops still found their way to her windshield, small beads of water hitting her car the only sound. She liked the quiet. This kind of quiet. She closed her eyes. How different this sort of silence was from the quiet that, until very recently, had defined her life. Then, it had felt as though she were imprisoned in a sinking car, panicked that the longer she stayed stuck inside, the less likely her chances of survival. There was nothing peaceful about that kind of quiet. But since her coffee with Marcie O'Dell last week, she had felt more free. More like herself. To finally break through a window and swim through the murkiness toward the surface was exhilarating after such a long struggle.

A light tapping on the passenger window made her jump; and Tammy opened her eyes to see Marcie, bent at the waist, damp hair hanging down around her face, looking in.

"Oh! Get in here before you drown!" Tammy leaned over to pop the door handle and Marcie slid into the front seat.

"I'm loving this rain, but I wasn't sure you'd want to come out in it today. Thanks for meeting me on such short notice."

"Oh, there's never a day that doesn't beg for a Sonic Happy Hour!" Tammy turned the key and lowered her window. "What do you want?"

"How about a cherry limeade?"

Tammy pushed the big red button and talked to a teenaged voice that crackled in the speakers. "One cherry limeade and one vanilla Coke. Extra vanilla, please."

Tammy turned to smile at Marcie. "My treat."

Marcie had already reached for her purse. "But I invited you. I'd planned to treat you."

"It's the least I can do, okay?" How long would it take before she could look into Marcie's eyes and not be wracked with guilt?

"Okay. This time. But next time it's on me. Okay?" Marcie put her purse on top of Tammy's bag of candy.

"Oh, I'm sorry. Here." She reached out as Marcie handed her the bag. "I brought that to give to the car hop. The last thing I need around the house is a lot of my favorite candy."

Marcie peeked into the bag before handing it over. "Oh my, dangerous stuff all right. M&Ms are my downfall too." And she went on to claim having once eaten three bags in one day. "I guess we've finally uncovered a way we're not alike. There's no way I'd have the restraint to give this away — or the discipline to take up Pilates, for heaven's sake. My hat is off to you, Tammy," and she nodded a little bow in deference to Tammy's self-discipline.

"Well, we'll see how long I keep up the Pilates. I don't have a great track record where exercise is concerned, either."

Just then, a skinny boy with acne skated up to the window to deliver their drinks, and as Tammy paid him, she handed over the bag of candy as well. He grinned his thanks and skated away as if he had won the lottery, the smile on his face practically daring the rain to dampen his day.

"So what was your big discovery last night?" Tammy queried, almost playfully, as she took a big swig of her vanilla Coke. "Ah perfect!" She turned to give Marcie her full attention.

"I'm guilty of being silent too."

Marcie's sober look and solemn tone were not what Tammy had expected, and immediately she shifted into a more compassionate posture, leaning in toward her friend and speaking out of concern as she asked, "What do you mean, Marcie?"

"All these years, I've tried really hard to help Jamie keep his secret. I've not spoken out against homophobic jokes that friends might make. I've not confronted bigotry in my presence, whether the stereotyping of gays or the outright vilifying of them. I haven't shared my own views about same-sex issues. And I told myself that by not drawing attention to the fact that I thought differently, I was somehow deflecting attention away from my son. Not singling him out as being different. Protecting him. But I see now what I was really doing."

Tammy waited a long moment before gently asking, "And what do you see now, Marcie?"

"I see that I have inadvertently taught him that it's not okay to be who he is in public; and, I hope I'm not right about this, but I'm afraid that I've taught him that, at least on some level, I am ashamed of who he is. And then, it's a slippery slope down from there."

"Oh, Marcie. Surely not. You are so loving and supportive and accepting of who he is."

"But on the surface, my silence out in public would look to him like he was only worthy of support in the safety of our home. Like the girl who begins to question her value when the guy she's dating only invites her over and never takes her out in public. Tammy, I've even been torn about what to do when another child's bullying was obviously meant to hurt Jamie for his effeminate characteristics. I usually chose not to call attention to it, for fear of the recriminations that Jamie would have to face. How protected could he have possibly felt?"

Tammy waited. And as she waited, she watched a panoply of emotions play over Marcie's face, until finally she brightened and looked up with resolve.

"Pat and I have come to realize that helping Jamie live his truth outside our home is the right thing to do and that means being silent no more. Jamie needs to see us going to bat for him and feel our support and know our pride in him — out in the world where he needs it most. He needs for us to stand up for, not just what we know about our son, but also what we believe about homosexuality. Jamie deserves to be loved and accepted for who he is and not be rejected for who others think he is."

Tammy smiled her support and reached out to squeeze Marcie's hand in encouragement. Marcie returned her smile and sighed deeply.

"Remember the chasm you spoke of last week? Well, it exists for my family too, only we've allowed it to be quarried by others, effectively dividing *us* from *them*." Their eyes remained fixed upon each other as Marcie continued. "And it frightens me to even imagine publicly crossing that gulf with all the hatred being trained on Jamie — and others like him — these days. But honestly, it frightens me more not to." She played with the straw in her drink. "And that's what I came to tell you. We're going to face our fears about going public, Tammy. We're going to a PFLAG meeting tonight.[7] It's a support group for parents, friends, and families of lesbians and gays — and bisexual and transgender persons too — and I'm a little nervous about it, but excited too. I wanted to tell someone, and then I realized the one I wanted to tell ... was you."

Tammy was touched to the core. A capacious welling of emotion took her by surprise. This woman, this mother, was not only big enough to forgive all Tammy's past transgressions, but big enough to include her in her own recovery. What compassion. What a risk. And how grateful Tammy felt to be the recipient of both. She reached over and hugged Marcie. "Oh that's wonderful. I can only imagine how scary it must feel to think about being so open ... around here especially." Tammy waved her arm in a broad stroke to encompass the ultraconservative community in which they lived. "And it means so much that you wanted to tell me. What made you decide to find a group?"

"One of Pat's co-worker's told us about them, but our family therapist has also suggested that we find a local chapter and attend. And after last night, we knew we were ready to go. We're having to drive nearly all the way to Austin to find a group, though. It's all the way down in Cedar Park. But you know, it's worth the drive if it helps us help our family. It's one thing for Pat and me to work out any fears we may have about being so openly supportive of Jamie, but we have to think about Alexandra too. We want to know how best to explain to her how to handle things she may overhear at school or in the neighborhood." Marcie then told Tammy about the unpleasant encounter that Jamie and Alex had experienced on Halloween night.

Tammy's mouth fell open in shock. "Are you serious? What's wrong with people? They're just kids! I can't believe someone would say that kind of thing to their faces."

"Well, believe it." Marcie shook her head. "So you see, coming out isn't just Jamie's responsibility. It's something that our whole family has to do.

"PFLAG has a wealth of resources and information to help us on this journey and I'm hoping that we'll find the encouragement we need from other people who've already journeyed down this road. Pat and I are pretty sure about our roles, but when it comes to Jamie and Alex ..." Marcie looked out the window. The rain had let up, nothing more than a light sprinkle now. "At school, Jamie has been immobilized by his fears — first of being excluded, then of being harassed, and now of the constant threat of outright bullying." She looked straight at Tammy. "We weren't prepared for any of that. And we just don't want to make the same mistakes again with him now, or with Alex. And that is why we're going to PFLAG."

"I can't tell you how much I respect that. I mean, everything that you're doing. As hard as it is, it's the right thing for your family." Tammy thought of that afternoon just after her last visit with Marcie. She would never forget the fear and shame that Michael had brought home with him from school that day. Sad that it had taken his becoming the victim of a similar ordeal for him to truly understand the suffering that bullying can produce. It had deeply affected Michael and Tammy both. Yet the O'Dells had struggled with that same kind of heartache on a continual basis. *How had they survived?* "And it's the right thing for all the rest of us, too."

"What do you mean, 'the rest of us'?"

"I mean people like me." Tammy put her Coke down in the drink holder and turned in her seat to face Marcie. "Marcie, I'm done. I really am. I can no longer ignore, much less tolerate, any type of discriminatory behavior or statements in my presence. I think I finally fully realize that not taking action is just as bad as being an active participant. I thought I was there, but now I know I am." She had to look away for a moment before continuing. "You see, we've experienced some things with Michael that have just brought all of this too close to home. It's a real part of me now too. All of it." Ironically, it had been Michael's cruelty and Ed's pious defensiveness that had brought this into the Sloan household in the first place, not Jamie. But it was getting to know Marcie, and then Michael's becoming a victim himself, that had cemented Tammy's convictions. "I now know what it feels like on both sides of all this hideousness. And I want to learn how to respond to bullying, in all its forms, in ways that will create healing for everyone. The bullies, the victims, and the families — all of them."

Marcie smiled as Tammy continued.

"I want to become educated in how to empower others, people like me and you, to take the necessary steps to help themselves and their loved ones. But how? And then where do I find people who need help?"

"We've learned in counseling that one in four families has an immediate family member who is LGBT, and that most people have at least one LGBT individual in their extended circle of friends. It won't be as difficult as you think to find people who need your help."

"Really? I had no idea it was that many."

"That's because those individuals want it that way. It's difficult to live in the closet, Tammy, but it's also difficult to step outside. You see, your first reaction on learning that your loved one is gay or lesbian can range anywhere from anger to sadness, from fear to hurt, from utter confusion to deepest grief. And anywhere in between. We've learned that all the emotions we experience as our loved ones navigate their coming out process are perfectly normal — for them and for us. Isn't it sad how hard we make it on ourselves and those we love the most? Our kids? It's hard for me to comprehend, actually. Something else we've learned — did you know that one in every ten people in this country, and across the world, is lesbian, gay, bisexual or transgender?"[8]

Tammy's eyes widened. *How could that many people hide from society? From their families?*

"Because you and I can remember the excitement we felt when we first realized we were attracted to our boyfriends, and later our husbands, and then the sheer delight of learning they liked us, too, we can really appreciate the contrast that's there for someone like Jamie — the confusion, the loneliness and the intense fear that his attractions bring him. It's not too great a stretch for us to imagine that people attracted to someone of the same-sex are just as joyful inside as we are, but our society has taught them to be ashamed of their feelings. Taught them that their feelings are not natural — evil even — and has driven them to hide, or even repress, those feelings. Well, Tammy, you and I are no longer going to be a part of that system. I'll send you some of the things our counselor has shared with us. She's very good. And if you're really serious about this, you should consider going to a PFLAG meeting yourself."

Tammy was taken aback. Go to PFLAG herself? She wasn't a parent of a gay child. But then she quickly realized she could go as a friend. She wanted to be a friend — their friend. And she could gain a lot of insight by attending such a meeting. She was floored by what Marcie had just shared. Imagine what she might learn from the people at PFLAG. "You know, that's not a bad idea. I've just never thought about that before." As soon as the words were out of her mouth Tammy realized the absurdity in her statement. There was certainly a *lot* that she had never thought about until recently.

"Our counselor says that at PFLAG people are encouraged to ask questions — all kinds of questions. Nothing is off limits. They talk about sexual orientation and about their faith communities and about governing bodies at the local, state and federal levels. They're all about education and advocacy. And they provide the support and resources to help on whatever your journey happens to be."

"I want to learn how to respond to all the negativity out there in positive and transformative ways. If I can help just one mother avoid the unnecessary pain that you and I have endured — because of acquiescence, silence, or just plain old misinformation — it will be worth it to me."

Marcie's smile was wide. "I think you've got the makings of a counselor, Tammy."

"Oh stop it. Don't joke!"

"I'm not joking. I'm serious. It's our passions that bring about the biggest changes in our lives and in the world. And you've certainly got that."

"Well, we'll see." She swatted the air with her hand to dismiss Marcie's words, but Tammy's thoughts were already swirling with a myriad of possibilities. She had certainly said things recently — to Ed, to Bill Pritchett and even to the kids — but she hadn't actually done anything to back up her changing convictions. Her old ways of thinking had been exposed to a new way of living, and she now truly recognized and embraced the changes within herself. Walls of submission, insecurity, and exclusion had begun falling down around her, but it was no longer as frightening as it had been just a short time ago.

Driving down the highway toward home, the sun began to shine. Breaking through the clouds, its beams reached down to touch the earth, and Tammy could feel its comforting warmth cutting through the chill in the November air. The upcoming holidays already on the horizon, Tammy uttered a prayer of thanks. *This Thanksgiving looks to bring with it a multitude of unexpected blessings out of what I first thought were only disasters. Thank you for giving me the wisdom to listen and the strength to grow.*

Change does not roll in on the wheels of inevitability,
but comes through continuous struggle.
— Martin Luther King, Jr.

Chapter 12

PFLAG

Tammy picked up the phone without even looking at the caller ID. "What are you doing tonight?" It was Marcie.

"Ed's got a late night in Austin, so I was going to order Chinese for everyone and then curl up with my book. Why?"

"Tonight's our PFLAG night, and Pat just called to tell me he won't be able to get away early enough to go with me this time. Wanna go?"

Hannah and a friend from school came running into the kitchen, cackling like chickens. "I'm on the phone." Tammy pointed at the phone and motioned to them to quiet down; then she moved the phone to her other ear. "What time?"

"Seven. But it'll take us over an hour to get there with traffic."

At twenty minutes to six, Marcie pulled up the long gravel drive at the Sloans'. Tammy jumped in and they were on their way.

"Thanks so much for thinking to invite me. I'm really excited about this."

"Well, I knew you were wanting to broaden your horizons, and this seemed a perfect way to introduce you to the real-life issues LGBT individuals and their families go through. Besides, I really enjoy your company, and we don't get much opportunity to get together."

"I agree, and we need to rectify that. I love our coffee dates, but this sort of thing is fun, too. Although, I guess most people wouldn't think this kind of seriousness is fun!"

Marcie laughed and agreed wholeheartedly. Then she spent the next hour filling Tammy in on what she might expect from the meeting and on the sort of people she would probably meet. "They're from all walks of life, Tammy, and everyone is at a different stage in their coming out — as a parent of a gay child or as the gay 'child' themselves. Some have made peace with it; some embrace it; and others really struggle to make sense of it. The ones who have the hardest times are those who have grown up in a church that judges homosexuality as sinful — evil even. But all of them are there because they love their children and they're trying to figure out a way to make their relationship work. You'll like them."

Although she had chosen the group closest to her home, Marcie still had to drive more than forty miles before pulling into the parking lot of the Red Oak Unitarian Church in Cedar Park. It wasn't a large building, but there were several entrances, so Tammy was glad to have Marcie there to guide her. She wasn't nervous. Why should she be? But she had to admit that she hoped no one would recognize her and connect her to her well-known husband.

The room was pleasant and inviting. The smell of fresh coffee brewing and the convivial sounds of friends happily greeting one another after a long week's absence filled the space, which was large enough to accommodate the four tables and twenty-odd chairs that had been set up in a square in the middle of it; yet it was not so large as to lose the intimate, cozy feeling the room conveyed. They were a few minutes early, but it was already filled with more than a dozen people. Some were standing in small clusters visiting. Others were already quietly seated. After Tammy and Marcie got their coffee and mingled a bit with those at the refreshment table, they found two seats together and joined them.

Tammy couldn't help but notice the man seated directly opposite her. From the flag and battle helmet tattoo on his arm, she guessed he was a veteran, and based on his age, she reckoned that he had probably been in Vietnam. He sat in silence with his arms folded across his chest; and, although he wasn't really scowling, he certainly wasn't inviting interaction. *But he was there. Good for him.* There were several couples, moms and dads, of varying ages. And several college-aged kids.

But there were definitely more women than men. Nobody seemed to recognize Tammy, or if they did, it didn't seem to matter. Tammy felt welcomed.

The speaker was an older gentleman — mid seventies maybe? Bob had retired from Xerox two decades ago and had followed his high level executive position with going back to school, earning his second master's in counseling, and then using his passion and newfound expertise to help individuals and families deal with coming out. Extremely successful at work (over the years he had led hundreds of others to reach their full potential) he, on the other hand, had felt an ironic disconnect in his own personal life. Bob had remained in the closet for his entire career. He hadn't even told his mother and brother until he was well into his fifties. He had been the quarterback in high school and college, student-body president, and a regular Sunday school teacher. He never married, hadn't dated a woman in twenty years, and had lots of male friends. But living as he did, in Alabama at the time, he saw no reason to risk the possible professional and social fallout of coming out any further.

He went on to explain how the release of any secret (coming out as gay being only one example) occurs in three stages. He drew three concentric circles on the white board behind him, labeling the inner circle PERSONAL PHASE, the middle circle PRIVATE PHASE, and the outer circle PUBLIC PHASE. "When we as individuals become aware that out of fear or shame we are hiding something," he elaborated, "we find ourselves in this personal phase. We keep it to ourselves, revealing our innermost thoughts and feelings to no one. Some, in fact, bury the reality so deeply and are in such personal denial that they can't even admit the truth to themselves." Then he got personal. "I, for one, stayed in that phase of personal hell for a decade or more. I knew I was different when I was about six, but I didn't really understand *how* I was different. Yet, even at six-years-old, I knew enough to keep it to myself. Imagine. Knowing that at six."

Tammy shook her head in sorrow and disbelief. She thought of Michael at that age. So innocent. So secure in his sense of belonging. So confident in himself. No, she couldn't comprehend his feeling shame and having to hide who he was — even from his mother. They had been so close, and he had been an open book to her. Her heart grieved for Bob — and for Jamie — and for all those others yet unknown to her who were living with such pain even now.

"I was around sixteen or seventeen when I finally began to recognize and accept who I was, but I still didn't tell a soul." Now, Bob looked around at the mothers and fathers, sisters, brothers, and grandparents who were there. "And remember, this secret-keeping phase is true, not only for the individual who is struggling to accept his or her own sexuality, but also for you — families and friends — once you've been told. Once you've learned that a loved one is gay, you may feel you need to keep it a secret too, in order to protect yourself, your reputation, your community standing, whatever. Remember, no matter the secret, the phases are the same." Marcie and Tammy exchanged glances — Marcie acknowledging her own culpability with a sigh, and Tammy whispering, "I know." Her heart ached for dear, brave Marcie.

Bob then went on to describe the private phase, the time when one might actually consider telling another person. "Most people will have a 'safe person,'" he asserted, "a parent, a sibling, a good friend — who they know can handle the truth and still love them. Unlike me. Growing up in Alabama in the fifties, nobody talked about gay people, and I wasn't about to talk about myself like that to anyone I knew. My 'safe person' eventually came in the form of a lady that I sat next to on a flight to Chicago. I was twenty-eight years old. She wasn't from Alabama, and I was on my second beer! That was safe enough for me!"

People laughed. At first, Tammy was hesitant to join in the laughter. Wouldn't that seem insensitive to find humor in this man's struggles, no matter how long ago they happened? But then she looked around the table. So many understanding expressions … And they were smiling, laughing, and making humorous comments of their own. She realized their journeys must not be so different from Bob's.

Then he posed a question to the group. "What do you think makes us capable of reaching that point? Of wanting or needing to tell someone?"

The lady sitting next to Tammy answered. "Isn't it all about safety?"

"Yes, safety plays a big part. But just as important is feeling empowered to take that first step. And that is where PFLAG plays such an important role. When every fiber of our being tells us that ours is a solitary road to travel, we hear others' stories, and we realize that we are not alone — that there have been countless others who have walked this journey before us. In seeing them affirmed within the group, and their feelings and struggles accepted, we are emboldened to share our own reality. In watching how others handle and survive the 'tellings' in the outside world which have not gone well, and in seeing the support they receive from the group, we are encouraged that we too, can overcome. And then ultimately, after we have risked and survived, we find we can be there —here — to help all those who come after us."

One man from the other side of the table spoke up. "That's why Sandy and I march in the parade every year. We want to let all those people know that we are their family — maybe not of origin, but of choice. I can't tell you how many times people have reached out to hug us, tears in their eyes, just to say thank you."

"Just like we are family to each other." This came from a woman who had come in by herself. "I can't even talk about this with my husband. He doesn't want to talk about Claire and Judy at all."

"And, Connie, your's is a perfect example of being stuck in the privacy stage. You feel you can talk freely here, and nowhere else. It doesn't matter if you are the LGBT individual or a friend or family member. We stay where we feel safe. Many people live their entire lives in this stage." Bob turned and placed his finger on the middle circle he had drawn on the board. "But staying there means you're constantly editing your life, afraid to tell the truth about yourself— or your loved one — for whatever the reason." Again, Tammy and Marcie caught one another's eyes. This was hitting awfully close to home. Neither had any trouble identifying with how much energy such a life demanded.

The room became quiet. "Does anyone have any questions before I go on?"

No one said a word and Tammy became lost in her own thoughts. She had told Ed and the kids how she felt, and Henry and Amber — and even Edith and Marcie. Most of those she had known would be 'safe,' but it had taken all the courage she possessed to tell Ed and Edith. She had known to expect conflict with Ed and had had to steel herself to face it. That was scary; but it had actually been harder talking with Edith, since she really wasn't sure how Edith would respond, and she wanted to preserve their good relationship. *Bless her heart, Edith had come through beautifully.* That was her inner circle, but what about her greater circle of friends? Was she ready to risk possible social repercussions from her conservative friends in the community and church? *And I'm just the friend of a parent!*

Her breath literally caught in her throat when she realized the risks — personal, professional, and social — that the others in this room had faced, and would continue to face, each time they decided to live true to themselves or their loved ones.

"Once you truly go public, there's no going back." Bob's words broke through her reverie and startled her back into the present moment. "How true," she sighed.

Bob was now straddling the back of a chair, preparing to tell a story. "There comes a time about halfway through my 'Coming Out' workshops[9], when everyone is expected to share a 'telling story' with the group. For some, this is terribly difficult since it revisits so much pain. I could tell you a multitude of horror stories, and some of them, sadly, would sound all too familiar. But there is one that stands out from all the others. A young woman in her early twenties had attended the first three classes and had worked all the self-acceptance and empowering exercises that we cover in those weeks, but she was still quite fearful of telling her family, her mom in particular. Her reasons were typical: 'I don't want to disappoint her.' 'I'm afraid she won't accept me.' 'Our church says it's a sin,' etc. Well, when she came to the fourth class, she was a completely different woman — bright, sunny, full of hope. I noticed the difference in her demeanor immediately and guessed that she must have had a good experience sharing her truth. Of course, I also assumed that the good prep work I had provided had helped make it so. So when it came time for everyone to share how they had taken steps toward wholeness that week, the young lady shared her story. She said that she had been so stressed about telling her mom that her girlfriend had suggested a fun night out. They went to Sue Ellen's, a popular lesbian bar in the Oak Lawn area of Dallas, where they could enjoy some good food, good drinks, and live music. And who did they see when they got there?" Bob paused dramatically and looked around the table. "Her mother!"

One lady laughed so hard she nearly cried. "Well, I guess that made all their 'family telling' a little bit easier for everyone!"

Bob laughed himself. "Now, I don't recommend waiting for such a rare stroke of luck as that, but it is a lighthearted way to look at what it is that we are really looking at. Did that make sense? What I mean is, we're just talking about being honest — with ourselves first, then with the people who love us the most in this world. When we can do that, then the rest of the world just kind of falls into place."

In a way, Tammy felt she had already 'gone public,' what with all the awfulness that had been spread via airwaves, newsprint, and social media. Then it dawned on her. She hadn't gone public at all. Everyone else had. Ed's position in politics had driven what would have been a private matter, for the O'Dells and her own family to work out for themselves, into a matter for public fodder. Yet, she hadn't said a word. Not publicly at least. She looked over at Marcie, wondering if her friend could possibly tell what was going on inside her head.

"Being public means being honest — in all circumstances, with all people."

"But what do we do when we feel we can't be honest at church?" A young man, probably high-school aged, had posed the question. "I mean, I've heard people at my church say that they would leave the church if gays were accepted there."

"That's a hard one. In ancient times, a failure to offer hospitality was a serious transgression. One of the worst, really. In fact, it was a lack of hospitality by the townspeople that was at the crux of the whole Sodom and Gomorrah story. All ancient cultures practiced it, including the Israelites, and it was adopted by the early church as a defining principle of Christianity. And what did it entail? Simply put, it meant bringing the stranger into your household and offering them what they needed for their journey.

"When someone threatens to kick another out, or leave the church over issues of inclusion, they are being inhospitable. They are failing to practice the very discipline that is at the root of Christianity. And this includes you or me leaving a church because we don't feel welcome." Again he paused, this time to let that thought sink in before he continued, "People leave the church over a social policy or a theological interpretation, but we have to remember that we are not an issue or a policy. We are people. All of us — on both sides of any issue."

He stood up and walked over to the young man who had posed the question, placing his hand on his shoulder and giving his listeners time to internalize this truth. "And the only way *we* are going to help others out there get to know us is by being honest, open, and willing to stay the course — even when *we* may not feel welcomed. It's up to *us* to be the change we want to see in the church. In our families. And in the world."

"Wow. That was powerful," Marcie whispered.

Tammy could only nod her agreement. Her thoughts crowded her mind. She was learning so much, and she had only been here forty-five minutes. Coming to this group, she realized, was about as public as she had risked so far in letting her opinions be known. And Bob's last part on hospitality reverberated within her. He had articulated so well what she had been intuiting, but could not express. *Thank you, God, for Bob's words. Give me strength to live them out. Help me to know how to do so.*

Bob wrapped up by inviting anyone who was interested to a six-week workshop he would be holding at St. Luke's Methodist in Austin. It was open to anyone — LGBT, family members, or friends. Several people pulled out pens to jot down notes while Marcie and Tammy made their way, first to the ladies room, and then to the coffee and cookies.

"Are all PFLAG speakers this powerful?" Tammy asked.

Marcie told her that some were professional speakers, like Bob, but that many were simply gay individuals who shared their personal stories in hope of helping others — struggling family members (not unlike their own) and individuals who were still in the process of coming out. "And there's an unbelievable amount of power in that too. Family members are able to ask them questions they can't ask their child, and the speakers can tell them things it's hard for them to share with their own families."

"Hmm. I don't doubt it. There have been times when I'd have benefited from having a set-up like that myself, especially as the twins were approaching puberty. And you said the second half will be everyone sharing their stories?"

"Yep. We'll go around the circle, but you can pass if you want. Lots of people do that for a while until they've established trust within the group. Pat and I passed at our first meeting, but some don't speak up for a lot longer than that. Everyone is respectful of one another's privacy and protects that space. Speaking of which, we'd better get back to our seats. Want another cookie? Or something to drink?" Marcie was already helping herself to both.

"I'll just get some water and be right there."

They went clock-wise. First to speak was Herb, a man whose daughter had come out some time ago. His daughter was now twenty-two, and he feared for her safety. "I've never had a problem with my daughter's sexuality. She came out to me and my wife when she was about fourteen, and I've really been okay with it all. Maybe things were easier for us because our daughter was fully open and fully accepted all through high school and college. We live in a part of Austin that is very progressive, and that is where she went to high school; then she attended a small 'liberal' liberal-arts school. But now that she's out of those relatively safe environments, I'm not so sure anymore. She'll be moving to Midland for her first job next month, and that's right in the middle of the Bible Belt. This should be an exciting time for her, and for me as well, but I'm worried, instead."

The next to speak was a woman who found out two months ago that her thirty-seven-year-old son wanted to become a woman. Millie struggled with pronouns, using "he" and then correcting herself each time by substituting "she" instead. Tammy could tell she was trying hard. She broke down and cried when recounting their initial conversation. Her son had told her, "Mom, I just can't be who I'm not anymore. If I don't do something about it, I just don't want to live anymore." Having him/her in California was making things even worse. She was his mother. She wanted to help him, to lay eyes on her, to comfort him/her. But instead, they were both going through their journeys alone. "You are the first people I've had the courage to tell about this," she snuffled. "I'm so glad I found this group."

Many people teared up listening to Millie's tender account, but the stern-looking vet sat, still with arms crossed, apparently unmoved by her emotional story.

Another man spoke next. Clearly uncomfortable, Charlie talked about his only son, Eliot. "I knew before he did. When he was only two. You know, some things you can just tell. Anyway, he's in high school now and he likes to dance. He does ballet. And more and more people can see it now. I understand this is who he is, I really do. But we don't have the luxury of living in an open-minded area. I'm really worried about him. We read about hate crimes — muggings and beatings, or even worse — and I know that could happen here. I just wish he would show more discretion."

A woman named Sharon detailed an encounter she had experienced at her church. "I was on our local missions committee and a special task force had been put together to reach out to troubled and homeless youth in our area. One of the committee members offered his homophobic ideas about why these youth were homeless in the first place. And that's all it took. Nearly everyone on that committee eventually chimed in with their prejudiced attitudes against gays, lesbians, and transgenders. But I sat there, paralyzed, not saying a word. I wanted to have the nerve to speak up, to defend my son and others like him, but how could I stand up against an angry group like that? And that's when I knew I had to do something, because I couldn't live with myself for denying my son in that way. And that's when I found PFLAG. It's been a godsend for me and my family. I've learned ways to offer my perspective, which often challenges untruths, without resorting to confrontation. I feel better about myself and my son does too."

Tammy made a mental note to get to know Sharon better. They had a lot in common, and she could prove a great ally, and perhaps mentor. She'd ask Marcie to introduce her to Sharon after the meeting.

Marcie had also identified with what Sharon had said, and told a story of when she had failed to speak up. "I was at a pack meeting with Jamie when he was just a Tiger Cub — so we're talking about ten years ago. He would have been just five. He had already told us that he knew he was different from the other boys, and Pat and I were just beginning to suspect what that difference might mean. Well, the meeting room had been decorated with multi-colored balloons and at the end of the evening, one of the dads began passing them out for the boys to take home, and Jamie chose a pink one. The dad grabbed it back and gave him a red balloon instead. When Jamie started to pout, the dad told him to man up, that no manly boy would choose pink, and then he turned to another guy and laughed. He said something like, "That's the problem with kids these days. They're seeing things on TV that make them think it's okay to be fruity." And he said this right in front of Jamie. Then he went on to talk about the Don't Ask Don't Tell policy that was popular and in force at that time, and I just walked away. I'm not proud of that moment. I wish I had had the courage then to stand up to that man. But at least I know that now I do have the strength to support my son, not just at home, but also in public. And I have this group to thank for that."

Now it was Tammy's turn. She swallowed hard before speaking. "I don't have a relative that's gay. But I think it's really sad that families, churches, governments, and our society as a whole are so willing to advocate bigotry like this. I don't think they're all intentionally cruel, although some may be. I just think most people are uninformed. And that's why I'm here tonight. I want to educate myself and then help educate others. I've come to realize that's the best way I can help my friend and her son."

Everybody clapped. Although Tammy felt good about what she had said and the response her statement had received, she was a little embarrassed. To her it felt like getting a participation award in the Olympic Games. All the others had faced so much more than she.

Next, a young man, barely out of high school, spoke of his coming out. "I knew I could tell my mom. She's always been very open about her views on everything — this included. But when I finally told my brother about a year ago, it was a risk. I really didn't know what his true feelings were. I guess I shouldn't complain, 'cause it's not like he got angry or ugly or anything. And we're okay and everything. But he treated it like it was no big deal. Once again, I know that's not a bad thing, considering the alternative, but I had geared up for telling him for months. I was nervous. I was scared. This was a big deal to me. Telling my older brother was huge. But he was like, 'Gay, schmay. It doesn't matter to me.' And that was that. He went back to playing his guitar, and we haven't talked about it since. I guess I'd have liked to have heard something about him knowing how hard it all was for me. You know, something like that."

Many heads nodded. Perhaps the news itself wasn't a big deal to the brother, but the fact that this kid had to deal with divulging something so personal, with no assurance that he would still be accepted by someone who was so important to him, was. It was a very big deal, and everyone in the room seemed to get it — deep down, including Tammy. She envisioned the emotional tightrope being traversed by everyone involved when somebody comes out. Was there a right way to do it? The coming out and the accepting? Does anyone ever come out on the other side unscathed? She made eye contact with Marcie, and they shared a smile.

Now it was the veteran's turn. Still silent, still seated in the defensive posture he had maintained throughout the meeting, he passed.

The last person to share was a young dentist, probably in her early thirties — beautiful, successful, and a lesbian. Megan got up and began her story. "I'm pretty typical of someone who was trying to deny who I really was." She was an over-achiever in school, trying to make up for the shame she felt inside. Maybe if she worked hard enough, if she was respectable enough in other ways ... but no, what she felt didn't go away. She had come out to her family when she graduated from dental school. She was finally ready to tell them, but they weren't yet ready to hear it. Actually, they still weren't ready to hear it. Her parents just completely ignored that aspect of her life, acknowledging her partner of ten years as nothing more than a close friend. They simply glossed over the fact that they lived together, traveled together, and spent every holiday together.

"And just when you think you can be okay with the fact that they won't ever really get it, they come out with both barrels loaded and aimed at your heart." She choked out the words. "After including my partner in family gatherings for the past decade — as 'just my friend' — something made my parents blow last Father's Day. Apparently, some television personality they both love got talking about the sins of homosexuality, and that got them all riled up. They went off on us. Said we were going to hell, among other things. It was bad. My partner left in tears. I sat there in shock. My mother cried and my father yelled. It was terrible."

Several heads around the table nodded in sympathy. Some looked down.

"Since then, I've at least been able to talk with my mom, but still not with my dad. He won't come around. Won't even take my calls." She stopped and swallowed hard. "I haven't seen him since that day at their house. And we used to be so close. I was his 'little princess.'" She tried hard to compose herself, but her shoulders shook with sobs of grief. "I just want my family to love and accept me for who I am, and to love and accept Kate, and to see both of us for who we are together."

The poor girl. It was obvious that she was a happily adjusted and successful individual, but she deeply grieved the loss of the relationship with her father. And all of their pain was unnecessary. Tammy could see the way her story resonated with all those seated around the table. The young woman was sitting next to the vet, who uncrossed his arms for the first time all evening and leaned toward her as she choked back tears.

His eyes glistened as he spoke. "Give him a chance." And then as a sob escaped him, he whispered again, "Just give him a chance."

Nancy was the group's leader and the next one to speak, but she allowed a minute or so of silence before she did so. Something powerful had just happened and they needed to honor that. She closed the meeting by telling her own story. "Our daughter, Julie, was a university basketball coach in Tennessee. When they found out she had a female partner, she was fired. The very next day. Not because of the team's poor performance or for indiscretion with a student, but for loving a woman. She was told that she no longer met the moral standards of the university. Yet other coaches at her school somehow survived sex scandals involving of all kinds of improprieties, when all Julie was guilty of was love — and of being honest about her monogamous relationship of nine years." Those around the table who had not heard this story before shook their heads in disbelief. "But that terrible injustice was the best thing that ever happened to Julie and Liz, as well as for LGBT rights overall. Since then, they've adopted a baby, a precious little girl; and Julie has gone on to work for the Human Rights Campaign and has even testified before congressional committees on several occasions. They refuse to be beaten. And so do we. That's why we keep coming back. Groups like this allow us to work out our feelings and gather perspective from all sides without having to be defensive. And that can be a tall order, given that we all feel the sharp edge of bigotry every day — even though the majority of us who come to PFLAG are straight. What hurts our loved ones hurts us."

The last hour had passed quickly. Following the meeting, several gathered in smaller groups of two or three to continue sharing further. That's when Tammy noticed the grizzled vet holding the young dentist. They were both crying.

"Some find it easier to talk to someone other than their own parents or children, especially at first." The lady who had facilitated tonight's meeting tilted her head toward the embrace. "I'm sorry we didn't get a chance to properly meet beforehand. I'm Nancy." And she extended her hand to Tammy.

"Nancy." She took her hand, "I'm Tammy. What an amazing meeting tonight — the way everyone was so open about their situations and everything. It was absolutely compelling, and it certainly opened my eyes to something of what these dear people are going through. It opened my heart, too. Thank you for letting me attend."

"Come again, any time. I loved what you said about wanting to learn more about the LGBT world, and we would welcome helping you do that."

"Thanks, Nancy, I certainly will." And Tammy hurried off to join Marcie, who was already in a lively conversation with Sharon.

On the way home, Tammy asked Marcie about the old vet. She had found herself wondering about him throughout the meeting. *Was he there of his own accord? What was his story?* In his closed-off silence, he was so inscrutable — an enigmatic presence that continued to draw her attention from across the room. She had tried not to look over there too often, for fear of making him uncomfortable; and yet, she would catch herself studying him from time to time. She was intrigued. What was it about him? And then, his response to Megan? It had been so unexpected. So heart-wrenching. She had fashioned a story that would explain his behavior, but she wanted to know his truth.

"Marcie, what can you tell me about the old vet? I don't even know his name but he seems to be haunting me. I can't get him, or what he did tonight for Megan, out of my mind."

"Yes, Guy has that effect on people. I know the first time we came he was there and was just as stoically removed from all of us as he was tonight. You can't help but notice that and wonder why on earth he comes." Marcie looked over at Tammy conspiratorially. Eyes back on the road, she continued, "Anyway, after a couple of weeks, I asked Nancy about him. I had never seen anyone come with him and it made no sense that he would come on his own and then not participate."

"And?"

"Well, she said that he had started attending with his wife almost three years ago. They came, or rather she came, to learn how to deal with the news that their daughter was a lesbian, but it had seemed to all of them that he was coming just to mollify his wife. Apparently, he seemed to have a lot of anger back then. But no one pushed him to talk, or even to interact with them. They just accepted him where he was and respected his privacy. And he kept coming."

"There was never any movement, though? No change in affect? No attempt to socialize or share in the meetings?"

"Not that I know of. I certainly haven't seen any in the short time we've been coming." There was a moment or two of silence before Marcie added, "He must have gotten something out of the meetings, though, because he continued to come even after his wife stopped. And then, for tonight to happen. Wow! I think that really took everyone by surprise."

"It just goes to show that we really can't know what's going on inside another person." Tammy's words had the ring of hope to them, even as they reminded her, once again, not to judge. God had certainly been at work within Guy all that time, even though the fruit of that work had only manifested itself, for such a long time, in the most easily overlooked of responses: Guy had just kept showing up! That was all. Was God softening his heart all along for this moment with Megan? It certainly seemed to have been a real watershed moment for the two of them.

"So why isn't the wife still coming?" Tammy asked.

"I heard she's in a long-term care facility."

Tammy had a hard time falling asleep that night. She kept replaying the stories she had heard and the conversation she had overheard. She kept seeing faces — Sharon, Millie, Herb, Nancy, Charlie, Guy, and of course, dear sweet Marcie — all of them agonizing over the way their child had been mistreated, some of them worried still about their safety and security, each of them at various stages in the process of accepting and attempting to understand, and each of them struggling mightily with emotions of their own.

She tried to put herself in their place, imagining in turn each of her own children coming to her and telling her he was gay, she was a lesbian, "she" wanted to become a "he." And then, she envisioned the stories she had heard at the meeting as hers: Kelly, being shunned by her own father, his loathing withering her very soul; Hannah, half a continent away and undergoing a painful metamorphosis all alone; and Michael, being cursed and rejected by the very church family that had helped raise him, had made those promises to him — and to God — at his baptism.

An entire universe of feeling overcame her, and broken hearted, she sobbed — violently but silently — into her pillow, careful not to awaken Ed even as her grief threatened to consume her. He would not understand. He would tell her she was being silly and making herself sick over something that wasn't even real. But the fact was, it was real. Megan, and the young high-school student were flesh and blood children of someone. Jamie was the son of her dear friend. And if she were to believe Jesus Christ, then they were her children, too.

She ached for them all, but there was something about the story of the young man who'd asked Bob how he should respond to his church's anti-gay sentiments that demanded she attend to it. There was such pathos in that question. She imagined what it did to Jesus' heart that one of His children must feel so rejected by the community that bore His name, a community that was intended to accept Jew and gentile, master and slave, male and female into the unity of brotherhood. It had to have been the church, she reasoned, that had nurtured the young man's spiritual growth over the years, or he would not have referred to it as "his church." How hard it must have been for him to hear the very ones who had taught him Sunday school, who had taught him that God was love and that we were to love one another, who had taught him to sing *"red and yellow, black and white, they are precious in his sight"* — how hard to hear those same ones say, "King's X! We are to love everyone except those like you."

And that got her thinking about the church's overall response to "the gay issue" in recent years. Certainly, there was increased awareness with so many of the mainline churches raising issues of inclusion and ordination within their denominations. There had been lots of dialogue over the years which had brought several of those denominations into a more open stance. But there had also been loads of dissension over those decisions and even strident divisions within the church.

Tammy thought of the story Sharon had told about the church committee meeting, and she cringed. That could so easily have been her husband who had said those things. Who was she kidding? Ed *had* said such things, and in doing so, had incited just such judgmental, fear-based fervor in others. She felt guilty by association and then angry that she had allowed herself to be cast in that camp. She would rectify that beginning tomorrow. She may not know enough yet to have solidified all her beliefs about homosexuality and all the issues surrounding it, but she knew where her heart was leading her. And she would trust that since it was leading her by love toward love, it had to be of God.

She would go see Jimmy, her pastor, tomorrow and let him know where she stood. She would tell him how she desired to have a more hospitable heart and how she hoped that same thing for their congregation as well. And she would challenge him to lead their congregation in study and prayer around the gay issue. She owed Jamie and Megan, and that young boy whose name she didn't know, that much. And with that resolved, she drifted off to sleep.

"**S**o if someone is gay and wants to serve the Lord, would they be allowed to do so here in our congregation?" Tammy was seated in the study of her minister, Rev. Jimmy Smith. The Sloans had been members of Bethany Presbyterian for almost twenty years, and Tammy had the sort of relationship with Jimmy where she could be very direct and get very personal.

Jimmy looked down at his desk before lifting his gaze to meet Tammy's. "The question I have to ask you first, Tammy, is why do you feel you have to place a qualifier in front of anyone who wants to serve the Lord?"

"But isn't that what we do every day? Categorize and qualify? And our churches do it too." Tammy had called as soon as the church had opened this morning to schedule this meeting with Jimmy.

"Yes, Tammy. We Christians do many things every day — some good and some not so good. But one thing we don't do enough of is emphasize mercy. The mercy, of course, that comes through Jesus Christ."

"So are you saying that we need to forgive homosexuals for their sins and let them serve? Or are you saying that their love isn't sinful in the first place, thereby making it an irrelevant point?"

Tammy was still troubled by all that she had heard at the PFLAG meeting. Almost every single person there had talked of feeling ostracized by their families and churches — and all in the name of upholding Christian morality. Tammy could not condone the cruelty of such treatment, but she especially didn't appreciate that her Christian faith, which had been such a cornerstone in her own life, was being used to instill hurt and shame, rather than to bestow love and acceptance.

"That, Tammy, is the real question. And the answers are evolving, for individuals, as well as for congregations and entire denominations."

"You can say that again. I'm certainly an evolution in progress." She saw the questioning look on his face. "Jimmy, I need to tell you what I've been going through." And with that, she began telling him of her journey, sharing with him the many ways she had been affected by recent events and their repercussions. She ended by describing the call she had felt on her life, first to find her own voice, and then to reach out in a reconciling way to those who were being maligned by so many others. He listened for a good twenty minutes.

"So, where are we, here at Bethany, with regard to attitudes on all this? I think I'm at the point where I would like to see a class that offers information and encourages open discussion, not just arguments. I haven't seen any opportunities for something like that happening."

"And I have to take responsibility for that, Tammy. I am pastor and counselor to everyone in the congregation; and regardless of what they, or I, may believe, I have taken a vow to minister to everyone. Because we have a wide diversity of thought on the subject — with some very heartfelt beliefs behind the opinions on both sides of the issue — I have struggled, not unlike you, as to how to be authentic, remain true to the gospel as I understand it, and become a reconciling presence ... all the while honoring the strong convictions to which others' faith has led them."

"What do you believe, Jimmy?"

Jimmy leaned back in his chair and searched the ceiling of his office for the right words before he began. "Where am I exactly? That's hard to say. But I can say that I admire all the gay and lesbian people out there who have kept their faith in God, and who continue to pursue service in His church, despite all that we fellow Christians have done to exclude them. I believe that the overarching message in the Bible is one of love and acceptance, rather than law and judgment. And I also believe that if each of us were to more faithfully follow Christ's example, we wouldn't find ourselves embroiled in so much debate."

Tammy valued the friendly relationship she had with her pastor, and she was very relieved to hear such openness coming from him. Jimmy had been preaching about acceptance in general for the last couple of months. He had encouraged members to look beyond their own life experiences, which would necessarily limit their understandings. He had exhorted them to be more receptive to change as it came into their lives. And, he had entreated them to reach out to help those who were on the margins of society. He had mentioned those experiencing racial discrimination, those suffering from addictions, and those trapped in the cycles of poverty and abuse. He had come so close, but he had not yet mentioned the issue that lay on the desk between them now.

Last Sunday, Jimmy had made a strong point about all the division in the greater church as he talked about the age-old squabble in the church over Holy Communion. "We can't even agree on how to bless and serve these elements, and we've been arguing about it for over a thousand years. Do we celebrate the Sacrament once a year or every Sunday? Do we use intinction or pass the cups? Do we use wine or grape juice? Bread or wafers? Do the elements actually turn into the body and blood of Christ, or are they merely a memorial event? Or do they symbolize Christ's very real presence with us, feeding us for our journeys? And, the big one: who is allowed to partake and who isn't?" He had been on a roll and had gone on to challenge the congregation: "If we, as the church, and therefore the body of Christ, can't even come together on things like this, how can we expect to live into the unity we've been called to when we deal with much more difficult social issues that polarize our families, our churches, and our societies today?"

Then, he had pressed to his conclusion. "Does that mean we just give up our position? Or that we must bang the other guy over the head until he is in agreement with us? Neither. Instead we must remember what brings us to the Table in the first place. A desire for community — with each other and with our Risen Christ.

"Next to that, none of the rest should matter all that much. We are all sinners and, apart from His grace, are all lost to Him. The better question to ask ourselves is, 'Do we want to be found?' And if, once found, will we help others on their own quests to be found? Or will we resolutely remain a hindrance to them? Will we open the door or close it? " It had been a powerful sermon, yet it still had stopped short of naming the elephant in the room.

The clock chimed on the wall behind Jimmy's desk. "In all honesty, Tammy, I've been faced with a dilemma that I would have liked to avoid. You know I don't like conflict. Who does? I was trained in an 'old school seminary.' And so, I've been hesitant to engage in studying the issue myself, let alone facilitate congregational discussions. But there is a book I recently read," Jimmy stood up to reach the upper shelf of the book case next to his desk. "And I think you'd find it very interesting, too. It's helped me a great deal: *Jesus, the Bible and Homosexuality* written by Dr. Jack Rogers.[10] He's a Presbyterian minister, seminary professor, and former moderator of the General Assembly in the Presbyterian Church (U.S.A.). There was something he said that really resonated with me." Jimmy turned around and plucked a book off the shelves behind him. He opened it straight to the page he was looking for. *"During this period of study I didn't change my Reformed theology or my method of biblical interpretation. For the first time, however, I had to apply them to the issue of homosexuality. That has led me on a journey that in some ways has been uncomfortable and in other ways has resulted in growth and satisfaction."*

"And that's where I am, Tammy. I know that I'm growing, yet there are times when growth is quite uncomfortable for me. I've been reading scripture anew, as Dr. Rogers suggests. Not with the lenses of my prior understanding, which allowed me to insert culturally conditioned opinions of my own, but with the intent to read it apart from any socially biased assumptions — ours, or those of the one writing the words. And, I've been interpreting each passage in the context of Jesus' ministry of love and reconciliation. That is the true lens through which we should read scripture. If we remember to make Christ's love for His Father, and for all humanity — *all* humanity, no exclusions — our model for living, then how can we possibly exclude anyone from serving Him? Christ himself said, "I am the Way." And then He said, "Follow me." Maybe that's the question we need to be asking ourselves, instead of questions we like to use against each other in judgment. How can I more fully live as Christ lived and love as Christ loves?"

"That is exactly the question that I feel has been burning in my heart these last few months, Jimmy. How can I represent God's love to these people society has made outcasts?"

"Some folk challenge Rogers' conclusions, just as others, like yourself embrace them. But in the end, he gives his readers information and insight that can help them in their journey. And that is what I would like to do here at Bethany. Give information that will help everyone on their individual journeys. Something that would educate — not push any agenda — but just teach. Thank you, Tammy, for giving me this kick start."

Tammy smiled. "You've given me plenty of those in the past. It's about time I returned the favor. It just seems that being better informed will help us be better able to dialogue about the issues and not just attack one another." She fell quiet, reflecting for a moment. "Do you think we, as a church and a society, can ever get past all our differences when it comes to all this?"

"The controversies over homosexuality will probably be around for a long time. But just as the church struggled with issues regarding minorities, women, and divorce in the past, maybe the church will find its Christ-like perspective on issues of sexuality over time. The difficulty for me is in trying to bring about change without forcing individual members to believe this way or that. Each must come to his or her own understanding in their own time. And we may have to agree to disagree in the meantime. That's where I have to be careful. Like I said before, I am the pastor to every member, and as you know, we live in a very conservative area. So we have to take small steps. But as long as we all end up in the same place, living our lives as examples of Christ's love, then I think we are being the children of God that He would like us to be."

"I agree wholeheartedly. But Jimmy, I have a confession to make. Whenever someone starts quoting scripture at me to defend anti-gay morality, it just shuts me down. I get so frustrated because I don't know what to say to them. I guess because I am unsure myself. I do believe that the whole of the Bible is God's word to us, but I also believe, like you said, that the gospel of love is paramount. It seems to me that sometimes the teachings seem to contradict each other. I guess that's the context thing you were talking about?"

"Yes. A seeming contradiction can be cleared up when you read what is said with an eye to the context in which the verses were written. And also, when you interpret what is said within the context of scripture as a whole. There are numerous passages in the Bible that can be taken out of context and used in hurtful, even dangerous, ways. But when we take the scriptures and interpret them through the life and teachings of Jesus, we can gain a better understanding of what they're really saying to us today, several thousand years after many of them were originally penned.

"Truthfully, Tammy, a lot of what is now being seen as problematic, was written through the lens of the patriarchal culture of the times. The idea of male superiority, and concomitantly, the need to keep gender roles separate and *not* equal, was of utmost importance in that place and time. And so, a good, moral family was defined as: man, the provider, decision-maker and holder of all power; and woman, his *helpmeet* and homemaker, subservient to him in all things. That's one very big reason that the early church, with its emphasis on gender equality and its inclusion of slaves and masters as equals, was so radically subversive. It broke down the hierarchies a patriarchal society requires in order to exist."

"Hmm. I'd never thought of it that way. I can see why the early church was persecuted."

"And one reason Jesus himself was crucified. People in power don't take kindly to that power being undermined."

Jimmy leaned forward and steepled his hands. "And that's part of our problem today. We're not altogether free of the patriarchal system and its hierarchies in our *own* culture. There are those who still hold strongly to this "biblical" image of family as being the only legitimate one, and preserving family, as it's understood in that strict definition, becomes all important. From there, it's not hard to understand how homosexuality would be seen as a threat. Not only would it undermine the very essence of that definition of family, but it would also be considered a threat to the concept of masculine prerogative. But, when we base our beliefs upon Christ's examples of inclusivity and the breaking down of hierarchies, we can then see the invitation in Him to be open to all sorts of relationships and family units. This could include stay-at-home dads, blended families, multicultural or multi-racial marriages, and yes, even marriages between members of the same sex."

Tammy immediately thought of Ed. She was having trouble listening to what Jimmy continued to say. He may as well have just dropped a *Duh!* bomb on her. Could this be why Ed was so antagonistic toward gays? Was his anger being displaced? Was he really just defending the masculine prerogative? There was no question, all right, that Ed was a true believer in male superiority. *Good grief!* The entire Texas legislature was full of conservative-minded men in leadership positions, and many of them were friends they had known for years. And they were all just like Ed. And their wives were just like Tammy — or rather, just like what she'd always been before last September happened. All of them harboring this same mentality. It's all they had known.

But recent events had facilitated so much inward change within her that Tammy wondered if she still resembled them and their outlooks on life at all. She had begun to look past these constraining viewpoints and make real progress toward accepting herself as an equal in her marriage, which in turn had brought about her desire to accept all individuals and their families as equals, regardless of their gender or sexuality. But which had actually come first? Her sympathy for the plight of the outcast? Or her desire to stand on her own two feet? It was a *chicken or the egg* kind of conundrum. Jimmy's words finally disrupted her tumultuous thoughts.

"But it all comes down to how an individual, or an entire denomination, interprets scripture. And that is a constant work in progress. So we've gone full circle now, Tammy, and we're back at square one ... what do we believe? And I'll go back to my very first answer. I believe in mercy. Christ's compassionate mercy in forgiving us our misinterpretations, our judgments of others, and our often misguided deeds. All in the name of believing in Him."

Everybody is a genius. But if you judge a fish by its ability to climb a tree,
it will live its whole life believing that it is stupid.
— Albert Einstein

Chapter 13

STATE FAIR

Bill Pritchett walked right through the door of Ed Sloan's office. Ed was on the phone and screwed his face into a knot of obvious disapproval, not at all happy for the interruption. He pointed to the phone and shook his head. But Pritchett plopped down in the wingback opposite Ed's desk anyway and smiled like the Cheshire cat, completely ignoring Ed's apparent irritation. He picked up the bronze Texas boot on Ed's desk, turning it around to read the inscription: "Congratulations Commissioner Sloan, a Texan dedicated to Conservatism." It was a congratulatory gift from the Young Conservatives of Texas who had endorsed him in the last election, touting Ed Sloan as the most conservative candidate in the race. Pritchett wondered at the symbolism of *giving him the boot* — not an idiom typically used in an endorsement of support.

Ed plucked the bronze award out of Pritchett's hands and returned it to its proper place on his desk as he continued with his phone conference. But Bill remained nonplussed. He leaned back, crossed his long legs, and placed his folded hands in his lap. He had decided to wait out this interminable phone call and to wait out Sloan, who finally hung up and acknowledged him with a grumble.

"If you've got more of your usual bad news, Pritchett, I don't have time to hear it. Just save me the misery, okay? I'm up to my eyeballs here."

"Well, let's see if your misery-filled eyeballs can read this. Looks like we may have finally turned things around." And he tossed the reports on Ed's desk.

Ed's demeanor changed dramatically at this promise of good news, and he eagerly grabbed up the papers and began reading quickly, looking for any word that could offer the encouragement he was so hungry for.

"Someone ... ahem," Pritchett coughed and then cleared his throat dramatically, "leaked the news about the progress of the immigration deal and credited your office with ending the deadlock caused by all the political games played out in the past. Oh, and look at this report on the Desalination Project. All of central Texas will be on your side now, Ed. They love your ideas and they want the Governor to back whatever funding is necessary to make it all happen."

Ed listened, but continued to do his own reading as well. This was too good to be true, and he needed to see those beautiful words himself. With each word that he read, the furrow in his brow eased noticeably; and after a few minutes of processing what he had read, Ed leaned back in his chair, loosened his tie, grinned broadly, and declared Bill Pritchett a magician.

"This is cause for celebration, Pritchett!"

"Hold on now. We're not in the clear by any means ..."

Ed interrupted. "I know, but this shows that the tide has turned. That I can get back to doing the work of the people of Texas. And, I didn't have to sacrifice my ideals to get here. No surrender needed, my friend. I've been vindicated by the public and these reports prove it."

Bill flinched at such boldness. "Well, let's not think that this means you can continue to do as you've said and done for the last couple of months. You don't have carte blanche here, 'my friend.'" He threw Ed's words back to him to underscore his point. Bill knew Ed could negate all of this good will if he spread his homophobic feathers again. Political polls were a delicate thing.

Pritchett had already contracted additional pollsters to begin the process of learning where they stood for the next election. Their first set of numbers had come in right after the Supreme Court, those nine oligarchs in robes, had heard the DOMA and Prop 8 cases. And although representing nothing more than a snapshot of current public opinion, the numbers had alarmed Ed. Younger Texans were increasingly supportive of same-sex issues — up to sixty-seven percent in this poll — as were Texans living in Houston, Austin and Dallas — the biggest voting blocs in the state. Both demographics were pivotal for Ed, whose opponents would be a Democrat and the newest Bush. Whoever turned out to be the Democratic contender would surely split the Hispanics with Bush and also take the gay vote and their supporters. What did that leave Ed? His rural constituency and their shared "Crusade for Conservative Values" as Ed had been putting it recently. He had always been his local constituency's darling, but now he realized he needed to broaden his base. And Pritchett's leaks causing all this recent positive publicity might do exactly that.

Ed slapped Pritchett on the back. "Come on, Bill. This ain't my first rodeo. Give me a little credit." Ed's huge smile covered his face, his white teeth gleaming with satisfaction and long-awaited relief. Handling political pressure was nothing new to Ed, but this whole thing had been a catastrophe. Caught between his personal convictions and his desire for success, this had nearly brought him down — both personally and professionally. Now that things were getting better at work, he figured things would get better at home too. He couldn't wait to boot Pritchett out of his office and call Tam. This should turn her around too.

It had all been Ed's idea. He may have missed the State Fair at Gracie's school, but he could create their own fair, for cryin' out loud. And, why not? He *was* Big Tex after all, wasn't he? Pritchett's news had solidified that fact. And besides, he had wanted to celebrate. Ed was keen to create some positive family time, and he knew this would do the trick.

Wearing a very loud, red and yellow plaid shirt, Ed lumbered down the wide steps of the porch in a bow-legged swagger, bellowing out "Howwww-deeee, fo-o-olk-s!" in an exaggerated drawl, the little ones' squeals of laughter encouraging him with each 'thunk' of his size-sixteen boots.

"Uncle Ed! You look just like him!" Gracie shrieked as she sprang from the car and ran toward the great house, yellow mane and new cowgirl hat streaming out behind her. Savannah kicked her legs with excitement, wanting to follow her older sister as Henry wrestled with the car-seat straps in order to set her free.

"Yes, he does, Gracie." Tammy muttered sadly to herself as she leaned against one of the tall white columns at the top of the porch. "Your dear Uncle Ed is just like Big Tex — steadfast, yet inflexible: resolute, and unbending." Then speaking much louder for Grace to hear. "Isn't he tall and handsome? And what a big booming voice!"

Ed puffed with satisfaction upon hearing his wife's words of praise, thereby increasing his resemblance to the broad-chested Big Tex even more. Basking in the simple pleasure of knowing she still found him attractive after all these years, and in spite of their recent difficulties, he threw out his chest and walked even taller.

The real Big Tex was a fifty-two-foot cowboy who sported a seventy-five gallon hat and size seventy boots. And his hinged jaw and booming voice had welcomed fairgoers to the Great State Fair of Texas since 1952. Ed was about the same age, but his thirty-six-inch inseam was no match for the seventy-two yards of denim that the real Big Tex required for his jeans. Such details didn't matter to little Gracie and Savannah, though, and they gleefully skipped and twirled around the long legs of their oversized great-uncle before he could bend down, scoop them up one at a time, and lift them high to the heavens, while booming another "Howww-deee, Gracie! And howww-de-do to you, too, li'l Savannah". To them, he seemed every bit as big as the real thing.

Once Ed returned Gracie to the ground, she bounded toward Michael, who had been put in charge of the makeshift midway that he and the girls had spent the last few days crafting out of odds and ends they'd found around the place. Before he could explain how the game worked, Gracie grabbed a handful of beanbags and began enthusiastically tossing them toward the brightly painted washtubs, squealing with delight when she finally hit her mark. "Look at what I did, Momma! Daddy, come see!" Abandoning his own plans for how the game should work, Michael began to retrieve her errant bags; and, as he returned them to Gracie, he knelt beside her and patiently instructed her in the finer points of taking aim. "I'll do the fishing game, next," she announced, when she finally tired of Michael's ministrations, and she skipped off to the kiddie-pool-turned-fishing-pond where Kelly was ready to take her on to the next great adventure.

"And then you can pin the hat on Big Tex," Hannah cried after her, hoping to corral Gracie and steer her enthusiasm toward the huge cut-out of the famous cowboy that she had glued onto foam board herself. She had also created several hats from which the children could choose — a fireman's helmet; the tall, white toque of a chef; a Rangers baseball cap; and, of course, the traditional Stetson — and she was eager to get the fun started.

Ed watched all these goings-on with great pleasure, his hubris in this moment almost as big as the ten-gallon hat atop his arrogant head. It had been good for the kids to work together on the preparations for the fair, and now they seemed to be really enjoying themselves. *Good! Good! Good!* ... And it was so good for all of them to have had something positive to do on a Friday evening for a change. Everyone had seemed to enjoy the diversion that getting ready for today's big event had brought —himself included! And he had been the one that had made this all happen! It had been his idea, after all. *I'm definitely back in the saddle,* he thought. He spent a moment or two longer in self-congratulation; and then, hitching up his belt, he proudly turned to make his way up to the porch where the others were gathering.

"Have you heard from Edith yet?" Amber arrived at the porch with a colorful bouquet of helium balloons and began tying them to the chair backs.

"Yes, she'll be here in a bit. Her hair appointment took longer than she expected." Tammy reached over to take a handful of the balloons from Amber, intending to help speed the decorating; but a bright blue one slipped through her fingers in the transfer, rising quickly out of reach.

"Boon! Boon!" Savannah had come running at the sight of the escaping balloon, but in reaching for it, had outrun her feet. Shod as they were in new cowgirl boots, she lost her balance and toppled to the ground, right in front of her great-aunt. Tammy snatched her up before she could even register that she had fallen and lifted her onto her hip. "Don't you look pretty today, little one," she cajoled. Distracted by her great-aunt's compliments, Savannah beamed up at her and patted her chest proudly. She and Gracie were both dressed for the occasion, in matching denim skirts and boots, but it was Savannah who was most pleased with the new finery. She now took the opportunity to point out each element of her ensemble to her doting aunt, soliciting just the appreciative "oooohs" and "aaahs" that she had hoped for as she, first, showcased her "Aat" and then, kicked her red boot out for Tammy to admire.

"And what's this, sweetheart?"

"Nekkus!" she happily sang out as she fondled her most prized accessory. "Nekkus!" she repeated again. "Nekkus! Nekkus!"

As he thundered closer, Big Tex bawled: "Henry my boy, what's that li'l cowgirl saying?"

"It's her necklace." Henry clapped his hands together and held them wide, an invitation for her to jump from Tammy's arms into his. And she did so quickly, losing her hat in the transfer and jingling and jangling all the way.

Savannah was happily wearing a set of oversized teething keys, the brightly colored plastic kind. They were hanging on a string of snapping beads, thereby avoiding any choking hazards, and they dangled beautifully down the front of her little paisley blouse. With two blonde poufs of curls atop her head, she looked like Chirin, the little lamb from the children's movie, *Ringing Bell*. Ed remembered watching that movie with Michael and Kelly while Tammy tended a newborn Hannah. Despite a rather dark and disturbing storyline, it had redeemed itself by presenting a good moral of sorts. What was it the little lamb's mother had said? *When we are young, we don't know a lot of things, but the small amount of knowledge we do possess makes us happy.* That certainly seemed the case with Savannah. Come to think of it, he certainly felt happier these days, too — youthful or not!

"You sure have strange ideas about accessorizing, little one. You're supposed to lock a door with those, not wear them like a necklace. Let your Uncle Tex get you a pretty bandana or a proper bolo tie, ya hear?" Ed set off to the porch where he hoped to find something more appropriate for his great-niece to wear to the Sloan State Fair.

Meanwhile, Savannah continued to proudly fondle her colorful keys as if they were jewels. "Nekkus," she smiled, while looking into her daddy's face.

Tammy studied the toy which was draped around the baby's neck. Individual keys on a ring. They didn't resemble any key fob, push button, or key pad that existed, or would exist, in Savannah's life experience. Keys these days already lived in your purse, or pocket, and had sensors that knew how to unlock your car. Ignitions started with the push of a button and many doors opened with the swipe of an ID card. Why would she try to open a door with them? She didn't recognize them as keys.

Henry put her down in the grass as Ed returned.

"Here you go, now. I've brought you a pretty red bandana to put around your neck. It'll even match your boots!" Ed got down on one knee, removed the plastic toys, and began tying the red gingham in a loose knot around her tiny neck, which prompted Savannah's face to cloud and her lip to protrude.

"Ed, she already has a beautiful necklace," Tammy warned as gently as she could. Ed looked every bit as wounded as the toddler upon hearing Tammy's words. "But, thank you for trying, dear. That was very nice of you." She handed Savannah's "nekkus" back to her and they all watched as Savannah promptly restored it to its proper place.

Ed wouldn't get this, of course, thought Tammy. In his eyes, it was a set of keys, utilitarian objects meant to lock a door or start a car. And that was all there was to it. He couldn't see beyond his own interpretation of the thing. Tammy hadn't seen it right away either, but then it had dawned on her. Ed had seen something so plainly in that toy that was fully invisible to the child. And Savannah had envisioned something totally incomprehensible to him. Two realities existed side by side: one conditioned by the culture's penchant for naming, defining, and valuing and being fettered by the need to conform; the other, free to see with new eyes, to experience the outside world directly.

Hmm. She suddenly realized that perhaps her own ability just now to honor both Ed's and Savannah's truths, without having to choose between them, signaled that she herself was growing toward that freedom too. Wasn't it Richard Rohr who had talked about a "both/ and" type of thinking in one of his recent daily devotionals? What he'd said about living with paradox and needing to live within the tension between two mutually exclusive truths had made a lot of sense. There was such mystery in the world and it couldn't be contained within the boxes of our "either/or" style of thinking. None of us had the exclusive truth — as though there ever were such a thing.

Just then, Trey and Becky Jones pulled up with their son, Robert, and Tammy went out to greet them. Bill and Ginny Pritchett were in College Station visiting Greg, and Holly was still out of town and not able to make it, so Trey and Becky were the only ones at today's festivities who weren't family. Trey had been out with Ed on numerous work-related occasions, but this was their first invitation to the Sloan homestead. Tammy wanted to be sure they felt truly welcomed. She guessed he might be feeling a little nervous.

"You have such a beautiful home, Mrs. Sloan." Becky took in the beautifully landscaped property and elegant home which stood before her.

"Well thank you, but we aren't very formal here at the ranch. Everyone calls me Tammy." Tammy reached out with both hands and welcomed Becky and Trey with a warm smile. Then looking down to acknowledge their son, "And who is this fine gentleman?"

"I'm Robert. But you can call me Rob." His soft voice was barely audible, and he kicked at the rocks on the gravel drive, taking a quick glimpse at the Midway games the others were already enjoying before thrusting his hands deep into his pockets.

Tammy got down on her knees to meet his shy eyes. "It's awfully nice to meet you, Rob." Then looking toward the hodgepodge of games the kids had come up with, "We've got lots of fun things to do over there under the trees. Why don't you come with me and I'll introduce you to all the others?" She offered her hand, but Rob obediently glanced up at his mother for permission before placing his small hand in Tammy's palm.

Becky nodded at her son and silently mouthed the words, "Thank you," to Tammy as she rose from her knees and led him toward the other children.

Edith arrived an hour after everyone else. "Hello darlings." Gracie and Savannah ran toward her, and she folded her precious granddaughters in her arms.

"Come see Uncle Ed, Gamma. He really turned into Big Tex for me!" Gracie was filled with excitement and practically bounced as she pulled Edith by the hand, leading her to where Ed was standing.

"Howww-deee, Edith!" He addressed his older sister with a monstrous roar. Ed was hamming it up for all it was worth. Assuming the posture of the fifty-two foot version, he stood with one arm bent at the elbow, palm facing forward as if taking an oath, his other arm extended out to the side. "Welcome to the Great. Sloan. Fair of Texas!"

"I'm so proud of my dad, the statue." Michael cut his eyes over to his posturing father and shook his head resignedly, before greeting his aunt with a hug and submitting to a peck on the cheek.

"Don't laugh too loudly, sonny. You look just like him!" Edith winked and then her eyes crinkled into a compassionate smile. "How are you doing, hon? Things getting any better?"

"Yeah, I guess. Just trying to make the best of it."

Gracie grabbed the hem of Edith's skirt and pulled. "C'mon, Gamma. Now you have to come play the games!"

"Maybe we can talk later, okay?" Edith waved at Michael as she was dragged over to Hannah's "Pin the Hat" game. Michael breathed a sigh of relief. He had no intention of talking with his aunt about any of this. He could talk with Kelly, of course. That was like thinking out loud. And even to his mom — some. But, no, he wasn't about to pour his guts out to anyone else about all this. He was still heavily vested in the Sloan tradition of suppressing one's emotions.

The weather was perfect. Some of the leaves were just beginning to turn, and the smell of a distant wood-burning fire filled the air. Shouts of glee and explosions of laughter erupted across the spacious lawn as the younger kids chased each other blowing noisemakers left over from last New Year's Eve. Tammy asked Michael to shepherd their shenanigans while Ed conscripted Kelly to serve as deejay for his special surprise. She had created a playlist of his country favorites on her iPod earlier in the week and now had set up the speakers on the front porch. As she set it playing, Ed waltzed to George Strait and two-stepped to Kenny Chesney with each lady in turn, starting with Edith, who kicked up her heels gaily, as much into the play as was her brother. He even managed to pull Kelly away from her duties to dance to Tim McGraw's "My Little Girl." But when "Can I Have this Dance" by Anne Murray appeared on the playlist, he sought out his wife.

Once again assuming the posture of Big Tex, he extended his left hand in invitation. Tammy bowed to the crowd and then to Ed, as she gracefully twirled into his arms. Ed held her close as he waltzed her in circles across the lawn. *"I'll always remember the song they were playing the first time we danced and I knew ..."* And as their bodies warmed from their exertions, he breathed in deeply the scent of her clean, warm flesh. It took him back to their early dating days, days spent inner-tubing the Guadalupe and nights spent dancing at Gruene Hall or enjoying a romantic dinner at the Grey Moss Inn. *"When we're together / it feels so right."* That was true then, and it was true now, even after all these years. He was overcome with love for his wife. This beautiful woman who had been by his side for the past twenty-two years and who had given him his three great children. What would he do without her? Oh yes, he definitely wanted her as his partner for the rest of his life.

But he was happy to let Anne Murray confide these innermost feelings of love and devotion, instead of attempting to find the words himself. After all, she could say it better than he ever could. And besides, Tam already knew he loved her. And so, he danced on in silence, willing her to know his heart.

Anne Murray's melody faded into something by Kellie Pickler, and Ed bent Tammy in half, planting a deep kiss on her full lips as he held her in a suspended back-bend. Everyone hooted their approval and she went limp in his powerful arms, laughing. It felt good to have him hold her like this. It was so uncharacteristic of Ed to show affection in front of others. Must be that he was still playing the Big Tex thing for all he was worth. Looking up into his dark eyes, however, she was surprised to see love and real passion there. Ed had kissed her for real. She searched his eyes again, seeking signs of tenderness, but found there instead, a fierce glint of obsidian that seemed almost to be a challenge. As she pushed against him to right herself, he held her captive a moment longer, and it was in that moment that she recognized the flint in his gaze for what it was.

Ed was telling her and their world that she was his. *Interesting,* she thought. There was a time when such a show of possessiveness would have thrilled her, but now? She registered a smoldering coal of resentment flickering behind her breastbone, which she quickly tamped out. Once upright, she patted Ed on the cheek playfully, thanked Big Tex for the dance, and started for the porch to ring the dinner bell. She needed to get the attention off herself and her confused emotions.

"Come and get it, everyone!" she called as she clanged the triangle she had bought especially for this occasion. "Dinner's served!"

Several long tables had been set up along the length of the porch, set with red-checkered tablecloths and topped off with pots of bright yellow mums. The serving table was full of such staples as would have been found at the real State Fair in Dallas: corny dogs, fried cheese, fried pickles, corn-on-the-cob, and chicken legs. Turkey legs would have been more authentic, but KFC had made better sense. And for dessert, there were lots of choices. Kelly had made her own version of funnel cakes and Hannah, insistent that there be a "Kid's Dessert Menu" to include ice cream on a stick and caramel apples, had actually made both herself, spending half the day in the kitchen.

"I've wanted to ask you all day. Where in the world did you find that shirt, Ed?" Amber laughed as she speared a bit of corn dog with Savannah's fork and handed it to her.

"Bite." Savannah announced, bobbing her head up and down. "Bite. Bite. Bite." She plucked the bit of food off her fork and fisted it into her open mouth.

"Do you like it?" Ed twisted back and forth so that everyone could see all sides of his flashy shirt, which was completely unnecessary. To fit Ed, it had to be the size of a small tent, and its bright red and yellow pattern could have directed traffic in the dark.

"I bet he got it at the Big and Tall Shop," Edith opined, "but I must say, I thought they had better taste there than to carry that excuse for a hot-air balloon!"

Reaching across the table, Kelly helped herself to another piece of fried cheese. "I actually found it on the internet. You'd never believe how many hits you get when you Google 'loud shirts.'"

"Seriously?" Becky had to lean around Trey in order to see Kelly. "That's how you found it?"

"Oh, yeah. Anything you want to know? Just ask the internet." Kelly was the internet queen. She could look up football scores, book titles, the electric company's phone number — whatever you needed — before you could barely finish your request.

Tammy sat just to Trey's right and leaned around him to speak to Becky. "And she's shown me how to shop online, too. This Christmas is going to be so much easier. Now Christmas lists can be as easy as sending me a link. Amazon is amazing."

"Uh-oh! Becky doesn't need to hear about anything that makes shopping any easier." Trey leaned in, obstructing their line of sight, and jokingly held up his hands in each lady's direction.

"Oh you!" Becky laughed. "What you don't know won't hurt you. I've been shopping the internet for years."

"Maybe I should have Kelly get me another shirt just like it?" Ed questioned the table at large, but flashed a grin toward little Gracie, his even white teeth displayed in dazzling rows.

"Yes!" Gracie's head nodded in approval, and she threw both arms in the air as if to signal a field goal.

"I don't think so." Tammy rested her elbow on the table, her wrist bending under the weight of the iced tea glass she held in her hand. "Remember, dear, Big Tex went up in flames, and his shirt wasn't nearly as fiery as yours.

"And now, in case you've forgotten, little brother, he's being rebuilt and newly outfitted in something a lot less flammable. I advise you to take his woes under consideration before you make your next purchase." Edith parodied maternal concern beautifully.

"Talk about going up in flames." Trey gnawed on his third chicken leg. "What a relief that this football season is finally over."

Ed shot Trey a look that could have brought down an eight point buck, but Trey munched on, completely oblivious to being in the sites of his boss's deadly gaze. Becky tried to warn him by squeezing his leg hard underneath the table, and Trey looked up, startled as any deer, at first not comprehending the danger, nor the reason for the tense silence that had descended on the once festive table; but then, as he realized his gaffe, reddening quickly — a deep crimson blooming at his shirt collar and then spreading all the way up to his receding hairline. He attempted to stammer out an apology, but in his fear and confusion, initially could only sputter.

Michael, who had been a full participant in most of the day's earlier activities and the conversations throughout dinner, had jolted upright as soon as the words were out of Trey's mouth, locking eyes with him for a brief moment before dropping his gaze to stare fixedly at his plate. After a moment, Michael looked up again, searching the faces of those around the table, his eyes ultimately finding their solace in Kelly. Ed couldn't, or wouldn't, meet his eye.

"Oh my God!" I didn't mean to ... I was just ... Michael, I'm sorry. I didn't mean to embarrass you. I ..." He blanched a greasy white as he struggled on under Ed's glare. "I just meant ... that because of this whole gay thing ... even our local team has been adversely affected. Personally, I don't approve of any of that being brought into our school, let alone protecting those who do." It was a desperate appeal to get back into Ed's good graces.

"The 'adverse effects' that issue has on our children is the whole point." Ed hissed his disapproval in a hushed voice, but the color rising in his neck showed the deep-seated emotions that Trey's comments had so easily spurred.

Tammy watched Michael curl further inward, drawing a protective shroud around himself as he conscientiously avoided eye contact with all those seated around the table — those who willed him to see their compassion and find comfort there, and his father who was incapable of showing such mercy. She had seen him flinch at Trey's thoughtless comments and his father's blooming temper. Each was as difficult for her to witness as the other. A black cloud was descending once again on her precious son, and there was nothing she could do about it. Not here. Not now. A mother's comfort would be the last thing he would want and would make things even harder for Trey. She let Michael excuse himself from the table, knowing that Kelly would follow after him shortly.

Tammy had lived this scene many times during her marriage. *The lion and the lamb, the wolf and the deer.* Trey leaned over to whisper in his wife's ear. The inevitability of a swift and furious attack was certain. Successful hunters wait for their best shot, when the deer turns broadside away from the rifleman, and Tam sensed that Ed was lifting his barrel for another round.

"Hey, Big Tex, why don't you go fetch us all some dessert? I'll bet Gracie and Rob would love some ice cream." Tammy met Henry's eyes. She was sure he had been just one step behind her in trying to defuse this volatile situation.

"Whee!" They screeched in unison. "We'll help, too!" They hopped off their chairs and skipped around the table.

Ed placed both hands on the table, stood up, and took a deep breath. With his eyes still trained on Trey, he opened his mouth to speak just as little Savannah lifted her shirt up over her head and shouted loudly.

"Pee Boo!"

She then lowered it to reveal her expressive face, smiling with all three of her teeth. One of her pigtails had come undone, and her blonde curls had come to life, springing in every direction, but on only one side of her face. She lifted her top again, trying to engage someone in joining her little hiding game. Gracie and Rob laughed raucously at the baby's silliness, and the adults smiled their relief, grateful for some release from the tension that had settled over the table.

Henry stifled his grin and gave his daughter a stern look. "We don't do that at the dinner table, peanut." And he patiently smoothed her shirt back into place. "But you know, maybe she's got the right idea! We could use some more fun around here right now! C'mon, Uncle, let's go get that ice cream Tammy talked about."

The children had changed the stakes, so to speak, and without access to his ordinary tools of intimidation and control, Ed was left with no choice but to acquiesce to Tammy's request and accept Henry's invitation. He pushed his chair away from the table, the tense muscles of his clenched jaw still visible as he stalked off with Henry to retrieve the ice cream. The children followed him like puppies, trying their best to keep up with his long strides.

Tammy's heart ached as she watched Ed leave the porch. Playing with everyone this afternoon, he had given her a glimpse of the man he had once been and could be again; and yet, in this unfortunate incident, he had also reminded her of what he had become. She did not fear a similar outcome for Michael, for he had been making some real progress before this evening, and she was confident he would again. But Ed really was like the friendly giant from Fair Park — stuck in an unchangeable position for decades, with no real updates other than a new flannel shirt every year. Like Big Tex, Ed was a charming and endearing icon, a fixture everyone looked to to get their bearings. But more often than not, he just stood there, watching real life go by, untouched by the heartfelt undercurrents of human compassion that led others to accept, to broaden, to include, to connect. Ed had built for himself a tidy house of self-righteousness. He had gone inside long ago and had slammed the door shut.

The evening had ended soon after the ice cream, funnel cakes, and caramel apples had been served. Like any toddler, Savannah's internal weather was as unpredictable as that of Texas itself. Her mood had turned quickly, from happily nibbling apple cubes to suddenly being fussy, ready for a bath and her bed. Amber washed her sticky face and lifted her by the armpits, making the announcement that Savannah would soon turn into a pumpkin. Trey and Becky were also eager to retreat. Little Rob waved goodbye out the back seat window as his stone faced parents drove down the long drive, then hurriedly turned and sped off down the highway. Tammy and Edith walked Amber out to the car while Henry and Gracie gathered up a few of the helium balloons to take home. There wasn't anything to pick up out on the lawn. Michael and Kelly had taken care of the Midway Games before dinner.

"So, I'm going to tell Ed tonight." Tammy rested her arm across the top of their car.

"Are you sure that's a good idea? I mean after what happened at dinner and all? I'd wait for a better time if I were you." Edith knew her brother well and had accurately calculated the depth of his displeasure. He would be hostile for some time to come.

"Edith, honey, you know with Ed there is rarely a 'better time,'" Tammy laughed. "Living with him is like living inside that old short story we read in school. You know, 'The Lady or the Tiger?' The door opens and you just don't know which Ed will walk out — the friendly, caring one, or the antagonistic, aggressive one. There's always the possibility of it going either way — and he can turn on a dime. Right now, I'll just have to weigh a few uncomfortable minutes at dinner against the rest of the day — which really was wonderful — and take my chances.

"What do you think he'll say?" Amber handed Tammy the diaper bag as she opened the back door and leaned over to put cranky little Savannah in her car seat.

"I have a pretty good guess." Tammy looked out across their beautiful acreage. So many wonderful times had been had on this great lawn. Birthday parties, barbecues, campaign announcements, and even one wedding. And today would stand out as another pleasant remembrance, with the exception of the last half hour. "But I can't really know."

"And you know this is a reputable organization?" Although Edith didn't usually keep up with daily news, she knew something of the dangers that gay activists and their supporters could be up against. "You know he'll want to make sure you're safe."

"As do we." Amber smiled shyly.

"Oh, stop it, you two." Tammy casually waved her hand at Edith and Amber, dismissing their fears. "Not to worry, okay? For your information, The Trevor Project[11] is very reputable. In fact, it's the leading national organization that provides crisis intervention and suicide prevention to LGBTQ youth."

"And who are they, pray tell? No need to go all alphabet soup on me, Tammy. I'm a plain woman and I like plain speech." Edith cocked an eyebrow and peered out from under it. "I assume you meant gay kids?"

"Well, yes, but the letters are more inclusive than that. They stand for lesbian, gay, bisexual, transgender and questioning youth. Each population has its own unique issues as well as the many they hold in common, and I learned at PFLAG…"

"There you go again."

"I'm sorry, Edith. Parents and Friends of Lesbians and Gays. It's the support group I've been attending." She shook her head and smiled at Edith's mock disapproval. "You're right, of course. I guess every cause has its jargon, but it's not meant to exclude anyone. In this case, it just gives us an easy way to remind ourselves of an important truth. What we lump together as the 'gay issue' is really quite a complex system of needs and injustices and those differ a bit among the various groups. The acronym reminds us to remember each orientation and each individual's special circumstances and needs."

Amber spoke up, "You're learning a lot at those meetings, aren't you?" She reflected a moment longer, "Good stuff!"

"Yes, I certainly am. And, yes, it certainly is."

Just then, Gracie came running up. Henry was following at a slower pace, bearing two chosen balloons for safekeeping. "Daddy helped me. I got a yellow balloon for me and a red one for Savannah. To match her boots. There wasn't a white one to match mine. But that's okay. I like yellow." Gracie made her announcement, beaming up at the adults who beamed back at her and her little-girl enthusiasm. She then gladly climbed into the back seat and reached out to take the proffered balloons into her own custody.

"Good night, my sweethearts. Gramma loves you so much!" Edith kissed her fingers and lightly touched them to each little girl's cheek, before offering her own to Henry as she returned his bear hug. "And good night to you too, son. You've had a busy last couple of weeks. Get some rest."

"Will do, Mom. I love you."

"Me too. Now get out of here!" and she popped him on his bottom.

"Not before I thank Tammy for this fantastic gathering," and he leaned in to give her a kiss as well. "This meant the world to Gracie, Tammy. Thank you for everything."

"Well, it was Ed's idea, you know, and the whole family pitched in to make it happen, but I'll gladly accept your thanks on all our behalves."

"Good. Uncle Ed had a hard time doing that just now. Poor guy. He just can't let some things go. Good luck tonight."

"Yes, good luck, Tammy," Amber repeated with added emphasis. "And thanks for everything. This was such a fun day. " Amber looked around for Ed, finally spotting him on the porch steps. She shouted out to him, "Hey!" and offered an exaggerated wave. "Thank you, Ed! You were a fabulous Big Tex!"

Silent and unmoving, Ed stood on the steps and raised his hand, his stiff figure offering a benediction on the day.

There were more hugs and kisses, thuds of car doors closing, and the crunch of gravel under tires as they drove away. And then it was quiet, except for the sound of the crickets beginning their evening song. Tammy turned and sighed a deep sigh as she began to make her way to the porch. What awaited her? Tiger, or something more benign? She straightened her shoulders, bracing herself for whatever would come, and walked unhesitatingly toward her husband.

She had learned of the Trevor Project at the last PFLAG meeting she'd attended, and when she'd excitedly told Marcie about her wonderful discovery, she'd been surprised to learn that Jamie was already well acquainted with them. In fact, he had recently opened something similar to a Facebook page on their social networking community, and just making that connection with others like himself was already making a difference. Marcie's grateful description of his more buoyant spirit brought tears to both their eyes. Thinking back on it, that was probably the moment when this idea had germinated within her. She wanted to volunteer in whatever capacity they could use her.

Using Kelly's advice to always "ask the internet," she had learned even more about Trevor on her own. She had learned, first of all, that there were many aspects to Trevor. She learned that the program Jamie was using was called "Trevor Space" and that its world-wide platform had made it possible for young people to connect with other LGBTQs across the globe, helping them make friends and find much needed support. For those in need of a safe and judgment-free place to talk, there was "Trevor Lifeline," a 24/7 hot line where trained counselors offered support to those with questions or concerns. And Trevor Chat was for those who didn't have access to a phone or who just preferred communicating through instant messaging. This is the area where Tammy had decided she wanted to volunteer. She would be trained by a professional on the Trevor staff.

Tammy arrived at the steps and patted the arm of the statue, which was Ed. "Help me clean the kitchen?" And she continued walking into the house, turning out lights as she went. Ed turned and followed. Tammy didn't believe in luck; she believed in hope. And that is exactly what Ed's show of affection earlier in the day had been for Tammy — hopeful. Perhaps Ed was softening? His hardened shell might not be so impenetrable after all. She and Ed removed the tablecloths together, each holding one end and shaking off the crumbs. Tammy gathered up the dirty dishes while Ed collected the rest of the helium balloons. They moved together now, just as they had danced earlier in the day, each flowing naturally with the other. Their mutual silence as much a conversation as anything they could have spoken. They moved to the kitchen and stood together at the sink. Tammy washed; Ed dried.

Tammy rinsed a plate, but then just stood there and held it against her body instead of handing it to Ed. "I want to do something significant with my life, Ed."

"You mean this isn't significant enough for you?" With a dishtowel in one hand and a dinner plate in the other, he held them up to Tammy and tried to smile. This was his way of apologizing for tonight. Being pleasant, maybe even making a joke or two, then never mentioning the issue again. That was Ed's M.O. "I think we had some significant fun today, don't you?" He put down the plate and picked up another.

"Of course I do. And I loved it all! Thank you for making this wonderful day happen, sweetheart. But Ed, I need a different kind of fulfillment too, and I think I've found it. I've recently learned about an incredible program called the Trevor Project and I want to volunteer to help out in their online chat room. It's for LGBTQ youth, and their friends and allies, and I'd be a supportive voice when a hurting or confused child called. Ed, I want to become one of their allies."

"Here we go," Ed sighed, "So much for a pleasant rest of the evening! You know I hate it when you start spouting all those letters at me. LBGQ or YMCA. I don't give a damn about any of that, and I'm tired of you bringing it into our home all the time." He threw the damp towel onto the counter and crossed his arms disgustedly across his chest, almost daring her to go on. Here he had been feeling pretty good about everything and she had to go ruin it all by bringing up those damn gays again! How long must he continue to endure these struggles just to keep his family insulated from depravity?

"I don't want to talk about this, Tammy. You know where I stand."

"But do you know where I stand?"

"You're damn right I do, and I've had it with all your liberal concerns about people who are deliberately flouting God's laws. I don't even know who you are any more, Tam." He took her by the shoulders and stared long and hard into her eyes. "You seem to care more about total strangers, just because they're gay, than you do about me — and our family." He picked up a stack of plates and carried them to the cabinet, plunking them down without much care for their safety. "A flesh-and-blood relationship should be more important than other people like that out there you want to save."

"But that's exactly the point, Ed. I do have relationships with 'other people like that.' And so do you. They're everywhere; just look around. I don't even like saying 'they' anymore. It just feels wrong. We all need to start saying 'we.'"

"But you only have one husband." He walked over to the fridge, grabbed a beer, and took a couple of swigs before he sat down at the table. She could see the muscles in his jaw clenching. "And what about your kids? Have you even considered what the kids will think of this?"

"It's called empathy, Ed, and I think they will respect me for reaching out to help others who really need it. I agree that Michael still has a way to go, but he has come so far already. Have you talked with him?" She searched his eyes but already knew the answer. "He has matured, and I think he's feeling true remorse for what he did." She scrubbed a little harder than was necessary. "In the past, I've done my best to duck controversial conversations. I've changed the subject more times than you know because I didn't want to cause a stir. And, I've been careful not to go too far, all because I *do* care about you and the kids. I've been changing, yes, but I would love it if each of you could come along with me. I know I can't expect us all to evolve in the same time frame, or in the same ways even, but I desperately want us to make room in our family for each of us to become who we need to be. And I do *need* to make a difference, Ed. And I want to make a difference alongside other people who want to make a difference, and that's what The Trevor Project is all about."

"I've had enough. Do what you damn well please, Tammy. I'm going to bed." He stood up to leave, but Tammy grabbed his arm and held him."

"Please, Ed, hear me out," she pleaded, "Please." Surprisingly, after a moment's hesitation, he acquiesced and sat back down at the table, where she quickly joined him.

"Thank you. She reached over and gently patted his forearm. "It's just that if I, and other people like me, who believe Christ came into the world to break down the barriers between 'us' and all the 'thems' we've manufactured, don't speak out, don't do our part to be reconciled, to create a bigger 'us' that includes everyone, then I believe we've failed as Christians. Jesus spent most of his time with the marginalized of his world, and He preached love and compassion and reconciliation. Then He asked us to go out and do the same. That's what I'm trying to do."

"Tammy Sloan, savior. Trying to save the world. One gay kid at a time." His tone was sarcastic. Still, he stayed. And he listened.

"Ed, I'm serious. We'll all benefit when we can choose reconciliation over discord. And to do that, we have to start listening to and learning about those who are different from us. I want to begin by helping these poor kids who can't even turn to their own families for help. I mean, in most of these cases, it's the kids' families who are causing the biggest problems for them."

Ed lifted the longneck to his mouth and batted an errant balloon back into the fold with the rest. "No, Tam. It's not the families that are the problem, but those 'kids' who expect their moms 'n dads to open their arms and accept those immoral and repulsive lifestyles."

"But, Ed, don't you see? Love for one another should trump everything! Our differences. Our judging of one another ..."

"Now that sounds like you're watering down the Bible to me, Mrs. Sloan. Making it more palatable for the weak-willed. I mean, who defines what's right and what's wrong any more? And who should be doing it? Current culture — or the Divine Creator?" He bored into her with a steady gaze, challenging her to refute the immutability of divine law.

What exactly did she want from him? Did she expect him to become other than what he was? A man so entrenched in maintaining authority, and so habituated to living by absolute standards, that he could not envision any other way of relating? Not only was that impossible, but she realized now, it was also unfair of her to ask. She needed to practice what she had just preached, but how to do that? *Please God*, she prayed, *help me to be more loving and accepting here in my own marriage.*

He stood up but continued to stare at her, his face still as stone. Were their hearts really that far off course these days? "How am I supposed to survive in my political world," he asked her, "when my wife and I don't agree on something so basic as this?" He clutched the chair he had just vacated, white-knuckled, lest he let it fly across the room.

"I'm not asking for your permission, Ed, but I had hoped for your acceptance of who I am and what I need and want." Tammy tried to tame the uncharacteristic anger in her voice. "I'm just asking that you respect my opinions and my interests, even when they are different from yours." She searched his face, looking for any sign that could give her hope, but what she saw there stabbed her in the gut. Ed was chiseled stone. Steely. Cold. He had closed off all access to her. Had she gone too far? Could she really disagree with the "home team" this way and come out unscathed? Could she wander off the playing field, as Ed saw it, and still wear the same uniform that he did?

Ed walked out. She could hear his heavy footfalls against the stairs as he made his way up to their bedroom. Tammy remained seated at the table, her eyes drifting around the room, landing on various objects which brought her comfort: the African violet Edith had given her for her birthday that now rested on the window sill, the mugs from past family vacations hanging under the cabinet, magnets on the fridge handmade by children who had grown far too quickly. She exhaled, audibly, and returned to the sink to finish the last of the dishes.

By morning, the only remaining evidence of today's festivities would be the balloons, and they would be tired and used up. By then their colorful shells would be devoid of any buoyancy, and they would sadly bob along the floor, their lonely dances a stark reminder of what once was.

Chapter 14

FREE AT LAST

"Holly? Where are you? Come look at what just came in the mail!" Anne tore into the oversized envelope from the Province of Ontario, but did not remove its contents just yet.

"I like the way it's addressed." Holly had walked into the kitchen and now stood next to Anne. "Holly Anderson & Anne Nelson. There's something about that little ampersand that makes all the difference." She slipped her arm around Anne's waist and squeezed her close. Then, together, standing hip to hip, they pulled their marriage license from its encasement and just stood there staring at it. Even after more than a month of being legally married, there was still something surreal about seeing their names on this official document, this document that told the world they were legitimate.

"I know we've both been married before, but I don't remember feeling this kind of impact the first time around. Do you?" Anne posed the question to her new wife. "Were we just too young to truly understand the enormity of it all?"

"Or did we simply take it for granted? You know, that whole societal expectation that we *could* get married to the person we loved?"

They each knew the answer to both questions was *yes*, but they had to ask themselves these things nonetheless. They were like that. Neither had entered into their first marriage lightly. Although both were married in their early twenties, they were young women of integrity and spiritual depth, and the vows they had made to their husbands were made in love and with sincere commitment. They had intended lifetimes together and could not have foreseen that tragedy would strike down one young man and that life could change the other so drastically. Marriage was much more complicated than either had realized at twenty-one and twenty-three.

But there is something to be said for finally attaining that which had previously been unattainable. When the impossible is finally achieved, an increased appreciation develops, making it all that more precious. And their new partnership in marriage was exactly that. Something they never thought possible — never imagined would be legal.

Holding their marriage license in her hands, Anne shook her head in disbelief. "I can't believe so many people disregard the importance of a marriage license. They say that it doesn't make their love any stronger or more faithful to be legally married." She looked over at Holly. "I don't think they really get it."

"Maybe people don't think they need that substantiation because they've never had their relationships defamed and defiled." Holly remembered the cruise they had taken about a year ago. They had chosen something called "My Time" dining which allowed them to adjust their dinner times according to any planned excursions they had for the day, and they had signed up for tables for two for some nights and tables for six for the remainder. They really enjoyed meeting people and looked forward to getting to know the different individuals they would break bread with each evening. But on their first night in the dining room, they were seated at a table for four instead of six. "Oh well, this will still work," Holly remembered telling Anne.

But it hadn't worked at all. A couple was brought to the table by the hostess, but the woman had refused to sit down. She had stood there, right beside the table where Holly and Anne sipped their cocktails, and argued with both her husband and the dining room hostess that the table was undesirable and that this wasn't what she had had in mind at all. What Holly had felt at that moment went well beyond embarrassment and discomfort. Here was someone denigrating the person she loved most in the world, not to mention herself; and there was nothing she could do about it without drawing even more attention to the calumny being perpetrated in the crowded, very public, confines of a cruise ship dining room.

She could tell the husband was embarrassed by his wife's behavior; but nevertheless, after several long and uncomfortable minutes, he ultimately acquiesced to her objections and the discontented couple had been seated just two tables down from Holly and Anne. Just feet away, really. Evidently, location had not been the problem. The hostess had returned to apologize "for the misunderstanding," but no other guests had been brought to dine with Holly and Anne. And they had remained by themselves at a table for four for the duration of the evening. After that initial mortification, the women had decided to stick to tables for two for the rest of their cruise. Apparently, meeting people on cruise ships was not an option for some couples.

"Well, no matter how others regard a marriage license, this piece of paper means everything to me," Anne asserted. For her, it *was* a validation of their love and commitment to each other, something they didn't receive from the community in which they lived. Anne reverently held the license a minute or two longer, absorbing all that it meant, before moving to put it in their closet safe.

Holly watched Anne fumbling with the combination on the safe's door. "To me too, hon. I don't care if it can't bring us the opportunities and benefits that everyone else gets. That isn't why I married you."

Anne shut the door to the safe and stood to face Holly. "How romantic to know that you didn't marry me for the income tax credits, insurance benefits, or inheritability of my estate — or to avoid death taxes. Not all newlyweds can be so sure of their loved one's motives, you know." Anne winked and gave Holly a kiss on the cheek.

"Well, sorry to rain on your romantic parade, darlin', but there's another piece of mail I picked up today that I need to tell you about. What you just said made me think about it. I got our wills back from the attorney's office today, and I'm going to attach a letter to mine before I send it to Alicia and David." These were Holly's siblings, and they had agreed to serve as executor for Holly's estate until her children were old enough to handle the responsibility themselves.

"So what are you going to tell them?"

"I don't want to tell them about *us* in a letter, but I plan to highlight the obvious changes — that you are now executor with them serving as co-executors, and about the house being put in your name upon my death. Let's just think of it as a really big clue"

Holly grinned widely, but Anne had trouble appreciating the humor in Holly's statement and stared wide-eyed before finding her voice. "Big clue my foot! That's practically telling them 'Read between the lines. Anne and I just got married!' And they don't even know to think of us as a couple, yet."

"But it also respects their readiness to hear it or not. Remember how you handled the *sex talk* with Mark? You gave him bits of information as he was ready to hear it and sometimes you gave him big clues that just lay there because he wasn't at a point to take them in just yet. And I did it the same way with Amanda and Stephen. I kinda hope that's how it will work with this letter."

"I guess that means I need to send Julie a similar letter to go with mine, but I'm not sure that I'm ready for that yet. Once it's out there, it can't be taken back."

"True. But until something is out there, we'll continue to live in this limbo and with the tension that creates. Is that what you want?"

Anne didn't even have to think about it. "You're right, of course. Darn it. Then how about using your letter as a template for mine? You can just change the names and everything. You'd do a much better job, Holly. I'd just stumble over my words and say too much or not enough. This whole thing makes me so nervous."

"Done!" Holly smiled; and she went right then, before Anne could change her mind, to get her MacBook. When she returned, Anne was still mulling over their situation.

"I know when men and women marry and create blended families they have to go through some of this too, but I just hate having to do all this extra stuff just because no one will recognize that our marriage is valid. It's just so unfair."

"I know. It really sucks. And I hesitate to think that we may not know the half of it even yet. Remember how clueless we were when Adam and Charles started filling us in last summer on the legal discrimination they'd had to face as a couple? Who's to say there aren't more injustices that we just haven't run up against yet? Or that there won't be more to come, given the current attitudes of our governor and state legislators."

Anne remembered that night all right. It had been an eye-opening conversation that still sent shock waves reverberating through her whole being when she thought about it. They had met Adam and Charles back in August at a fundraising dinner for the Make A Wish Foundation, and the conversation had grown out of the complications the men had experienced that night trying to make a donation. Holly and Anne had watched as they first discussed the exact amount they could give as a couple, and then had figured out the percentage they each would contribute, and finally had gotten out separate checkbooks and had written separate checks.

Adam had looked up and noticed their quizzical expressions. "A gay's gotta do what a gay's gotta do," he had quipped as a means of explanation, but seeing no evidence of further enlightenment in either of them, he had continued, "You know, to get a charitable deduction for income tax purposes." They must have continued to look stupefied because he had tried again.

"You're a couple, right?"

The question had felt like a frontal attack and they had looked at each other like frightened rabbits, alarmed that it *showed*. But they had faced Adam and Charles and had courageously come out to them, even if it was only by mutely nodding their heads in unison.

"Well then," he'd pressed on, 'Surely, you know that there are all sorts of ramifications to the simple fact that our unions, married or not, are not recognized as legal." He'd paused for confirmation, but seeing none, he had spelled it out for them. "Starting with the fact that, even though we've been together for thirty-five years, and are legally married now in the state of Vermont, we still cannot file our income tax jointly. Hence, this jockeying around of funds you just witnessed."

"Not to mention the hundreds of thousands of dollars we've paid out over the years since we can't take advantage of the standard marriage deduction," Charles had added.

That had gotten their attention. Anne remembered gasping out loud when she'd first heard that astronomical sum. She'd never thought much about it and had no idea that filing as individuals could make that much of a difference to their finances.

She remembered being embarrassed by their naïveté and feeling compelled to explain why they didn't know these things that Adam had taken it for granted they would — should! Looking back now, she couldn't believe she had actually told those perfect strangers about their coming from heterosexual marriages and their still needing to find their way in this new, unfamiliar world. She had become a veritable Chatty Cathy, but Holly had cut to the chase.

"We're getting married soon, and we need to know this stuff. What else can you tell us?"

And Adam had obligingly fallen into his professorial role. He was a bio-ethics professor at Southwestern University, if she remembered correctly.

"Okay. Do either of you have children?" he had begun. And when they had told him they did, he had launched into his first lesson. "Since neither of you can legally be called a spouse, the law would see your cohabitation as being 'overnight guests' in one another's homes. And did you know that most divorce decrees have clauses that disallow parents from having 'overnight guests,' even for one night? There was actually a case in the Dallas area where this happened. One partner was forced to move out of their home when the ex-husband of the other decided to go for custody on the basis of moral turpitude. It was either lose her partner or lose her children. That's a *gotcha* of the tallest order."[12]

They were dumbstruck. All they could do was plead, "Oh my God!" and then thank God that their children were no longer minors. But even as they were congratulating themselves with having dodged that bullet, Adam had come back at them with more.

"So Texas is a community-property state, right? And any couple with children from previous marriages, who bring separate property into their new union, must decide what will go to the new spouse and what will go straight to the children. Generally, this is done to protect the kids, since all income and every asset that is earned during the second marriage is community property, entirely inheritable by the new spouse. But in Texas, a 'legal marriage' is only between one man and one woman, so you guys are going to have to create your wills in much greater detail than 'traditional' couples do. You'll have to spell out everything that you intend the other to inherit, because the state won't recognize your having a community estate at all."

That had been disheartening to hear, but before she could assimilate what they'd just been told, Charles had added to Anne's stress. "And there's more. Much more. Like not being eligible for each other's Social Security benefits. Or my not being able to make Adam the beneficiary on my pension plan because I'm not allowed to list him as a spouse — never mind that we already had a legal marriage license at the time and that we had cohabited for some thirty-odd years. I find it ironic that a common-law man and wife are recognized in the state of Texas, but we are not. And all they have to do is *say* they're married."

Holly had blurted out, "What a farce!" And she had had to agree. They had gone home that night and Googled common-law marriage in Texas only to discover that Texas was one of just nine states that still allowed these unions, but that "all states — including those that have abolished the contract of common-law marriage within their boundaries — recognize common-law marriages lawfully contracted in those jurisdictions that permit it."[13] They had stayed up late into that night consumed with questions. So why is one covenant that is made within human hearts respected, while the other is not? Why is one couple given all the protections of a legal marriage, and one is not? And why, in one situation, is the State of Texas willing to recognize what another state has sanctioned, and in the other, be adamant in their refusal to do so? Why is only one considered a threat to traditional marriage and family?

She had felt so bombarded after Charles' comments that it was hard now for her to recollect everything else that had been said that night. There was something about spousal beneficiaries on IRAs and 401(k) s getting perks that non-spouse beneficiaries were denied. *What was it?*

"Holly, do you remember what Adam told us about retirement accounts and the beneficiaries?"

Holly stopped typing and looked up at Anne. "Of course I do."

"Well, what all did he say? I don't remember. There was just too much for me to take it all in."

"Well, he said that a surviving spouse can just take over the account as their own. But a non-spouse beneficiary has to either take a lump sum or liquidate the account — within five years, I think it was. Remember how he said that they'd amassed a good-sized nest egg? And that when one of them died, the other would have to begin drawing large sums out of the inherited accounts? How they'd have to pay outrageous tax bills since it would all be taxed at ordinary income tax rates? And how he said the survivor would have to take it out before the deadline whether he needed that money then, or not? Holly shook her head in disgust. "Pitiful!"

"Wow. So if you die before me, and let's say it's before I retire, then I would have to take the money out and pay taxes on it then, even though I might need it more later on for my own retirement?"

"Yep. And then you'd be limited in the amount you could put back into a tax-deferred account. And to add insult to injury, you'd have to continue paying taxes on any growth of the part you couldn't put back into your IRA."

"I can't tell you how angry that makes me. I feel like we're being robbed."

"Want to get even madder? I've since learned that *you* have to get renter's insurance for everything that's *yours* since *we're* living in *my* home, because our homeowner's policy won't recognize you as my spouse, either. And, for the same reason, we'll have to keep our separate car insurance policies, so we can't save any money there. I've heard that there are problems with HIPAA and medical releases, too, but I haven't had time to research that yet.

"And all of these headaches and financial losses are due to the Texas Legislature imposing their moral standards on everyone indiscriminately, no matter that the 'givenness' of some lives is radically different from their own."

"And don't forget about DOMA. Texas isn't in this alone."

"How could I ever?"

Holly went back to her typing and Anne got up and went to see what she could muster up for dinner. She pulled out the left-over ham and put it, bone and all, into the Dutch oven to simmer. She would quick-soak the beans in the pressure cooker and then put together some cornbread to go with the soup. A perfect November supper.

Once she got both on the stovetop, she leaned against the kitchen counter and watched as Holly continued pecking away. "How are you doing, hon? Is it all coming together?"

"I'm getting close. I'm just being very careful with my word choices, making sure that I'm telling them but also making sure that I'm not telling them. I'll be ready for you to read my first draft in a few minutes."

While she waited for Holly to finish up, Anne found herself going back again to that evening with Charles and Adam. Nothing had ever dismayed her more than that moment when she first saw just how far-reaching the tentacles of prejudice were. Anti-gay legislation was not limited to conservative state governments. It was pervasive; it went all the way up to the federal government. She had never even heard of DOMA — the Defense of Marriage Act[14], and yet it stood, seemingly unconquerable, between her and her inalienable rights.

It was DOMA that prevented them from filing joint tax returns or receiving each other's Social Security benefits. It was DOMA that prevented her from making Holly her beneficiary on her church pension or IRA. And she remembered what Adam had said about its insidious, all-encompassing effects — how the surviving same-sex spouse of a soldier killed in action can't receive a dime, because they aren't considered married. And how an immigrant can be deported because his marriage to a gay U.S. citizen isn't recognized. And how DOMA's omnipotence and omnipresence invades even the smallest details of a gay couple's life. They couldn't even give a joint pledge to their church without one of them sacrificing the charitable deduction.

When she'd first heard all this, it had felt like a sucker punch to the gut — and to her heart. She'd been knocked to the mat by all that Adam had said. And, now, as she remembered that hopeless feeling, she relived lying there, out for the count. And the same question she had asked then rose within her again, "Can anything be done?"

He had told them that Bill Clinton had signed DOMA back in the mid-nineties, but recently had made a public apology for doing so, saying point blank that he had been wrong. He was now advocating for its repeal. Surely that would make a difference. Maybe it already had. Adam had told them that he heard the Supreme Court would hear arguments next spring on a case that would test DOMA's constitutionality. It had to do with inheritance taxes. Something about a surviving spouse of a same-sex marriage, who had been with her partner for over forty years, having to pay something like three hundred grand in estate taxes since she wasn't considered a legal spouse in the eyes of the federal government, all because of DOMA. DOMA had rendered the federal government unable to recognize New York's sovereignty in what should have been a state matter: marriage. [15]

Driving home that evening, they had resolved to take the necessary precautionary steps to protect and provide for each other. They had since met with their lawyers and had had their wills changed. And now, with the arrival of today's mail, they had taken the next step, the risky step that would begin their official coming-out process.

Anne began to read over Holly's shoulder as she was putting the finishing touches to their letter, the letter which would explain things — more or less.

"They're going to be curious, don't you think? I mean, why would we do this after all these years? Up until now they've thought of us as just being roommates."

"Well, if they're curious enough, hopefully they'll just say something." Holly kept typing. "And that will make it just that much easier on us."

They had each begun to drop subtle hints, just in the last week or so. Their photographs on Facebook were beginning to resemble those of a couple, rather than just what good friends would typically post. They had tried to infuse the collective pronoun 'we' into their conversations whenever they could; but each had struggled with when it felt safe and when it didn't, so they weren't very consistent with that. And they had begun to be purposely careless with their occasional use of a "Sweetie" or a "Hon" in the presence of others. But no one had yet taken their bait. No one had stepped forward with "the question," or an even kinder "I know."

"So do you remember that lady who said something to us the morning after we got married?"

"Of course I do. I can still see her face. I remember being ecstatic afterwards and for some reason, it didn't seem so scary being transparent in that moment."

Anne was referring to a woman who had been seated across from them at dinner on the evening of their wedding. They had eaten at the hotel's finest restaurant overlooking the falls. The colored lights had splashed across the thunderous water, but neither Holly nor Anne had noticed them. They were lost in conversation and in one another's eyes, completely oblivious to their surroundings. They had forgotten to be careful and had allowed themselves to appear, as any newlywed couple would, undeniably in love.

The next morning, as they were leaving breakfast on their way to the rest of their adventure through New England, this same woman had waved them over, beaming as she sat sipping her coffee. "I think we have something in common," was all she had said. But it was enough. Holly and Anne had known what she meant. And Holly had jumped at this unexpected opportunity. "We got married yesterday!" A hearty congratulations was given and received — and that was that. They didn't really remember any further conversation at all. But what had touched them more than anything else was the simple fact that this woman, this stranger, had recognized their love and their relationship — and had dared to say so.

Everyone else in their lives was so respectful of their privacy. Anne thought about that a bit. Although their marriage was still brand new, their relationship certainly was not. But they had been guarding themselves, and their hearts, from everyone who knew and loved them for several years now. No wonder no one had approached them on the subject. And it had become exhausting living this lie. Still, there would be risks ... Anne could feel her heart speed up as she thought about Julie, David, and Alicia opening the letters that Holly was so busily composing.

She thumbed through the documents still on the kitchen table, the new Last Wills and Testaments and the Durable Powers of Attorney. That seemed to soothe her somehow. Funny how those legal instruments, and the marriage license now housed securely in the safe, seemed almost sacred to her. Perhaps it was just the safety they were providing for her and her dearest love, but she didn't think so — even if they did offer protection the laws of the land could not. No, it went deeper than that. It was ... it was that they were tangible proof that the unbelievable had been made real. They grounded her. They grounded her in their new reality, and she realized now that was the reality she wanted desperately to share with her son — and her sister, and her mother, and her friends at the church — all those dear ones whom she wanted to keep close. She could already feel the separation from them that her secrecy was creating, and she couldn't abide that. Whatever the cost, it would be worth the risk to regain the intimacy, the authenticity, that had always defined her relationships with them.

She looked over at Holly. Theirs was an uncommon love for sure, but not just due to their genders. Theirs was a unique bond based upon deep respect, absolute honesty, and total commitment. And it had found them when they weren't even looking. If she were honest with herself, she knew that everyone who loved her would be overjoyed that such a love had found her.

"I wish that everyone who's in a closeted relationship could let go of the fear of judgment."

Holly looked up. "Well, wishes do come true, sweetie. If you're good with what I've done, I'll drop these in the mail tomorrow."

They were on their way.

Avoiding danger is no safer in the long run than outright exposure.
The fearful are caught as often as the bold.
— *Helen Keller*

Chapter 15

BUNKO

"Hi!" A breathless little voice giggled.

Tammy knew that Alex O'Dell was younger than Hannah by a couple of years, but she wasn't exactly sure what their age difference was.

She smiled. "Hi yourself. Is your mama home?"

"Yeah, Mommy's here. We're all home right now! Daddy came home early and we're all gonna put up the tree after our meeting."

"Well, good for you, sweetie. That sounds like fun. Can I talk with your mommy for a minute?" Tammy guessed they were on their way to a family therapy session.

"Sure." Some muffled scraping sounds covered up more giggling. "Mommy! Someone wants to talk to you. Mommy!"

Marcie took the phone from Alex. "Hello?"

"Hey, it's Tammy. Have I called at a bad time?" She could hear voices in the background as she spoke.

"Oh, hi! Well, we're actually trying to get out the door, so I've only got a minute."

"Okay, I'll be fast. I just got an email from Tonia Bolton, you know the Civic League President? They need some extra players for the Bunko Fundraiser this Thursday night and I wondered if you wanted to come."

"Bunko? I've never played before."

"Oh, that won't matter a bit. It's not a serious game or anything, just a way to raise money for a good cause. And it's fun. I think you'll really enjoy it. How 'bout if I forward you the email so you can RSVP to someone on the Board? Everything you need to know will be in Tonia's email, okay?"

"You know, that actually sounds like fun. Thanks for thinking of me. How will I ..." A loud squeal of laughter cut her off in mid sentence. "Oh, shoot, Patrick just came in and 'potato sacked' Alex out to the car. I'm gonna have to go or we'll be late. Call ya later to work out details."

"No problem. Talk to you later then." As soon as she hung up, Tammy ended the call and went straight to her computer to forward the email. It would be nice to do something light and fun together for a change.

Tammy arrived early, so as not to miss Marcie, and waited at their agreed-upon meeting place, just outside the main entrance to the fellowship hall. She waited until just a few minutes before seven, and then, after trying to reach Marcie on her cell but getting no answer, she decided to go inside to see if they had somehow missed each other.

She sensed the unrest as soon as she walked into the crowded room. Although it was early December, it felt like a summer thunderstorm was brewing. As she searched the large hall for her friend, she noted numerous dark and clouded countenances gathered together, building strength and swirling in the dangerous, ever-increasing energy of chattering gossip. Tammy pressed on, working her way around the knots of women spread across the room and practically ran into Pam Long as she held court. Pam, the President-elect of the League, had lightning in her eyes as she sucked the air right out of the room with bolts of white-hot resentment. "If they want to start their own organizations, churches, and what not, that's their business. They can have their own communities. But they damn well better stay out of ours."

What was going on? Tammy turned away from Pam's unpleasantness as quickly as she could, only to encounter Tonia Bolton, whose hair was practically standing on end as she twirled this way and that, touching down in as many conversations as possible. "Declaring something no longer immoral does not make it so. If we don't stand up against this "anything goes" liberal nonsense, we're in for a complete breakdown of our families and communities." Tonia was certainly ensuring widespread damage with that kind of vitriol.

And then there was Dawn Skaggs, Pam's minion, dutifully following the others' lead and spreading verbal debris like sheets of rain. "You know that when homosexuals…"

So that's what all this was about. What a night to have invited Marcie with such a brouhaha going on! It had all the makings of a real disaster. She redoubled her efforts to locate her friend and warn her of the impending maelstrom. Marcie had been through enough already and certainly didn't need this hostility on their supposedly fun night out. But Marcie was nowhere to be found. Instead, she recognized her sister-in-law, Edith, standing along the back wall, filling her plate. She made her way over to her.

"Edith!" She waved enthusiastically as she approached.

"I feel like the emperor with no clothes on." Edith turned to look at her backside, raised her eyebrows and pursed her lips. "And I just got found out." She looked around the room. Eyes darted in their direction, and then were quickly averted as soon as Edith attempted to make eye contact. "What's going on anyway?"

"I'm not really sure, but I've got a guess it has to do with my inviting Marcie tonight. I couldn't miss all the anti-gay sentiment circulating around the room as I walked through. But people rarely work up a mad like this without due cause. There's got to be more to it than that. Have you seen her yet?"

"Who?"

"Marcie."

Edith shook her head. "You mean they're acting like this because of Marcie O'Dell?" Edith was truly surprised by this revelation. "But everybody knows who she is. And they know us, too! Why are they so upset with us? I just don't understand what this is all about."

"It's about judgmental people trying to stir something up, Edith." Still searching for Marcie, Tammy looked around for the rest of the story and then saw Bella McLoughlin, the reporter from News 25 and *The Daily Telegram*. Her voice caught in her throat and she took a sip of iced tea to find it again, surprised by her visceral response to Bella's mere presence. *Well, well, this is going to be an interesting evening,* she thought as she leaned in closer to Edith and whispered, "The gal who interviewed Ed last September is over there, and that can't mean anything good."

The climate across the U.S. was one of hot debate, with news topics like the Defense of Marriage Act, the Boy Scouts of America's policy changes and California's Proposition 8 all keeping the "homosexual agenda," as it was being termed, front-page news for the last many weeks. Muckrakers, like Bella McLoughlin, were working overtime whipping up polemics on both sides, and Ed's words, more than three months old now, kept having new life breathed into them whenever it suited some pundit's personal agenda. Pritchett had been right. Even though Ed was experiencing some good news in the polls, this wasn't going to go away. The public had been aroused.

And she had Bella to thank for all this. Bella had put her long, pointed nose into the fray and, sensing a kill, had taken advantage of Ed's initial raw emotion and subsequent careless words. Then, she had relentlessly continued to poke the proverbial stick into his tiger's cage. Tammy narrowed her eyes at the recollection. She had no love lost for Bella McLoughlin.

"And I bet Pam Long invited her. Oh no, poor Marcie. I've got to find her." And she scanned the Fellowship Hall again.

"Oh, for heaven's sake." Edith rolled her eyes and exhaled deeply before plunging into the artichoke dip on her plate. "Can't we just come here and have some fun without everything getting all political?"

George and Pam Long's son, Phillip, had been one of those suspended and sent to the Miles Academy for the infraction against Jamie O'Dell, and they both had been vociferous in their blaming Jamie for all their son's troubles. It was Phil's senior year. The opportunity for college scouts to see him play was now lost forever. And in Texas, where football comes second only to religion, this was an injustice beyond forgiving. *But just what were Pam and her cronies hoping to accomplish with all their ugly rhetoric? And why was Bella McLoughlin, with her take-no-prisoners journalistic style, here tonight?*

"People like Bella destroy lives. With all that she stirs up, we're not even given an opportunity to make things right." Tammy leaned over the table, spooning some ranch dip over the veggies on her plate.

"We?"

"Well, you know what I mean." And Tammy popped the remainder of a deviled egg into her mouth and once again scoured the room for Marcie.

Yes, Edith knew what she meant. Things were obviously different between Tammy and her little brother. Ed had been a rock-solid presence, consistent and reliable over the years — for Tammy and the kids and for Edith and Henry too. There was no denying his loyalty. But as wonderful as he could be, he harbored a stubborn streak that was not at all flattering. Ed was always right. And even when he wasn't, he still was.

Or had Tammy meant making things right within the community? There certainly was a long way to go there, too. Edith opened her mouth to have Tammy clarify for her, but was drowned out by a voice that filled the room.

"Okay ladies, we're fixin' to get started, so now's the time to see which table you'll start at." Tonia Bolton's voice rang out over the speaker system of the First Baptist Fellowship Hall. She was the outgoing president of the Civic League and tonight's fundraiser would be her final duty before passing the mantle to her successor, Pam Long. "Look on the bottom of your cup, and you'll find your table number. But please fill your plates before you sit down. We'll be starting as soon as everyone gets settled. Let's say ten minutes?" Across the room, about eighty women lifted high their cups full of raspberry sherbet punch or iced tea to discover their table placement and pairings. "And after we've played for a bit, we'll take a little break in order to give everyone another chance to check your bids."

"I'm table two. Woo-hoo!" Edith was a veteran player and knew the benefit of her table placement.

"Guess I'll try texting Marcie to see where she is." Tammy declared, and then wrinkled her nose as she checked the underside of her cup. "Pooh! I'm at number thirteen. Looks like I won't see you again till the night's over."

"I'll try catching ya at the break, Tam. Bye now. I've got prizes to win for the little ones."

Bunko is a silly dice game meant to facilitate conversation and fellowship, nothing more. Many Bunko groups hand out cash prizes for winners of various award categories, but tonight's game was raising money for the Girls & Boys Clubs of the Texas Hill Country. Every Christmas, the First Baptist Bunko group hosted a charity auction in support of their mission, and all proceeds of the auction, plus any cash prizes from the Bunko game, would be donated to one of the area clubs located in Boerne, Fredericksburg, or Comfort. The ladies rotated their support among the three clubs from year to year.

First Baptist's regular group consisted of about twenty-four players, enough to fill six tables; but the Bunko Christmas Charity, known as the BCC, brought in women from about a fifty mile radius. Being part of such a collection from several small towns was similar to attending a family reunion with distant relatives. You might not see the attendees frequently, but everyone knew each other, and most knew a little bit about everyone else's business. The longings to be part of something greater than yourself and larger than the small community in which you lived, reflected twin values in most rural communities. And a gathering like this, which created fun for the greater good, easily had become tradition.

Pam Long and Bella McLoughlin were already seated when Tammy reached Table Thirteen. *What were the odds? This had to be a setup of some kind.* Pam's quick glance over to Bella gave way to a satisfied smirk as Tammy pulled out her chair and sat opposite the media hound.

"So it looks like we'll be partners tonight, Bella." Tammy didn't look at her as she spoke, but punched out a quick message to Marcie instead.

"It will be a pleasure, I'm sure, Mrs. Sloan." Bella had short, cropped reddish hair and wore stylish pointy shoes. Her lips were darkly outlined and filled with a much brighter shade of red. Her ultra-lush lashes looked like small rakes rimming her ice-blue eyes, and she pointed her chin at people when she spoke.

Tammy wondered if her over-the-top appearance was an attempt to make up for the fact that her readers and viewership consisted primarily of sleepy little towns. *Legitimate correspondents didn't try so hard.* But even so, she did have a faithful following.

"Hello there, ladies! Sorry to hold things up." Jo Brown's cane dangled from the crook of her arm as she leaned over to deposit her plate on the table. Her other arm was busy balancing her purse and a glass of punch.

Tammy reached out for Jo's cup and put it on the table for her. "I haven't seen Marcie O'Dell, Pam. I got Tonia's email about needing to even out the numbers, and so I invited her. Have you seen her tonight?" Tammy was sure Pam would know the answer. *After all, wasn't that the reason Bella was here?*

Jo, taking everything in, slowly removed her heavy brown sweater and draped it across the back of her chair. Jo was a big woman, and it took her a while to get settled.

"Yes, I know all about that, Tammy." Pam politely spat through her pursed lips. "But it turns out we didn't need her. Dawn let her know that the BCC is only open to experienced bunko players." Dawn Skaggs was a shallow imitation of Pam, a pawn desperate for social inclusion and subsequent status.

"When did you tell her?"

"When she showed up tonight. Dawn met her at the door and let her know that she wasn't needed."

"She went to the trouble to come here tonight, and you just turned her away?" Tammy was incensed at Pam's less-than-charitable treatment of her friend, but she masked her outrage and asked nicely instead. "Isn't this night all about the charity?" Two could play at this game. Tammy looked toward Bella, whose eyes were on her lap, those lashes nearly touching her sharp nose.

"Well, yes. But we weren't about to tell *her* that." Pam dabbed the corner of her mouth with her napkin. "Jo, dear, this is Bella McLoughlin. You may recognize her." Pam reached over and placed a familiar hand on Bella's shoulder. "She's a reporter for *The Daily Telegram* and a special edition correspondent on News 25."

"Well, I'm sorry to say that I don't."

Tammy checked her phone. Still no response from Marcie. She was livid. Every fiber of her being wanted to leave. Right now. *But isn't that exactly what they want me to do? Make a scene? Leave in a huff? And prove to them that I am unfit for membership in the Civic League, just as they had already insinuated Marcie was?* It was obvious. Tammy's association with Marcie and Marcie's being the mother of a gay child were compelling enough offenses to deem them both "undesirable."

Finally established in her seat, Jo took a mouthful of congealed salad. "I quit watching TV a while back. It was taking up too much of my time. Of course, I'll still occasionally fit in a little quality programing, like *The Bachelor.*" She winked at Bella and let out a little laugh. "I can miss a couple a shows and still get caught up pretty quick. But everything else on TV? I just don't care for it." Pam opened her mouth to speak, but Jo talked right over her. "And I can't remember the last time I subscribed to the paper. It's just too hard to have them deliver out to my place."

Jo lived outside the little town of Cameron, on a two-hundred acre ranch that had been in her family for centuries. The Brown family pockets were deep, their fortunes made by previous generations from oil and cattle. But Jo Brown put on no airs. She wore oversized floral dresses with sensible shoes and still canned her own vegetables. To the casual observer, the similarities between Cameron's Jo Brown and Mayberry's Aunt Bee were striking. Jo was a good one.

Desperate to drive the conversation to a more sophisticated plane, Pam brought up the auction. "Have you seen all the wonderful items we have tonight? I've placed a generous bid on the autographed Laura Bush biography. I've heard it is very moving."

"Oh, you'll love it, I'm sure." Bella crowed. "I've had the privilege of meeting the President and Mrs. Bush in Crawford on several occasions. She is simply a delight."

Tammy was having trouble sitting still. She sent Marcie another text, "I just heard what happened. I'll call as soon as I can." She still wanted to bolt right out the door in support of her friend, but that would be playing right into their hands. No, she would stay and take the high road.

Pam practically sang back to Bella, her voice deliberately accenting certain words for their import. "*I* think she was one of the *classiest* first ladies *ever*. And it's the *one thing* here that I *really* want to go *home* with tonight."

"Well, I'm not a fan of biographies." Jo removed a tissue from her pocket and wiped her nose, obviously not impressed with Pam's opinion or Bella's acquaintances. "And I don't like reading books about politicians, their families, or people who are dead, either. Give me a Paula Deen cookbook any day. I bet her words have caused more tears and inspiration than anything I can think of." Jo let out a hearty laugh, her whole body shaking.

Tammy laughed with her old friend. It felt good to see someone put these uppity women in their place for a change. Pam quickly got busy attending to one of her oversized pearl earrings, acting as if she didn't hear. But Bella's antennae were raised.

Inflamed with the possibilities in this moment, her hair seemed even more red. She lifted her chin and cleared her throat, getting everyone's attention. "Don't you find it *limiting,* to exclude yourself from thought-provoking sources of news and information which can bring so much growth and insight to your life?"

Jo returned the tissue to her well-worn purse and clipped it shut. "Well, with all due respect, Ms. McLoofin, I like to buy *my* cookies from the lower shelf of life, if you know what I mean." Jo gave Tammy a little wink.

Had she just butchered Bella's name on purpose?

"And that doesn't mean that I'm happy to hide out in the sticks with mud between my toes. But there's something worthy in the simple life of country folk like me. We ordinary people are like leaves on a tree — we hang together. And I've found that most everyone's happiness is within their own reach. I've not seen a lot of happiness on the top shelf of life, have you?"

Bella and Pam were both struck dumb with a rare and exceptional muteness, their salvation coming from the bell at the Head Table signaling the beginning of Round One.

"I'll keep score." Tammy reached for the pad and pencil in the middle of the table, and instead of rolling herself, she handed the dice to Pam. "You guys can start." She checked her phone once more. Marcie must still be driving home. She would call her during the break.

They played their rounds slowly. Bella, as Marcie would have been, was not a regular player and was unfamiliar with the game, while Jo was a constant source of conversation, cracking corny jokes like a bad stand-up comic. "What did the tortilla chip say to the unlucky cheese? It's nacho day!"

Pam sat to Tammy's left and cast covert glances her way, attempting to bait her into dangerous waters. "Phillip has had a very hard time this semester thanks to that O'Dell boy." She paused for effect, but receiving nothing but a noncommittal, "Hmmm," she went on. "The people over there are so unkind and he's just devastated at the loss of his college prospects. So uncalled for, don't you think?" When that did not elicit the sought-after response, she resorted to a direct question: "And how is Michael doing?"

Tammy flinched at the unctuous, falsely solicitous tone of Pam's inquiry and hoped it wasn't noticeable. "Just fine. Michael is doing just fine," she replied serenely. "Thank you for asking." She would kill them with kindness.

"Of course, the entire community lost when our boys were removed from the team. But that's what happens when we invite degeneracy into our schools and homes."

Tammy wasn't foolish enough to return Pam's look and avoided talking to her by staying intently focused on the roll Jo had just made. "Is that so?" was all that she ventured, as she continued notating each point and indicating when each player's turn was over.

Pam tried one last time, "Is Ed going to run for Land Commission again? I've heard rumors of strong opposition." Bella looked up from her play, ravenous for a scoop.

This time Tammy did make eye contact with Pam and then smiled sweetly at them both, "Surely, ladies, you know that is an announcement that my husband will have to make." She was proud of herself. She had deflected their rancor and stood her ground. Pretty good for having just learned how to stand up for herself.

But when it was Pam's turn again, she left the dice untouched on the table in front of her. "So Tammy, how are Jamie O'Dell and his family faring these days?" She clicked her red nails on the table, then slowly gathered her dice, one by one, and held them in her hands before rolling.

"Why do you ask, Pam? And why do you ask me? If you really cared maybe you shouldn't have prevented Marcie from coming tonight." And she snapped off the end of a carrot between her teeth, with a loud snap and chewed it thoroughly. It felt good to put Pam Long in her place. Tammy was always so careful not to offend. But what had she done, really, other than state the facts at hand?

Pam's eyes slowly widened. "Well, it's just that I've heard you two have become overly friendly of late, despite problems it may cause for you. And for your family." This time her sideways glance was intended for Bella, and it hit its mark. After successfully ignoring Jo and her homegrown humor, the reporter sat up and leaned in closer to the table, once again attentive to the ensuing storm and any chaos it might produce.

But Jo opened her umbrella wide, not allowing any rain on this night's parade.[16]

"I know just what you mean, Pam. You have to be careful these days. My late husband, Davis, had a niece that was gay." Jo clucked her tongue in apparent disapproval. "You just can't imagine how thoroughly gays can threaten the traditional order of things, you know."

Tammy groaned silently. *Not Jo too!* And she steeled herself for another onslaught.

Pam wiggled in her excitement, shifting her position toward Jo now, instead of away from her as she had been seated most of the evening. Eager to hear what Jo had to say, Pam Long was panting with delight.

"My biggest complaint about those girls … " Jo took a deep breath and exhaled loudly, "had to do with their power tools. After all, we're proper southern women, and we should never pick one up, except to put it in a Home Depot shopping cart."

Bella's heavily penciled brows immediately creased, coming together in a severe "V" as Jo continued her discourse. And Pam's face sallowed — to the very same degree that Tammy's spirits lifted.

"Not having a man around the house, they had to fix things themselves, you see. And they did." Jo's eyes widened in sarcastic surprise. "And they were so brazen about it. Sometimes they even used their tools in the front yard. Where everyone could see!" Jo took the time to look at each face around Table Thirteen, condemning such outrageous behavior with a firm and steady shake of her head. Tammy had never discussed same-sex issues with Jo. She had never discussed them with any of her friends other than Marcie, and she had not known about Davis' niece, nor had she held any idea of how Jo felt about such things. "They would often engage Davis in conversations about their honey-do projects and the tools they would need to use. Why, he even borrowed some of their tools once! Can you believe the gall?"

Pam shriveled like a used-up balloon, and her eyes darted over to Bella, whose steely countenance was now controlled, offering no emotion whatsoever.

"Another thing they did was grill. With *charcoal* no less!" Jo slapped the table with her large hand. "When they had us over, they would insist that Davis sit in a chair on the deck. A deck which they had built themselves, by the way. And they had him drinking beer while they tended to the grilling." She leaned back in her chair and exhaled loudly. She was obviously enjoying this. "Not cooking cornbread in a cast-iron skillet wearing an apron, mind you, but grilling steaks — with tongs and spatulas!" She shook her head in mock disgust. "And did I tell you they used *charcoal?*"

Jo leaned into Tammy and placed her hand over Tammy's, patting it tenderly. "Tam, gender roles are collapsing all around us. You have to be careful with your associations these days. You have to think about your daughters. You don't want your girls to see someone like Tricia or Faye dressed in fancy clothes and driving a fancy car home from work, do you? They might begin to think, 'Hey, when I grow up, I can get a good job too, and not have to rely on a husband to provide for me.' She released Tammy's hand and huffed. "Everyone knows that's a man's job. And look out, or they might even take 'em to see a Lady Longhorn basketball game or something. You don't want them to think that women's sports can be just as exciting as men's, do you?"

Reclining heavily in her chair again, Jo deliberately placed her hands upon her large abdomen, then clasped them together to deliver her final blow. "But the worst that might happen would be if your girls ever mentioned, 'I wish those ladies had children, because their kids would be really cool to play with.'"

Pam's face was now crimson, the same color as Bella McLoughlin's hair. They looked quite the pair. Two lobsters in a pot, simmering in their own juices.

"Really now, be extra careful, Tam, or Ed will have you out there slaving over a hot grill, drilling holes, and fixin' fences before you know it." And she winked at Tammy as she took a long drink from her cup.

Tammy couldn't help herself, and she laughed out loud. Dwelling on negativity did not suit her, and Jo's timing had been impeccable. It was so nice to find some humor in all of this for a change.

"I believe it is your roll, Ms. Brown." Bella's voice was cool, a direct contradiction to her boiling insides.

Jo happily scooped up the dice and rubbed them together, blowing on them for good luck before throwing them down in the middle of the table. Three of a kind. "Well, Heaven's finally here! I thought I'd mildew in this chair before I'd roll me a BUNKO!" She called out louder still for everyone else to hear, "BUNKO!" She received twenty-one points and women across the hall answered with whoops and whistles. Jo continued her turn only to immediately roll another set of fives, for a second BUNKO.

"I have never seen that happen before." Pam's voice was barely audible.

Tammy stood up. "BUNKO! Jo rolled another BUNKO!" Once again, the Hall erupted.

"That'll be another twenty one points, thank you very much!" Jo's large frame leaned against Bella again, spilling into her space at the table. "I feel crazy as a bedbug, I swear I do. Maybe you can put *me* on your ten o'clock news now!" Apparently Jo did indeed keep up with her fair share of current events, despite her earlier admission of lackluster interest in the world and its happenings.

The Head Table bell rang, signaling the end of Round One, and Jo huffed as she lumbered out of her chair, signaling to Pam. "Come on girl, we're movin' on up..." She sang it just like the theme song to *The Jeffersons*, "... Movin' on up ... to the Top!"

Bella and Tammy remained at Table Thirteen, but the protective shield that Jo Brown's delightful performance had provided remained in place for Tammy for the duration of the evening. It thwarted Bella's continued attempts to ruffle her and get a great lead-in story for the newscast. The cleansing rain of Jo's humor had washed away the troubled energy Tammy had felt earlier in the evening's pursed lips and clipped words. And Tammy felt renewed. Just knowing that there was someone who had her back made all the difference.

She called Marcie on her way home. "This night was an emotional storm that I'm glad you didn't have to endure. But you would have loved the unexpected rainbow that was Jo Brown." And they both shared their accounts of the evening's events, Marcie explaining how she had chosen not to take Dawn's public rebuff personally — "Thank goodness for all the counseling sessions I've attended. Before we started seeing

Teresa, I would have been reduced to a puddle from the humiliation, but now I can see it is more about them than about me." — and Tammy recounting all the ways she had deflected Pam's malice and Bella's prying aggression.

Tammy's mind wandered as she maneuvered the car toward home. She remembered the explanation of the stages of secret-keeping that she had learned at her first PFLAG meeting: Personal, Private ... and Public. Jo Brown was certainly in that public phase. She hadn't hesitated to let her opinions be known, even in that hostile environment so ready to condemn. And because Jo was confident in disclosing her true feelings, Tammy now knew she and Marcie had an ally they could trust.

Weathering destructive storms, Tammy reflected, was a part of life in tornado alley. It was not unusual at all for the sirens to go off multiple times a season. And since cellars are scarce in the shifting Texas clay, all Texans knew to run to an interior closet for safety when the warning sirens blew, preferably one framed tightly on all four sides, perhaps even hidden under a staircase. Tammy had huddled with her children in a closet like this during many springtime storms over the years.

A flash of lightning in the distance caught her eye. Yes, riding out threatening storms, not unlike the one she had survived tonight, was definitely a part of life where she lived — and knowing where your safe places were was a must. She had found such a safe place tonight, and it had been found in the company of a trusted friend, not inside a confining closet. *How sad*, she thought, *that it's still in the closet where entire families find themselves, waiting for the terrifying storm to pass.* She had met such frightened families at PFLAG. She had seen in their eyes the uncertainty of survival. She had heard the sorrowful cries of those who believed they or their loved ones would fall victim to society's ravaging winds. *What they need is their own Jo Brown*, she thought.

And yet, she had also seen those who had hope, who then courageously shared their hope with those paralyzed by fear. Bob ... Nancy ... Sharon ... There were good people in the world who were trying. But Tammy understood what it meant to hope against hope that the funnel would hopscotch over your hiding place. To believe that your concealment might spare you from the cloud of debris that scatters bits of innocent lives in its wake.

She drove the rest of the way home in an almost meditative state as faces played before her and connections dropped into her lap. As she turned into her driveway, she realized that in some odd way something had settled within her. She felt hope, not a Pollyanna-like optimism, but the deep abiding hope of faith that has seen the pain and counted the cost and is prepared to work to bring about God's good in the world.

She entered the kitchen, dropping her purse and keys onto the table before following the sound of the television into the family room, where she knew her family would be gathered. She entered the room, smiling from a new sense of peace and purpose.

It was a live shot. Bella McLaughlin, with a microphone in hand, stood in the parking lot of the church, its well-lit, giant steeple soaring behind her as an impressive backdrop. "Many of the area's local Bunko groups gathered tonight for the annual Bunko Christmas Charity, a big fundraising event which was held at First Baptist Church where over eighty ladies were in attendance. I'm here with Pam Long, who will begin her tenure as president of the Civic League on January first. Pam, you must have been very pleased with the large turnout and the many generous donations from the surrounding communities." The camera turned from Bella and zoomed in for a close-up of Pam Long. Bella extended her microphone to her guest.

"Yes, Bella. As a group, we were able to raise over $8,000 for the Hill Country Boys and Girls Clubs tonight. We have always strived to maintain our reputation in the community and we work very hard to preserve the values and principles that every Texan holds dear to their hearts. Although we've had some members recently make demands that our group lower its standards and offer membership to those who don't abide by these same values, we believe that by our results tonight, we have been affirmed in our stance to uphold a certain level of integrity and morality." Pam's words slithered through her tightened lips. "There is just no place for gays in what we are trying to accomplish here."

The camera turned again and found Bella's heavily painted face. "As we have seen all too often of late, the lives of decent and respectable people, and the fine organizations which they lead, are continually being forced to withstand the undercurrents of depravity and corruption being propagated by liberal agendas. Perhaps our local resident, Commissioner Ed Sloan, needs to focus his attentions on matters a little closer to home these days."

The live shot was then sent back to the studio, but Ed and Tammy sat in their living room, stunned.

"What the hell is she talking about? What happened tonight, Tammy?" Ed came out of his chair and now stood in front of her.

"Absolutely nothing. I didn't lower myself to their level and I think that's why they're all mad. I just can't believe they actually let her say all that on the newscast. Nothing happened!"

The weather was on now, and the weatherman was standing in front of a map of central Texas, pointing at the line of storms which Tammy had seen earlier.

"Something had to have happened! Dammit, Tammy!" Ed stamped and spat as he yelled. "Everything's been going so well for me! And now this? Goddammit, Tammy! Tell me what you did!"

As Ed continued his rant, Tammy battened down, more fully understanding just what it was that made so many choose to live their lives in the closet. Like so many of those she had met through PFLAG, she now was being persecuted, being blamed for simply being who she was. She was having things attributed to her that were not accurate and were not true. And she realized for the first time that there really was no defense against what someone else was determined to believe.

More strongly than ever, she resolved to become a safe friend to the hiding ones and to help free them from those walls of supposed safety.

Freedom is a gift of God. And the hope of every human heart.
— *George W. Bush*

Chapter 16

VAUGHN CHRISTMAS

I t was the week before Christmas. The time that all of Holly's extended
family gathered to celebrate the holidays together. When the kids had
been little, each nuclear family had wanted to create traditions of their
own, and so Holly's late mother had come up with the idea of moving
Christmas. They had begun celebrating as an extended family the weekend
before the actual holiday, and that move had worked out beautifully
for them. For twenty-three of the last twenty-six years, all thirty-plus
members of their clan had managed to celebrate 'Vaughn Christmas'
together and they did it without conflicting with in-laws or Santa Claus.
And the three years when someone had to miss could be accounted for by
a case of flu, an emergency appendectomy, and the arrival on December
14th of a brand new grandchild. Although the kids were all grown now,
some with families of their own, this date was as sacrosanct as the 25th itself.

For years, they had all gathered at their parents' house, but now that
the elder Vaughns were both gone, they had moved "Vaughn Christmas"
to Alicia's lakefront home in Lago Vista. As the oldest sibling, she had
asserted the firstborn's prerogative; but more to the point, she and
Rick had the biggest house and the most outdoor space, both *musts* to
accommodate all the family festivities and accompanying frenzy. For
years now, the Vaughn Christmas dinner had been a sumptuous Tex-
Mex *fiesta*. After so many years of carrying out this tradition, no one
had to ask anymore what they could bring. It was a given that Alicia
would make her famous lime soup, her own rendition of the *sopa de
limon* she had first discovered in Cozumel some thirty years before.

And it was a given that Sherry would make her famous *enchiladas suizas*, that Rick would grill his chicken and beef fajitas, and that David, the family baker, would bring both a Mexican chocolate sheet cake and his crème de menthe brownies. Melinda, of course, would bring the traditional Christmas cookies, already cut out and baked and ready for the little ones to decorate before dinner. And her husband, Joe, never came without several tins full of Ranger cookies.

And not to be outdone, in recent years the younger generation had gotten into the act also. They had taken over making the homemade salsas, guac, *queso*, and *pico de gallo,* and their specialties were already being received as "famous" too.

No one else would ever consider trying to compete with their budding culinary talents. Certainly not Holly. Holly was famous in this family of near chefs for *not* cooking, but she had a friend at work who made the most incredible homemade tamales, so her contribution to the family fiesta was always one of the most highly anticipated. Since Anne had been attending these gatherings for four or five years now, she had also developed a specialty. Her *charro* beans were to die for. And as she and Holly walked down the lovely *luminaria* lined walkway toward Alicia's front porch, she made her way carefully, so as not to spill any of the pot liquor.

"Alicia always does things up right," Holly observed as they drew closer. Not only were there *luminarias* lining the walk, but there were more outlining the spacious flagstone porch, not to mention fairy lights twinkling in the post oaks that dotted the property. Two giant red poinsettias flanked the massive oak door providing cheerful contrast to the limestone walls, while a single spotlight illuminated the rustic metal angel which graced the door, arms wide open in welcome and blessing.

"She certainly does. And isn't it all beautiful? It all just beckons you to come inside and get warm."

"Well then, let's do just that," and Holly set the tamale cooker down on the porch so she could get the door for Anne. "Ho! Ho! Ho! Merry Vaughn Christmas, everybody."

Two of her little great-nieces came running and grabbed them both around the knees, "Aunt Holly. Come see the tree!" "Auntie Anne. I found my ornament already! I was the first one!"

"Good for you, Ainsley. Hi Lily. My, you girls are growing so fast."

When they were all little, Holly's mother had made a special ornament for each of her four children, and when the grandchildren started coming, she had done the same for them — and then for the "greats" as she had liked to call them. When Vaughn Christmas came to Alicia's, so did those ornaments; and now, the youngest generation ran to the tree first thing, vying to be the one to locate his or her teddy bear, snowman, or angel first, just as Holly and her brother and sisters had done so many years ago. It was one of many family traditions that made their celebration so special. And they would get to them all tonight — everything from setting the table with their mother's holiday pattern, to doing the stockings and gift exchange the way they had always done them, to announcing this year's recipient of the memorial donation they always made in their parent's names, to ending the evening singing carols around the piano while Holly played. She sighed. With all the change she had been experiencing lately — good change, for sure, but stressful nevertheless — it was so good to have this grounding, this continuity with her childhood. *Ah, the goodness of family.*

"Have you guys started decorating Aunt Melinda's cookies yet? Holly barely had time to grab hugs from the girls before they scampered off calling, "Aunt Mel! Aunt Mel! Can we do the cookies now?"

Holly and Anne started making their way to the kitchen via the family room but their progress was slow. They stopped multiple times along their way as first one and then another of Holly's relatives came up to greet them with hugs and kisses, and offers to help carry their loads. As the girls pressed on toward the kitchen, the others went back to their conversations. They were already engrossed in catching up. "So when is the baby due? Do you know if it's a boy or a girl yet? Have you chosen a name?" "I hear you got a job as host at Outback and they're *mucho* impressed. Keep up the good work, son." "When do you start that internship down in Houston? Do you have a place to stay?" Everyone was talking over everyone else in their excitement and in their efforts to be heard.

"Now I know I'm at Vaughn Christmas," Anne laughed. "Where's Rick?" The decibel level at a Vaughn family gathering could be overwhelming to those not born into such noise, and Rick was known for his excuses to get out of the house when the cacophony got to be too much. Often he would invite Anne with him into the yard or on an errand. She called him her "sanity saver," but truth be told, she loved these gatherings. They were so full of life and love.

"Holly! Anne! Come in here and give me a kiss. I'm up to my elbows in *masa*."

Holly set the tamale cooker on the stove top and ran up to hug her big sister from behind. "Alicia, you're wonderful. Homemade tortillas no less!" And she squeezed in to give her a big kiss to go along with the big hug. "I love you! And I've missed you, big sis."

"Love you back, sweetie. And where is Miss Anne?"

Anne was right behind her, and kissed her on the cheek too. "Right here, Alicia. Your place is just gorgeous, as always, and everything smells so good. What can we do?"

"Yeah, we're here to help."

"Well, then let's get this show on the road."

Dinner was wonderful. All thirty-two of them had gathered in a circle and held hands for the blessing before scattering all over the house to enjoy the feast. The stockings and gift exchange had been great fun; the memorial gifts to The Capital Area Food Bank and Sierra Club were very fitting; and now everyone was gravitating to the back patio for a complete change of pace before caroling and goodbyes. Some had brought their dessert with them; others, a nightcap. And still others had followed Rick and the children over to the fire pit to watch them roasting marshmallows and making s'mores. There was plenty of seating in several different conversational groupings, but now the voices were much more subdued. There was something about the wide open vista, the starlit skies, and the gibbous moon reflected on the lake that stilled all their earlier energies, turning them inward. People talked in low voices, or not at all. Even the children were quieter as they concentrated on making the perfect golden-brown marshmallow.

Alicia looked for Holly and found her seated with Amanda and Stephen and Stephen's fiancé, Chloe. They were talking a bit more animatedly than the others, but still in *sotto voce*. Probably talking about the wedding, she guessed. She had been glad to hear that they were waiting until after they both graduated. Long engagements were good things, especially when you were that young. As she moved toward their table, she saw Amanda's friend, Ryan, approach them from the other side; and as she watched, he leaned over and kissed the top of Amanda's head affectionately. Even in the dim light of twilight, it was easy to read Amanda's response. She positively glowed. Alicia wondered if another wedding was in the offing. Not the right time to get Holly off by herself, she decided, and so she changed course, heading for the fire pit instead. She would have to look for another opportunity. But she was determined to have the conversation before the evening ended.

Too much time had already elapsed since she had received that letter, and her thoughts had been getting away from her ever since. When she had first opened that manila envelope, she had laid the copy of Holly's will on the table, and had begun reading the accompanying letter with some confusion. *Why was Holly changing her will now?* When she came to the part where she was making Anne the executor and wanting to leave the house to her, her stomach had clutched. It sounded for all the world like they were a couple. But that couldn't be. She had known her little sister for forty-five years, had watched her grow up and mature into the wonderful woman that she was, and she knew Holly was not gay. Holly had been happily married. She had grieved Bruce terribly... and Alicia knew just how terribly since she had helped her through that time, talking on the phone every night, listening to her pain and anguish, offering words of comfort and hope. She must be mistaken. It just couldn't be.

"Rick, come look at this," Alicia had called. "Come read this and tell me what you think?" She could count on Rick's perspective. He had a way of cutting through emotions and honing in on the reality of a thing. He obligingly scanned the letter and tossed it to the table.

"Think about what? How she chooses to leave her estate is completely up to her, Alicia."

"I know that, Rick. But the fact that she's making Anne an executor, and leaving the house to her ... that's what you do when you're a couple."

"Well, what do you think they are?"

Those words had set her head spinning. Sure, they had lived together for three or four years now, but Alicia had had a good friend live with her while the friend was recovering from a divorce and getting on her financial feet again. It had been good for them both. And that's what she had thought was going on with Holly and Anne. She had thought of them as good friends. Best friends. Soul friends, even. She had seen their emotional intimacy, and had even thought of them as lifetime friends and housemates who could meet one another's needs for emotional and spiritual intimacy. But she had never thought of them as being a *couple*. That bent her mind in ways it did not want to go.

She had thought a lot about that letter ever since and about what it portended. If Holly really was gay, then she couldn't stand that her little sister was having to carry such a big secret without the understanding and support of her family. Without *her* understanding and support, in particular. Holly and she had always shared a special closeness that meant the world to her, but now she worried that their intimacy would be threatened if a secret so essential to Holly's being were allowed to lie between them. If Holly wasn't gay, then her own questions, left unspoken, could have the same effect. Either scenario was simply untenable, so she had determined that she would take advantage of the upcoming Christmas gathering to talk with Holly.

Besides, what if the letter had been a plea for help? It had certainly felt like a tentative telling and she had certainly gotten the message it had been careful not to spell out. Was Holly testing the waters, so to speak?

Well, big sister Alicia wasn't going to leave such a plea unanswered, and she certainly *was* going to let Holly know how wide and deep her love for her was — wide and deep enough to handle any eventuality.

I'll see if I can't catch her alone when we go back in to clean up, Alicia told herself. She sat back in one of the lawn chairs and gave herself over to the stars and to the hushed voices all around her. *Pax Noel,* she thought. *Merry Christmas, Mama and Papa.* As she settled into the quiet, she heard David's clear tenor and Anne's beautiful soprano lifting into the night, "Lo, how a rose e'er blooming, from tender stem hath sprung ..."

Beautiful. Jesus, she prayed, *give me the wisdom and the words.*

"**Y**ou're not going to believe this," Holly paused before turning the key in the ignition and looked over at Anne, her expression a mixture of amazement and relief. "Alicia just asked me if we were a couple."

"*What*? And you didn't tell me?" Anne was stunned.

"I'm telling you now. But what was I supposed to do? Tell you right there in front of everybody while we hugged everyone goodbye?"

"All I mean is, you seem so calm and I'm about to jump right out of this car! I'm sorry. Tell me what she said." Anne could feel goosebumps all over her body.

"Well, if I seem calm now, I certainly didn't then. I felt like a deer caught in the headlights of an oncoming eighteen-wheeler."

"So what did she say? Hurry up and tell me. I'm dying here."

Holly started the engine and began rolling down the long driveway. "She brought it up in the kitchen first. She said she'd read the letter I'd attached to the will, and she said the way I had worded things sounded like I was telling her we were a couple. I had been washing my hands at the time and at first I just froze there, looking down at the sink. When I looked up at her, I must have looked like I imagine a wild animal does when it first realizes it's been caught. My heart was pounding so fast I thought it would explode out of my chest. When I finally found my voice, I tried to make light of it, joking that her past life as an English teacher was paying off and that she had interpreted my words correctly.

She hugged me to her and told me she'd known you and I were close friends and life companions, but that lately she'd felt we were sounding more and more like a couple. She wanted to know so that she could support us — if that was indeed the case. Then just now, as we were hugging everybody goodbye, she whispered in my ear that nothing could ever come between us. That she was very happy for us. Can you believe it?"

"You know, I thought it seemed like she held me a little longer than she usually does when we hugged goodbye. " Anne shook her head in disbelief. "Wow. No, I can't believe it. She knows. Which, of course, means Rick will know too. But I'm okay with it. I really am. I can't believe that I am so okay with it."

"Actually, she told me that Rick has known for a long time, long before she started to suspect it."

"I don't know if that makes me feel better or worse. But go on. What else did she say?"

"Well, she said that getting my letter made her realize that if that *were* the truth, she wanted me to know that my happiness meant everything to her, and that if our relationship is what brought me happiness, then she wanted us to know that she was not only okay with it, but that she was truly happy for us and for our future together."

Anne just stared straight ahead looking at the empty countryside. "Wow." It was all she could muster. Her emotions whizzed in every direction almost as fast as the car in which they were driving. The dormant grass along the highway was a drab tan. The skies overhead were a dark and dreary gray. But the many colors rushing through her psyche lit up everything in her mind. The occasional houses with strands of Christmas lights adorning their rooftops and fence lines were no match for the electrifying emotions which lit up her mind and dazzled her senses as she tried to make sense of all that she had just heard.

Holly broke the silence, interrupting Anne's reverie.

"I thought I was ready. I was so sure when I wrote all those letters. But when Alicia broached the subject tonight, I just froze solid. Honestly, I could hardly breathe. I don't even really remember much of what I said." They had hoped that someone would just open that door for them, and now someone had. "I just didn't realize how difficult it would be. Until I was there. Facing my sister."

"I can't even imagine. And boy, am I glad it was *you*, and not *me*. But you know, now that I'm getting over the initial shock of it all, I'm feeling nothing but excitement and joy. Just knowing that Alicia knows and that she supports us is so amazing. She knows and nothing has changed. And yet, I feel like everything has changed — exactly what we told Karen DeVita we thought it would be like when she asked us about telling our families. I've been so afraid of this first step, and now it feels like I've been released from prison."

"Me too. I'd always thought that we'd tell the kids first, but I'm really glad that it worked out this way. Telling them puts the most at risk for us, and I think that's what has been crippling me. But being able to disclose the truth in a less risky relationship, and receiving such a positive response, has been freeing, and encouraging, and really empowering." She was silent for a moment. Then laughed and sang out, "I am woman. Hear me roar!" Holly took one hand off the steering wheel in order to make a one-armed victory sign and grinned over at Anne who was laughing heartily. "Thank you, Alicia!"

"Telling the children. That's the next big step, you know." They hadn't told them yet because they had wanted to wait until they could each have those discussions face to face, and one on one. And with everybody already on their own, or off at college, they knew that wouldn't happen any time soon.

"Does Alicia know that we haven't told them yet? I'd hate for the kids to hear in a round-about way."

"She knows. And she knows to be very circumspect until we do tell them. We can trust her discretion, Anne. I think this just means that we need to gather our courage and make plans to talk to all of the kids as soon as possible, though."

"Before the euphoria of this moment fades entirely away," she added, "and we let ourselves get locked in by fear again."

Now that someone *knew* — not just suspected their being together but actually *knew* the truth of their being married — it was both exciting and frightening. They had kept their secret so close, so private, so protected, for such a long time, that it was no small feat to release it from captivity. As she thought about that, she suddenly realized that just as she had kept the secret captive, so it had kept her. And there was no way to describe the liberation she now felt.

That first step into freedom was a feeling of inexplicable joy. Anne and Holly talked the entire hour's drive back home, knowing that their lives had just taken another unexpected, and yet not at all unpleasant, turn.

Chapter 17

THE TREVOR PROJECT

Marcie and Tammy were spending the morning together shopping. The after Christmas sales were still in high gear, and Tammy was eager to find just the right outfit for her first day at Trevor next week. She hadn't dressed for a first day on the job in more than twenty years, and she was nervous. So she called Marcie, "How about being my personal shopper for the day?" They had agreed to meet at the mall.

"The Great Un-vitation," as Tammy contemptuously termed Pam Long's behavior at the Bunko charity event last month, had only solidified their growing friendship. It was one more thing they could shake their heads at and learn to laugh about. And that shared experience of growing beyond the community's ostracism had cemented their bond. They were stepping out more and more of late, disregarding any raised eyebrows they might incur as they laughed over their lattes, or shared stories over a soup and salad lunch. And, of course, they continued to pour their hearts out to one another in private, either over the phone, or when they shared a ride on the long drive to PFLAG. Their friendship was a welcome and important support to both, but it was becoming a life raft for Tammy.

Marcie, of course, had Pat. And he was a gem. He had been a consistent source of strength and stability for the entire family and a true confidant and partner for Marcie. His even-keeled personality and rational approach to the issues they faced had provided her with perspective, direction, and a sense of safety, while his willingness to be vulnerable and to let his feelings show had made the strong bond they shared possible. They could be real with one another, shelter and support one another, and that had made all the difference in how they had come through the adversity that had come their way, both as individuals and as a couple. Adversity, it seemed to Tammy, had brought the O'Dell family even closer. But the gulf between Tammy and Ed was widening.

"To tell you the truth, Ed and I had another fight about it just last night." Tammy picked up some pink flats, size five, and put the box under her arm.

"What started it?"

"Well, to be honest, he wasn't thrilled when he overheard our plans to go shopping today. He actually asked me if I was deliberately trying to wreck his political chances by parading my defiance around in public. Can you believe that? And then, when I tried to explain our friendship and defend my right to select friends and have a life apart from his, it escalated. He brought up Trevor and demanded to know if I was really planning to go through with "this Trevor Project thing." The derision in his voice was so demeaning that I really did become defiant. I jutted my little chin out just like Michael does when he's trying to rebel and announced that I certainly did. And then, of course, he went ballistic. It wasn't my finest moment, but Bella did me no favor when she raised the specter of the disobedient wife whom the strong politician could not control. Now he is super-vigilant in monitoring my behaviors and attempting to control my every move. It's… it's … it's untenable, is what it is."

"Tammy, if our seeing one another is a problem for you, we can …"

"Don't even think it, Marcie! For one thing, our friendship means everything to me. And for another, I can't afford to let Ed control me like that. It's not healthy for either one of us."

They walked up and down the rows of shoes, but Tammy didn't see anything she liked any better than the pink flats already nestled under her arm. "These are the ones. Let's go find a sweater, now."

Tammy was quiet for a bit as she replayed the tension from last night. Then she looked up sadly and heaved a big sigh. "I'm really not trying to be defiant, you know. I love Ed and I want to keep our family together."

"I know."

"But it's so difficult when Ed has no bend to him. He just can't hear that my moving out in these new directions is not about trying to hurt him but about my trying to follow my own truth."

"Do you think that's especially hard for him since he's a politician, and his livelihood depends on how others view his image?"

"Well, of course that plays into it. But there are all sorts of examples of married political couples who ended up on different political spectrums. And *they* found a way to work it out. James Carville and Mary Matalin come to mind, but there was also FDR and Eleanor Roosevelt, and Betty and Gerald Ford, and even Laura and George Bush."

"The Bushes? Really?"

"Yeah, she kept a low profile during his presidency, but she's come out for marriage equality and abortion rights since then."

"Really?"

"Yeah, and that's what I'm trying to do too. I don't plan to speak out publicly in opposition to Ed's views. In fact, I've been very circumspect in what I've said and left unsaid in public, in deference to his position. I mean, just look at the supreme effort I made not to give Pam or Bella any fodder for their gossip mills at Bunko last month. Not that my discretion did me any good." And Tammy borrowed Kelly's signature eye-roll to emphasize her point. "But, like any other woman on this earth, I want to be able to lead a full, if quiet, life — going out with the friends of my choice, thinking for myself, sitting in a cubicle and anonymously texting someone who needs support. Where's the rebellion in that?"

"Well, if you put it that way!" And they both laughed out loud, causing several nearby shoppers to look their way. They delved into the racks again to deflect the attention and collect their thoughts.

Tammy picked up and rejected several sweaters before she spoke again, quietly this time. "You won't believe what he said last night, Marcie, when I was trying to help him understand where I was coming from. Right in the middle of my pouring out my heart about finding, for the first time in my life, an issue that I care deeply about and telling him that I felt compelled to help in the small way that I could, he actually stopped me mid-sentence with, 'Your job, Tammy, is to stand by *me*, as my *wife*. Just as you always have!' And then, with all the dismissive sarcasm in the world, he snarled, 'Or is that asking too much of you these days?' It was like hitting a brick wall. All the air went out of me."

"That must have been really painful."

"It was beyond pain, actually. More like plummeting to the depths of despair. How on earth can we remain a family when he wants me to give up my very self to do so?"

Marcie let some silence settle over that question before she asked a question of her own, "Have you ever stepped out like this, against Ed's wishes I mean, on anything before?"

"No, not really. I've never felt the need to, honestly." Tammy shut her eyes. "But, I guess, over the years I fell into lazy thinking. Instead of thinking for myself, I borrowed the prevailing views of my community, and most especially Ed's. But that won't do for me anymore." She folded the sweater she had been considering and replaced it on the table. "It's not that I've been unhappy being his Tammy Wynette. It's just that we'd both quite forgotten that I have dreams and convictions of my own that might not always be in line with his."

"And now that you're remembering?"

"It's wreaking havoc in Ed's world. I see now that I've carefully, if inadvertently, taught him it's okay to think for me. And now that I'm trying to think for myself, it's like I've broken all the rules of the game. Underneath all his wrath, he's probably just as lost as I am."

She had tried to be conciliatory last night. When he had boiled over about her determination to follow through with the Trevor Project, she had followed him into the bathroom and had stood behind him as he leaned over the sink. She had wrapped her arms around his middle and felt him tense up. "Helping someone else doesn't mean that I'm against you or your career, Ed. Believe it or not, I've taken your need to preserve your image into consideration in choosing to volunteer in the way that I have. I'm not going to be out there with a microphone and a camera. In fact, I'm going to be behind a computer in a little cubbyhole where no one will even see me except a handful of other volunteers and counselors. I just want to help these young people who have to face the constant cruelty that's spewed at them almost every day."

She waited for Ed's response, but he had continued the thorough cleansing he was giving his incisors and then had spat. As he straightened up, he had removed her arms from around his waist, had gargled and had spat again.

"Ed, please listen. This is important to me. And I want you to know why it's important, so that you can understand why I need to do this." Ed hadn't turned around but had continued to look at her reflection as she spoke.

"So talk."

That hadn't been the encouragement she had hoped for, but she had taken what she could get. "It comes from everywhere in their lives, Ed, this cruelty. They get it at school, at church, even in their own homes. Many of these kids don't have anywhere else to turn, and I can't stand the idea of their being so alone. If I can be there when they turn to the Trevor Project, then that's where I'm going to be. I want to be a beacon of hope for them. We all need hope, Ed. I need hope. I need to see that you can respect what is important to me — just as I'm trying to respect what's important to you."

"Tammy," Ed had finally turned around to face her and had slowly pointed a finger at her chest, "you're asking me to respect a lifestyle that I just cannot condone. And I won't. And I would appreciate it if *you* would understand that that's what's important to *me*."

Some overexcited preschoolers came whirling around the end of an aisle just then and ran straight into Tammy, bringing her back from the unpleasantness of last night's argument.

"Ed wants nothing to do with what I consider a call on my life, Marcie. I'm not even sure he really wants anything to do with me anymore."

Marcie pulled a hanger off the rack and held a cardigan up for Tammy's approval. "So you're still sure you want to do this?"

"No, on the sweater. But yes, on the Trevor Project."

Marcie put it back and continued rifling through scores of other choices while Tammy leaned against a nearby clothes rack.

"You know, I haven't gotten here overnight. But now that I've come this far, I realize I can only be happy if I'm true to myself. I've never shied away from a just cause, or from doing what's right. It's just that Ed and I were usually in agreement as to what 'right' was. If I cave to Ed's wishes on this, I'll be losing much more than just my aspirations. I'll lose my integrity."

Marcie affectionately patted Tammy's arm, "And that's not something you can afford to lose."

"I know. And I also know I can't really fix any of this, but I want to bring my 'grain of sand to God's building site.' I read that once in a Joyce Hollyday book[17], and it's an image that has lived with me ever since. And I do believe that our efforts to bring acceptance into this world are part of God's building plan. I know I don't have any magic or anything. But I want to try."

Marcie smiled at Tammy's courage. "The fact that you're even willing to try will speak volumes to those whose lives you touch."

"Well, it's certainly speaking volumes to Ed right now."

She and Ed were growing further and further apart. She knew it. She felt it. It seemed to her that whenever they were together these days, they were arguing about something, and it was always her fault. "He still blames me for all those comments that Pam and Bella made on TV. He just won't let go of it."

"And he still won't believe you? That you didn't say or do anything that night?"

"No, it's as if he's decided that I'm a liability now rather than an asset, and you know his black-and-white thinking. He doesn't give any credence at all to anything I say any more, since a liability isn't to be trusted, you know." Tammy gave an angry little flick of her hair and focused intently for a while on flipping through the sweaters on the rack in front of her, using more force than was necessary to shoot the hangers along the rod one after the other — not really seeing the sweaters at all. "It's just so infuriating!" She looked up at Marcie, indignant tears shimmering in her eyes. "How could he possibly believe that simpering, conniving, sorry excuse of a journalist over me, his wife of twenty-two years? I mean, he *knows* what she did with his comments last September, twisting them to say way more than he meant. Why can't he give *me* the same benefit of the doubt?"

Marcie's heart broke at the forlorn look that she saw taking up residence now on her friend's face. "I'm so sorry, Tammy."

"Me too." Tammy clutched a hunter green Audrey sweater close to her chest, hanger and all, and sighed. "I guess it's really true that you can't change a mind that doesn't want to be changed, even when someone believes something about you that you know is not true. Their perception is their reality, no matter the truth — or what you say or do. If Ed chooses to believe my involvement in Trevor threatens him, or our marriage, there may be nothing I can say to change his mind. I guess I just never really believed it would come to this."

A woman with her arms full came around the large rack they had been browsing. "Excuse me, ladies. I'm just going to look over here." And with that, she squeezed past them, thumbing through every single item, just a few feet away.

Tammy temporarily suspended her search and rested her hand on the row of hangers. "I feel like I'm living someone else's life, Marcie."

Marcie met Tammy's eye. "You know, Tammy, you *are* living a different life now. You've learned that you can trust what your inner self is telling you. And you no longer rely solely on external approval. You're thinking for yourself. You've found a cause you believe in. You've found your voice. And you're negotiating a hard place in your marriage. You have grown and changed. And our counselor explained to us that when one member of a family changes, everyone in the family must change also. It's just that we can't predict or control how any of the others are going to change. Will they grow along with you? Will they grow in a different direction? Or will they choose not to grow at all?"

"Thanks, Marcie. But that's not much of a consolation given Ed's attitude so far. I'm afraid I'm gonna be stuck with door number three."

"Maybe so, but you never can tell. When Pat and I realized that the silence we thought was protecting Jamie was really protecting us, we changed — we came out as parents. We began to publicly affirm Jamie in his sexual orientation and to address bigotry whenever, and however, it presented itself. And then Jamie began to change. He became less moody and sullen. He no longer hid out at home. And he began to stand up taller and to handle the taunts and snide remarks without taking them personally. All because we had shown him that we loved and valued him in his totality."

"That's really wonderful, Marcie, but I don't see that kind of change happening in my family. I'm just trying to come out as a friend and supporter, which is not that big a risk. And yet, my morality has been questioned, and I've certainly gotten my share of judgment."

"There's always that risk when you speak up for social justice. But then, there are those, like Jo Brown, who just come out of nowhere and offer unexpected support. I just wish there were more people like her who had the courage to speak their minds. That's what it's gonna take for our society to stop vilifying gays and begin accepting the gifts they have to share and the service they want to give."

The woman sifting through a rack of discounted skirts searching for the perfect ensemble had not been far from them, and it was perfectly clear that she had overheard at least part of their conversation. She glanced at Marcie and then started a slow retreat. She gingerly touched a few more hangers as she made her way further away from them, careful not to draw any more attention to herself than was necessary.

Marcie noticed the woman's successful retreat and just smiled. *There it was again.*

Tammy settled on a sweater and they moved to the checkout, but as they stood in line, Marcie's phone rang. She held up a finger, mouthing the words, "Jamie's counselor," and excused herself to take the call and then phone Pat's office to coordinate a change in one of their family therapy sessions. Tammy's thoughts drifted once again to her own troubles. Ed's hard lines would be tough to soften, if they could be at all. *Why did she continue to give her opinions when they weren't wanted? Why did she ask him to support her hopes, which obviously contradicted his?* The temptation to be beaten down by his resistance was strong. But she was in too far. Tammy was vested now. She thought back to just four hours ago and how resolute she had been then. "Ed, we musn't focus on what our relationship has always been, but rather on what it is now. This is where we are, and this is what I need to do." These had been the words she had left him with this morning. Then she watched him leave, the taillights of his Escalade disappearing in the early morning darkness.

"Did you find everything you want?" the sales clerk asked, but didn't wait for Tammy to respond. Instead she immediately started removing the hangers and scanning the bar codes.

"Everything I want? Is that even possible?" The gal behind the register had no way of understanding Tammy's black humor.

Tammy pushed back her hood as she entered the building and held her ID card under the tiny laser of the key lock, listening to the soft click as the exterior door unlocked. The rain had mostly subsided, but even so, the February sky had remained dark. She had become accustomed to this new morning ritual. Three days a week she would take the girls to their schools early, dropping Kelly off first; then, Hannah. Kelly spent the extra time in the band hall, practicing. She really wanted to make the varsity band next year. And Hannah was a school safety patrol, so she had to be there early anyway. It was no real inconvenience for any of them. Even so, it would be nice when the twins received their driver's licenses over the summer.

As she entered the Trevor Project Call Center, Tammy was enveloped in the now familiar hum of soft one-sided conversations and the tapping of computer keyboards. This would be her first day flying solo — taking calls, or messages as it were, without a supervisor's watchful eyes monitoring the conversations. The past month had gone by quickly. Tammy, thinking herself rather worldly, had never considered herself a Pollyanna. But in the short month that she had been volunteering at Trevor, she had realized just how sheltered her life had been — how much innocence she still had to lose.

"Yes, Mrs. Sloan," the coordinator had told her during her initial interview back in mid-December. "Our phone volunteers answer calls from young people all over the U.S. who are struggling with a myriad of issues surrounding their sexual orientation — coming out, family and relationship troubles, bullying, depression, anxiety. You'll hear it all, I'm afraid."

"I'm sure that I will, but I'm prepared for it. When can I expect to start taking calls?" she had tentatively asked. She wanted to be accepted and was fearful that her age and station in life might preclude that acceptance. "I really believe in this," she added.

"I don't doubt that for a minute. Of course, you'll have to undergo extensive training, but I feel you will be able to handle live interaction with callers before too long. Let's have you start training on January tenth." They both stood, and she reached out to shake Tammy's hand, saying, "I admire your desire to help others, and that is something that we never take lightly here. When you're talking to someone in crisis, you may very well be their only hope. Sometimes even their last hope."

Tammy had thought she'd understood the desperation of someone in true crisis, until she began hearing these crises day after day. She would never forget her very first encounter. Her trainer, Anthony, had handed her a headset so that she could listen in to his calls. He said it was important for her to hear the voices calling in, so that when she transferred to the online messaging service, she wouldn't forget to "listen for the tone of voices" hidden behind their written words.

Tammy had barely gotten settled in that first day of training when Anthony's first call of the day had come through.

"I just can't see any way out." A girl's voice came from the other end of the line.

"I'm sure that whatever it is you're feeling right now seems too big to overcome, but maybe if we talk about it together for a while I can help. My name is Anthony, by the way. What's your name?"

"I'm Morgan. I guess it can't hurt to talk about it. That's why I called, right? So yeah, I don't know how to get past the fact that tonight — at the dinner table — my dad actually said that he wished I had never been born. He called it depraved and immoral that I chose to be gay. Chose it? Hel-lo? He even said that being this way will damn my soul and destroy my life."

Tammy had been paralyzed by this awful cruelty. How could a parent be so brutal with their own child? Until witnessing this devastating alternative, she hadn't realized just how blessed Jamie O'Dell was to have grown up in such a loving and supportive family environment. She thought she had understood until being invited to sit around the dinner table with Morgan's family.

"Unfortunately, things usually escalate around the holidays," she remembered Anthony telling her. "Additional seasonal stresses just pile onto what is already going on in many of these families. Not a very happy New Year for that kid."

As a TrevorChat counselor in training, Tammy had been exposed daily to the destruction that parents could inflict on their children, and she was pained deeply by each and every caller's sad story of rejection. Every day she listened as a multitude of different voices plaintively asked the same two questions: "Is it a choice? And can I change it?" The Trevor counselors proposed to questioning youth that, just like the color of their eyes, their sexuality was determined prior to their birth. They hoped to instill an understanding that they were God's creation just exactly the way they were, despite what they were hearing from others, especially from those whom they loved the most. Tammy often thought of that little girl, Morgan, imagining which pain she would choose to endure — that of a closeted life, or that of rejection?

As she continued toward her cubicle on the far side of the room, Tammy nodded greetings to several people with whom she had become friendly during her training. Cassandra was a large and imposing young woman with spiked hair and tattoos, but she had the gift of compassion. Tim was an older man who had lost his son to AIDS ten years ago. His ability to connect with family members was invaluable. Mary was their shift supervisor, the accredited social worker and single mother who managed their multicultural and multigenerational six-member team. She couldn't see Roberto or Amy, but she knew from the glowing lights of their cubicles on the other side that they were already taking calls. And then there was Father Blair, the Episcopal priest. He came every Monday, his day off from the church, eagerly serving a flock of lost sheep. Father Blair looked up and smiled as Tammy approached, and he winked as she dropped her purse onto the work station just opposite his.

"You ready to go, girl?"

Tammy turned with a start to see Mary's broad smile. Mary had followed her all the way to her desk and now stood there, holding a wireless headset in her sizable hands. She was at least twenty years younger than Tammy, but her age belied her maturity.

She had worked her way through college, earned her master's degree during night school, and was currently raising two young sons whose father had walked out on his young family when the youngest was just a newborn. Mary also had an older brother who was gay. He had killed himself when she was a teenager, and she had been the one to find him hanging from the clothes rod in his bedroom closet. Being born the son of an East Texas Baptist minister, a gay black man would have had many obstacles to climb. Unfortunately, Mary's brother had lost his footing early on, and his precarious climb toward adulthood had proven more treacherous than he could navigate. But his struggles against hate had inspired Mary's efforts to help others like him.

Tammy took the headset from Mary and adjusted it to fit over her thick auburn hair.

"Okay, you're on your own now." Mary's soulful voice crackled through the headphones. "Remember, I'm here if you need me."

Tammy nodded and smiled nervously at Father Blair as she continued to tuck in her hair. "Well, here I go," she mumbled to herself in order to calm her excited nerves. "This is it." She smoothed out her skirt, positioned the keyboard on her desk, adjusted the brightness of her screen. And waited.

Father Blair watched her anxious preparations. "You'll do just fine, Tammy." His entire face, plump and pink, crinkled into an ebullient smile. "I've got faith."

Tammy smiled back at him, appreciative of his kind words and encouragement. He didn't look like a priest. He wore his usual — jeans, Top Siders, and an open-collared shirt. His wiry hair sprung out around his headset in short silver spires. He actually had a disheveled look about him, maybe the same type of casual appeal that Jesus himself had possessed. She wondered what it must be like to attend his church. To have such a progressive minister, both in word and in deed, leading an entire congregation must be invigorating. After all, this was his day away from the church. But because his call was so strong, he chose to offer hope and acceptance, and maybe even some peace, to people who were struggling to accept themselves or their loved ones. And like Christ, he healed on his day off. He truly was an inspiration.

Bloop. Bloop. The two-tone alert brought her attention back to her computer screen. Her first young visitor shared an all too common feeling among questioning youth. Justin was only in the sixth grade. "I want to tell my parents, but I am afraid to because I

know what I am feeling is wrong. I don't want to hurt my
parents and have them be ashamed of me."

Tammy began typing her response immediately. "Justin, if I
can help you with only one thing, I hope that you will
begin to understand that you are not wrong for being you.
It may be difficult, and it may be painful at times, but
it is never wrong to live the truth."

Tammy wondered. How can we dare to denigrate the truth of
another human being's existence? For one's identity is exactly that —
the truth. A fact. A given. And it doesn't have to necessarily impinge
on another's truth. It's perfectly possible to have two disparate truths
traveling a parallel path. Tammy shook her head. If only we could
accept that in each other, there would be a lot less destructiveness in
the world.

Justin had decided to talk to his aunt. He felt close to her, and if
that went well he would have an ally when coming out to his parents.

"Promise to let me know how it goes, okay?"

"K. Thanks."

Father Blair had been watching Tammy's fingers feverishly click
against the keyboard and he looked at her, his white eyebrows raised in
question. She leaned back in her chair and gave him two thumbs up,
their beaming smiles mirroring each other.

Bloop. Bloop. This was Mandy, a high school senior. "I was afraid
to come right out and tell my mother, so I started out by
informing her that I had been reading up on current events
and such, including homosexuality. Well she interrupted
me before I could finish my sentence and told me not to
read that type of material anymore, and certainly not to
associate with or talk to anyone else about it because
she was afraid that I might 'turn gay' if I did. She
really thinks it is contagious, or something! WHAT DO I
DO NOW???"

"I know, Mandy. Unfortunately, Myths like that are
very common, and yet as we both know, they are also very
incorrect." Tammy's manicured nails pecked out a staccato beat as
she answered. "It's her ignorance that drives her fear more
than anything else. Most people are uncomfortable with
the extremism they see in caricatures on TV and in the
movies. But what she doesn't know is that there are gay

people already in her life leading such ordinary lives she doesn't even notice. Maybe it's her chiropractor or hairdresser, or her CPA or counselor. Let me suggest a few websites and books for you to check out which may help bridge the gap toward better understanding between you and your mother."

Mary's voice came through the headset over Tammy's ears. "How you doin'?"

"I'm okay, so far. Thanks, Mary. I'll let you know if I need something." Tammy continued her message to Mandy, and included the links to PLFAG, Rainbow Family Network, and the 24/7 number for Trevor Lifeline.

"Come visit us again if you have any questions after you've had a chance to look at what I've just sent you. Remember, Mandy, we are here for you."

Tammy felt a rush of excitement. She was really doing something meaningful. She had already helped two kids!

Her next call came from a parent. *Bloop. Bloop.*

"Last night my son told my husband and me that he is gay. He is only twelve. How can he know he is gay at such a young age? He is too young to think about having a family and about safety. What do we do?"

"First of all, I hope you can appreciate the courage it took to actually come out and tell you. A young person's desire to keep their sexuality to themselves is very strong, especially if they have any questions about your views on homosexuality. What is your son's name?"

"Ross."

Tammy looked down at her notes on the stages of sexual identity. "Ross has probably known he was different since he was 6-8 years old. Kids don't always know what it is that sets them apart from their peers, but they know they don't fit in."

"Can I really say this, Mary?" Tammy checked in and received a "You bet" almost immediately.

So Tammy proceeded. "Please refrain from wanting to talk him out of his feelings. If he has gotten this far, by telling you, they are real and should be respected. He may not experience any identity confusion if he feels love and support from his family. By opening up calm and honest conversations with Ross, you may be able to arm him with the emotional tools he will need whenever he faces any difficulty in the future."

"I'm afraid for him."

"I'm sure you are. And the best thing in the world you can do for him is to A) Learn everything you can about homosexuality; and B) support him, both privately and publicly." Tammy thought of Marcie as she wrote these words to the desperate mother on the other end of this connection. "All parents dream of happiness for their children. And you still can too. I recommend that you find a support group. PFLAG is a good one. I'll send you a link. Remember, by telling you, Ross demonstrated a great trust in you both. That alone speaks volumes about your family's relationship and possibility for happiness in the future."

By the time Tammy finished her conversation with Ross's mom, she was beat. The emotional energy it took to juggle calls, each of them pleas for help and understanding was astounding. Frequent break times were necessary in such a high-intensity work environment, and their lengths were typically determined by the length and gravity of the calls received. If each volunteer was indeed a lifeline to their callers, Mary was surely the lifeline to each of the volunteer counselors.

"Tammy?" Mary's voice materialized inside her headset. "Break time, girlfriend. We're putting you on a short leash since it's your first day on your own, okay?"

Bloop. Bloop. The ascending tone beeped in Tammy's ear again. "Okay, thanks, Mary. I'll sign off after this one that just came in." The fulfillment Tammy experienced in providing comfort, as small as it was, had her buzzing.

She picked up the next call and typed. "My name is Tammy, and I'm here to help you today."

"I'm afraid there's nothing anybody can do to help me." Tammy could almost hear the despondency in the words as they slowly popped up on her screen. "I'm beyond hope, or so says my dad, anyway."

"Don't ever give up hope, my friend. Do you mind my asking your name?"

"I'm Seth."

"Hi Seth. I'm really glad you called, and I'm here to listen to you. Can you tell me what happened to make you feel so bad?"

"My dad happened, that's what is wrong. He's been sending me to some anti-gay counselor and is threatening to kick me out of the house if I don't get my head on right."

Tammy had learned of conversion therapy like this in her training. Many families had turned to this intense, pseudo-therapy that purports to fix the gay person by turning him or her straight. But most mental-health associations had gone on record to say it was incredibly dangerous, especially for kids. In fact, Tammy had read in the training materials that the American Psychiatric Association had warned that the "potential risks of reparative therapy are great, including depression, anxiety and self-destructive behavior."[18]

"How old are you, Seth, and what made him decide to do that?" Tammy asked.

"I turned fifteen a few months ago and my dad is kind of a high profile person you could say." Seth's words stopped appearing on Tammy's screen. Maybe he was summoning the courage to continue? Tammy waited on Seth and made eye contact with Father Blair across from her, unconsciously seeking guidance from her mentor. Then Seth's words began again. "I don't exactly know where to start. So okay I've been in scouts since kindergarten and I have known Jeremy since about third grade when he joined our troop. Well I've been working on my Eagle Project for the last several months and he's been helping me. I'll be a sophomore next year and wanted to have it all done before then." Once again, he hesitated briefly before the characters lit up Tammy's screen. "We've always been best friends but recently we told each other how we feel about each other." Then Seth stopped typing. Over a minute went by.

"It's okay, Seth. you can trust me, I promise."

"Well," he continued after a long silence, "It turns out that some of the other guys heard us talking. Everyone wondered, you know, but they never really knew for sure until they heard me and Jeremy talking that night. So of course one guy tells another guy who tells another guy and then some of the parents go to the troop leader. And now I'm being

thrown out of scouts because of everything. My dad is
pissed because I've brought shame to the family."

This was proving to be the most intense call that Tammy had
fielded. She took a deep breath and began typing her response. "Seth,
I want you to remember that this is just his opinion, as
hurtful as it is. You have done nothing other than be
true to who you are, and I hope we can work together to
help your family accept this new truth."

"Fat chance of that happening!!!" And Seth painfully
recounted his father's initial reaction to the news: "He blames Jeremy.
He thinks Jeremy made me gay and that he (Dad) can make
me straight. He got me transferred out of all the classes
we had together and won't let me talk with him at all.
At school. On the phone. Nowhere. He thinks keeping us
separated will make me stop feeling like I do."

Tammy blanched simply reading about the father's diatribe and had
trouble imagining herself in Seth's position, having to face his father in
his tirade. Seth continued typing before Tammy could respond.

"He wants to put a stop to it now. That's why he's been
sending me to that crazy shrink. If he only knew the kind
of stuff that guy says."

"What kind of stuff does he say, Seth?" Tammy hurt so
deeply for this poor kid.

"Well he says things like it's usually a bad relationship
with the dad that makes a kid gay."

"Seth, I find that general statements like that are
generally untrue. I know a young man who has a wonderful
relationship with his father and always has. Yet he knew
he was gay when he was five."

Tammy had learned of therapists who had adopted this theory that
although the influence of mothers in the developmental and adaptive
process is given its importance, the more compelling role in determining
a boy's subsequent homosexuality is that of an inadequate father-son
relationship. This theme is then corroborated, through questionable
tactics and intense counseling, and becomes a salient theme in reparative
therapy. "Let's blame somebody" and "Let's fix it" — the common
battle cries of ultra-conservative camps.

"That's how I've felt too," typed Seth. "I don't ever remember feeling any different than I do now. It's just that my dad used to love me and now he hates me."

"I don't think he hates you, Seth. I think he truly believes that he is acting out of care and concern for your well-being."

"So you're taking up for him now???" She could hear his shouts. "He refuses to see me for who I am and he hates who I am so much that he sent me to this quack!"

"No, no, no. Hold on a minute, Seth." Tammy typed as quickly as she could. "Hear me out, okay? Many times, when a family member is upset by a loved one's coming out, they react by wanting to 'fix' the problem. What they don't realize is that it isn't the gay person who needs 'fixing'. It is their attitude toward their loved one that needs the adjustment." Tammy's fingers furiously tried to keep up with her thoughts. "So when parents block access to gay friends, or force reparative therapy, they believe they are acting out of care and concern and don't realize how hurtful it is to everyone involved. Your dad still loves you, but he is afraid of this new picture of you he has created in his mind, and therefore he wants you to go back to the Seth he thought he knew, and was comfortable with."

"Well fuck it!!! I can't go back because I was the same back then too." Seth's agitation had obviously increased. "He's never known me and he never will. What am I supposed to do? He says if I don't change he will disown me. If he ever catches me with Jeremy or anyone else like that he will kick me out of the house. But don't you see?? I can't change. Now what am I supposed to do with that??"

Bloop. Bloop. The descending tones signaled the connection had been broken. And with that, the call ended.

It isn't the action of bad people that we remember, but the inactions of good people.
— Martin Luther King, Jr.

Chapter 18

CHALLENGE TO CHANGE

T ammy turned on the coffee maker and waited for their six cups of morning salvation to pour through. She had to stand on her tiptoes in order to peer out the kitchen window. "Will you get it finished today?" The deer stand they had been building looked like one of the creatures from *Star Wars*, boxy body set atop long spindly legs. Ed and Michael would perch high above their prey, hidden from view and armed with lethal weapons, to bring down their blameless targets. *And this was sport?* She would never understand the pleasure they received from carefully and methodically gunning down an innocent creature.

"I think we should." Ed was at the table reading the paper. "But it depends on how late Michael sleeps in this morning. All that's left is building the interior shooting shelves." Although the deer season had ended in early January, Ed and Michael had extended their father-and-son season by taking on this project together.

The coffee was almost ready, the gurgling of the machine giving in to the last whines of hot steam being pushed through the filter. A winter wind was whipping the branches of the great oaks outside, and she could feel the cold morning air seeping through the windowsill. February always seemed to be the coldest month of the year. She could hear her wind chimes playing melodies with their long cylindrical tubes. There was something delicious about enjoying a winter morning and a cup of freshly brewed coffee. And she felt a smile creep up onto her face.

"Good God!" Ed snapped the newspaper in his hands, nearly tearing it in half.

"What in the world?" Turning to see what was wrong, Tammy spilled the coffee, nearly the entire carafe, all over the counter.

"The Boy Scouts have really done it now. They voted to allow openly gay scouts.[19]"

"Well, it's about time." She instantly thought of Seth, as she began sopping up the puddle of coffee before it crept off the counter and onto the floor. *Maybe this decision would make things easier for him at home and with his friends. One could only hope.* She poured what was left into her mug and started another pot for Ed.

He lowered the paper and peered at her, looking over the rim of his readers. "I hate to think what the newest badge will be about."

"Oh for heaven's sake, Ed." Tammy placed his eggs and toast on the table and then pulled out her chair to sit next to him. She knew all this was hitting him hard. Scouting had played a big part in Ed's formative years, and he still held the ideals of scouting to be the measure of the man. In high school, as a scout who had best exemplified living the Scout Oath and Law in his daily life, Ed was inducted into the Order of the Arrow — a prestigious honor revered among scouts and their leaders for its observance of one's service and brotherhood. She had seen pictures of him at the Brotherhood ceremony — so handsome in that distinctive khaki uniform adorned with his new pocket flag insignia and OA sash. But this morning, wearing his bathrobe and slippers, his thick black hair sticking out at odd angles all around his face, he looked quite vulnerable and not at all dignified.

"Tam, parents have the exclusive right to raise the issues of sex with their children." He folded the paper and put it on the table. "But only when they think it's best for their child and their family, and not when some openly gay boys bring it up around a campfire." He buttered his toast and took a healthy-sized bite off one corner.

She watched him chew, his cheeks bulging. "And you think straight boys don't talk about their girlfriends while on campouts, Ed? Pul-leese!" She had sounded so much like Kelly it was alarming. Over the last six weeks she had talked with so many teenagers through the Trevor

Project that their youthful expressions had apparently rubbed off on her. "Would you pass the jam?"

He looked at her in disbelief. "Tam, this is serious stuff. Even the local chairman of the Hill Country District has resigned over it. He says he is considering creating another character-building group for good young men as a positive alternative."

"Well good for him. But I shudder to think what kind of character he plans to instill in any boys who enroll in his program." And she pointed at the jar beside him. "The jam, Ed?"

"Mmm." He scooted the jar to within her reach with one hand as he picked up his empty mug with the other. His mouth was full so he asked his question with raised eyebrows.

"It's almost ready. I spilled the first pot when you yelled out."

"Just look around you." He swallowed, his head turning to follow her as she got up to check on his coffee. "The world is going out of control because everyone is becoming more accepting of immoral lifestyles. No rules. No structure. Look around, Tam. The further we get from morals and the Bible, the more disasters and heartache. It's a sad day."

Tammy made a face, standing at the coffee maker with her back turned to Ed. He was referring to a statement that had been made on the news last night. Anti-gay pundits had related recent weather-related trends, both drought and floods, and the rash of natural disasters on the developing acceptance of same-sex issues across the country. The interview they had seen was with John McTernan, the writer of a blog on the "cutting edge of prophetic events." According to him, Super Storm Sandy and the devastating tornadoes in Oklahoma were visible signs of God's wrath regarding wickedness — all of it blamed on the LGBT community and their supporters. She couldn't help but picture Dorothy's house being dropped on the striped stockings and ruby slippers of fractious conservatives like McTernan. It would be humorous if it weren't so appalling. Did people really believe that stuff? Did Ed?

The flip side to that story had been a report on a tweet by Maya Angelou: *It is sad but true that sometimes we need a tragedy to help us to see how human we are and how we are more alike than we are different. The unspeakable devastation in Oklahoma has brought human goodness to the fore.*

Men and women from Kansas, from Missouri, from Arkansas, even from New York City, have rushed to offer themselves as aid to the stricken Oklahomans. I sit watching the television and am proud of how we are able to sympathize with each other and saddened that the only way we come to that understanding is when a tragedy affects us. I have not seen one person ask if the injured were black, or white, or Jewish or Muslim or gay or straight. Don't you wish we could think of each other in kinder ways all the time?

"Well, Ed, I believe that if the Boy Scouts are really built upon the values of faith and family like you've always said, then they have nothing to worry about by creating a more inclusive organization." Tammy filled his mug to the top, silently wishing that Ms. Angelou would consider taking over the Boy Scouts of America. "I'm just glad that they'll now be serving *all* kids."

Ed's face tightened, and he took a long, scalding swallow of his coffee, regretting having started this conversation in the first place. The last thing he had intended was to turn this into an invitation for Tammy to go off on him. He didn't want any more of her preaching. Any more sob stories. And he certainly didn't want to give her the wrong idea — that he was in some way supporting this reckless rebellion of hers which, in fact, was causing nothing but problems for his career and consternation in their marriage.

"What's for breakfast?" Hannah staggered into the kitchen, her tangled hair as rumpled as her pajamas.

"Hey, dew drop!" Ed wiped his mouth and reached out to pick her up. His countenance instantly relaxed with gratitude for his younger daughter's timely arrival.

"But I'm your cupcake, Daddy."

Ed gathered her into his arms. Her long and lanky legs resembled those of a pony and already predicted that she would inherit her father's height. Any other ten-and-a-half-year-old would be too big to sit in their father's lap, but Ed's large frame was more than accommodating.

Tammy loved watching Ed show their youngest the physical affection that had already become difficult for him with both Kelly and Michael.

"Today is Olivia's birthday party. It's a boy/girl party. I've never been to one."

"Really? Do you think it will be different?" Ed tried to smooth out her dark waves.

"Not for me. But some of the girls like some of the boys. You know. They're 'goin' out' and everything." She yawned, a wide, open-mouthed, gaping yawn. "But I don't like any of them. They're immature. Just 'cause some of the girls like 'em doesn't mean I have to."

"Of course it doesn't." Ed smiled and kissed the top of her head in dismissal so he could get back to his eggs before they got cold.

Tammy held her mug with both hands, inhaling its buttery hazelnut smell. *Hannah sounded like Kelly too.* She was growing up so fast. "But it will be fun to go to a new kind of party, won't it?"

"Oh, sure. I can't wait." She poured herself a bowl of Kix. No milk. No spoon. Just the dry cereal that she began eating one little crunchy bite at a time. "I wanna see if anyone acts stupid or anything."

Tammy just shook her head, and Hannah smiled. No longer clouded from sleepiness, her eyes shone with an endearing mischievousness.

"I'm gonna go watch TV." And she took her bowl of cereal into the den to eat in front of a *Wizards of Waverly* rerun. It was Hannah's favorite show, focusing on a typical family. The Russos — mom, dad and their three kids — all appeared to live normal lives. But what their friends didn't know was that the kids were actually wizards in training, their dad a former top-notch wizard.

Apparently, there could be only one Family Wizard per generation. The others would, at some point, end up losing their powers and become mortals, so the three teenage siblings were in constant competition to see which of them would ultimately keep their powers forever. Because of this, the dad was on a continual quest to teach his children responsible use of their powers; but also, he was concerned that they not become dependent on their magic, as two of them would at some point have to learn a new way of living. It wasn't clear to Tammy why the dad, Jerry, no longer held any magical powers of his own. Did his marriage to Theresa, a mortal, force him to relinquish his powers, or had he lost his abilities long ago to a sibling of his own? Either way, because they lived in a mortal world, the Russo family was required to keep the existence of their wizardry a secret. There was a Wizard Council which monitored such things.

"Hmmm," Tammy smiled at a sudden insight. There were a number of similarities between Hannah's show and what was going on with the scouts.

The Russo children knew that they were different in some ways from other children, but they had learned from the governing bodies that they had to keep that difference a secret. Ditto any gays who happened to be in scouting — up to this point anyway. And the Russos weren't the only magical beings in Waverly. One of the daughters was dating a werewolf, for heaven's sake. There were probably closeted wizards throughout their fictional community, and everyone knew there were large numbers of undisclosed gay scouts in dens and troops all across the country. What good did keeping them a secret, or excluding them altogether, do anyone? Simply recognizing gays, or wizards, didn't make either of them dangerous. Nor did continuing to keep their identities a secret make them disappear.

Hmmm. Lots of similarities all right.

Once again she thought of that boy, Seth. He had been invading her thoughts for several weeks now. She was worried about him, and she couldn't get his father's barbaric treatment of him out of her mind. How different it might have been for Seth if his dad had been more like Mr. Russo. Jerry Russo wasn't threatened by his children's difference, even though he no longer had any magic powers of his own. He honored their differences and mentored them, preparing them to seamlessly adapt to the mortal world in which they lived. Unfortunately, their true identities were forever closeted. *Why do we do this to ourselves and to one another? And even more disturbing, why do we believe that it is okay?*

The banging sound was coming from outside. Ed and Michael had worked steadily through the afternoon on their deer blind. Ed had wanted to build it here at the house, then transfer it over to the lease with Bill Pritchett's pickup. It was nice to see them spending so much time together, but Tammy was having a difficult time concentrating, so she shut the door of her study to keep their hammering from echoing up the long hallway. *Maybe that would help.* She sat at her desk. Her stationery was still blank. Her pen was still lying there on the burled oak veneer. She picked it up but then put it down again, realizing that she'd been tapping to the rhythm of the hammer that was still sounding through the closed door.

The last six weeks had been exhilarating, yet wrought with anxiety. Her work at Trevor was rewarding, and the new friends she had made, people she would never have encountered anywhere else, were becoming very dear to her. But she could not shake the concern, and the responsibility she felt, with regard to Seth and the troubling conversation they had shared. Other than his combustible home life, she knew so little about him. Nevertheless, he crept into her activities during the day and filled her thoughts as she tried to sleep. *Could I have done more to help him? Did I make things even worse? What is happening in his home right now?* She had rewound their conversation numerous times, but to no avail. She never came up with an answer that would quell the irresoluteness she felt.

The minute that he had terminated the call that morning, Tammy had gone to the break room.

"Wow, your last call must have been a tough one." Father Blair patted the seat next to him, and Tammy gratefully plopped down. Tim was sitting opposite them on the other couch.

"Tell me about it," Tammy began. "I've been talking with a fifteen-year-old who is going to be kicked out of his house if he doesn't conform to his father's way of thinking. They sent him to a conversion therapist." She leaned back and crossed her legs, resting one foot upon the large square table between the two couches. "And I thought I was prepared to hear all of the hate that families spew at their kids out there."

"We're never completely prepared for all that we witness here, Tammy." Father Blair patted her hand. "Rejection by one's family for any reason causes deep-seated pain and problems for anyone, but the impact on those struggling with their sexuality is monumental. They're being rejected for who they are, not just what they've done, and the damage to young psyches is catastrophic. Unfortunately, we get to hear way too much of that sort of thing way too often here."

Tammy had read the statistics in her training materials. Those who faced strong rejection were eight times more likely to commit suicide, nearly six times as likely to report high levels of depression, and more than three times as likely to use illegal drugs as those who were accepted or only mildly rejected by their parents.[20]

"Ah, another instance of 'pray the gay away.'" Tim was older than the rest of them. He was a spindly man with long arms and legs and an unsteady gait. His perpetual attire of faded jeans and worn boots was in keeping with his weathered face and gnarled hands — and the frayed shirt collars and threadbare cuffs that dressed them. You could tell, just looking at him, that life had been hard. He was still married to Beth, but the death of their son had put a strain on the marriage from which they had not yet fully emerged. He had felt alone in his grief, his wife blaming him as she did for their son's death, and he had found a much-needed salve in comforting others. Not at all what one would expect from this crusty old cowpoke. "Have they used any aversive treatments on the poor kid yet?"

"Not that I know of. It sounds like the counselor is just messing with his mind right now." Tammy rested her head against the back of the couch. "It just makes me sick."

They all knew what this type of counseling could turn into. Conversion therapy relied on reconditioning through social skills training, psychoanalytic therapy, and spiritual interventions, such as prayer, support, and group pressure.[21] But as misdirected as this approach was, it often escalated into something even more dangerous, a form of operant conditioning called aversion therapy.[22] Tammy had heard of "therapists" administering nausea-inducing drugs and even applying electric shock to the hands and genitals of a gay individual as they showed him or her homoerotic stimuli. Supposedly, the patient would, consequently, associate extreme discomfort with homosexuality and would give up homoerotic behavior.

"How did we ever get so screwed up?" Tim was always rather matter-of-fact with his opinions, but his leathered face carried a pallor now, and his gray eyes took on a haunted look. "You know, I experienced two losses when my son died. The loss of a future with him in it and all the dreams we had around that, but also the loss of the present and any opportunity we had to fix our past. We lost so much time together while he was still living because he thought I wouldn't understand or accept who he was. All because I was too comfortable with my own take on things. I was an intolerant SOB." He swallowed hard. "I found fault with just about any group that was different from me — the blacks, the Hispanics, the guys on welfare, and the liberals who put them there. But mostly, I condemned the gays. I actually referred to them as 'those faggots' more than once in his presence. Told him I would be embarrassed to be the father of a gay son. I never would of said those things if I'd of known."

Tim's voice cracked with emotion. His eyes turned glassy. His toughened exterior belied the tenderness which lay underneath. "One more week. It'll be ten years in one more week. You look back and you wonder where'd the time go." He picked at the knee of his jeans.

Tammy's mind shot instantly to Ed. *Would there be something one day that would trigger a softening in him, a desire to understand and accept? Or would he be faced to live with regrets over choices he made — or refused to make? Would the door in his heart eventually open, or remained closed?*

Tim's change of heart had come about for the same reason that millions of others have taken a fresh look at this issue — someone close to him had come out as being gay. In Tim's case, it was his adult son, Will, as he was battling AIDS. And for Tim, the previously theoretical issue, which now involved his son, had been metamorphosed. He could no longer view 'the gay issue' through the lens of abstract thinking and judgment. It had become intensely personal. He now knew himself to be the father of a gay son who was dying, and he was not embarrassed at all. He was too busy passionately and fiercely loving him.

"Of course I would give anything to have him back now, but I would give just as much to have all those lost years of his living, when we were estranged through our dishonesty with each other."

Mary had shuffled into the room, her large frame instantly filling the area with her energy. "Tim, my love, you're up. Cassie needs to come sit for a while. Shoo, now."

Tim sniffed loudly and wiped his nose with the back of his wrinkled hand. He slapped both knees and stood, stretching his back in a long sinewy arch. He then dipped his head toward Tammy as he left the room. Mary settled into the place on the couch he had vacated. Her bright eyes usually bounced out of her sable complexion, as bright stars twinkle in a night sky. But now they were dimmed. "Tammy, I reviewed the transcript of your call. You did as good as you could. That poor boy is just strugglin'." She smoothed the wrinkles of her voluminous skirt. "So his daddy is some muckety-muck who appears to be more concerned with his career than the feelings of his own son." She shook her head and rolled her soft brown eyes to emphasize her disdain.

"I don't know what bothers me the most. His dad forcing him to go to that counselor or his threats to kick him out." Tammy rolled her neck and massaged her shoulders. She hadn't realized how tense they'd become.

"Counselor, my shoe!" Mary spat. Her face drew up as if she'd just bitten into an unripe persimmon. "No, I pray he can have a 'come to Jesus' talk with his daddy. Problem is, Daddy's actin' like he is Jesus himself — come to judge the quick and the dead." Once again, Mary's head shook, her beaded cornrows knocking against the sides of her rounded cheekbones. "All this because that boy desires a relationship with someone his daddy doesn't approve of."

"What relationship?" Tammy gestured into the empty air with her hand. "All they did was talk, and as I remember, one of the tenets of scouting is honesty. And it sounds like all Seth and Jeremy have done was to talk honestly with each other about their feelings, nothing more. Is that a crime?"

"Well, a big problem is that the majority of those complaining about the whole Boy Scout thing assume their own children are all straight." Cassandra had just walked into the room. She filled her mug with coffee and began aggressively stirring in the sweetener. "Another problem is that they think they know everything — they give you this big plastic smile and tell you you're going to hell. First, they can't see that sexuality is not a choice, nor a preference. No one wakes up one day and says, 'Hmm. I think I'll be gay today.'" She poked a finger into her cheek and looked toward the ceiling pretending to deliberate some heady thought. "'Or now that I think about it, maybe I'll be straight!'"

As a child, Cassandra had been the victim of intense bullying from her peers, as well as harassment from some adults. On one occasion, a seventh-grade teacher had separated her name from all the others when taking attendance. 'I'll call out all the girls, then the boys. And then we'll check for Cassandra.' Everyone had laughed. Cassandra had begun cutting herself and had attempted suicide twice. She grew up in a family who had taught Sunday school. She had gone to church every Wednesday and Sunday. But she found no solace there. The grace they talked about would not extend to her, unless the mansion He had prepared included an ample closet.[23]

"Second, they act like it's contagious ... and third, they act like all gay kids are sex fiends. False, false, and false. Besides, if their kids act as ugly as their parents do, I doubt any gay scouts will be goin' after those closed-minded bigots."

Mary made a face at Cassandra, then looked at Tammy. "Some do believe it's a crime, dear." She folded her arms across her ample bosom. "But the real criminals are the parents who treat their children like insubordinate dogs in need of obedience training. And then, when the training doesn't work, they kick 'em to the curb."

Tammy squeezed her eyes shut at the memories of that day, a vain attempt to keep the tears from spilling down her face. Slowly, she became aware again of the loud hammering, this time close by. The decibels had definitely increased. She opened her eyes and was stunned to see Ed standing in the doorway to her study.

"Were you asleep?" He could tell he had startled her.

"No. You're not building that thing in the house now, are you?"

"Of course not. I just knocked." Ed declared, although he still held the hammer in his hand. "What are you doing?" He looked around. It was unusual for Tammy to lock herself away like this.

"Oh, I'm just trying to relax before I pick up Hannah from the party." *What an understatement*, she thought. She needed more than relaxation — she needed to de-stress. She was undeniably edgy, jumping like that when all he did was knock on the door.

"Well, Pritchett is on his way, and Michael and I are going to take the new blind out to the lease. I just wanted to let you know we'll be home before suppertime."

Tammy had not shared her concerns with Ed. She had learned that the less they talked about her involvement with the Trevor Project, the better. They had established a *de facto* "don't ask, don't tell" policy of their own, and because of that, they had achieved a fragile rapprochement of sorts that she didn't want to shake up. Besides, she certainly didn't want to give him any reason to argue that she should quit. She knew that if she let on how much Seth's situation had disturbed her, he would hear it as a complaint, and his "fix it" mode would kick in. He would try to get her to stop volunteering there. But all their talk about the Scouts that morning had once again brought Seth back to the forefront of her mind, and she needed to process that with someone.

After Ed left, she called Marcie. She needed a lift.

"Of course I heard. Jamie is ecstatic. He's been planning to start work on his Eagle next year, but was afraid that getting approval for his project would prompt his being thrown out of the troop. Now, as long as he waits until everything goes into effect, he won't have to worry about that."

"As you could predict, Ed thinks it's a sad day." Tammy did her best to imitate Ed's booming voice, 'They're throwing away a hundred years of tradition, all in the name of political correctness.'"

Marcie laughed at her imitation. "Well, I think the greater error would be such a wonderful organization turning away a child who wants their guidance and direction. It can only be a good thing whenever everyone is given a fair chance in life. Equal opportunities. Without prejudice."

"I'm right there with you. I just hope they can embrace this decision and start moving on." Tammy breathed heavily. "All this hoo-hah in the news today about the Scouts has really made me think about that kid that I talked with a couple of weeks ago. You know, the boy I told you about? His whole life blew up because of an incident with other scouts."

"I remember." Marcie waited a minute; but when Tammy didn't continue, she asked, "And you're still carrying him aren't you? I'll bet this isn't the first time you've thought of him since then."

"You know me well, Marcie. Guilty as charged. He enters my thoughts several times a day. Every day. I can't seem to get him out of my mind. He sounded so alone and so helpless. So desperate. And it just kills me that I don't have any way to reach him to make sure he's okay. That I can't help him. Can't give him hope. Can't help him see that it won't always be this way."

"You're such an empath, Tammy, and that's what makes you such a beautiful person. But you're gonna have to learn to detach if you don't want to burn out — if you want to remain an effective listener."

"I know. If only I knew there was someone else out there who was giving him that hope. Giving him the love that he needs, then maybe ..." Tammy's voice trailed off into silence.

"Maybe there is. Maybe his mother is supportive. Or an aunt, or a grandparent, or even a teacher. There are a lot of adults in most kids' lives, and maybe someone out there has seen his distress and is reaching out."

"I sure hope so. That would make this a lot easier."

"Then believe it, or at least believe in the possibility of it. And while you're at it, think about the fact that God loves him even more than you do. Perhaps you could practice placing him in God's hands. That's how I turn over things that are too big for me to handle."

"Hmmm," Tammy smiled to herself. "You're absolutely right, Marcie. Thanks so much. I can and will pray for him, and I'd appreciate it if you would too."

"Of course I will. And you know, something else just occurred to me. As much as it hurt that he hung up still angry and hurting, take it as a good sign that he reached out to you at all. It's a huge step that he called into Trevor. You know what they say, 'Asking for help is the hardest thing we do.' Hopefully he'll continue to reach out. And who knows, maybe this new development with the Scouts will give his friends and family new encouragement to accept and support him. Today's news could be really good for him."

"You're right. I have to look at this differently. It's usually so easy for me to find the positive in a situation, but something about that kid has just stuck with me." Tammy visualized what Seth must look like. She saw him as a ginger, tall and thin, with pale skin and freckles. Somehow that made him seem more vulnerable.

So you're saying there are two kinds of marriage — the full marriage,
then this sort of skim milk version?
— Justice Ruth Bader Ginsburg, SCOTUS

Chapter 19

SPEAKING THE TRUTH

There was a gentle bustle at the Land Office as the afternoon drew to its close. Holly moved quietly, clearing her desk in preparation for another long day tomorrow. They were nearing the deadline on the Desalination Proposal and there was still a great deal of work to be done. Years of drought had placed a tremendous strain on the state's water supply, and the increased demand of a burgeoning population was rapidly depleting the Edwards Aquifer, once the source of abundant spring water for the whole of the Texas Hill Country. Water, and how to come by more of it, was a hot topic. The entire state was living just one step away from crisis. Ironically, at the same time that anxieties about serious water shortages were escalating, Texas was sitting on a massive amount of brackish groundwater. Far less salty than the ocean, it was still too salty to drink, and therefore, completely useless in the state's efforts to mitigate the effects of the drought.

Ed Sloan, extremely aware of the fierce competition he would be facing in the next election, had needed something big to cement a victory. And desalination had fit the bill. Just as Ed thirsted for positive PR and votes, the residents and businesses along I-35, between Austin and San Antonio, thirsted for water. And bringing water to the Texas Economic Miracle would just about ice his re-election. "Texas may be short on water, but we're not short on innovation!" Ed's quote had made it to the cover of *Texas Highways* magazine and would be on the coversheet of the proposals which would be sitting on every Texas lawmaker's desk next week. Desalination would be a game-changer, a commonsense fix for the Texas water crisis, and Holly had been instrumental in the successful marketing of this plan from day one. Things looked very promising.

Ed lumbered out of his office, his jacket draped over his arm. "I'm fixin' to leave for the day, folks. But before I go, I want y'all to know I've had Mary Anne make reservations for all of us at Truluck's. We need to celebrate all our good work and the completion of the Desal Proposal. Two weeks from Friday at seven-thirty!" Ed leaned over to punch the elevator button. "And Trey, bring the wife." Having now decreed the celebration, Ed Sloan promptly entered the elevator and disappeared.

Their desks faced each other and Trey still sat at his, reports on hydrology and geology stacked high. "Ye-ess!" Trey checked his calendar for any conflicts and then pumped his fist. "Yep, that Friday's all clear for me. I'll ask Becky to get a sitter so she can join us. Whadda ya say?"

Afternoon shadows stretched across the polished oak floor as outside the sun hung lazily on the horizon, its beams bursting into pink, orange, and purple hues, leaving the clouds awash in color. The slant beams of sunlight that made their way into the office, though, retained their golden color, striping everything in the room.

"I wish I could, Trey, but I've already got plans." That Friday would be April 4, and Holly and Anne had made it a point to go out together on the fourth of every month to celebrate another anniversary. They had started so late in life they wanted to celebrate as many anniversaries as they could, and their monthly observations had become a precious tradition.

"Come on, Holly, this has been a big project, and I think we deserve a celebration the minute it's over. And Ed's gonna treat!" Truth be told, Trey didn't relish the idea of an evening alone with Ed Sloan, but it would be bad form not to accept his boss's invitation. Besides, the prospect of a free dinner at Truluck's was too good to pass up. He was desperate to have Holly attend.

"I really can't, Trey. I'm doing something with Anne. But thanks." Trey was a good friend as far as colleagues go. He had met Anne on occasion and knew that she and Holly were longtime friends, but he didn't know their true relationship. Holly stood up, tossed back her hair, and brought her purse up over her left shoulder. She was now eager to leave before Trey could question her further, her old habit of protecting their secret kicking in before she could consciously recognize it.

"Tell her you can't make it. This is a big deal, Holly. Bigger than dinner with just a friend. C'mon, cancel it." Holly's willingness to place her good friend ahead of their work celebration irritated him. "It's not like you're married or anything," he grumbled.

She winced as though suddenly pierced by a sharp object. "I — I just can't do that, Trey." Clearly upset, she wanted to bolt. But instead, she was frozen in place, unable to move or speak further. *Just let it go*, she counseled herself. But she couldn't. Not this time. She had avoided situations like this so many times in the past, situations that begged her speaking the truth about her love and relationship with Anne. She had distracted, deflected, diverted, or exited when things had gotten too close before. But she realized now that in doing so, she had consigned Anne and the love they shared to the subterranean places secretiveness always creates. It was subtle, but insidious. And she hadn't even realized the effect such hiding had had on their psyches until they began telling others the truth and began experiencing the freshness — the goodness — that moving into the light had brought with it.

They had spent almost two years in subterfuge, being overly cautious during their children's visits not to let their intimacy show and continuing to worry that anyone who saw them together would sense the change in their relationship. The dissimulation had been wearing on them both. It took so much energy to live a lie. And then, to have to remember — a thousand times a day in a thousand different ways — to protect that lie. Their efforts to hide their love had been simply exhausting; and so, ever since Christmas and Holly's conversation with Alicia, they had been gradually letting down their guard.

They had told all three of their children now, various winter and spring breaks having afforded them with opportunities to find time alone with each. Of course, there had been the initial awkwardness that talking about any new relationship with adult children can bring — no matter the genders involved. Each conversation had been emotionally and physically draining, but with each telling, it had gotten easier.

And each telling had brought with it a freedom that neither woman had anticipated. It was thrilling. Everyone's response had been loving, enthusiastic, and congratulatory. And not a single one of them had been surprised. Most important, though, all three of them — Amanda, Mark, and Stephen — had given their sincere approval, without any hesitation at all. How that loving acceptance had lifted their hearts.

Fortified with acceptance where it counted most, their next step had been to begin telling other family members, and they did so in piecemeal fashion, starting with Anne's mother and stepfather, and then catching each of their siblings, nieces, and nephews as they could. Everyone had responded exactly as Holly and Anne had predicted they would back when Reverend DeVita had asked them what they might expect back home. Love had trumped, indeed.

Even though some had experienced difficulty assimilating this new information, not one had pulled away emotionally or physically. There had been several long, honest, heartfelt conversations where family members had thanked them for their openness and had searched for greater understanding. Humor had even entered one exchange. When Holly's brother had noted the number of second marriages in the Vaughn family and had suggested that, if they were to stay with the keeping of Levitical Law, they should *all* be stoned, a teenaged niece, not privy to the beginnings of the conversation, had then exclaimed, "But I've never even tried the stuff!" They had all laughed until tears streamed down each face.

Neither Holly nor Anne had felt any diminishment whatsoever in the love and affection extended to them and, in some ways, felt more connected than ever. Knowing they were accepted for who they were, and so loved that family members were willing to learn and grow for their sakes, Holly and Anne had rediscovered their open, carefree natures, and their relationship blossomed into an even more joyous union.

She couldn't deny Anne ever again. And brushing off what she was sure had been a throw-away comment on Trey's part would be doing just that — throwing away something so precious to them — since it went right to the heart of their reality. She couldn't deny their marriage. Not now. Not ever.

It would be a big risk telling Trey, though. She was aware that he had conservative leanings and that opening the door here at her workplace could bring about unintended consequences, but she also knew that she couldn't deny their truth and face herself tomorrow. Too much was at stake, and they had come too far. Facing Trey and his conservatism was a risk, but it paled in comparison to the risk of losing her own integrity and cheapening what she most treasured. Trey had certainly been right. This *was* a big deal.

"Seriously? You won't cancel? Aw, c'mon, Holly. Anne will understand that this is important. And you guys could get together some other night, or she could even come to Truluck's with you." When Holly didn't respond, he pressed on, "C'mon, Holly. Get a grip. This is a command performance with your boss, and you're choosing to go out with a friend instead? Where are your priorities? I'm gonna call Becky and get her to start working on that sitter." And he reached for his phone to call his wife.

Hot fear clutched her. It made its way from her stomach, creeping up her chest and down each arm, before it finally reached its destination and her face and neck flushed a fiery crimson. *This is it*, she told herself. She took a deep breath and heard Reverend DaVita's wise words as if they had been spoken yesterday: "You are merely speaking the truth." They had the same calming effect on her now as they had then. Nevertheless, her voice quivered when she finally spoke.

"Trey, don't call Becky just yet. We need to talk." She slowly set her purse back on her desk and sat down, facing the uncertainty this conversation would bring.

"What? Are you okay?" He was still holding his phone, eager to get his wife working on the sitter.

"No, I'm not. It's something you just said." Her hands were clasped together and resting on her desk, the ring on her left hand clearly visible. "You've been a good friend to me for a long time now, and I need to tell you something."

"Something I said? I don't know what you mean." Trey shook his head, his eyes searching the office for what he could have said that had upset her. "I just suggested we go celebrate. That's all."

She took another deep breath and looked out across the office as the afternoon shadows made their way further across the room.

"Oh, I get it. This has to do with Anne, right?" He leaned back in his chair, resting his large hands on the arms of the chair. "I know you're good friends and all, and I shouldn't have said what I did about breaking your plans and all that. But I did say to invite her." He looked up at her, a mock sheepishness on his face, "We still friends?"

It was now or never. Just say it! She could hardly breathe, but she knew she had to tell him. She knew she couldn't live with herself if she didn't take advantage of the moment. She made her mouth form the words before she could second-guess herself.

"Trey, my relationship with Anne has changed." There. She had said it! She had opened the door and there was no going back.

"What do you mean?" Trey tilted his head to gain a better understanding of what Holly was saying. She looked really serious. Maybe even a little scared. *What was going on?* "You two are still best friends, right?" He nodded his head, assuring himself of her answer, but his eyes drifted down to her slender hands, fingers laced together, and for the very first time, he noticed the gold band on her finger for what it might represent. "Oh ..." He drew out that simple two-letter word into a descending scale of several notes before his voice trailed off altogether.

"Yes." She looked down at her ring before meeting his scrutinizing gaze. "To both the question you asked, and the one that you didn't."

"Wait, this is throwing me off a little, Holly." He continued leaning back in his chair, but put the phone down. "So what exactly are you telling me?"

She laughed, if a bit nervously. "This threw us off a little too, Trey." But then, looking him in the eye and with a steadiness in her voice that she had not anticipated she could muster, she began. "Our relationship has turned into something much more than it's been in the past. It scared us initially, but after a while, we embraced what we'd found in one other." She sat up a little straighter in her chair. "Trey, I'm trying to tell you that Anne and I are a couple."

"Well, that's a bit surprising to be honest." And he also sat up straighter, no longer lounging as he had been previously. "Back when I first heard that she'd moved into your house, I'd thought that might be a possibility, but I honestly figured that would be the very last reason, ever, that you guys would be living together."

"Why do you say that?"

"Well, because you just don't look the part, Holly. And neither does Anne." He had to look away, as he shook his head in astonishment. "I just can't believe this."

"Well, I can tell you that there are a lot of couples out there who don't 'look the part.' All you have to do is look around, Trey."

He picked up a pen and began clicking it repeatedly. "Why are you telling me all this?"

"I'm telling you because hiding my personal life from my work colleagues has become increasingly difficult for me. I hear all of you talk about your spouses and the wonderful things you do together, the joys that you share, and I can't do the same. I couldn't even tell you just now that the reason I can't change my plans with Anne is because April 4th is our six-month anniversary."

"Wait a minute. Spouses? Anniversaries? You can't equate your relationship with Anne with what I have with Becky."

"Actually, I can, Trey. You see, we went to Canada in October to become legally married. In a church. With a minister. That was important to both of us. I'm just as legally married as you are. The only difference is that our marriage isn't recognized here."

Trey stopped clicking the pen, but continued to grip it tightly.

"Holly, you're my friend, but I have to tell you that I am strongly opposed to same-sex marriage. I don't believe it's biblical, and the Bible is what I stand on on questions of morality." He shifted again in his chair, this time leaning his elbow on the armrest and clasping his hands together. "Bottom line: If you profess Christ to be your Lord and Savior, then you need to confess your sin and repent. Turn away from that sin. That's not to say there aren't areas of my own life that I have to repent from — and I do — but I strongly believe that, as believers, we are called to live our lives according to scripture ... and what you and Anne are doing is not scriptural." And he punctuated his position with a curt nod of his head.

Holly was stunned. She kicked herself for not being ready for this. She had heard his conservative political views before, and she knew he attended a fundamental Bible church. He had shared his take on things many times over the years, but she really thought that since they had been friends for so long, and since he *knew* the kind of person she was, he would have responded with a little more understanding, if not a hesitant acceptance. She had never anticipated such harsh judgment.

"It's all in the teachings of scripture, Holly. Leviticus 18:22 and 20:13 are very clear. Homosexuality is an abomination. A detestable act. Then there's Romans 1, 1 Corinthians and 1 Timothy. You should go back and read your Bible more carefully." He stared at her, asserting Biblical authority — with nothing but contempt in his eyes.

She swallowed hard, willing herself not to respond in kind. She was tempted to come up with a retort to his using scripture as an injurious tool, rather than a means of grace. But how could she defend herself against his, or anyone else's, beliefs. Beliefs that were perhaps as deeply rooted as her own? Holly knew that what she and Anne shared was not evil. Was not sinful. Was not an abomination. It was love. Pure. Simple. Love. And for that, there shouldn't be a need for defense or repentance.

She tried instead to reach some sort of rapport. "Trey, like you, I love and follow Christ and I'm guided by scripture. We just seem to have different understandings of what that means."

"I'd say!"

She could feel him closing off from her in judgment and disdain. He now sat with his arms crossed over his chest, but he might as well have been holding a cross out between them to ward off the evil he perceived. Maybe she could find some common ground on which to stand. "Look, can we both agree that Jesus was somewhat radical for his day?" She so wanted him to listen to her point of view.

"Radical? What are you saying? He was peaceful and loving, not radical."

"He was radical in the way he sought peace and loved others, Trey." She moved forward in her chair and leaned further across her desk, attempting to close the distance growing between them. "He taught 'turning the other cheek,' compassion, and mercy. And He tried to break down divisions between people".

"And you call that radical?"

"Yes, I do. All of that challenged the status quo of an 'eye for an eye' culture: strict adherence to literal laws, judging others, and creating hierarchies of who was 'in' and who was 'out.' He came to teach us a better way, and it got him killed — because it was so radically new."

"He came to die for our sins, Holly. To *save* us. That's what got him killed. It was God's plan. But we have to admit our sins and repent if we want to be saved."

"And I'm not refuting that. I was just wanting you to understand that when I read scripture, I take Jesus' *life* and what he *taught* us as my measuring stick for how I am to interpret it. And often, what He does and what He teaches challenges the status quo. It begs us to expand our thinking — and open our hearts, to ..."

"Now you're rationalizing. If you think you're gonna get me to condone homosexuality when the Bible clearly states that it's a sin, you're wrong. Jesus didn't mean for us to 'expand our thinking' into an 'anything goes' sort of namby-pamby Christianity. He said He didn't come to abolish the law but to *fulfill* it!"

"Trey, I'm not trying to get you to agree with me, nor am I saying that 'anything goes.' And, I do agree with you that Christ is the fulfillment of the law. That's why I look to Him as the 'Way' we are to follow. And what I see, Trey, is that He befriended the lost and the lonely. He loved and accepted those whom the rest of society ignored at best and, at worst, abused. He lifted up the poor and kissed the leper and brought healing to those whom society deemed unclean — like the hemorrhaging woman. It wasn't just her bleeding He cured her of, but her designation as 'unclean,' a stigma that her culture had laid on her undeservedly. So much of what He did seemed to be about bringing all of His sheep into one fold — especially those that others deemed unworthy. I believe that in His very living, Christ was teaching us how to treat one another, especially those who need it most — those we don't understand, those we despise, and those with whom we think we have nothing in common."

"H-uh." Trey sighed resignedly, arms still crossed. "And He told the adulterous woman 'to go and sin no more.'"

"Yes, He did. Jesus was very concerned with our sin, especially with our making idols of the gifts that God's given us. He cautioned us about greed and self-preoccupation and warned us about all those things that keep us separated from God, but He never once mentioned a loving, committed relationship between two people of the same sex as being one of them. In fact, that's not mentioned anywhere in the Bible. It's neither condemned nor praised. It's simply not mentioned."

"You're wrong. It says it many times, Holly. The Bible says it's a sin and that you must repent in order to be forgiven. How do you get around that?"

"For some reason, people over time have come to equate loving, same-sex relationships with the promiscuous and the perverted, condemning us *all* to sin and shame. Well, I don't believe that, Trey. I believe in love, not lust. I believe in commitment, not promiscuity. I believe in acceptance and understanding, not exclusion and judgment. And I believe that God made me, just as He made you ... the way He wanted us both to be. And I don't feel the need to repent for simply being true to who I am, or true to whom I love."

"And if I'm true to who I am, then I've just lost all respect for you, Holly. You can't be a Christian, have a right relationship with God, and then live in and defend blatant, unrepentant sin like this."

That one really hurt, and her hands began to tremble. She couldn't believe he had actually gone that far. She felt the flush return to her cheeks, but surprised herself with her quick response. "My relationship with God, with Christ, is exactly that. *My* relationship. And honestly, Trey, I don't understand how you can feel qualified to question that at all."

"Like I already said, it's all right there in the Bible. Luke 13: *But unless you repent, you will all likewise perish.*" He shrugged his shoulders. "All you have to do is read the words and then walk the walk."

"But that is exactly what I'm saying, Trey. The words obviously don't mean the same thing to me that they do to you."

He threw up his hands in a parody of concession, screwed his large face into a sarcastic smile, and modulated his voice into a sing-songy lilt. "Okay. So you want to *interpret* everything differently, and assume that your 'love' isn't sinful ..." And then he dropped the façade and leaned in for the kill. "But ... when you act upon it, your feelings for Anne that is, it *is* a sin. And then, when you want to defile the sacred act of marriage, which God created to be between one man and one woman ... I just can't abide that, Holly. I'm sorry, but that's how I feel."

This was proving to be much harder than she had bargained for. But each condemning comment Trey threw at her energized Holly even more. In the past, when hearing insufferable zealots like this hammer their opinions home, she had retreated in fear. But not this time. This time she was angry, not afraid. And she felt that she had stood her ground well.

"Well, I think the reason you feel that way is because you already have the right to marry the person you love. And, when you exercised that right, it was legally recognized — everywhere. Well, I can't do that." She held up her left hand, proud to show him the symbol of love which had been given in love and then blessed with love. "You can't understand what it's like to be barred from marrying the person you love because of someone else's personal opinion about it. So you can see why marriage equality is a big deal to me."

"That's crazy, Holly. Gay marriage isn't the same thing at all. And that's a lot more than just a personal opinion."

"But it *is* the same thing, Trey. Marriage is marriage. Period. There are legislators out there who don't believe that our love is legitimate; therefore, they legislate against it. And there are many more who are afraid to vote their conscience because they don't want to risk re-election. And yet, with the same stroke of their pens, they allow divorced people to get licenses and remarry. Isn't that a sin too? According to the Bible? Or am I interpreting that wrongly also?" Clasping her hands in front of her and leaning toward him again, she took a different tack. "Let me ask you something. Would you ever consider, even for a minute, voting for a candidate if he said that your relationship with Becky wasn't good enough to justify your marriage?"

He swallowed, but said nothing. He had positioned himself as far from her as he could get by pushing his chair back from his desk and leaning back almost to the tipping point in his oversized chair. *Where was all this coming from?* He'd really thought that he knew Holly.

She took a deep breath and then rested her hand upon her chest, "Trey, you know me, and you know Anne. Do you really think we're wicked people?"

He looked down at his hands, "I think you are two really nice people who have made a mistake by sinning against God."

She waited until he met her eyes, "Anne and I were married in a Christian church by a minister of the Word and Sacrament, just as I assume you and Becky were. Do you believe that God was any less present when we shared our vows?"

He finally had no answer. And when he could no longer hold her gaze, he dropped his eyes for a detailed inspection of his desk.

Neither of them spoke, and the silence that rose up between them became uncomfortable, and then unbearable. Neither wanted to make eye contact with the other. Too much had been said. Holly let her gaze fall on all the familiar accoutrements of the workspace that had been her life for so long. Everything looked the same, but she knew now that it really wasn't and probably wouldn't ever be again. She sighed. All the colors had gone from the sky. She finally rose and pushed her chair back under her desk.

"If you disagree with someone, there's no need to shame them, Trey. Nor do you have to judge them." And once again, picking up her purse and placing it on her shoulder, she said very gently, "You don't have to compromise your convictions in order to show compassion."

She then turned and left him, still seated and still looking down into his folded hands.

"So what happens now?"

Holly had called Anne the minute she left the office and told her everything that had transpired in her conversation with Trey.

"I have no idea." Holly put down her briefcase and leaned over to give Anne a peck on the cheek. "I don't know what this is going to do to our working relationship. I mean, I know I'll be able to set it aside and work collegially. After all, how he defines our relationship doesn't change what we know is true, but I'm not sure how Trey is going to react to me from now on."

Anne was already preparing dinner, so Holly picked up a paring knife and began slicing zucchini. "I'll just have to continue to be who I've always been and not take anything he might say personally. Who knows, in time he might even grow accustomed to us."

Anne just shook her head as she continued arranging the eggplant in the baking dish. Her wife's optimism was one of the things she loved about Holly, but she couldn't help but feel that it would get her in trouble. *Sometimes it truly did seem that she had both feet planted firmly in the air.*

Holly picked up a second squash but paused, knife suspended mid-air. "You know, having everything out in the open with Trey actually feels pretty great, even if he did give me a really hard time about it. I love the freedom and the fact that we're on honest terms with one another now." She slid the zucchini over to one side of the cutting board and started working on the onions. "But I feel like I've only just started."

"How come that worries me to hear you say that?"

Holly laughed affectionately, "Because you wouldn't be you if it didn't."

Anne arched a brow. "Well it's just that there are some very real risks involved in being so open at your workplace, and you know it. I'm just really nervous that you've opened that door."

"I think you'd feel differently if you'd been there."

Anne looked askance at Holly, her mouth turned down in obvious disagreement.

"It was really gratifying, hon. I mean, it's the first time I've had to defend *us*. And I was able to do it with strength and confidence and still try to offer Trey some understanding." Holly popped a slice of squash in her mouth and crunched it with pleasure. "It felt really good."

"Well, I still can't believe he would say all that to you. After the way you've been so helpful and supportive of him? I mean, you're always available to him. He calls or texts you all the time about work. And sometimes he calls just to talk. But you're always polite and respectful, and you make time for him. And then Ed pulls him along, spends time with him, — grooming him for what? I don't know."

"C'mon, sweetie. Don't let him get to you. Trey is really a nice guy. His filter just isn't all that great. We know that. We just have to be able to disagree with him and go on. This is his to work through now, not ours. Anyway, I'd rather be caught being over-generous than be caught excluding and judging. We're better than that."

"I know. But I'm insulted and I'm really angry that he disparaged my wife. It's one thing to say he doesn't agree with same-sex marriage, but to question your 'rightness with God' because of it, and then tell you that you need to repent? Who is he to judge the relationship you have with God? I'm having trouble letting that one go." She picked up her knife and came down a little too hard on the Big Boy tomato in front of her, splattering it all over her apron. "Yuk!"

"Careful there, love." Holly chuckled and leaned over to massage Anne's tight shoulders. Anne was usually such a mild-tempered person, and to see her this worked up was sweet, even if a bit out of character. Holly had to admit that it felt good having Anne come to her defense this way.

Anne put down her knife and turned to face Holly. "Why does that not bother you?"

"Maybe because he said it to me. Maybe because I had the opportunity to defend my faith and explain our relationship. But, it hit me pretty hard too when he first said those things."

"That kind of reaction, attacking you and rejecting us, is exactly what I've been afraid of. You are no different now than you were the moment before he knew this about us. And yet, he went from begging you to join him for dinner to practically demonizing you before that conversation ended. How could this one aspect of your life make you so bad in his eyes?"

"I don't know, and maybe it's a good thing that I don't. We expected that we'd probably face this kind of reaction from somebody. We knew it was a good possibility — a probability even."

"But there's no way to prepare for the hurt that words like that bring." Anne wasn't ready to let it go. "Look what he's seen us do with that children's hospital every year for the last seven." The Land Office employees adopted a facility for critically ill children every Christmas, collecting toys, books, and clothes and taking them there the week before the holidays to throw a big party for the kids. Because of his portly build, Trey usually dressed as Santa Claus. Holly would take her keyboard and play while Anne led them all in Christmas carols. Holly and Anne hadn't missed a single one of those celebrations. "He knows you. And he knows me. And I'm hurt, and I feel betrayed by all of this coming from him. There! I've said my piece. And now I'll try to be a big girl about it, okay?"

Over dinner, they returned to the subject again and again, and by dessert Holly had helped Anne come to the realization that it really hadn't been a setback at all, but rather a triumph of the first order. They had finished eating, but still sat and enjoyed their wine.

"I have to tell Sloan now, you know. I don't know how it will go, but I don't want to risk having him find out from someone else. It needs to be me who tells him. I want it to be me."

"I know. I've been waiting for you to figure that out." Anne brought the glass up to her lips and took another sip. "Are you ready for it, though? I mean, not just the telling, but ready for whatever Sloan may dish out to you?"

"Yeah, I think I am. How about you? It could affect you too, you know."

"Well, has anything changed with ENDA[24]?" Anne was referring to the Employment Non-Discrimination Act: legislation that would prohibit discrimination in the workplace with regard to the hiring and firing of persons based solely on their sexual orientation or gender identity. This same type of legal protection had been proposed in the United States Congress every year since 1994 — save one. But either it never made it out of committee, or it was defeated soundly each time that it did.

"Nope. As it stands, there are still twenty-nine states where our bosses could fire the both of us simply because of who we love."

"And you still want to take that chance? I mean, telling Ed could put your job at risk, right?"

Holly gave a crooked smile and slowly nodded her head. "It certainly could." She swirled the cabernet in her glass — thoughtful. Then she took a sip. "But I don't think it will."

Anne's expression remained grave. "Holly, don't you remember that news story a month or so ago about the teacher who was fired just because she announced she had a partner and they were expecting their first child?"

"Of course I do. Out around Lubbock, wasn't it? As I remember, they tried to make it sound like she had resigned. But then later they came out with a statement saying she was incapable of committing to the high moral and ethical standards of the school, or something like that."

"And even though she was a good teacher and all the students loved her, when push came to shove, the school district was just too uncomfortable with 'her lifestyle' to keep her on staff anymore. So they just fired her. I don't want that to be you, Holly."

Texas, of course, was one of those twenty-nine states who still legally protected this kind of prejudice. Ed would have every right to discharge her if he wanted to, and Holly would have no recourse — no protection under the law whatsoever.

"I would hate for Ed to do that to you — all because of us."

Holly listened and took her spouse's caution to heart. Her decisions of whom to tell and whom not to tell would always affect Anne too. Even if the rest of the world was unwilling to accept them as a married couple, that is what they were. And they lived their lives as such.

Anne looked deeply into Holly's eyes. "I don't know how I feel, honestly. I go back and forth with everything. A part of me wants us to tell the whole world. And I understand why you want to be honest at work. But then the sensible part of me screams out — 'Why? Why risk the possible outcomes?' Isn't it reasonable to assume that people will eventually have their epiphanies without us having to open our personal lives up to everyone for possible persecution?"

"Believe me, I'm right there with you, sweetie. I feel all of that too. But I can't tell you what a difference it made just telling Trey. There's real empowerment in standing in the face of rebuke and not getting defensive or angry, and I hadn't realized that until I did it tonight. And then, driving home, I let myself imagine what it would feel like to be totally open about us when I'm at work. Just to be honest, to have everything out in the open so I could talk about our kids, our trips, whatever. It would be so good getting to use 'we' instead of 'I' from now on. I think it would be worth the risk just to be that free."

"I get it. I really do. But just be careful, Holly, not to alienate your co-workers. I imagine most of them are as conservative as Trey, and you don't want to be accused of 'rubbing their noses in it.'"

"Don't worry, I'm not going to fly a rainbow flag at my desk or anything. I'll probably just continue to follow our rule: 'If it's in the way of the relationship, it's time to tell. And if they ask, we'll answer honestly.' That worked great for us when we were telling our families, and actually, now that I think of it, that's probably why I felt like I had to tell Trey tonight. His saying, 'It's not like you're married,' was tantamount to his asking. And I had to answer honestly. And now, it's in the way of my relationship with Ed. So here we go again."

"Well, I'm with you on this one hundred percent. I really am. You need to tell Sloan, and I'm okay with that. It's just scary, that's all." Anne suddenly realized what she had just admitted. "Isn't that sad? That we feel such fear when all we want to do is share our happiness with the people in our lives?"

"Well, if we can't make a difference here at home by showing everyone we're just like them —and just like we've always been — we can always go back to Canada. They won't fire us there." Holly winked. "We know they're happy for us there."

They clicked their glasses together in a toast.

Chapter 20

MORE TELLING

The next morning, she was as ready as she could be.

"Ed, can I have just a moment please? There's something I would really like to discuss with you."

"Um. Sure, Holly. I've got a few minutes."

Trey watched from across the room as Holly disappeared into Ed Sloan's office, closing the door behind her.

Telling Trey the previous night had been invigorating. Until then, she had not had the opportunity, the necessity really, to defend her beliefs, her life, or her love. When they had each told their children and other family members, the outpouring of love and support had been overwhelming. It was much more than what they ever dared to dream. But yesterday, when forced to defend her relationship with Anne, she experienced a high she had not expected, and she had ridden the crest of that wave for most of the previous evening.

This morning, however, the familiar constrictive apprehension was back. Once again, she felt vulnerable carrying the heavy weight of their secret. *This was real life, and there were no clean getaways.*

Ed was preoccupied with the papers on his desk, and he continued to shuffle through them as she stood there. "We've worked together for a very long time, Ed, and I've enjoyed our working relationship," she began. "I really have. But there's something that has gotten in the way ..." Her voice trailed off.

"Wait a minute, now." She had gotten Ed's attention and his head shot up to face her. "You're not telling me that you're leaving are you?" There was desperation in his eyes as he searched hers. "Not now, Holly. You're an invaluable asset to this office. To *me*, for God sakes. I need you, especially now."

"Hold on, Ed." She raised her hand, using her palm to signal, *Stop!* "That's not it at all. If you'll just listen to me a minute." Holly played with her wedding ring, turning it in circles around her finger. "I love the Land Office. But it has gotten increasingly difficult for me."

He bristled. "Holly, I don't have time for guessing games. What are you talking about?" He picked up one of the files on his desk.

That was the push she had needed. "I assure you, Ed, this is no game. This is my life. Our life."

He continued holding the file, but looked back up to meet her eyes. "Whose life? What are you talking about?" He was extremely busy and didn't appreciate this type of interruption.

She had wanted to ease into this, but Ed's impatience was making it impossible. So she gritted her teeth and said it. "Ed, I got married."

He instantly relaxed. A smile spread across his face and he tossed the manila folder down on his desk. "Are you kidding me? And I thought you were trying to tell me something I wouldn't want to hear. When?"

"Quite a while ago, actually." She leaned back on her heels, a little unsteady for having told him, realizing that he still didn't know just whom she had married. "It was back in October when I took that extended vacation."

"Seriously?" He rolled his chair back from his desk and rested his hands on his long legs. "Who's the lucky guy? And why haven't you told me before?"

"I guess I was afraid that you'd disapprove of my choice, and I just wasn't ready to hear your, or anybody else's, negative reactions to my marriage. I guess I've believed that seeking others' approval would affect our happiness."

"What are you talking about? I've hoped you would find the right guy for a long time, Holly." His brows gathered together, a wrinkle of concern amid his apparent joy. "There's not something wrong with him, is there? He's not a convict or something, is he?" Ed laughed at his joke and then relaxed. "You're such a looker. You're smart. Successful. You've got it all, Holly. And you deserve the best. Can I come kiss the bride?" And he came from behind his desk, put an arm around her and gave her a kiss on the cheek.

"Thanks, Ed."

"Why wouldn't I want you to be happy, and why do you think I wouldn't like whoever it is? So stop the suspense already and tell me. Who's the lucky guy?"

"Well, actually there is no guy, Ed." She caught herself involuntarily squaring her shoulders and lifting her chin, as if bracing for the volley that was sure to come, "It's Anne."

He blinked at her. He was stunned into silence, paralyzed. The wide grin he'd been wearing froze in place before it began to melt around the edges as his brain started registering what his ears had just heard.

"I'm sorry. I wasn't planning on being so blunt, but it's hard to get a word in once you get going. The truth is, Ed, Anne and I have been together in a committed relationship for about eight years. We love each other, and we recently got married."

"Wha-? How'd you —?" He looked at her in complete shock as he choked on these few syllables. She was bombarding him with one preposterously bad piece of news after another. *What was she trying to do, kill him?*

"We went to Canada last October. We were married in a church and everything."

Ed's eyes darted here and there across the room, as though looking for a way out — an escape from all that she had just revealed. This couldn't be happening. Not Holly. He'd known her for years, for Christ's sake. He'd seen her with Bruce, and you couldn't fake that kind of love. She'd been crushed when he died.

"But you have kids. You ..." He looked up at her, giving her one more chance to take this all back. To rejoin reality.

She held his gaze. "We both have kids. Yes."

How the hell did this happen? he wondered, but he caught himself before blurting out the question. He didn't want to know. He didn't want to know any of this.

"Anne is such a big part of my life, Ed ..."

She just wouldn't let it go, dammit.

"... that not being open about us has gotten to be extremely difficult. Painful, even..."

He didn't want to hear it. Didn't want those images in his mind. If she had to act in this deplorable way, why hadn't she just respected his views and kept quiet about it?

"... Hiding such a big part of who I am has created a distance between me and the people I care about. And I just can't do that anymore."

Too bad you couldn't, Holly, Ed thought. He was finally gathering his wits and collecting himself. *'Cause the distance is about to grow even wider, now.*

Holly watched his slackened jaw tighten, his mouth go grim, and his eyes take on the steely squint of command and control that was so familiar to those who knew Ed Sloan. And all those who knew Ed Sloan knew what this taut and coiled visage presaged.

Holly braced herself again. *Could Anne be right? Was he going to fire her now?*

He looked her in the eye, inscrutable as he continued to stare her down, but she held his gaze unflinchingly. It felt like forever. She could feel her heart knock against her ribs, so loud she thought surely he would hear it. She heard the clock on the credenza behind his desk ticking away the seconds. And still they stood there. She could see the little muscle in his right cheek twitch as he ground his teeth together. And then, just as she was about to say something, say anything, to break the tension, Ed looked down and shook his head. She followed his gaze and their eyes met again, this time as reflections on the surface of his finely polished desk. He looked back up at her.

"I don't know what to say. And I certainly don't know what you might expect me to say."

She was dumbfounded. This was not the Ed she knew. Could it be possible that their history together had made a difference? That he could let his feelings for her — she knew he cared for her and had held her in high regard all these years — that he could let *those* feelings for her soften his hard-line stance? Her heart leapt with hope.

"I'm not asking you to say anything. I just wanted to tell you who I really am. Who *we* are. So that you wouldn't be blindsided if you heard it down the road."

He studied her for a moment longer, then cleared his throat.

"Well. I guess that's all, then." And he turned and made his way around the desk to his chair. Sitting down, he picked up a thick file and began perusing its contents, no longer acknowledging her presence there.

Dismissed. Just like that. How humiliating. She felt a slow burn ignite deep down inside and then explode into full fledged outrage. How dare he belittle her — belittle Anne — like that!

"Yes." She gathered her dignity around her. "I guess that *is* all." And she turned on her heels to exit, head held high. *So this is how it was going to be*, she thought. *Out of sight, out of mind. Her marriage, because it was to another woman, would be treated as nothing more than an irritant that is best ignored.* Everyone would follow Ed's lead, and her personal happiness would be purposefully ignored, as though her marriage had never happened. She would be no freer to join in the break room conversations about family life than she had been before. *Ironic*, she thought. She'd been prepared for Ed to fire her on the spot, figuring he would believe she was now a threat, a detriment to his career. Somehow his total dismissal of her wonderful news came as an even bigger blow.

With her hand on the doorknob of his office door, she turned to face him. He was still seated, concentrating on the piles neatly stacked on his desk. "By the way, I've already talked with Trey, and although I don't plan on making any grand announcement or anything, I'm not going to hide who I am anymore. Y'all mean enough to me that I wanted to be honest with you. And to share my happiness. That's all." Then she opened the door and walked out.

As soon as he heard the door close behind her, Ed put down the folder he was holding and, crossing his arms on top of it, leaned his weight heavily onto his desk. He stared at the closed door for a long while and then shook his head. "Good God! She's crazy!" was all that he could manage. She was deliberately going about ruining her life, and he would have to make damn sure she didn't ruin his as well.

But that would have to wait. What was most important right now was getting the proposal finalized and on the desks of every Texas congressman by the end of next week. It had promised to be a time-pressured day even before Holly's little interruption, and now he would be even more hard-pressed to meet that deadline. He mentally chalked up that transgression to Holly's account as well, before he picked up the file once more and began to read.

But try as he might to concentrate on the facts and figures in front of him, Holly's words kept intruding, and unwelcome images crowded his mind. He found he was just flipping pages, not comprehending or remembering a thing he'd read. *Holly and Anne — married! And in a committed relationship for eight years, for Christ's sake.* The thought nauseated him. It had been going on right under his nose and he had been oblivious. Hell, he had met Anne a number of times and had seen them together at office picnics and parties. *How the Sam Hill had he missed it?* He felt foolish. All this time he had thought Holly a noble, grieving widow and dedicated mother. He had held her in high esteem, had tried to care for and protect her. *Come to find out, she was nothing but a fornicator. And a lesbo to boot!*

Disgusted, he tried once more to focus on his work, but then the thought hit him. *A Trojan Horse.* That's what she was — a Trojan Horse right here in his own office — and she one of his most trusted assistants. She knew his politics and she knew his crusade to keep Texas on the moral high ground; and yet, she had deliberately led this underground life that was diametrically opposed to all that he stood for. She had brought the enemy inside his gate, and her duplicity made him wonder what else he didn't know about her. Well, one thing he knew for sure; he couldn't, wouldn't ever really trust her again.

A third time he picked up that same file, but this time he didn't even have time to open it before the next thought hijacked his will. *What if this got out?* He would be a laughingstock. It was bad enough that he had to deal with Tammy's rebellion at home, but now Holly was bringing it into his workplace too. There was mutiny within his own ranks, and that could only undermine his carefully crafted image as the strong, in-control leader he wanted others to see in him. He should fire her on the spot. She no longer fit his campaign culture, and he shuddered to think what Bella McLoughlin would make of his having a married lesbian on his staff.

But she was invaluable to the Desal Project. *Shit.* She was invaluable to him. He needed her, especially in the marketing phase that was coming up. He slammed the file down, scattering papers across the desk and out onto the floor, then pushed himself up and out of his chair with so much force that it nearly collided with the credenza.

"Dammit, Holly," he cursed aloud. "Dammit! Dammit! Dammit! Could you have done anything that would have screwed with me more?"

And then he remembered her parting words about already having told Trey and planning to tell others. *Hell.* He couldn't put off damage control any longer.

Holly worked quietly at her desk until lunchtime. Trey had barely spoken three words to her all morning and had not once met her eye. Apparently, the rift in their relationship that had begun with last night's conversation was already widening into a gulf. She had only wanted to live with integrity. Now she wondered if the distance between them might prove impassible for Trey. And maybe for Ed? Would he be able to cross the divide she could already see him dredging? And what about any others at the Land Office that she might tell? Or those who would hear it through the office grapevine. She flushed hot at the idea of Anne's and her marriage becoming fodder for office gossip. It made her sick to think of what she held so sacred being profaned in that way.

Whoa now, Holly. She tried to calm her burgeoning fear and resentment. *Don't borrow worries from tomorrow*, she told herself. *Just deal with what you know is true today.* And the truth was she didn't know how this would play out. Would she be condemned? That was a real possibility, given Trey's reaction and what she knew about Ed's conservative position. Or would her long history of warm, collegial friendships win the day? Her relationships with everyone in the office had been good, healthy ones — at least until today. *The jury would be out for a while*, she guessed. After all, there were two worlds colliding here.

She did her best to remain in the present, to concentrate on the work at hand, to go about her interactions with others as though nothing had happened, because nothing really had happened yet, at least as far as she knew. She fought the temptation to wonder if Trey had said anything, or to imagine meaning lurking in the glances she had noticed being sent her way. Bit by bit, the long morning passed.

Just before noon, Ed peered out from behind his closed door. "Holly, would you step in here for a minute?"

She had been busily at work, putting the finishing touches on an important energy consumption chart, and her heart stopped on hearing his voice. *Uh-oh. What was this about?* If he had wanted to discuss anything work-related, he would have had her bring the appropriate file. She swallowed hard before entering his inner sanctum and closing the door behind her.

Ed cleared his throat and fidgeted in his chair as Holly stood just inside the doorway. Fixing his eyes on the empty chair in front of his desk, he summoned her. "Holly, have a seat." Even his best poker face couldn't conceal his irritation.

"I've been thinking since our talk this morning." He sent a counterfeit smile in her direction, his furrowed brow relaxing momentarily.

She sat up straight, careful to place her arms casually on the armrests when she would have preferred the defensive stance of crossing them in preparation for whatever was about to come down.

"I'm concerned about your desire to be so open about this relationship with Anne. Don't get me wrong. I like Anne. But I'm worried about what kind of statement such a public display will make. I don't want it to appear that this office approves of — or, uh — promotes this kind of thing."

"Ed, this 'kind of thing' you're talking about is *me*. I'm a person, and this is my marriage."

"Dammit, Holly!" His fist came down on his desk with force. "Don't you see that this kind of thing can cause us to lose all credibility with our friends over there under the Dome?" He pointed in the direction of the Capitol building across the parking lot. "We need their votes to get the funding approved for our proposal. And I need this proposal to turn into a project which may very well help me overcome all this past mess and win re-election. You're just gonna have to stay quiet about all this, okay? Now is not the time to be throwing a monkey wrench into the equation."

She let him finish. "So, when *will* it be time, Ed?" She was surprised at the composure in her voice. It didn't match the heat that she felt rising in her throat and causing her face to flush.

He bristled. "Look, you don't understand. I can't have another issue like this getting picked up by the press. Not now. Not ever again." He leaned forward and gave her his demand. "Bottom line: I don't ever intend to bring any of this up again. And you're not going to either."

She listened, wide-eyed, incredulous at the extent of his self-absorption.

"I'm firm in my convictions as a Christian, and I'm firm in my policies as a politician. So assuming that you don't have any questions ... we're done here."

Behind Ed's desk, on his credenza, there was a framed plaque, a quote from Martin Luther King, Jr.: 'Injustice anywhere is a threat to justice everywhere.' But next to the plaque sat one of those statues of the three monkeys: *See no evil. Hear no evil. Speak no evil.* What a bundle of contradictions. She so desperately wanted to scream at those three little apes. *Open your eyes! Open your ears! And speak up! You can't keep the world at bay by pretending it doesn't exist.*

In that moment of shock and disgust, she saw Ed for what he truly was — a bully, plain and simple: one who manipulated others into meeting his demands by cultivating, and then playing to, their fears. And in that moment, Holly realized that she was no longer afraid. By overreaching his locus of control, as he'd done just now, he'd exposed his tactics for what they really were, and they no longer held any power over her.

She rose from her seated position, coming to her full stature, and stood proudly in front of him. "You're right, Ed. We are definitely done here. But I do have one question for you." He squinted up into her clear gaze. "Should I submit my resignation to you, or to your three little wise friends over there?" She tipped her head in the direction of the monkeys, but she did not wait for his reply. She turned and left his office without speaking another word.

"Godammit! Well, what did she expect me to do with that bombshell?" Ed poured himself another drink from the decanter. "I was just trying to help her, and she up and quits on me!"

"Would it have been such a bombshell if she had told you she married someone named Anthony instead of Anne?"

"Come on, Tam. This isn't something to joke about." Ed clenched his fist and shook it, as though he held something in his hands he could rend into pieces. "Can you lay off for just this once?"

It was a windy, stormy night. A flash of lightning threw uncertain glances around the room and brought disquiet into the shadowy corners of the house, creating unrest rather than the comfort that usually came with nightfall.

"Okay." She would change tacks. "How *did* you try to help her, Ed?"

"I warned her. I let her know that if this got out all over Austin, all her good work on the Desal Proposal would be for naught. We'd lose all credibility with them. It would never become a project, and she'd be finished. I tried to protect her job."

It wasn't lost on Tammy who he was really protecting, but she thought it best to let that go. "So why did she quit then?"

"Hell if I know. I was just telling her I wasn't going to mention it again and that she shouldn't either and she got all red in the face and told me she was resigning. Said something about my three monkeys statue. What that was all about, I haven't a clue."

No, Ed, you wouldn't, she thought. *Hear no evil, see no evil...* The patron saints of denial. *Poor Holly.* She could just see Ed not dealing with Holly's declaration. He would have been too consumed with morality issues, and how it would affect him, to think about *her* feelings and respond to *her*. She just prayed that he hadn't been too dismissive in his self-protection.

"Do you understand how monumental it was that Holly wanted to share this with you, Ed?" A clap of thunder rumbled, causing the windows to rattle. "It speaks volumes about how much she respects you — and trusts you. I've learned a lot about the risk involved in coming out and how people always look for a safe person to tell. And Holly told you anyway, even knowing where you stand on the issue, and knowing that there could be life-altering consequences since you are her boss." *The living, the telling, the potential for acceptance or rejection — and the consequences that follow — are out of the 'tellers' control.* Tammy understood only too well how big and very personal the risk was.

Ed was uncharacteristically silent.

"You're the one making this such a big issue, Ed. Not me. And not Holly. What could you do to make this right?"

"Hell if I know."

"I've always liked Holly ... and Anne, too."

Ed turned away from Tammy, watching the light show on display outside. "So have I."

He threw his head back and emptied his glass. Still gripping it tightly, he considered the glass in his hand, but then thought better of the momentary satisfaction that hurling it across the room would bring. What would he do now — without Holly? He had come to rely on her for so much. Everything had just spun out of control so fast, and he wasn't even sure how it had happened. *Dammit all to hell!*

"Actually, it makes perfect sense when you look at their lives together. Honestly, I would have been more concerned if Holly had said they *weren't* together."

"Oh, I'm not concerned about *them*." He watched as the driving rain assaulted the windows. Then he poured himself another drink.

"So what is it you *are* concerned about?"

"It's just, how can a Christian church perform such a marriage? I don't understand what this world is coming to. By living in unrepentant sin, they're walking in open rebellion to God. How do I reconcile myself with that?"

"Maybe you don't have to." The wind was picking up outside. The sound of it tumbled down the chimney. "Maybe it's not your job to pass judgment on whether or not someone else is right with God."

"Here we go again." Ed slammed his glass down so hard that what was left of his scotch spilled out onto the buffet. He turned, leaving the mess just as it was, and stalked out of the room. As he began making his way up the long staircase to their bedroom, Tammy was right behind him.

"No, really, Ed. What you just said made perfect sense to me, believe it or not."

He stopped at the landing and turned to look at her, intrigued. "Well, that's a first! So what do we agree on, Mrs. Sloan? I'm eager to know."

"Maybe it would be a sin for you to enter into a relationship with another man ..."

He cut her off. "Well, whadda ya know? You're right. There *is* something we both agree on." And he resumed his march down the hall to their bedroom.

"Ed, please. Let me finish." She followed him into their room. "If you were to do that, it would be going against your own beliefs and your own sexual orientation for the sake of prurient interest. It would be lust, not love."

"The hell it would! That's downright perverted, Tammy. I can't believe you can even think, much less say, such a thing." He glared his disgust at her.

"Ed, I'm using a hypothetical to prove my point. Maybe the real sin that requires repentance is entering into intimacy with someone when there's no underlying foundation of love or commitment there."

Ed turned to look at her again with an exaggerated expression of annoyance.

"Couldn't that be what the Bible is talking about when it warns about sexual sin and lists fornication, adultery, sodomy, and prostitution as examples? There's no assumption of love in any of those activities. And if there is no real love for the other, but only a craving to fill your own appetite … that's where I think you find the sin and the sorrow. The Bible doesn't say anything against a loving, monogamous same-sex relationship, you know, so why are you so quick to equate what Holly and Anne share to those awful things?"

Ed's reply was to wad his expensive silk tie into a ball and throw it into the hamper. "Jesus Christ, Tammy. Who made you a Bible expert? I don't remember you ever attending seminary." He was tired and had had too much to drink. Her reasoning was confusing him, and it took all his effort to remain stalwart in defense of his faith. Best to deflect and divert.

But she ignored his taunt. "Isn't that what marriage is all about? Being able to declare to the world, and to each other, that you love and are committed to one another — and to want what is best for one another?"

Ed made a grudging, grunting sound.

"So then, who are we to feel we have to 'reconcile ourselves' to someone else's marriage?"

He turned his back on her, and she watched him undress in silence. Where had her loving husband gone? These days he was so much more ready to condemn than to be compassionate. She thought back to those earlier days and how he had really extended himself to help the young Henry heal and then nurture his growth into manhood. And she remembered when their own three were little, how he had balanced, as best he could, his career with family time. With Tammy time. Now it seemed that he had exchanged his humanity for an ideology, and that the only thing he extended himself for was his own aggrandizement.

Poor, dear Holly. What sort of denigration had Ed put her through? Tammy wanted so badly for Ed to reclaim his better self. She wanted so badly for him to grow. For his sake and for hers — as well as for the betterment of the world. Their marriage depended on it, she realized. And this is where it became very personal for her. Helping people overcome their fears by educating them is what she did at Trevor every day, and she was determined to do her best to help Ed do the same.

"Ed, what about Holly's announcement hurt you the most?" He remained silent for a while longer, but she could sense a different texture to the silence. Perhaps it was the slumping of his shoulders, the more relaxed bend to his back and neck.

"I really liked her and trusted her. And I thought I really knew her. I mean … after all these years together. It's like she's been living a lie or something."

"So you feel betrayed." She waited a moment before asking, "Did you ask her about her love life or her relationship with Anne? Did she evade your questions or mislead you in anyway?"

"What?" His head spun around to face Tammy. "Of course not. I didn't ask her anything."

"Why not? If you think her love life must revolve around your belief system?" She looked at him intently, willing the scales to fall from around his eyes.

"I don't want to know, Tam. It isn't my business and I don't want it to be my business."

"Then why have you made it your business?"

His prickly impatience came through in his voice. "Dammit, Tammy. I've had enough." He hadn't asked Holly to tell him. That was her own doing. Why had she involved him in her personal life? "Don't blame me because Holly chose to blindside me."

"I'm not blaming you, Ed. I'm just trying to help you see the good in Holly's news ... that's all. And it shouldn't be this hard!" *No. Love should never be this hard.* Tammy's eyes glistened.

"The good? Really, Tammy?" What possible good can come out of believing all this same-sex absurdity is socially acceptable and not a sin after all?"

"Because love is good, Ed. It always has been and it always will be." Her throat constricted around her words, pinching them as they tried to escape. *He just couldn't let himself hear himself. He just couldn't see beyond himself and the ideology he used to defend against having to grow and change.* It was hard to hold an ideologue close because all you got was hard edges.

Something turned over inside her, and she flared, "And I am not going to stand by and watch another life ruined because of your inability to let compassion guide you instead of moral fervor. Family values won't be eroded by the inclusion of good people like Holly and Anne, Ed, but they certainly will be when controlling and judging behaviors begin to eclipse loving, accepting ones. And that's true in *any* relationship — *ours* for example!"

Her tears started flowing now. "I'm tired of your making things your business which you've just admitted aren't your business. Who made you — or the government, or the church for that matter — God, that you would intrude on someone else's personal decisions about love ... or the way they choose to live their lives? God doesn't even do that. He gives us free will!" She snatched up her pillow from their bed and took a blanket out of the closet. "I'm sleeping in my study tonight."

Ed neither spoke nor moved. She had left the door to their bedroom open and he could hear the clock downstairs chime the half hour. His already surly temper burned in him like the fires of perdition. But even so, the stillness of night eventually settled over the house. And Ed, overcome with exhaustion, cursed his ill fortune and went to his bed, alone. *Surely, even the gloomiest of nights give way to morning.*

The distant rumbling suggested the worst of the storm had passed.

Tammy waited until the weekend to call Holly, wanting to allow some of the freshness of the incident to fade. But balancing her respect for Holly's privacy with her own strong desire, need even, to counterbalance Ed's insensitivity had proven difficult. *Was it really just insensitivity? Or had he been cruel?* She had never been able to discern exactly what he had said that had pushed Holly over the edge. But whatever it was, it had pushed her too.

"Holly, it's Tammy Sloan." She called Holly's cell, not the office line. "Can we talk?" Tammy and Holly had their own unique relationship, as many spouses and work wives do, and each respected and appreciated the ties that bound each of them to Ed Sloan.

"Umm. Sure." Holly took off her glasses and stared through the large window above her desk into the back yard where little green tufts were just beginning to bud on the big ash. "I'd like that, Tammy." Holly was in her office, one of the kids' bedrooms that she had taken over when it was abandoned for college. She was bringing most of her work home, leaving the Land Office at lunchtime every day. She was involved in the critical editing phase now, and nowadays her home, rather than the office, seemed more conducive to this type of concentration. Ed had not balked at the change in her routine.

"First of all, I want to congratulate you and Anne on your marriage. I am so very happy for you."

Holly was flabbergasted. She had just assumed that Tammy's views would mirror those of her husband, and she had not seen this coming. "Well, thank you, Tammy. Thank you very much."

"I really mean it, Holly. And it's important to me that you know that. You're both such wonderful people and I'm so happy that you have each other. So many people never find a soul mate, and I for one want to celebrate it when they do."

Holly had not expected this at all. She hadn't been surprised to see Tammy's number on the caller ID, but this revelation was truly unforeseen — a shocker really. She, more than anyone else, understood what it took to live and work with Ed Sloan, and she knew that differing with him on any subject brought with it the risk of censure or worse. Because of this, Holly's appreciation for Tammy's forthrightness came from a very deep well.

"It really means a lot to hear you say that, Tammy. More than you can know, actually. Thank you so very much."

It was clear that Ed had discussed her disclosure with Tammy and probably their subsequent exchange. *But what had he said? And what had he left out?* Holly couldn't think of anything else to say so she repeated, "Thank you."

"And yet, as happy as I am for you, I'm saddened to hear that you'll be leaving the Land Office."

"Yes, I am too. But I think it's best, given the situation."

"The situation being … you and Anne? Or you and Ed?"

"All of the above. I want to be able to work in an environment that will allow me to openly talk about my family."

"And Ed isn't going to allow you that privilege." It stung to speak the truth about her husband.

"No. But it's not just Ed. There are others who share his views too. And I've come to realize that, if I'm really honest with myself, it's as much the Texas legislature as anyone who is to blame. The laws they've passed, or refused to pass, allow any boss, not just Ed, to fire me simply because of Anne, and Anne simply because of me. Whether we were married or not. To his credit, Ed didn't do that, but we don't want to live with that kind of uncertainty. That's not a place to build a home — or a life."

"I totally understand." Tammy swallowed her sorrow. Holly was being forced out of her home just as so many of the kids at Trevor had been. And, she acknowledged with sadness, as she herself was being forced out of her marriage. If she had remained quiet, she and Ed could have continued on in an apparent peace. But at what cost? Because she had come to a point where self-identity and personal integrity no longer afforded her such an option, she, like Holly, had been forced to risk confronting the powers that be. The powers that were Ed.

"So, what are you going to do?" Tammy wondered about her own answer to this question as she waited for Holly's reply.

"I'm not sure yet. But we've got lots of options, and I've already put out some feelers. You know, Tammy, in a lot of ways this is an opportunity for us to strike out on our own. And frankly, we want to make good use of every single minute we have. We don't want to have to always be looking over our shoulders to see what's coming next, or preparing to defend ourselves and our happiness against other people's belief systems. Life is too short not to be living it fully and openly. So, if I can't live it at the Texas General Land Office, then I'll just have to live it somewhere else."

Tammy related to her comments more than Holly could possibly know. They both were weary of living their lives according to someone else's rules and expectations, and they both knew that change was in the offing. Holly and Anne were trying to live their lives authentically, just as she had been attempting to do lately by asserting her opinions and then acting on them. But Holly was displaying a courage that Tammy had not yet been able to muster. *She* was moving on.

She swallowed the hard knot that had risen up in her throat. "How is Anne doing with everything?"

"She's still pretty upset. But she's upset at the injustice of it all. We're definitely on the same page with everything, but she's mad that I had to face all of this in the first place. It's just so unnecessary. And as you can imagine, the whole thing's a little hard to swallow."

"I am so sorry. Thank heavens you've got each other."

Holly laughed. "Well, even that was a little touch-and-go when I came home and told her that I had quit my job."

Tammy didn't know whether to laugh or cry.

"Oh, Holly. I don't even know where to start. I'm sure I've only gotten half the story, but I want you to know, both of you to know, that I am so very sorry for what Ed may have said or done to drive you to the point…"

"Tammy, don't. We both know Ed. He is a strong personality, and he doesn't do well when things don't turn out the way he believes they should. And I just couldn't be who he wanted me to be any more."

That comment went straight to Tammy's heart. How many times recently had she wondered if she could no longer be the wife Ed wanted? But living *her* truth was bringing no comfort. Holly had Anne — they held their truth together. She had no one else but Ed. Suddenly she felt very alone.

"And yet, I feel some responsibility for his behavior, Holly. I guess you could say that I haven't been exactly who he's been wanting me to be lately either."

"Please don't go there, Tammy. Don't take responsibility for Ed. It's not your fault. I know better than that."

How many times, at Trevor, had she uttered those same exact words to someone else struggling with family acceptance? "It's not your fault!" Why was it so clear to see when it didn't involve *you* or *your* loved one? Why was it always so much harder to see when yours was the life affected? Wasn't it common sense to desire healthy relationships? To no longer live a lie? To live in integrity? *But sometimes,* Tammy realized, *even common sense requires courage.*

The way we talk to our children becomes their inner voice.
— Peggy O'Mara

Chapter 21

STRUGGLE WITH DARKNESS

I t was impossible for Tammy to conceive of any human creature more wholly forsaken than a child who has been betrayed by a parent. In her few short months at Trevor, she had learned things about humanity that she had never wished to know, and she had come to understand that betrayal has many faces.

It can lie hidden behind the mask of "the perfect family," a child's true nature subtly but routinely suppressed in order to fit the only image the parents and community can love. Or, it can materialize in a single crushing blow to the heart that wreaks instant havoc and destruction. More often than not, it was the latter that figured in the stories of the young people who reached out for help through the Trevor Project. They were children who suddenly found themselves utterly alone and vulnerable. And like stunned beachcombers paralyzed with fear as the tsunami approaches, these children and youth faced a destructive energy called condemnation which threatened to engulf them. With no resources or tools to defend against the tyranny of contempt, their sense of self was often at the mercy of hateful denunciations and intolerant attitudes; the innocence of their childhood swept away, lost forever in a sea of enmity and self-loathing.

Sometimes the constant stream of heartbreaking stories that popped up on her screen at Trevor became unbearable, and each time she felt hope wane inside her, she turned to Father Blair for solace and for counsel. He helped her to remember that even the smallest interaction that shows compassion helps to turn the tide of self-loathing that so many of 'her kids' were mired in. "Compassion is very akin to blessing," he had told her.

He had explained that the gay youth learns to hate who he is because that is what he is taught — that the young person's embarrassment and shame blend in his mind with his parents' disapproval and anger. Then, all too frequently, this gives way to confused — and stunning — high-risk acting out, such as turning to drugs or seeking relief through promiscuity or flamboyance. "Living *down* to their parents' expectations," is what he had called it, "the old 'you think I'm bad then I'll act bad' phenomenon."

"And that is what society sees and condemns," Tammy had realized. It was the birth of a stereotype, the root of a prejudice, the downward spiral of a child crying out for help in all the wrong places.

But he had also taught her that by looking beyond self-destructive and irresponsible behaviors and by looking beneath God-given differences to the worth and dignity of the human spirit, one could actually begin to reverse the spiral of self-hatred. He had shown her how, by addressing that person with the reverence and respect due a child of God, one could plant new seeds of self-understanding, and how from that foundation, healing could begin to occur. That was the blessing of compassion. His wise words had encouraged and guided her, and his presence attracted and inspired her. She decided he was more Christ-like than anyone else she had ever personally met.

She settled into her desk across from Father Blair. They were both waiting for their first calls to come through.

"Father, how have you kept from becoming cynical or judgmental yourself? I mean, being surrounded by so much sadness and abuse all the time has to take a toll, doesn't it?"

He leaned back in his chair, his folded hands behind his white spiky head, and pulled his lower lip in with his teeth as he prepared his response. "I guess you can concentrate on the ugliness and let that 'take a toll,' as you suggested, or you can take each of these sad circumstances and see the possibilities in them instead. God possibilities. There are so many instances in the Bible where a person has endured persecution of some kind or another, only to become someone of significance later on — sometimes in spite of, but sometimes because of the obstacles they'd faced before. Think of Joseph, son of Jacob. He was thrown into the pit by his jealous brothers and left for dead, only to become a great leader in Egypt who later showed mercy on his family and provided food for them and their people during great famine. And of course, there's Moses. At the time of his birth, all newborn Hebrew boys were to be killed. So hoping to spare his life, his mother placed him in the basket and sent him down the Nile. And we all know the rest of *that* story — Moses gained freedom for the Jews. He parted the Red Sea. And he received the Ten Commandments from God Himself.

Father Blair sat back and closed his eyes. "'As iron sharpens iron, so one person sharpens another' — Proverbs 27:17." He smiled gently at Tammy. "That's always been one of my favorite scriptures. It reminds me that we help grow one another through our encouragement, compassion, and guidance, but that God can use adverse situations, too — *if* we allow them to teach us, and *if* we allow God to work in us."

"I guess I just have trouble accepting the way some people continually create these adverse situations, Father. Sometimes I just want to scream. People say they're Christian but yet they still judge and choose hate. Isn't being a Christian about loving your fellow man? Isn't it about *not* judging? So many of the callers we get here have been persecuted by fellow Christians, and that really angers me. I don't like seeing Christianity being used as a weapon against others. That just goes against everything I've ever known and ever believed in."

"Well, here's what I know about people who judge others, Tammy. They have convinced themselves that they know everything. Therefore, their purpose in life is to criticize those who think differently. And they frequently use the Bible as their fallback because who would question the Word of God, right?" And his eyes twinkled conspiratorially.

Tammy nodded her agreement. She could listen to him for hours.

"Parents wrap themselves in the Bible while kicking their children to the curb. You're right, it's a mockery of Jesus' message of love and inclusion." He leaned in closer and his voice took on a more intimate tone. "Tammy, if you're dismayed by an injustice that you witness and you let the perpetrator know it, you're merely stating a fact and standing up for what is right. But there's a big difference between identifying an injustice and judging someone because of it." His eyes smiled and his smile crinkled into a gentle empathy. "And that's a trap that *we*, as advocates, must be especially careful to avoid."

"And that's a lot easier said than done." Tammy was aware that she was already perilously close to crossing that line.

"Believe me, I know." Father Blair sat back and reverted to a more didactic style, "But you know, we Christians make an even bigger mistake when, in attempting to be non-judging, we choose to stand by and say nothing when we witness mistreatment. In the first scenario we only hurt ourselves in that we become what we are railing against. But in the second scenario, we are complicit in hurting both the perpetrator and his victim."

Tammy thought a minute about what he had just said. She understood complicity in the crime against the victim. That was easy and she had heard it many times before. *But hurting the perpetrator?* And suddenly it became clear. "It's that sharpening thing from Proverbs again, isn't it?"

"Exactly. Those who judge not only cloak themselves in piety, they take our silence as agreement, and that encourages and empowers their continued malfeasance. If their unjust behavior is not questioned or challenged, they see no reason to change, and that keeps them from growing into all that they could be — all that God wants them to be." He held both hands in the air. "It takes both — speaking up for justice and refraining from judging those whose words, decisions, or actions are unjust. That's our truth and the tightrope we must walk, Tammy."

Tammy thought back over her own evolution. For so many years she had struggled to speak up, but now that she was, she realized she'd made a full pendulum swing. Her struggle at this point was learning how not to become overly zealous herself. "So how do you manage that tightrope, Father? I need to work on my balance."

"Well, first of all, we have to remember that the Christians of one generation tend to become the Pharisees of the next. And you remember how Jesus felt about Pharisees. He called them a brood of vipers, and he called them out because they were so careful in the little things — like tithing a tenth of their mint, and rue, and all other kinds of garden herbs. But they neglected the really big thing — seeking justice and showing mercy by seeing that the poor were fed and sheltered, and that the stranger was taken in. He accused them of loving the law more than they loved others and, therefore, God."

Father Blair brought his hands back from behind his head and rested them on the table as he leaned forward in his chair. "We must be wary not to let the keeping of the law get in the way of living for God." He stopped to let that sink in. "We tend to forget that the law was meant to draw the Israelites, and now us, closer to God — not draw a line in the sand between us and Him."

"Or us and 'them?'"

"Exactly! If we Christians aren't careful, our focus on outward cleanliness ... or in our day and time I guess a better word would be purity ... Our focus on purity can become an obsession, ultimately blocking out the more important part — the inner life of our souls. Jesus' words cause us to step back and look carefully at what we're doing and why we're doing it."

The inner life of the soul ... Tammy agreed that that was the better part. Mary had chosen well when she had sat at Jesus' feet, for what gives the soul life if not abiding in God and allowing Jesus to abide in one's soul? Abiding in love and incarnating that love here on earth. And there was the answer to her question of keeping balance: keeping Jesus as her center. Tammy glowed with this grace of insight, but Father Blair was on a roll, and she loved to hear him talk, so she concentrated once more on what he was saying.

"Yet we see this in the world every day. Have you ever noticed how many organizations with overly pious or patriotic names have formed to gather like-minded people around a purpose which, in effect, is nothing more than discrimination against one minority or another? People may think the virtuous name of the group renders all their activities virtuous as well. But they're bowing to the idol of purity rather than following God's vision of *shalom*, a vision of peace and justice for all. And I personally believe that type of deception to be misleading, misguided, and misanthropic."

Tammy shook her head. She thought of the many people she personally knew who believed an organization's statement or value system simply because it had "America" or "Family" or "Marriage" somewhere in the name.

"But even so, that doesn't give me the privilege to tell them they're wrong. Consistently trying to prove you are right, instead of empowering others to come to their own conclusions, is a perfect example of poor leadership and misguided direction. Once again, there's that judgmental trap we must work hard to avoid."

Tammy nodded in understanding. She hadn't realized just how much she needed to hear everything Father Blair was saying.

"Part of what we do here at Trevor is help folks learn that gay people exist in our day-to-day lives and that they are good people, not odious specimens of the human race as some would believe. Opinions such as that foster ignorance and fear and then use the closet as a weapon. 'Speak up about who you are, and we will punish you.' 'Silently hide in the recesses of your life, and we might spare you.' Many people are thoroughly happy with the whole idea of 'don't ask and don't tell.'"

He was talking about people like Ed. Father Blair had never met him, but he was describing Ed perfectly.

"Our work here is to help people bring all of this out in the open. To create opportunities where 'iron can sharpen iron.' You and I can see the error in following false teachings, Tammy, but when someone doesn't, you can still let them know that you disagree without pointing fingers. That is the judgment of Scripture. If you do, point fingers that is, then you'll be no better than they are in their sanctimonious knowledge of what is verifiably right and wrong. If we are humble and truly love God and follow Him, we will desire justice for *all* His children. But in order to get there, we must submit our ego to a greater whole. After all, our strongest unity comes from our diversity."

Father Blair reached up and touched the headset covering his ears. "Looks like I've got a call. But Tammy, it all boils down to we're all God's children. That makes us all more alike than different."

She was so grateful to have Father Blair's insight and the benefit of his twelve years of experience with Trevor. Her 'mama bear' had already been aroused numerous times during the chats she'd had with her 'kids' and she'd been struggling ever since with how those families could drive their children to such painful places. Hearing the stories, it was hard not to begin pointing the finger, for she understood the import of each and every call she received. She had learned that when a child confides in you, through Trevor or any other medium, their problem is probably ten times worse than what they actually tell you. Many would have to be driven to a point of utter desperation to be willing to even talk about it.

Bloop. Bloop. The familiar tone rang through her headset.

"It's me again."

Her heart raced upon seeing who it was!

"Oh Seth, I'm so glad to talk with you again. I've been worried about you. Are things any better at home?" She had thought about him so much over the last several weeks. She had prayed for his safety and hoped that she would have another opportunity to help.

"Not so much. Today is probably the worst day I've ever lived."

She wanted to tell him that it couldn't be all that bad, but she remembered that whatever he was telling her was really only the tip of the iceberg. "Want to tell me about it?"

"Not really but I guess that's why I called. ☺"

Tammy was encouraged to see the little smiley face in his message. Maybe he had just experienced a bad day. "I'm here."

"Well did you hear about the whole Boy Scouts decision a couple of weeks ago?"

"Yes. I'm very familiar with that. Isn't it good news?"

"Well not for me. My troop leader resigned because of me. Said I was incompatible with the principles of the Scout Oath and Scout Law. But I haven't done anything!!!"

"Oh, Seth. I am so sorry. Did you tell your parents what he said to you?"

"I didn't have to. All the other parents did. Everyone is pissed at me cuz we lost our leader. And now a bunch of the other guys are joining up with a whole new group. It's called Trail Life or something.[25] My dad is really hot."

Tammy remembered the words that Tim, her Trevor colleague, had once spoken, about his regrets of past hurtful words and the lost

time with his now deceased son. He would have to live with that grief
for the rest of his life. Thank heavens Seth's father wouldn't follow in
those same footsteps. "I'm glad to hear that your dad is angry
about the way you are being treated. That is wonderful."

Tammy waited for his reply. What was taking so long? She knew he
was still online. The call indicator was still blinking. Had she somehow
said something wrong?

"Seth?"

"Are you there?"

"You don't get it at all. He is furious with me. Says
it is all my fault that the troop is gonna disband. And
now Jeremy is telling everyone he never liked me like
that. He says it was all me coming on to him, never the
other way around. And everyone believes him. And now my
dad is kicking me out. Says I'm no Christian and certainly
no son of his. I've got to be out of the house by this
weekend."

Tammy was stunned. Then another line came in before she could
gather herself to respond.

"I'm only fifteen. And my life is already over."

Tammy's heart lurched. She thought of Kelly and Michael. The
thought of them being sent to the streets sickened and terrified her. She
was infuriated at Seth's father. This was his son! How could he do such
a cruel thing to the child he had once held in his arms and promised
to love for the rest of his life? While that man repeatedly pounded his
chest with self-righteousness, his son was sinking into the depths of
hopelessness, with a polluted and self-defeating mindset put there by
the one he should trust the most.

"I'm so sorry, Seth. It must feel like everyone around
you is taking out their anger on you. But you are better
than that. We here at Trevor can help you find a place to
stay. OK? So don't panic. We can help you get a plan."

Tammy tapped her headset. "Mary, can you hear me? That boy
Seth is on the line and we need to find him a place to live. His dad is
kicking him out. He has to be out in three days."

"Okay. Find out where he lives. If he doesn't want to tell you, the best you can do is find out which city or state he's in. That way we can at least give him some relevant resources for places in his area."

"I'll try. Thanks, Mary."

"And see if you can get his phone number too. That way we can actually have someone in his area give him a call."

Father Blair was sitting across from her and upon hearing her one-sided conversation with Mary he looked up. There was a noticeable strain in Tammy's expression. "You okay?" He mouthed to her.

"I think so."

"I'm not panicked. I'm not even scared. I know what I have to do but I just don't want to do it alone. That's why I called you."

"But Seth, you aren't alone. If you'll give me your phone number, I'll have someone in your area call you with options. They'll have a list of places where you can stay. You'll get to choose."

"I can't give you my phone number. My dad took my cell. All I have is their land line."

"Where do you live?"

The screen was quiet for a moment. He must be wrestling with whether or not he should tell her where he was from.

"I live in a closet. In Texas."

Tammy mumbled to herself. "Oh Seth, don't believe everything your mind is telling you." But she was having a hard time with her response. She began by typing something about his life no longer had to include the closet, but she deleted it. Then his next message popped up on her screen.

"I told you I didn't want to do this alone." He had found the courage to face what he felt he must, and Seth removed the safety on his feelings as he 'talked' to Tammy.

"I told you, you're not alone Seth. I'm here. And there are many others who love you."

"Well, I don't know who they are anymore. Everybody I thought I loved hates me."

"I don't hate you. I know you're finding it hard to feel that support, Seth. But I promise you, it is out there."

"I. Even. Hate. Me."

Something about the way he typed out that last note alarmed her. Tammy could feel the steely cold pressure of society pressing against his innocent flesh. The cold barrel of anger pointed directly at his core — who he was and who he would become. Suddenly, Tammy felt sick.

"Seth?" She feared she now understood what he had not wanted to do alone.

Nerved with a strength found only in the desperate, Seth picked up the resolution to all his pain. He slid a round of clarity into the chamber. He gripped all their cumulative words of rejection into his hands and raised them up.

"Seth, please don't." Her hands trembled as she typed.

Facing them head on, he swallowed them. He would silence their pointing once and for all. No more menacing fingers would be aimed at him. He pulled the trigger on misunderstanding, hostility, and fear. The metallic taste of condemnation and judgment, the last thing he would ingest. The door would be closed on his father's revulsion for the last time, leaving instead the acrid smell of a decimated spirit, the demise of youth and promise.

"Seth!"

His potential swirled above in wisps, as smoke. Tendrils of possibilities that could no longer be pursued, supported, or praised. Seth's shattered hopes and dreams were all that remained. Splattered for all to see against the backdrop of his innocence.

"Seth! Answer me!" She desperately typed, hoping to receive an answer. He had not disconnected the call. "Seth, are you there?"

But the chamber, once filled with rounds of self-loathing, was now empty. No more lethal rounds would be fired.

The shot rang in her ears as if she had actually heard it. She rocked backward in her chair, locked in horror and disbelief. As she did, she felt Mary's hands on both her shoulders.

"Tammy, honey. I think we've lost him."

Instinctively, she looked over at Father Blair, desperately seeking her comforter, but she could not find his benevolent gaze, his wise strength. She could only see a desperate, haunted teen, an apparition that was too vivid to see beyond. He was sitting on the floor alone, his keyboard in front of him, the disembodied words on his screen the only support he had in the world. He lifted the gun, and she saw his face. "Dear God …" she pleaded before she doubled over, her arms wrapped around her middle as she tried valiantly not to be sick. The face she had seen was Michael's. She drew her hands up around her neck and fought back the sobs that were welling up inside.

The tragic news of Seth Graham, the Georgetown mayor's son, was everywhere. It made the headlines in all of the area papers and was "breaking news" on all three local channels. It was the subject of conversations and the object of speculation on Facebook and Twitter and around every table where people gathered, particularly in the area diners and coffee shops.

"Jim Graham's son couldn't come to terms with the fact that he was gay."

"He was from such a good family, but that couldn't save him from himself."

"He had struggled with his identity for so long, and nothing Jim could do seemed to help. I know he tried."

"It's heartbreaking. Dreadful. What a waste."

"Poor Jim and Betsy. They are heartbroken to have lost their only son in such a tragic way."

"There's a lesson in this for us all. When we veer away from God's plan, there is always a tragic consequence."

But Tammy knew the real story. And she felt beaten to her knees by the hopelessness of it all.

Henry and Amber attended the funeral that morning with Ed and Tammy. They all shared space on the pew, but they had kept pretty much to themselves. What more could be said? Tammy had already told them enough, and Henry was still stunned. He was sickened by the whole thing. This tragedy could have been avoided. Should have been avoided. Henry believed that with all his heart. The situation had cried out for love and understanding. That's all that had been required. Seth had needed these things from his family, and his family had needed them from society. Henry searched the hollow expressions of the hundreds of mourners and noticed Jamie O'Dell and his mother, hands clasped and leaning against each other. *Now that's the way it should have been for Seth. Why do we continue to withhold these simple things from one another? Why do we wait until it's too late? Too late to try for reconciliation. Too late to look beyond behaviors, or attitudes, or orientation? Too late to remember how much we love the person before us?*

So there he sat. At the funeral of a fifteen-year-old boy, all because his family and friends had refused to accept him. He pinched the bridge of his nose, trying to make sense of it all. He knew what he felt, but that didn't help make sense of such a senseless situation.

The congregation rose to repeat the Lord's Prayer and Henry stood up with them. "Thy will be done." *Oh, if only that would happen, and happen now. Open the doors of our hearts, dear Lord.* Henry was so tired of the way humanity gets in the way of God's vision of a peaceable kingdom where all His children are blessed with health and happiness and justice, where everyone has enough, and where the stranger is welcomed and the alien is included.

Henry had been the different one as a kid, the one without a father. Everyone else had *Leave It to Beaver* families, but not Henry. His family was missing a major player, and he had felt it every day of his life growing up. Had his father abandoned him? Run off by choice or circumstance? No. The cruelty of disease had taken him from his loved ones, but it didn't really matter. The outcome was the same. He was gone, and Henry had felt different.

He looked over at his uncle, seated next to him, his mouth no more than a grim line, his eyes staring fixedly forward. In so many ways, Ed Sloan was an unlikely candidate to be a harbinger of God's *shalom*, and yet, this prickly, self-important man had been the one to welcome Henry into his heart and to help mitigate the loneliness that difference always creates. Henry's eyes became moist with affection.

"Into your hands we commit Seth's spirit, a lamb of your own fold …" Henry was pulled back into the funeral liturgy. *If only Seth had had an Uncle Ed in his life.*

Henry loosened the knot of his tie and slipped it off, tossing it onto the books which were stacked on the coffee table in front of him. Jim and Betsy Graham had looked like zombies this morning. They were going through all the motions, shaking hands and murmuring "thank you-s" to the long line of well-wishers who offered them condolences; but there was no life in either of them. They were empty shells, ambulatory, but bereft of consciousness or awareness. He desired a similar disconnect and slumped down on the couch. Wearily he closed his eyes.

"Daddy! Look! We found another *Old Turtle* book at the library today!"

He opened his red-rimmed lids to see Gracie running into the den, her nightgown billowing out behind her, and he smiled at this precious image of life abundant. It was a good reminder. Life does and must go on. He wiped his eyes in order to better see the cherished storybook she now held in her hands and patted the place next to him.

"This one is called *Old Turtle and the Broken Truth*.[26]"

As he opened the book and turned the first page, Amber placed Savannah into her spot in Henry's nest and then joined them on the couch. This was usually her time to get something done without little ones underfoot, but tonight she needed to be with them in their special time. Too many painful realities had encroached upon her utopian outlook lately. She needed to be recharged. They all did.

Henry began the story. It was about a far away and very beautiful land where fell … a Truth. It streaked down from the heavens, creating a tail as long as the sky itself. But as it plummeted downward, it broke. One of the broken pieces blazed off through the dark night's sky, and the other fell to the ground in the beautiful, far-away land.

Henry read about a lot of different animals, each of whom would find the shiny piece of Truth and begin to carry it for a while, discarding it when they discovered its rough edges and realized it was broken.

Each time another animal picked it up, he or she would discover it was a burden to bear, and the unanimous sentiment had been, "We do not need this Broken Truth. We will find a better one, a whole one instead."

Gracie had listened enthralled, her eyes glued to the beautiful pictures of each of the animals as she helped her daddy turn the pages. Then Henry read with a somber voice how the Broken Truth was finally left on the ground and forgotten. He paused for effect and Gracie looked up at him questioningly. "It's not finished, Daddy," she instructed. "Keep reading."

Henry complied. He read how finally a human found it and because he could read, he knew that it said, "YOU ARE LOVED." As Henry read what was carved onto the rock, Gracie had looked up at him, her bright little face the picture of pure gladness. She had clasped her hands together under her chin, scrunching her shoulders up under her ears.

"That's 'The Truth,' Daddy. Isn't it?"

"Yes, sweetie, it certainly is. You, my little pipsqueak, are loved!" And he kissed the tops of both Gracie's and Savannah's heads. "You both are."

Amber reached over to brush back Savannah's disheveled hair and then kissed both girls' little hands. "You, my little darlings, are loved more than you'll ever know. By Daddy, and by me, and by Grandma, and by Mimi and Pop, and by Uncle Ed and Aunt Tammy, and all your cousins."

"And by God too," Gracie chimed in, in her best Sunday school behavior.

"And by God too, Gracie. That's for sure. Now do you want to hear how such a shiny and lovely truth could get broken?"

"Yes!" yelled Gracie in her enthusiasm.

"Yesh!" mimicked Savannah. "Yesh! Yesh!" And she clapped her pudgy hands together excitedly.

And so, Henry read on. They learned that the human had kept the Truth all to himself at first and then had shared his Truth just with his friends — all those people who were just like him. And they learned that the people began to worship and idolize the Truth and consider it their possession. As Henry began to read about how other people demanded to have the Truth for themselves, Gracie's face began to cloud, and as he told of how their discord resulted in wars and the ruin of all creation, she crossed her arms and perfectly imitated Amber's facial expression and tone, the one she used when needing to correct one of the girls.

"Daddy, the people are being bad. They need to put it down like the animals did."

Her parents shared an amused look over her head.

"She's got you pegged," Henry mouthed, eyebrows raised.

Amber had ducked down into a sheepish pose.

"But just remember," Henry had encouraged her, "There is a voice of wisdom in the midst of trouble.

"Yay! Old Turtle!" Gracie was once more her ebullient self. "Remember? She's a girl turtle, Daddy."

"Yes, I remember, Gracie." Henry remembered a lot about Old Turtle, actually. The original story had stayed with him, had resonated with him on a very deep level. The Earth and all its inhabitants had not found peace within themselves or with each other until they were able to recognize God in one another. And this second tale, about the Broken Truth, was proving to be just as insightful. A story more for adults than for children.

"Keep reading, Daddy. I want to hear what else Old Turtle says."

Henry picked up where they had left off, and they read even more about how the people got in trouble. They had become so busy trying to define and enforce their own interpretations of the Truth that they forgot to live the Truth. And they refused to see the Truth in one another.

"Where's Old Turtle? She needs to come help them right now."

But instead of Old Turtle, when Gracie impatiently turned the page, she found a picture of a little girl, about her age. Surprised, she flipped through several pages until she found the familiar form of her favorite reptile.

Savannah touched the picture on the page with her stubby fingers, "Tuh Tuh."

"Yep. That's Old Turtle. Keep reading, Daddy."

Henry quickly synopsized what Gracie had skipped: the little girl's frustration with all the fighting and her journey to find Old Turtle.

And then he read Old Turtle's advice which was something about all things being mended only when people were finally willing to meet others in different places, who may have different faces, or even have different ways.

Gracie wrinkled her nose. "Huh?" She was obviously disappointed that Old Turtle's advice didn't make more sense.

"I think Old Turtle is telling her that the best way to get a whole truth is to listen to one another's truths and learn from them."

Sure enough, on the next page, they read that Old Turtle had told the little girl that there are truths all around us and within us, but when we no longer see these truths in each other — no longer hear them at all — our own truths then become broken.

"You were right, Daddy!" Gracie smiled up proudly at him.

"You *do* have a smart Daddy, Gracie," Amber agreed and tousled Henry's hair. Having gotten his attention, she made a 'hurry up' sign with her right index finger and pointed to the slumping figure of Savannah, curled up in his nest, eyes drooping with heaviness.

So Henry moved the story along more quickly. Old Turtle taught the little girl and then gave her a talisman to take with her on her long journey home. Old Turtle had saved it for a very long time, for just the right person. "Look, she's just like you," he read, as he tweaked Gracie's nose and then turned the page.

It had been a very long journey; the little girl had seen and learned much and her heart had changed. When she got back home, the people didn't even recognize her. She explained about the Broken Truth and the need to make it whole. But they didn't believe her. The people didn't understand.

"Why don't they listen to her, Daddy?"

"I guess they're just not ready to hear what she's trying to say."

Finally, the Great Truth was brought out of the place where it had been kept and the little girl knew what she was supposed to do. She carefully took Old Turtle's stone from her pocket, where she had carried it throughout her long journey, and she tenderly added it to the old broken piece.

"It was a perfect fit!" Henry touched each word as he continued reading what was etched into the two broken stones, "YOU ARE

LOVED … AND SO ARE THEY." The people stared at the joined pieces in disbelief. Some of them frowned, some of them smiled, and some of them even cried. But then they finally began to understand.

"And look, Daddy! Old Turtle's smiling again!" Gracie finished the final page herself.

After the girls had been carefully tucked in, prayed with, and sung to, Henry and Amber found themselves back on the couch and in each other's arms.

"That book explains everything so simply. So clearly." Amber looked into Henry eyes. "Why is it so hard for us to get it?"

Henry shook his head. "I dunno. I ask myself all the time what it's going to take for things to change?"

"Maybe the real question is will things ever change? The whole time you were reading, all I could think about was that poor kid, Seth Graham, and all the others out there just like him."

Henry sat up and turned to face her. "Hon, I have to believe that things will change. We've already seen some progress. It's just that we tend to focus on what still needs to be done, instead of on what we've already accomplished. Think about all that's happened over the last fifty years regarding racial equality and women's rights. That change was slow, and sometimes very painful, but change came despite many obstacles. And I believe that we're on the right path here with gays and lesbians, too. Unfortunately, I think we'll continue to see a lot of suffering in the meantime."

Amber was silent for a minute or so, twirling a strand of her golden hair around and around her fingers as she thought about all that had transpired recently, not just with Seth, which was appalling enough in and of itself, but also with Jamie O'Dell.

"Where have we failed, Henry? I'm talking you and me, here. Have we in some way contributed to this whole tragedy?"

"What are you talking about? Everybody knows how we feel about same-sex issues."

"But maybe we have failed, Henry. We both talk a good game, but what have we really done? To make a difference, I mean. And I mean a real difference, not just you and me sitting around and talking with friends and agreeing on what we believe. Tammy's really doing something at Trevor, but what are we really doing? I know we've got two little ones, and that really limits what we can do, but I also can't sit and do nothing. I don't care how stretched I feel. I feel like we have to do something."

"Well, I guess we can begin by actually reading all those petitions that are highlighted in the HRC[27] emails we receive. And then we can take the time to sign the ones that make sense to us. And maybe we need to put our money where our mouths are. You know, give financially to organizations that reach out to the people we want to help."

Amber picked up Henry's phone and immediately began a Google search. "Wow. There are hundreds of groups we could support — by state, or nationally, or internationally, whatever we want to do. Of course there's PFLAG[28] and the Human Rights Campaign. But there are a bunch that I've never even heard of. Here's one called the Gay and Lesbian Alliance Against Defamation. They call themselves GLAAD.[29] There's even something called Stonewall Democrats[30], and then there's another group called Log Cabin Republicans.[31] Go figure."

Henry rested his head against the back of the couch and closed his eyes.

"And then there's a link to a whole separate site on anti-bullying organizations." She clicked the link to be amazed even further. "A lot of these have to do with programs at schools. These sound great. There must be about thirty or so groups on this one page alone. I had no idea there were this many places offering this kind of help."

"How about if you create a list of the ones you like the best and then we can sit down tomorrow night to see which ones we want to support and how."

"Oh, my gosh. It says here that twenty-three percent of elementary students report bullying incidents during a regular school year. Elementary school, Henry."

Henry just shook his head. What was his little Gracie already witnessing at school?

"Here is a story about an elementary parent who formed an alliance with the local high school. She got the drama team to come perform skits for the elementary kids. This mom actually wrote two of the skits herself, and the other ones were written by the drama team members: "You're Mean." "You're Stupid." "You're Weird." "You're Different."[32]

Henry opened his eyes. "What a terrific idea. Creating visuals like that for kids to see situations that they may not recognize as bullying."

"Don't you think the Westmont drama team would jump all over this? I mean, given all that's happened in this one school year alone?"

Henry didn't answer right away, but looked at his wife as she continued to scroll through the numerous options and organizations that lay before her. "Do it, Amber."

"Do what?"

"Do what that mom did. You would be great at getting people to work together. To really make a difference."

"You really think I should? That I could do that?"

"I know you could. And it would be a win-win for everybody involved. Just imagine how things may have turned out differently for Seth Graham if more of his friends had learned those kinds of lessons at a young age. Or if they had been part of the drama teams that presented them?"

"Oh, Henry. I love you." Amber slipped her arms around Henry's neck. "You're so good for me."

"And imagine what you'll be teaching Gracie and Savannah. To see their mom making a difference like that in their own schools. And with their friends."

"You can stop now. I'm gonna do it. I just hope you don't regret getting me started, that's all. You know how I can get."

"I know exactly how you can get. Why do you think I believe it's such a great idea?"

Chapter 22

DESPAIR WITHIN
DOCTRINE

I t was Tuesday morning, and the room was more crowded than usual. Typical Breakfast Club topics were covered by local businessmen and professionals from a variety of industries in and around the surrounding communities, but today's meeting was going to be different. Seth Graham's suicide had hit this community hard. Everyone knew Jim Graham, and most had been acquainted with his son, so this was a loss with wide sweeping effect. Already seated, Henry Keene looked around for the others. Holly was on the other side of the center aisle, seated with Anne. Trey was sitting with Ed's secretary, Mary Anne, a few rows behind Holly. He also saw Bill Pritchett near the front of the room and motioned to him, but Bill continued his conversation with a group of men that Henry did not recognize. Nonplussed, Henry continued his search for his Uncle Ed. It was unlike him to be late.

The sound guy from the Club was already placing a mic on the starched collar of the day's speaker. As mayor, Jim Graham had made a point of rotating the Club's meeting place among all the churches in town, both to stay in touch with his constituents and to avoid any appearance of favoritism toward a particular denomination or congregation. So it was no surprise when the mayor's office had announced that a clergyman from outside the community had been invited to speak today. Jim and his wife were still in seclusion. Neither

Jim nor Betsy had been seen outside their home since the funeral last week, and mayoral duties were being carried out by office aides.

Most everyone was seated now, and Mike Gamble, city councilman and newly appointed mayor pro-tem, was preparing to introduce the guest minister when Henry finally caught a glimpse of his uncle. Ed had just walked in the back and was hastily getting his coffee and pastry. Henry waved and when Ed saw the empty seat beside him, he nodded his head and put up one finger, indicating that he would join him in a bit. The refreshment table held his interest more than the promise of this talk.

"Good morning, ladies and gentlemen," said Mike Gamble as he greeted the assembly. "We are grateful to have everyone here this morning. We've gathered today with heavy hearts. Each of us here has been affected in some way by the tragic death of Seth Graham — because we are a community. And in a community, what happens to one, happens to all. We come to this Breakfast Club meeting today still in grief and in shock as we try to regain some sort of normalcy within our lives and community. In acknowledgement of our communal pain, we have altered our program for today. Dr. Marie Schmidt has graciously consented to being rescheduled so that we could directly address the issue that's in the hearts and minds of all of us today. And so it is with great appreciation and gratitude that we welcome our guest today, Brother Rick Brenton[33], former head of staff at Temple Baptist."

Ed slipped into the chair next to his nephew at about the same time that Bill Pritchett and Kevin Lloyd, a mortgage broker relatively new in town, sat down in the row behind them.

The applause was subdued in deference to the solemnity of the occasion.

"Thank you ladies and gentleman," began Rev. Brenton. "May we begin with heads bowed for a moment of silence."

"I almost didn't make it," whispered Ed. "Tam and I had another blow-out and I couldn't get her to stop arguing."

Henry looked up at his uncle and nodded, but did not respond.

"Let the words of my mouth and the meditation of my heart be acceptable in your sight, O Lord, our rock and our redeemer."

Henry opened his eyes to see Reverend Brenton surveying the audience with a benevolent gaze.

"I thank you for inviting me here today. There is a profound pain in this gathering today…"

Kevin Lloyd leaned forward from his seat behind Ed Sloan and spoke softly, "I certainly don't envy him this sermon today."

"Has anyone heard from Jim?" replied Ed between bites of muffin.

"I don't think so," whispered Henry in reply. "They're crushed from what I understand."

"I would be too." Kevin Lloyd had met Jim Graham on several occasions, but certainly didn't know him well. "I can't imagine losing a son, but to have this other news come out as it has for Graham … It's just shocking."

"Quite a blow, on top of everything else," Ed agreed sympathetically.

Henry was disturbed by the implication in Lloyd's statement and in his uncle's quick concurrence, but he simply said, "Let's let him talk."

"No death is ever easy for those left behind. And an untimely death is even harder for the survivors. But when friends and family must face the death of a loved one who has taken his own life, the pain and the guilt can become almost unbearable. My heart goes out to all of you who are grieving the recent suicide in your community and the tragic loss of such a fine young man as Seth Graham."

Ed's eyebrows shot up. "Humph," he snorted.

Henry glanced over at his uncle and from his crossed arms and sour look, Henry guessed that the term 'fine' had not gone over too well with his uncle. *Open your heart, Uncle Ed, like you once did with me,* Henry silently entreated. *The Seth's of the world still need you.* He turned again to concentrate on what Reverend Brenton was saying.

"They say that when a suicide is successful, the deceased hands his inner turmoil over to those who survive him. They are now the ones who must live with the rage and despair, with the helplessness and hopelessness that drove their loved one to such a desperate act. And so, we remember Jim and Betsy Graham in their grief. I know that you all will rally around them as a supportive and loving community in the days and weeks — and years — to come. And that is a very good thing. But there are others in your community who live in deep pain and mental anguish on a daily basis and they need your support too. I'm talking about the host of young people, if statistics are to be believed, right here in your own community — who like Seth, find themselves ostracized because they are different."

"What the hell?" said Ed, almost under his breath.

Again, Henry looked over at Ed. He had tucked his chin to his chest now and was peering up at the speaker from under a gathered brow. Henry gave him a quick couple of pats on the leg for encouragement and grinned, "Come on, Uncle. Give the guy a chance. He might say something you really need to hear. That we all need to hear."

"Right." Ed's curt sarcasm suggested he did not hold out much hope of that happening, but Henry figured he would take what he could get. As long as Ed was being agitated by whatever it was he heard, he was still engaged, and that was so much more promising a position than if he had stopped listening at all.

"Elisabeth Kübler-Ross famously taught us that guilt is a part of the normal grieving process that follows any death. At some point, the survivor begins to ask a series of 'If only' questions: 'If only I had called or gone by that day.' 'If only we had not argued.' 'If only I had taken her to the doctor when the symptoms first appeared.' It is part of the healing process to process what is our responsibility and what is not, and in the case of most deaths, we realize that this is something beyond our control. That we did not cause it and that the guilt we feel is false guilt. We can let it go. But in the case of a suicide, the guilt runs much deeper.

"It may seem that suicide occurs without warning, but the reality is that the state of hopelessness which can end in a suicide usually has been brewing for a very long time and has signaled its presence in identifiable warning signs all along. Immediately, the question becomes, 'Why didn't I see this coming?' Or, if the person had seen the depression, the isolation, the darkness of soul, 'Why didn't I do something about it while I still could?' Later, the question is one of soul searching. 'Did I compound his torment, her misery, their loss of hope through my actions — or inactions?' 'Could I have made a difference by doing differently?'"

"I'm having trouble seeing how all this talk about guilt is supposed to help Jim and Betsy. Or any of us, for that matter." Ed had leaned over to confide in his nephew's ear, but as in all things Ed, his whisper was loud enough to cause several people seated around them to turn and stare. Kevin Lloyd had reached out to give him the old "atta-boy" punch on the shoulder.

"My sentiments exactly."

Henry sighed. He was wishing he had not motioned for them to join him earlier. It was proving very distracting having to listen to all this play-by-play commentary and he was intrigued with where Brenton was taking this. He was thinking this guy was pretty gutsy and hoped he had the courage to take it all the way.

"Those questions are questions we all must ask ourselves, for as Hillary Clinton once said, 'It takes a village.' Recent research has shown that the characteristics of one's social environment figure prominently as contributing factors in all suicides. And never is this more the case than in suicide attempts within the gay and lesbian community, most especially among gay youths and young adults where 30 to 40 percent have attempted to take their own lives. But unfortunately, there isn't any concrete national data regarding suicidal ideation among the LGBT population because there is no agreed percentage of the national population that identifies as being gay — all because we have made any openness on their parts so difficult. But no matter the exact numbers, what all this means, according to the Suicide Prevention Resource Center, is that young people who live in areas with a more negative sociopolitical climate towards gay individuals and without the support of affirming resources are at an increased risk for suicide when compared with their peers in more supportive environments."[34]

"Is he trying to say this is all our fault? Is this guy for real?" asked Kevin Lloyd, just a little too loudly. Once more, heads turned in their direction.

Ed turned around in his seat in order to return Kevin Lloyd's volley, but Henry laid a staying hand on his uncle's shoulder. He was excited. Never before had he heard someone speak so boldly on the community's role in driving a young person to such desperation. This was important. This could make a real difference. "Listen, people!" He heard himself urging.

As he continued, Rev. Brenton's speech became more impassioned. "There is a crisis here, and we face tough challenges in our communities, our schools, our families, and our churches. We must offer love, acceptance, inclusion, and hope to those who live and love differently than we do. Belonging is one of the most basic of human needs. When people feel isolated and excluded, they often abandon all hope. And that is where we people of faith must remember that the greatest commandment is to love God — who is Love itself — and to love one another."

He continued with his charge to the community, especially to the churches, to surround all persons in the margins of society with the same love and support that was being offered to the Grahams that day. He said that this would be honoring the memory of Seth Graham in the best way possible and that such loving, faithful discipleship would be a revelation of the Christ light like no other. "Jesus came that we might know God's love in the world, that we might learn to be ambassadors of that love, and that we might learn how to break down the barriers that exclude any of His children — regardless of race, religion, gender, or sexuality — from that perfect love." With those stirring words, he closed his speech to standing ovations in some sectors — Holly and Anne and Henry among them — and polite acknowledgement in others. Neither Ed nor Kevin Lloyd responded at all, other than to remain seated, stump-like, their arms resolutely crossed in front of themselves. Guarded. Challenging. Defiant.

Reverend Brenton had noticed their resistance. He quieted the crowd and offered to close the meeting with prayer. "Creator and Sustainer God, we came before you today with humble and hurting spirits and you have met us here. Thank you. You have asked us to love — to love those who are easy to love and to love those You want us to love. Help us now as we leave this place to make a difference in the hurting hearts of others. Teach us how to better love our neighbors, accepting their differences and educating our children to do the same. Give us the strength and courage to stand up against hatred and misunderstanding. And help us to recognize and then minister to those who feel rejected, outcast, or despised. It is in Jesus' name, the one whose example we are called to follow, that we ask these things. Amen."

By the time the Reverend's homily was concluded, both Ed and Kevin Lloyd were sufficiently inflamed to challenge the man head on. Since last fall, Ed had refrained from making disparaging remarks about gays in the public arena. Bill Pritchett had helped him come to the realization that creating polarization among his constituents was not constructive, but his personal repugnance toward the whole idea of same-sex relations remained. And he was still all too happy to share his views within his inner circle. This cleric's defense of Seth Graham and his sexual orientation had really ticked Ed off. *How could a decent Baptist minister not condemn homosexuality as the intrinsically wicked behavior that it was?* It was downright irresponsible.

Henry and Pritchett shook hands with Rev. Brenton as Sloan and Lloyd began their posturing.

"So Reverend," asked Sloan, "I appreciate your message today, but it left me wondering if we read the same Bible?" His tone was not confrontational, but the sarcasm was not lost on any within earshot.

Henry remained standing next to his uncle as the inquisition began. This could be one of those difference-making opportunities that he and Amber had just discussed, but Bill had to step away, rolling his eyes in exasperation. "Excuse me while I go warm up my coffee," he said and then hastily left, eager to engage with a group gathered by the refreshment tables in the back of the room.

"Good morning. Rick Brenton. And you are?" He extended his hand first to Sloan, then to Lloyd and Henry.

"I'm Kevin Lloyd and this is Texas Land Commissioner Ed Sloan," he answered with pride as he shook Pastor Brenton's hand.

"Good to meet you all, gentlemen. And to answer your question, Mr. Sloan, yes we do read the same Bible. We just have to remember and accept that every reader interprets scripture through the lens of their own presuppositions."

"Meaning that we can make it mean what we want it to." Lloyd was first on the attack and gave a sideways glance at Ed immediately afterwards, his aggressive sarcasm rewarded by Ed's appreciative nod.

"No, not at all," said Brenton with a friendly smile. "What I meant is that our understanding of Scripture must rise above our own presumptions to factor in the historical situation the text originally addressed, the meaning of the Greek and Hebrew words used, and the understanding of the original audience."

Ed pulled himself up to his full stature and, in his most commanding voice, pointedly asked, "So are you saying that we can discount God's clear commandments because they are out of date and irrelevant? Do you really think that we can bend the word of God in order to satisfy our current-day definitions or to bow to social pressure?"

"I'll tell you what," Brenton realized that this conversation was going to require more than just the few minutes he had first supposed. "It sounds like we might have a lot to discuss. What if we were to have a seat over there?" And he gestured toward some empty chairs off to the side of the assembly hall. Most attendees were businessmen and women who had had to leave immediately after the prayer to get back to their respective offices, so the room was emptying quickly.

"What I'm saying," he continued once they were seated, "is that Scripture cannot mean now what it did not mean then." And he paused a moment to let that concept settle over the obvious gulf between their understandings.

"Meaning that it's all in the translations we use?" Henry was eager to clarify.

"In a way, yes," Brenton replied. "As we examine specific passages, we must remember that we modern readers are picking up the Biblical conversation mid-stream. We can't ignore the cultural, doctrinal, and historical context those scriptures addressed. Reading twenty-first century concepts into ancient scriptures will guarantee an incorrect interpretation every time."

"Well, with all due respect …" and somehow Ed managed to convey through his tone and expression that respect was the last thing he was offering, "there is one word whose definition doesn't change, and that word is *sin*." He leaned forward with arms akimbo, fists balled on his thighs — the stance of a dominant male protecting his territory. Ed felt confident. The Scriptures had grounded his faith formation since childhood and had determined his adult beliefs, especially his understanding of sin. He was rock-solid on that, and he was enjoying this. He might be learning to refrain from making outward judgments of others' sinful choices, but he could still take a stand on moral issues. He knew right from wrong.

"And in that, Mr. Sloan, we most definitely agree." Benton nodded his head agreeably. "Sin is what separates us from God, but it is most important for us to understand that Jesus Christ died to take away our sin. Not our sexual orientation."

"Oh, here we go." Lloyd leaned back in his chair in disgust.

"Bear with me just a moment, gentlemen, and hopefully I can explain the theology that supports what I just said."

Henry leaned in closer. This was exciting. He had never heard a minister offer a biblical defense of his opinions before and he didn't want to miss a word.

"First of all, I believe in the verbal inspiration and the plenary and the infallible authority of Scripture. But in order to better understand the meaning behind the written words, we must first accurately interpret the context which particular scriptures addressed, specifically those now used against gays and lesbians. Many Bible scholars believe the condemnations found in Leviticus, Romans, and 1 Corinthians are more a condemnation of idolatry than anything else. Leviticus addressed a particular culture and a particular historical situation — the wandering Israelites in the land of Canaan. And the people of Rome and Corinth, they believe, were being reproached for their sexual religious practices and idol worship."

"Now *that* makes sense." Henry's head bobbed in understanding. "In real estate, the three most important words are Location, Location, Location. An otherwise beautiful house in a bad location loses its value. And when interpreting Scripture, the three most important words must be Context, Context, Context. A verse taken out of context loses its intended meaning ..."

"Exactly the point." The theologian exuberantly thumped his Bible.

Ed rolled his eyes at that one. *Whoever heard of scripture losing its meaning? Why did they suppose it had been around for thousands of years? It had staying power precisely because it was the truth, dammit.* He couldn't believe Henry was falling for this stuff.

"Just as we parents set rules and limits on our toddlers for their own safety and well-being, God did the same for His fledgling nation. Certainly bedtimes, curfews, and limitations on dating and lipstick aren't decrees to be upheld into adulthood and forevermore? They are instructions given to a specific people, for a specific purpose, at a specific time. Moses presented the Law, which included 631 commandments, to the Jewish nation after the children of Israel had left Egypt and had naïvely wandered for over a generation throughout lands where people worshiped pagan gods — and did so in ceremonies involving cult prostitution and human sacrifice."

Brenton opened his Bible and thumbed its pages as one would a deck of cards, "From Genesis to Revelations, two themes are consistent: first of all, that hospitality, which means loving one's neighbor and caring for the stranger among us, is key; and secondly, that loving and worshiping the one true God is primary. To do otherwise is the real abomination, according to Scripture."

"So, as faithful Christians, how do we decide which commandments are still to be obeyed today?" Henry was sincere and wanted to resolve questions such as this which conflicted with what he knew his uncle had been taught as a child.

"Meaning, are we modern-day Christians still under the Law of Moses and the Levitical Holiness Codes?" clarified Brenton.

"So answer your own question, Reverend. Are we? Or are some of us above the law?" Lloyd's snide question was intended to trip him up, but it missed its mark.

"I can't answer that for you, Mr. Lloyd. You must first decide which theology you ascribe to." Offering his left hand, open palmed as option one, he explained. "If you believe in Covenant Theology, which is viewing Old Testament Law as representing an eternal standard, always in force and always reflecting the will of God, then you are obligated to obey The Law. And that means all 631 laws, not just a select few."

He looked straight into Lloyd's hostile eyes and then Ed's steely ones, allowing the import of his words to fully settle. "Full compliance would include offering blood sacrifices, no cutting of hair or beards, no eating shellfish, no remarriage post-divorce without being guilty of adultery, and many other laws which we have chosen not to observe over time."

"But in Dispensational Theology," he now offered his other hand as a second option, "believers view Old Testament Law as temporary, lasting only until God instituted a better covenant, which was Christ our Savior. In this way of thinking, Christians are no longer obligated to offer the sacrifices commanded under The Law because Jesus Christ was our ultimate sacrifice. In fact, The New Testament clearly states that we are no longer 'under law but under grace.' Romans 6:14."

"So," Henry summarized the lesson. "It sounds as though we Christians have been very selective as we've tried to define sin by applying Old Testament laws, but expecting some of us to adhere to the old standards while others of us don't have to. Sounds like a double standard to me."

"You are very insightful, Mr. Keene, and you are apparently quite open to considering new truths as well." Pastor Brenton smiled his appreciation. "Are we no more than modern-day Pharisees ourselves when we hold gay Christians accountable to covenant theology on one point, and one point only, of the Holiness Code, while we and they are free to employ dispensational theology with all other parts of the law? In other words, in all instances other than same-sex unions, it seems that we accept that we are no longer bound by the legalism of the Mosaic Law. It seems we understand that we are freed in Christ to interpret the precepts behind a law through the lens of his teachings. In all instances save one."

Brenton again surveyed his audience to assure himself that they had followed his train of thought. And he could see their wheels turning. He decided to press his point. "I believe it's tragic that the Christian church judges, dismisses, and excludes the LGBT community because Christ's teaching was all about inclusion. And I for one pray that the church can find room in her heart for gay and lesbian members of the family of God. That young man, Seth Graham, might not have chosen to take his life had he received love and acceptance instead of hatred and exclusion."

"But the Bible says in no uncertain terms that homosexuality is a sin. An abomination," demanded Sloan. "Are you suggesting that we disregard that view completely?"

"Gentleman, when these passages were written, the word 'homosexual' didn't even exist in Hebrew, Aramaic or Greek, the languages in which the Bible was originally written. As a matter of fact, it only first appeared in the 1934 edition of Webster's Dictionary, so for that very reason we must be extremely careful when inserting our modern definition of homosexuality into ancient Biblical texts."

Ed's brows furrowed more deeply. Kevin Lloyd scowled. And Henry grinned from ear to ear. This was too good to be true. He wished Amber and Tammy were here to see this. Maybe this conversation would be the thing that would finally crack his uncle's defenses and let some new light in.

"In fact, the accurate translation of the original words that are so often cited to condemn homosexuals, actually imply shrine prostitution and rape. Not a loving same-sex relationship. Therefore we cannot and should not try to equate them in any way."

"That sounds like mere semantics to me!" scoffed Ed. "Fancy footwork trying to twist the Word of God to your own understanding." He shifted in his seat so as to share a pointed look and knowing smile with Kevin Lloyd. Their double-teaming against this errant minister was working, and Ed wanted to keep up the momentum. He tipped his head, signaling a handoff to Kevin.

Brenton was unfazed, however. "Semantics, Mr. Sloan, are very important. Let me give you an example of how important using the right words can be. Would you agree that the terms 'rape' and 'making love' can both be used to refer to the act of sexual intercourse?"

Ed shrugged his acquiescence.

"Both would be anatomically correct representations, but each has its own connotations and if they were taken out of context and translated incorrectly, it would make for great confusion, would it not?"

Ed leaned back in his chair and exhaled loudly. Henry had never seen his uncle so flummoxed.

"Well, what about the whole 'one man, one woman' thing?" Lloyd jumped in to take up the slack in the argument. "How can anyone justify gay marriage when the model for marriage is so clearly stated in Genesis?" Lloyd did not like the way this conversation was going and wanted to get back to safe ground. His thin lips creased into a conspiratorial grin as he cast his eyes over at Ed. "Or is there another translation problem that I'm not aware of?"

Pastor Brenton opened up his well-worn Bible and began thumbing through the pages as he responded. "Not so much a translation problem, Mr. Lloyd, as one of misconstruing intent. I'm not so sure that the intention of the Creation story was ever to set up rules for the only way marriage was to be defined. Genesis 1 paints a much bigger picture. It is describing how creation came about and its intent is to establish God as author of all life and to show God's love for, and approval of, all He created. And I am bold enough to believe that that includes those created with a same-sex orientation."

"I can't believe you just said that!" blasted Lloyd. "God doesn't create those deviants. They *choose* to sin against God. This is pure blasphemy, and I just can't listen to any more of this bull crap." With that, Kevin Lloyd got up and marched out of the assembly hall, leaving Ed and Henry alone with the cleric.

Henry was stunned by Kevin Lloyd's animosity and embarrassed by his rude departure. He began to apologize for the man's behavior when he realized that Ed was also standing up to leave. He put out his hand. "Please don't go just yet, Uncle Ed. It's important to me that you stay."

Both Henry and Pastor Brenton could see the play of emotions cross Ed's face as he considered all the unsettling information he was receiving. What was he to believe — all that he had ever known and understood? Or the words and interpretations of a person he didn't even know? Ed Sloan was a man torn, but in the end he sat back down, amazingly no longer surly. Other than the three of them, only staff members remained, moving chairs, clearing tables, and removing the leftover danishes and coffee.

Brenton did not comment on Lloyd's exit, nor on Ed's election to stay. Instead, he turned his attention to the point he was trying to make and engaged Henry as he did so.

"It seems to me that whereas we want to focus on the outer configurations of a marriage, arguing about who is allowed to be married to whom, God always looks inward to the heart and blesses all sorts of marriage configurations when the hearts are right."

"That's what I've always felt." Henry leaned toward Brenton, his voice almost a whisper. "What I've always believed. That we should be looking at what's in two people's hearts — not at their genders. And I can't begin to tell you how helpful it is to have my beliefs defended by a clergyman."

"What church did you say you were from?" Ed still couldn't believe all that he had heard coming from this so-called minister. He had to be a fraud. And Ed was determined to expose him. His nephew's soul was at stake.

"I'm Baptist. Went to Baptist Bible College in Springfield, Missouri, but I no longer have a pastorate. I'm an author and a motivational speaker. But with regard to the greater church, I work primarily in the areas of outreach and spiritual growth."

No wonder he doesn't have a church of his own! Ed nearly said it out loud. *He certainly wouldn't last in any of the Southern Baptist churches around here,* he thought.

Brenton interrupted Ed's thoughts. "In Genesis, God is simply telling us what happened when He created the earth and the human race. A man and a woman are necessary for procreation. That is a given. But to infer that every subsequent marriage must exactly replicate the Adam and Eve model, when Scripture tells us otherwise, is folly."

"Okay, Reverend, I think you're really stretching things here." Sloan adjusted his tactics, modulating his usually bombastic style. "It isn't just an inference." He was eager to prove his authority on this matter. "The Bible states unequivocally that marriage is to be between one man and one woman, period. Everyone knows that."

"Well, it's all in the stories." Brenton answered slowly, choosing his words carefully. And he rapidly began turning the pages of his Bible.

Before Sloan could interrupt, he found the passage he had been searching for. "Just a handful of chapters past the story of Adam and Eve, we find Abraham whose wife, Sarah, may have been his half-sister. He claims her as such in Genesis 20:12. This sort of incest is specifically forbidden in the Holiness Codes, yet through this couple, God blesses an entire nation."

Ed's puzzled look betrayed him. *His half-sister? Really?* Why had he never heard that before?

Benton flipped a few more pages and then continued with additional references from the Old Testament.

"And as we read further, we find other examples of marriage blessings that don't fit our cultural norms of today. There is Jacob who married two sisters, Leah and Rachel, in addition to two other women. And he fathered children by all four wives. God abundantly blessed Jacob's polygamous marriage and even indicated His approval of Jacob's marriages by choosing the offspring from all four wives to form the twelve tribes of Israel."

Ed Sloan had attended Sunday school as a child, competing in Bible Drills on local and state levels. He knew his Bible. As an adult he had stood upon it; it was his foundation, and he had thumped it on numerous heads. But he had never really thought about the multiple wives of biblical times and how their mere presence was a direct contradiction of the one-man–one-woman model he had so confidently used to prove his point on so many occasions.

"But perhaps the most radically different example from Adam and Eve is that of King Solomon who had seven hundred wives and three hundred concubines but, nonetheless, was revered by men and blessed by God. I could go on and on."

"Please don't," Sloan said. He was growing weary of this lengthy discussion, which to him seemed to be going in circles. Still, he had to have the last word.

"But none of that says anything about gay marriage, which we know is wrong."

"You're right. There is nothing whatsoever in the Bible about gay marriage. Scripture does not speak to it at all." He closed his Bible and held it up before them, saying, "It's a grave mistake to assume that God implicitly condemns loving same-sex relationships when there is no mention of them in the scriptures. As I said to you earlier, we cannot make scripture mean now what it did not mean then."

"Maybe we put too much stock in words, and whether or not we understand them correctly, and not enough in focusing more on the living example of Christ himself." Henry's clarification was as much for Ed's benefit as his own.

"Henry Keene," said the clergyman, "you are a wise man. That is exactly at the crux of everything, for you can't follow Christ and not be changed in your thinking and your living. That's part of the cost of discipleship, letting go of the need to be right. And as someone once said, 'It takes much more courage to change one's opinion than it does to cling to falsehood.'"

Ed's thoughts were swirling. He was upset and unsettled by everything he had heard but quickly remembered his own past comments declaring he would never become a boomerang on this and other political issues. He couldn't afford to change his opinion.

The preacher then pulled out a carefully folded piece of paper from his Bible. "Long ago, Harriet Beecher Stowe so eloquently wrote: 'O, ye who take freedom from man, with what words shall ye answer it to God?' Perhaps, gentlemen, we risk the greater penalty when hatred and bigotry are allowed to thrive behind the pretext of Christianity than we do by being over-generous with our love, acceptance, and forgiveness."

Ed had taken all he could take. He stood, nodded a curt goodbye to Henry and to Brenton, and silently left the now-empty room. Though he had talked stoutly during most of the conversation, he left this prolonged meeting sourly, carrying with him the seeds of self-doubt and inner reflection. And he did not care a bit for the discomfort they created.

Ed and Tammy had retired for the night. She had been spending most nights in her study, but tonight she felt the need to be close to Ed, so when he had gotten home she had followed him up the stairs and into their room.

It had been an especially grueling day for Ed, and he longed for a relaxing evening at home with a good book, hoping to salve his nerves and loosen his tightly strung body. He couldn't seem to shake the uneasiness he felt. *Was it that kid's suicide? Or that minister from this morning?* He crawled into their giant bed, opened his book, and escaped into his retreat.

Tammy was resting on her settee in the bedroom, her legs pulled up and her book resting against them, when she turned to her husband and said offhandedly, "So how was Breakfast Club this morning? I heard they invited a guest minister."

"Yeah, some guy from out of town." His glasses sat near the tip of his nose, his eyes still fixed on the book in his lap as he shifted uneasily under the covers.

"Well, I ran into Henry and Amber while out to lunch, and he went on and on about the wonderful speaker you had."

"He did, huh?" Ed exhaled and turned another page, all the while looking down, intent on relaxing with his book and leaving the day's events behind him.

"I'd like to hear what you thought about what he had to say." And she peered over the top of her knees in order to see his reaction. It had been difficult for her, dealing with all the details that she had known about Seth, not to build resentments toward his family and all those who sympathized with their type of thinking. Ed included.

"If Henry told you everything, I would think that you know how I feel about it." He continued staring down at the volume he held in his hands.

"Ed, I really want to talk with you about this. Henry told me what the minister said, and I think it would be good for us to have a discussion about it." She tried not to plead, but she desperately needed to talk about her feelings with her husband. "Please."

Ed forcibly shut his book and looked up toward the ceiling, gathering strength to quell the storm that he felt Tam was brewing. "Look, all I wanted to do tonight was come home, spend time with you, and relax from a very long and very difficult day."

"So spend some time with me — by talking with me." The hiccup in her voice exposed her vulnerability, and this was not lost on Ed.

"Well, I don't see what there is to talk about. Henry liked the guy, and I didn't." Ed removed his readers and tapped his fingers on the cover of his book, eager to have this over with.

"But Ed, I want to hear what it was you didn't like. And I want you to know how I feel about what he said and about what happened. I think it's important that we share our feelings ..."

He cut her off. "We've had this same conversation for months now, and frankly, Tam, I'm tired of it." Although he kept his voice in check, his frustration was building up significantly, his posture straightening and stiffening in preparation for another debate that it appeared he could not avoid.

All she really wanted was an intimate relationship with her husband. But intimacy was next to impossible, given Ed's continued refusal to share his feelings or to listen to hers. She desperately needed a sense of belonging together, some affirming connection with him at a deeper than surface level. But instead, she had continued to experience a limited relationship, due largely to Ed's inability to be honest and open with her about almost anything. *Was it too much to ask of a partner in life? How had they gotten to this point? Could their marriage even survive?*

Tammy was determined to keep trying. She couldn't live with herself if she didn't.

"I don't know why you're afraid of talking about feelings — yours or mine. A man is not emasculated by giving acceptance and showing tenderness ..."

Once again Ed talked over her. "Just because I don't like to get sentimental, that doesn't make me a chauvinist; and just because I believe in the traditional definition of marriage, that doesn't make me a bigot!" He turned, propped the pillows he had been resting on, and gave them each a punch.

"I didn't say you were either of those things, but when you expect others to abide by the definitions you're comfortable with, that does beg the question."

"They aren't my definitions, Tam. They come straight from the Bible!" Like circling the wagons, he secured his defenses as he hissed at her.

"Ed, the Bible instructs us not to engage in interracial marriage also. But over time, we've come to realize that God's command was primarily about religion, not race. Like your minister from today pointed out, the people of other countries worshiped false gods. That was the real problem. God didn't want his people getting entangled with idolatry."

"Correction, Tam ... he isn't *my* minister. Thank God."

"Ed, we lived this. Remember when interracial marriage in the states was a felony? But since then, we've grown to realize that God loves all of us equally, and we've changed our laws and our ways. Looking back we can see how criminalizing those relationships was so wrong."

Ed leaned his head back against his pillows, looking to the heavens for saving grace.

"And the same goes with women. When the Bible was written, women were nothing more than a man's property, and there were all kinds of laws about 'shoulds' and 'should-nots.' But now, thank heavens, we've embraced the gifts that women can bring to the table. And that never could have happened if we hadn't realized men and women were equal in God's eyes and deserve equal opportunities."

"Is that what Henry told you he said? He didn't say anything of the sort. And he certainly didn't offer any comfort to those of us who are grieving."

"Don't even get me started on the grief aspect of all this." Tammy got up from the settee and walked over to her dressing table, unable to contain her agitation any longer. She stared at the mirror, studying her reflection. She knew too much. And she was angry. Angry at a society for creating shame where there shouldn't be any. Angry at fellow Christians who used the Bible and Scripture as weapons. Angry at parents who were unable to simply love their child for who he was, rather than for who they wanted him to be.

She wanted to avoid the trap that Father Blair had tried to warn her about. But there it sat, wide open before her, and she stepped right into it.

"That boy's death could have been prevented." She had to look away from the troubled countenance she saw in the mirror, no longer able to sustain eye contact with even herself. Closing her eyes she bent her head and rested both hands on the dressing table. "What I'm getting at is why do we insist upon the literal interpretation of a few biblical references about homosexuality?"

"Must we keeping talking in circles, Tammy? It makes me crazy!" Ed noisily threw back the covers, and his book tumbled to the floor. He got up and began pacing the room.

Tammy turned away from the mirror to face Ed. "I just don't get how you can be so rigid in this area, yet willing to bend in others just like it. What is it about same-sex relationships that threatens you … or our marriage, for that matter?"

He puffed himself up and sarcastically burst out, "I'm not threatened by a bunch of pansies, Tam!" He leaned over to retrieve his book and tossed in onto the bed.

"There you go again, poking fun, and minimizing others instead of really talking to me about what you're feeling." She walked over to Ed. Placing both her arms on his, she looked up into his face and implored him, "Ed, I'm serious. I want you to really talk to me. How does a same-sex marriage threaten ours?"

The internal struggle between tenderness and tyranny gave way for a moment, and Ed was able to reply with honesty, "Well, I guess nothing like that could really threaten ours, but in the broader scheme, I don't want others to get the wrong idea about what a committed relationship is all about. That's all. Okay?"

"What that sounds like to me is that you've decided that either two men or two women are incapable of love and commitment simply because they share gender."

And with that, his flicker of compassion was snuffed out. He broke free of her hold, turning away to face the window. "Well, it just isn't right. It isn't natural." *Why did she insist on making all of this about the two of them all the time?* It didn't involve Ed and it didn't have to involve Tammy either.

"Ed, a lot of people get married because they believe marriage is some kind of beautiful box filled with everything they desire in life: companionship, intimacy, friendship, and love. But the truth is that marriage is nothing but an empty box that gets filled with whatever the two partners bring into it. It's up to the partners in every relationship to define their marriage, Ed — not you, not me, and not the State of Texas or the federal government. Who are we to decide with whom someone else gets to build 'their box' with — or not?"

He turned back toward her now, "The Bible says ..."

"Ed, there is no love in marriage. Love is in people, and people put love into a marriage. They should also put in romance, commitment, hard work, and respect if they want a happy one. But those same people can also bring into their marriage things like estrangement, manipulation, and resentment." She realized she was talking about them now. She could no longer maintain eye contact as she continued. "People are people, regardless of gender, and they will get out of their relationships exactly what they put into them." She returned to her previous spot on the settee, but she did not recline. She was too upset.

"But I can't just throw out the Bible and all that it teaches, Tam. Don't you see that?"

"And I'm not asking you to. No one is. All I'm asking is that you consider putting yourself in a different position for a minute. The way I see it, the greatest threat to traditional marriage is traditional divorce. Wouldn't it be nice if we could start there, where our attention really belongs, instead of disallowing loving individuals who desire legalization in their relationships?"

Ed returned to their bed and plopped down, but whether in defeat or indignation even he did not know. He picked up his book again and placed it in his lap, but folded his arms across his broad chest, essentially willing Tammy to abandon the argument.

"I think it would help if we could pray together about this, Ed. About us. About everything."

"I don't think talking to anyone, not even God, is gonna change anything. He's been pretty clear, it seems to me, as to how He thinks we should live."

They sat in silence, listening to only the rise and fall of their breathing and the beating of their own hearts. But after a few minutes their eyes met, and Tammy found the strength to continue despite the hurt she felt so deeply.

"Just for a minute. Let's assume that we had marriage equality in Texas." She sat with both elbows on her knees, leaning toward Ed as she continued in a much softer tone. "Would that mean that you would have been tempted to fall in love with another man instead of me?"

"You're being ridiculous now," and he picked up his book again, but did not open it. "You know me better than that. No."

"My point exactly. Giving everybody the same rights to marriage would in no way diminish ours. Would it be different than ours? I don't know. I guess it would depend upon what they put into their box." Her eyes creased into a crooked smile, but he shook his head in exasperation as she continued. "But that would be the only way their marriage would be different from ours. Do you see?"

"I see, all right. I see that the relaxing evening I had hoped for has just turned into another argument with you instead." And thumping his book down on the nightstand he announced, "I'm going to sleep now. Maybe I can find some peace in my dreams."

Just what was so unacceptable about the way he was, anyway? Had he not participated in a multitude of conversations about everything gay for months now? Had he not agreed to let her get involved with that Trevor Project despite his reservations? Had he not endured the discomfort of today's meeting and subsequent discussion? What else did she want from him? *It's just another night of not getting any,* he thought. Ed turned off his bedside lamp and, turning away from her, burrowed into the mattress, gathering the covers about himself to better incubate his festering anger and frustration.

Tammy remained on the settee, hugging her knees and watching her husband's immobile bulk for quite some time, but eventually the rhythmic rise and fall of the bedclothes told her that Ed had fallen asleep. She knew he might never be comfortable sharing his secret dreams and darkest fears, but she so needed him to listen to hers. She pulled the lap blanket off her feet and drew it around her shoulders as silent tears spilled down her cheeks.

Chapter 23

A LIVING LEGACY BEGINS

They were the Pink Dragons and they played soccer every Tuesday night. Gracie Keene was a standout player even though she was only six years old. She was extremely athletic, like her mother and father, and her natural abilities allowed her aggressive play to lead the team in both goals and steals.

Henry had driven straight in from Austin. The northbound traffic on I-35 had been heavy and he had barely made it in time. As they awaited the starting whistle of tonight's game, Henry found himself standing in front of a little girl from the opposing team.

"Will you tie my shoe?" she asked him.

He smiled back at her as he looked around for parents that he did not see. "Can you say 'please'?"

To which the little girl, who now looked rather sheepish having known better than to leave out that very important word, answered him quietly. "Mister, will you please tie my shoe?"

"Of course, young lady." Henry responded with a wide smile. Then bending down on one knee, he gathered up the long laces of her cleats. "Do you know how to tie your own shoes?"

"No, sir. I don't." Her eyes were hidden under the flutter of her long, dark lashes.

"Well, these laces are very long and that makes them harder to tie. If the game wasn't about to start, and we had more time, I'd teach you."

She grinned at him. Her bright white teeth played against her dark skin, but then she looked down again, embarrassed to look him in the eye for too long.

Since Henry had come straight from work to the soccer fields, his necktie was dangling in front of her shoes, making it hard to avoid tangling them. So the little girl lifted his silk tie in order to help.

"I like the way it feels." She caressed his tie, rubbing the smooth silk between her hands as if to keep it warm. She gently traced the colorful striped pattern with her fingers, first the yellow then the blue. She outlined the entire length of his tie until she was up to the knot and very close to his face. "My daddy used to wear ties like this. But he's with Jesus now."

"Oh, honey, I'm so sorry." He remained on her level despite the dampness he was beginning to feel in the knee of his trousers.

"Oh, it's okay. I'll see him again." She released his tie but continued to stand there, facing Henry. Their eyes locked, communicating without saying any words.

One of the great gifts of childhood is the ability to live in the moment, Henry thought. Kids are still so deeply engaged in their daily experiences that the past and future have almost no meaning. Yes, she would see her father again. The fact that it would be an entire lifetime before their reunion took place was beside the point. She would see him again. Period. Henry realized at that very moment that most of the pain resulting from his own father's death occurred as he had grown older and had become more acquainted with what concepts like 'time' and 'loss' and 'grief' could mean. Though this little girl didn't yet know it, her last truly innocent moments were behind her. From now on, her life would be forever marked into chapters of 'before' and 'after' Daddy died. But it was a small comfort to imagine that, at least for now, her young age might somehow be lessening her pain.

"There you go, sweetheart. You're all set." He patted her shoe.

She looked him in the eye, for some reason no longer embarrassed. "Thank you, Mister. Your tie is pretty. And so is your hair!" She gave him a big hug, almost toppling him over, and then turned and ran in the opposite direction toward her teammates, who were already gathering on the field.

He absentmindedly ran his hand through his hair. It was too long for his liking right now, but he was glad that she had liked it. He smiled as he watched her bound across the field, her childhood innocence so apparent. With no yoke of inhibitions to chain her, she could share her loss, still find beauty in her surroundings, and express affection — all in about three minutes and with a perfect stranger. Was it blind optimism? Or blissful ignorance? Or just unadulterated joy of living? Either way, it was a better way to live life and that little girl had just taught him a valuable lesson.

"What was that all about?" Amber moved Savannah's diaper bag to make room for Henry as he found his way into the bleachers.

"Just a little girl needing some help, that's all." He waved to Gracie who was taking practice kicks into the net.

Savannah, wearing a little smocked top with an owl embroidered on the front, kept herself busy by climbing the bleachers. She didn't yet have the confidence to climb back down by herself, though, so their conversation contained multiple interruptions as one or the other of her parents climbed up to retrieve their daughter.

"Well, for what it's worth, I think your tie is pretty too," and Amber grabbed the silk from around his neck and pulled him closer for a quick kiss.

The whistle blew and the game started.

"Holly's leaving the Land Office." Henry undid the knot of his tie and pulled the smooth silk though the collar of his starched white shirt.

"What?" Amber turned her attention away from the soccer field and looked at her husband.

Savannah again scrambled up the bleachers beside Henry, and he playfully popped his little one on the behind. Her bloomers, padded with a thick diaper, resounded with a loud thud. Savannah turned and wagged her finger at him. "No. No. No." She apparently didn't want her progress impeded by her father. "No."

"Yep. She's going to see that the desalination presentation gets finished. But then she's gone."

"What happened?" Gracie made a steal and immediately turned the ball up the field. Amber cupped her hand to her mouth and yelled, "Go, Gracie!"

"I'm not really sure. But she told Ed that she and Anne were a couple. They even got married." Henry got up to rescue Savannah from the top bleacher yet again. "They went all the way to Canada to do it. Isn't that great?"

"Wow. I didn't see that coming. But how wonderful for them. I really like them both."

"That's exactly how I feel. But you know Ed." Savannah, now weary of the constant up and down game, sought refuge where she always found it — in her father's 'nest'. But it was gone, covered up with stuff. Frowning, she began to push his jacket and tie out of her space.

"Whoa there, honey bunch. Let me help you." Henry handed Amber his things and patted his thighs in invitation. "Hop on up here, sugar." Savannah climbed her father's legs, and with a helpful boost to her bottom, installed herself on his knee as a substitute. Henry wrapped his arms around her and drew her in close. She was growing, but she still had that wonderful baby smell. He inhaled deeply. It wouldn't be too long before he couldn't enjoy that smell anymore. Savannah abided her captivity by outlining his face with her tiny hands. His bright blue eyes, his ears, his nose. When she got to his lips Henry nipped her fingers and she squealed with delight. Then they started the whole game again.

Amber watched them and smiled deep down inside. Savannah's curls were the same as Henry's when he was a baby. Edith still had several pictures of him on display at her house. "Oh, no. What did Ed do?"

"I'm not exactly sure." Henry took the tie and draped it around his neck so it wouldn't get lost.

"Well, I can only imagine." Amber made a face and turned to reach for Savannah's bag. "I know he's your uncle, and yes, he's been good to us, Henry. But Ed can be an ass sometimes." She retrieved a sippy cup out of the bag and gave it to Savannah, who immediately tilted her head way back, nearly falling over backward as she drank.

"Only sometimes?" Henry laughed. The baby thought he was laughing at her so she joined in too. "Well, whatever the reason, Holly feels that she can't work there anymore. They're even making plans to move to Massachusetts."

"Are you serious? Massachusetts? Why there?"

"Benefits, Amber. They're legally married, so if they go somewhere where same-sex marriage is actually recognized, they'll be eligible for state benefits. And if DOMA gets repealed, they'll be able to get federal benefits as well."

"What's DOMA?"

"The Defense of Marriage Act. It's before the Supreme Court right now. The justices have already heard the case and they're expected to rule on it in the next few months. If they repeal the Act, the federal government will no longer limit marriage to between one man and one woman. In essence it would open up all sorts of possibilities for same-sex couples, like filing their income taxes together. They can't do that now here in Texas. But if they move to a state where it's legal, and DOMA gets repealed, their rights would be the same as ours."

"But they're married now, right? I don't get it."

"But they aren't married in everyone's eyes, Amber. When we got married, who issued the license? The state of Texas. Not the federal government. So in order to receive federal benefits, assuming DOMA is repealed, they would have to live in a state where their marriage is recognized. That's why they're going to move. They're afraid it will never change in Texas. This way they can really start their life out together and be able to protect each other with all sorts of shared economic benefits."

"Well, I don't blame them one bit. Good for them." The crowd roared and they both jumped to their feet. Gracie had scored the first goal of the game.

"We should have a going-away party of some kind, Henry."

"Funny you should say that. Ed's already made reservations on the fourth, at Trulucks in downtown Austin. It was originally planned as a celebratory dinner for completing a big project, but now I'm making sure it will be Holly's send-off party instead. It's been a little frosty over there lately, and I don't want her to leave without a proper goodbye. And of course, I'll get Anne to come too."

"Ooh. I love that place! You're the best."

"Well, I don't know about that, but I'm certainly yours." Before he could kiss her, the crowd roared again. Gracie had scored her second goal.

They continued to talk throughout the rest of the game. Her parents were coming down from Little Rock for a visit. And since they didn't get to see the girls that often, Amber wanted to make sure that Henry's schedule was flexible enough to accommodate all the plans that she was making for them.

"Okay." Henry made a mental note to clear his schedule for the 29th. "So let's make sure to get out on our bikes before they get here. It's supposed to rain a little later tonight and into tomorrow, but this weekend is supposed to be really nice." Savannah had thrown a shoe, and Henry got off the bleachers to retrieve it. "We should get out and ride around the lake on Saturday. Maybe even have a picnic. What do you think?"

They had gotten new bikes at Christmas. Now that Savannah was big enough to ride in a seat behind Henry, and Gracie was finally big enough to keep up with them on her own, they had been taking family rides together.

"Oh darling, that's a great idea. And we don't have any soccer games next weekend. I love this time of year!" Amber worked the shoe back onto Savannah's foot as the toddler struggled to free herself from Henry's grasp.

"And tomorrow is Library Day." She playfully "beeped" Savannah's nose, then Henry's. "Get ready for another round of literary intrigue when you get home, Daddy!"

"I can't wait." Henry smiled. *Was it possible to be any happier than he was now?* Theirs was a terrific relationship, compatible in every way. After ten years of marriage, when for many the excitement has worn off and the drudgery of every-day-living and parenting begins to take its toll, he and Amber still found delight in each other and in all of their family activities. They shared laughter and weren't afraid to share tears. They shared many interests, yet weren't threatened when one or the other needed quiet time to recharge or reflect. He would need to be careful not to let the demands of his expanding career interfere with this wonderful family life of his. He knew what he had was rare, and he didn't ever want to take it for granted — or risk losing any of its precious moments.

After the game, in which Grace had scored three goals, he scooped her up and held her in his arms. "That's my girl! You made so many great passes to Emily and Samantha tonight. And I loved that great steal you made near the end of the game when it looked like they were about to score." Henry made it a point not to focus on the flashy goals that she had scored, but to reinforce instead the teamwork, both offensively and defensively, that she had displayed throughout the game.

Since he had come straight from work, they were in separate cars. Reliving the highlights of tonight's game as they walked, Henry held Gracie's hand as they made their way toward Amber's Toyota. He held Savannah in the crook of his arm. Amber took care of the stroller and Savannah's diaper bag while Henry opened the car door for Gracie, giving her time to fasten her seat belt before closing the door behind her. Once he had Savannah safely tucked into her car seat, he breathed in her familiar scent as he always did when kissing the top of her head. He then leaned in to kiss his wife through the open window. She looked into his eyes with the intent of sending a message of love, but ruined the moment by saying, "Oh, honey, I just remembered, we're out of dog food. Do you mind stopping by the store on your way home?" The girls were both already yawning.

"No bother, darlin', I'll be right behind you. But you girls might have to do tonight's books without me then. I need to stop for gas too." And with that she drove off. Watching him in her rearview mirror, she smiled as he stood there with his hands in his pockets, sporting his famous grin.

It was almost an hour later when the doorbell rang and she immediately breathed a sigh of relief. She hadn't realized how late it had gotten. With two baths, bedtime books, and multiple drinks of water, she had been distracted. It started raining after the girls had gone down and Amber had tried his cell. But Henry hadn't answered. She had just begun to worry, but instantly felt at ease when she had heard the bell. *Silly man, how had he let his phone die AND lock himself out of the house?* She unlocked the deadbolt and opened the door expecting to see an embarrassed and bedraggled Henry, but instead she found Ed, Tammy, and two uniformed police officers standing there.

"Amber, there's been an accident." Ed Sloan choked on his own bitter words.

"Oh, God!" she said, and before Ed could reach out to catch her, Amber had instantly dissolved onto the floor of the entryway, a puddle of despair and disbelief.

Tammy offered to stay at the house with the girls, and the policemen drove Amber and Ed to the hospital. They were headed north on Interstate 35. They must be going to Scott & White in Temple. Amber knew they had a Level One trauma center.

It had been raining hard for some time now, and the flashing lights of the lead patrol car carried with it little colored halos of mist as they drove. There were no sirens, just lights.

They were nearly there when she finally spoke. "You can tell me what happened now." One of the officers sat beside her in the backseat. Ed was on her other side. They had started to tell her back at the house, but Amber had waved them into silence as Ed struggled to pick her up off the floor.

"Well ma'am, we've got a witness and another victim. It had been raining and an elderly man lost his brakes. He came around a blind turn at a high rate of speed, and it appears that your husband swerved to miss the head-on collision. But when he did, his car ended up in the trees on the opposite side of the highway. We got the call from a student at Southwestern, and they brought your husband up here on a CareFlight. But I honestly can't tell you the status of either your husband or the other driver. That's why we want to get you to the hospital as quickly as we can."

She felt a spark of hope and looked up at Ed. But his pained smile told her nothing.

They ushered them through the ER doors where a doctor introduced herself to Amber. She thanked the officers, excusing them for now, and then accompanied Amber to see her husband. Ed shadowed them, several paces behind. But instead of following the corridor to the regular patient examining rooms, they turned down a more secluded hallway. And Amber knew.

The female doctor opened the door and there he was. Her beautiful Henry, his blonde hair awry and his countenance peaceful. His strong body appeared to be resting under the thin sheets just as she had seen it so many times on a late Saturday morning. But this time, he would not awaken to her tender kisses. Her cherished husband, soul mate, lover, and best friend would never again wake and demonstrate his love to her as he had every single day of their life together.

She must have floated into the room. She didn't remember walking to his bedside and sitting in the chair next to him. She thought of breakfast that morning. The laughter they had shared. The kiss he had given her — just as he had always given her — when he left the house. She looked down at his hands. Those strong but tender hands that would never again grasp the tiny fingers of their girls. That would never again hold her in the night. She choked on her thoughts. *This can't be real.*

She caressed his shoulder. His shirt had been yanked open and his tie, the one that had caught the attention of that little girl, was missing. She stroked his head, pushing back the blond wisps that hung down his forehead. He needed a haircut. She had made the appointment for next Thursday. Once again, she felt strangled by her own breath. She brought her hand up to her throat and swallowed. Desperate to defeat the anguish that was rising from the pit of her stomach, she breathed more rapidly. But a devastating grief twisted her heart and her lungs with its miserable grip. *This couldn't be happening.* She looked around the room, hoping for a way out. But there was only the one door. The one she had entered through. And Ed was seated just outside it.

Ed sat alone in the hallway, a stone-faced sphinx, his eyes opened wide and staring straight ahead. Unmoving. But not unfeeling. Ed's appearance was still carefully put together on the outside, his stony façade perfectly hiding the pieces of him that were literally crumbling away on the inside. His heartbreak was not revealed to anyone, save himself.

Amber felt terribly alone. "My darling. Don't leave me." Her lips brushed his ear, his cheek, the corner of his lips. Then she saw it. "Ed! He's breathing. They've made a mistake! Ed!"

Quickly leaving his post in the hallway, Ed entered the room.

"Ed! Hurry! Call the doctors! Look! He's breathing! They've made a mistake!"

Amber was fumbling in the bedclothes looking for the call button as Ed placed his hands gently on her shoulders.

"Honey, I don't think so." He felt his own chest heave as he tried to continue. *How could this keep getting worse? Why must he be the one to tell her?* "It's just the machine that's helping him breathe right now." He thought she had understood what that doctor had told them. The trauma had ruptured his temporal artery causing a massive brain bleed, and they needed to keep him breathing to keep his organs viable. Ed's eyes were brimming with sorrow, and he couldn't keep Amber in focus as he spoke. "He's gone, darlin'."

He felt her go limp under his hands. He had never faced anything this difficult, never felt anything so awful.

She leaned toward Henry's bedside and slowly drew her hands up to her face, covering her mouth and nose in utter horror. She closed her eyes tightly and rocked back and forth. *How could this be real?* Her hands began to tremble as they cupped the pain that was taking up residence in her very soul. She closed her eyes tightly, hoping to keep this awful reality at bay.

But she knew she couldn't close it out forever. She willed herself to open her eyes once more and to watch as Henry's chest deceivingly rose and fell, the gentle whoosh of the ventilator the only sound in the room. She couldn't help herself. Her heart fluttered with a confusing and desperate hope. But then she looked again at the slender tube. She couldn't remember exactly what Ed had just told her, but she knew what his words had meant. That small tube was the only visible hint of tragedy, and it was from that merciless reminder that his lifeless body now received its oxygen. How fragile that little conduit was. Carrying with it the very breath of life. Or death. Henry was only one breath away, but to see him again, she now knew she must cross an eternity.

Surprisingly, her tears did not come. Her loss was so devastating, so all-encompassing, so overpowering, that the much-needed release of tears could not yet be summoned.

She was allowed to sit alone with Henry for almost half an hour before the door once again opened. But even the soft whir of the respirator could not drown out the voices in the hallway. The sound of their footsteps stopped well behind her so as not to intrude into this most intimate of settings. She turned and faced them, her permission for them to speak granted. And as she did so, she saw the tips of Ed's shoes in the hallway. Still seated. Still guarding. Still her protection. She registered a small, warm gratitude for his faithfulness.

But he was silently imploding. Ed had gone back into the hallway earlier to phone Edith again, and just as he had feared, the awfulness of this night had certainly continued. How do you tell a widow that her only son has also died? Certainly not on an answering machine. He had tried calling her multiple times since he had heard, each time bracing himself for the worst. Finally he had gotten her, and she was on her way. He would remain in the hallway until Edith arrived.

"Mrs. Keene," said someone she would never remember. "I am so sorry for your loss." He handed Amber a small zippered bag that contained Henry's wedding band, car keys, and wallet.

"Ma'am," said the other person, whose identity was equally unimportant to her. "It's only because the timing of these things is so vital that I bring this up to you now, but your husband's driver's license indicated that he wished to be an organ donor, giving the gift of life to others. And I must ask for your consent in order for the doctors to proceed with his wishes."

All she could do was stare at them. Those two nameless and faceless people were nothing but ghosts in her nightmare. But even so, they produced a real clipboard and a real pen. And they waited for her to give a real answer.

Being willing to act on the intellectual knowledge of death — without yet coming to emotional acceptance — may be what makes organ donation possible at all. Amber consented without hesitation. She signed the necessary papers and was allowed another thirty minutes with her beloved. She slipped his wedding band on her finger where it nestled next to her own. She left his keys in the bag. She would give them to Ed. And then she opened Henry's wallet. A Sak-n-Save receipt dropped onto her lap. She picked it up and saw the charge: $12.42 for dog food. And she laid her head against her husband's arm for the last time and wept bitter tears that brought no comfort, tears that would not stop.

Never underestimate the pain of a person, because in all honesty,
everyone is struggling. Some people are better hiding it than others.
— Will Smith

Chapter 24

WE MEET ANDREW

The phone rang and woke him from a dead sleep. It was 3:17a.m. Careful not to tangle the tubes which ran from the oxygen tank into his nose, Andrew slowly reached across the bed to retrieve the special cell phone issued to him by Baylor University Medical Center at Dallas.

"When?" Cradling the phone under his chin, he used both arms to struggle to an upright position and leaned against their headboard. "Coming from where?"

At first, the phone's ring and Andrew's sleepy voice had sounded like it was coming from underwater, but Taylor was now fully alert, turning on the bedside lamp and propping up the pillows behind himself and then Andrew.

"What will I need to ..." Andrew succumbed to a horrible coughing fit, struggling to breathe while simultaneously stifling the impulse to cough up his toes. His deep brown eyes were now red-rimmed and watery, and it took several long minutes to catch his breath in order to continue the call. Taylor handed him the water glass from the nightstand, pushed dark curls off his forehead, and then watched hopefully as Andrew's spasm settled down. Despite his temporary inability to speak, Andrew still communicated with Taylor, his dark eyes bright with hope and his sunken cheeks lifting into a broad, mustached smile. The mustache was a recent addition, grown since the oxygen tubes had made it difficult to shave. Andrew handed the glass back to his partner and put the phone back up to his ear. "I'm back," he wheezed on an exhale and then paused to catch his breath. "When do you …" — sentences of more than just several words were difficult — "need me to get there?"

Taylor crawled closer to Andrew and turned to face him. He sat with his legs crossed, elbows resting on his knees, chin atop clasped hands, resembling for all the world a child at bedtime prayer.

Finally, Andrew drew the phone away from his ear and looked at it in disbelief as he punched the button to end the call. "We've got lungs." The words were barely audible. Andrew was so full of emotion and so short on oxygen that he couldn't summon the strength to say more. Tears rimmed Taylor's lids. He leaned forward and gently gathered his partner into his arms. And they cried. They wept tears of joy and gratitude. They wept out of relief and for the hope welling up inside them both, and they wept for fear of holding out hope. This had been a very long journey, and no words were necessary now. They sat in silence in one another's arms as their tears mingled.

Andrew had grown up the only son of a humble farming family just outside McPherson, Kansas. The Colsons had been planters there for generations, so there had been much celebration when he was born, the youngest of Don and Madge's four children and their pride and joy. The family finally had its heir. The land that had been theirs for over one hundred years now had a caretaker who could carry their faithful husbandry into the next generation.

But their parental aspirations were not long-lived. The infant proved to be sickly. The toddler did not thrive. And so Don and Madge began the almost weekly treks to the doctor that would come to define young Andrew's life.

Originally thought to have inherited his mother's digestive delicacies, Andrew saw a variety of specialists and underwent numerous tests before a diagnosis of cystic fibrosis was finally confirmed. He was only six years old. This devastating diagnosis, handed down by his physicians, coincided with his emerging recognition that he was different from the other boys and his own self-diagnosis of "being wrong," a verdict which was equally as devastating. He didn't yet have a concept of sexuality and had never heard the word "homosexual," but he already knew that he didn't feel the same way about girls — or boys — that his friends did. And he learned very early on that he needed to hide this difference from everyone, including himself.

Throughout his childhood and youth, his sensitivity and softness were easily explained away by his physical maladies, and he was content to have others regard these early manifestations as nothing more than that. Instead of the taunting and bullying others received for being any kind of different, he was usually treated with deference and compassion. The other kids' parents, and the teachers at school and church, would brook no mistreatment of any kind of the "poor little sick boy," and his female classmates loved to nurture him. Of course, being singled out for such special treatment created distance between him and many of the other kids and left him feeling "less than." But that was still preferable to others seeing what he now thought of as "the bad" that lurked deep inside him, a growing attraction to other boys that he resolutely rejected. And thus began a life of hiding behind his disease.

As he entered his early teen years, his doctors learned how better to control his CF symptoms by introducing digestive enzymes into his daily diet, and Andrew's physical strength improved. He was finally functioning well enough to enter the world that had meant "belonging" for so many of his peers — sports. His doctors had advised him that swimming would be a healthful activity to pursue as it helped with both mucus clearance and ventilator function when practiced on a regular basis. So he became an avid swimmer.

At first, he was simply attempting to keep his symptoms at bay, but as he and his coaches realized the extent of his natural talent, he was encouraged to join the only competitive swim team in the area, the McPherson Aqua Pups. Soon he was competing in all of the Missouri Valley sanctioned swim meets throughout central Kansas and regularly winning the freestyle and breaststroke events.

For the first time in his life, he felt like he was being seen as more than just his illness. He was a real person, a teammate, a swimmer. It was a heady feeling and swimming became a real bright spot in his otherwise difficult early teen years. When he was swimming, he could forget all about the nagging worries and anxieties swirling around his budding sexuality. So he swam a lot and eventually ended up on the varsity team in high school where he lettered in his freshman and sophomore years.

Although not symptom-free, he was relatively healthy during these years, suffering only occasional lung infections. Each infection, however, took a cumulative toll on his long-term health, for each episode left damaging scar tissue which built up in his lungs and, in turn, intensified his breathing difficulties. He would sometimes have to stop in the middle of a practice and cough, his dark curly hair shaking off pellets of water as he convulsively hacked. But he knew that swimming was helping him socially and emotionally, as well as physically, so he pushed himself to do as much as he could for as long as he could.

Of course, bad days still came, and on those occasions his family would resort to performing chest physiotherapy on him. It was called "clapping," and his sisters and parents did this anywhere from one to four times a day for as many days as Andrew needed it. And they continued these ministrations for many years, cupping their hands and striking his chest rapidly and firmly — front, back, and sides — to break up the congestion in his lungs. It was very tiring for them, and so they took turns relieving one another, but no one ever complained. And as odd as it may sound, he found in this skin-on-skin touch the intimacy he could not find anywhere else. He was still struggling with his sexual leanings, unable to reconcile who he was and who he wanted to be. He felt terribly alone, and so very lonely, outside his family circle. And even within his own family, he sometimes felt like he didn't belong. He had hidden who he was for so long that it was as if they were all relating to someone else, a figment of his and their, creation.

Despite his difficulty gaining weight, Andrew grew into a tall, strong young man, though very slender. And, though lacking the rough bark of manhood already evident in many of his school friends, he did catch the eye of several young women in his class. They were drawn in part to the tragic aspect of him, a nice-looking, romantic figure who everyone knew would die young. And they were drawn in part to the gentle boy who listened so well and seemed to understand. Afraid to act upon his true desires and hungry for the companionship he saw others enjoying, he began casually dating some of these "girl friends," always careful to keep things on a superficial basis. Knowing as he did that he was not true boyfriend material, whenever 'just dating' seemed to be on the road to something more, he would break off the relationship. He never wanted to hurt those girls he really liked the most. Dating was fun. It got him out of the house, he made some good friends, and it provided him with good cover. But each time that he came home from one of those dates, he descended even deeper into despair. He plummeted into a profound sense of alienation. His heart, his soul — his very self — was drowning in longing and loneliness.

Upon high school graduation, and much to his parents' dismay, Andrew moved to the Dallas area to attend the University of North Texas. Their concern had little to do with his leaving and everything to do with his going. Since his diagnosis, they had known that Andrew would not continue his father's legacy of farming. The physical demands on a working farm were more than Andrew could possibly handle, and besides, they knew the farm would be well taken care of. Two of his sisters had already married local boys eager to carry the load for their new father-in-law, and Don and Madge had raised all of their children to lead lives independent of them, Andrew included.

No, they weren't upset that he was leaving home. They were anxious that he was going so far away, out of reach of the doctors who had cared for him since infancy, out of reach of the hospital staff and respiratory therapists who knew him by name. And they were worried about how he would manage his already advancing chronic illness in a big city where he knew no one. Madge had gotten the names of specialists and a good primary-care doctor from his current doctors, and Don had researched the Dallas hospitals and pulled together contact information on emergency services. It was all they could do now for their son — that and pray — for he was intent on going to Dallas.

But they were concerned. As Andrew had grown older, his lungs had become weaker, and they knew that this was the inevitable progression of the disease. He had already had to give up his beloved swimming, and the only reason he could strike out on his own like this was because of the new 'ThAIRapy' vest he'd gotten at his last visit with Sue, his respiratory therapist. The vest, connected by hoses to an air pulse generator, vibrated his lungs in the same way that they all had when they were clapping him. *But what if something went wrong with the machine?* Madge had worried.

"I'll be okay," he had assured his parents from the seat of his Jeep Wrangler as he prepared to drive southward toward Texas and his new life. He had thanked them for the reference notebook they'd handed him and had hugged them all goodbye. As he backed out of the driveway and onto the road, he turned to return their last goodbye wave.

"Call us when you get there," his mother had called out.

"We love you, son," Don had said as he waved. "Be safe!"

They had been good parents. And as he drove off down the street, he felt a hard lump in his throat and a burning in his chest that had nothing to do with his CF. But he had made up his mind. He had no intention of returning to Kansas. In Kansas, his life had been doubly defined by conditions that had marked him out as different from everyone he had ever known. He wanted desperately to fit in, and Dallas, with its gay neighborhoods and strong gay presence throughout the city, called to him more loudly and insistently than the sirens had called Odysseus.

His self-esteem had been crushed in Kansas, crushed under the weight of harbored anxiety and repressed drives too deeply secreted away. He wanted to make a clean break with all that and to become something new: a gay man who could live in the light, not hide in the shadows. He knew he could achieve this transformation much more easily in a place where no one had any other expectations of him. The reality of his shortened life expectancy gave a sense of urgency to this desire. He didn't want to die having never experienced romantic love and intimacy. Therefore, Kansas, and all those he left there, remained in his rearview mirror except for when he made infrequent Thanksgiving or Christmas visits. But even these were short stays, nothing more than condensed versions of his former life. It was now very hard for Andrew to feel gratitude for, or find joy in, living a lie. Especially when the lie was as much a part of family tradition as the turkey and the tree.

His first-ever hospital stay without one of his parents there was at the age of twenty, and although it was initially a frightening experience, it gradually became just a fact of life. Andrew received his degree in accounting and then accepted employment as a lower-level executive of a large non-profit in downtown Dallas.

He met Taylor one Sunday at the Metropolitan Community Church.[35] Andrew had found this open, welcoming mainstream congregation shortly after he had arrived in Dallas. He had been impressed with how the ministerial staff and congregants alike worked a triage of sorts, offering solace and treatment to those who had been injured in the conservative holy war against gays. Countless visitors had come to MCC bearing deep wounds to their psyches and their souls, wounds inflicted by lethal doctrines and inhospitable churches. And they were nursed back to emotional and spiritual health by this loving congregation. Many of the healed would remain as wounded healers, continuing this saving work in the war zone that was the Bible Belt. Some would move on to create healthy, happy lives from what had previously been battered and broken ones.

Taylor was one of these wounded healers and had served as the church's coordinator for Austin Street, a therapeutic homeless community funded entirely by volunteers from Dallas area churches. He organized a monthly meal which was provided, prepared, and then served by church members to the hundreds who found respite in the downtown facility.

"You know, some of the people who end up there are forced out of their homes by families unable to deal with their sexuality. They're lonely and scared, and often they turn to drugs."

They had been bagging sandwiches assembly-line style with about twenty-five other men and women the first time they had met. Despite the peanut butter that had splotched the front of Taylor's shirt, Andrew had taken notice of the attractive young man opposite him and had been taken aback by the passion he displayed for the marginalized in their community.

"They really don't have anywhere else to go. I know because I was almost one of them when I was in high school. My dad kicked me out when I told him I was gay, and I spent the next two years sleeping on different couches. I could've easily been one of them, using drugs and sex to create a false sense of belonging. And if it hadn't been for someone who invited me to come to MCC, I *would've* been one of them. Just another statistic. Just another casualty of a judgmental society. That's why I do this. I think it's important for them to see that gays and lesbians can actually be successful and happy. Unlike what they may have been taught at home."

Andrew hadn't been as physically limited at that time, and he was able to contribute a good bit of time and energy toward this outreach, which also afforded him a good bit of time to get to know Taylor better. Andrew had moved very slowly. Having never been open like this before, he had been reluctant to share too much of himself too soon. Taylor's ability to live his truth, even as a teenager, had been completely foreign to Andrew — and even a little frightening. He still had not even told his parents so how could he let himself be vulnerable enough to love another man? Yet there was no denying that his feelings for Taylor were growing in intensity, and even though they felt like the sentiments of a stranger, these very feelings had pushed him to the brink of a life-altering decision. He could either face his fear and gain what his heart most desired, or he could continue what had been the safe path up until then, a path built of denial and lies.

Taylor's compassionate nature had proven hard to resist, and their friendship had eventually blossomed into something more, with Taylor whispering the words first, "I love you."

These were words Andrew had never heard addressed to him before, other than by his parents or his sisters, and he had certainly never dreamed he would hear them from someone like Taylor, someone so kind, so honest, so real.

"Do you? Really?" Trust had proven difficult for Andrew in the beginning. "I'm not sure I really know how to love someone. Maybe because I'm not sure that I've ever been able to really love myself."

But Taylor had been both patient and persistent. He had been able to see beyond Andrew's insecurity and worsening infirmity, and over time, that tentativeness had given way to cautious trust — first, trust in Taylor and, finally, trust in himself.

Their months together had now turned into years, and Taylor had grown increasingly concerned watching Andrew's symptoms worsen, his fears only slightly allayed when Andrew was finally placed on the transplant list. Andrew's lung capacity had dropped to thirty percent, and just a month before, his physician had diagnosed ventricular enlargement due to obstructions caused by the scarring in his lungs. So now he was a heart patient too, and neither man knew whether to take that as good news or bad. One had to get sick enough to warrant being considered a priority recipient before he could be bumped to the top of the list, but he had to remain healthy enough to survive the eight-hour surgery. There is stress upon stress when your loved one is on the list, and there is nothing you can do but wait. The risk of each passing day brought Andrew closer to death, but every day that he survived also allowed him another opportunity for life. It was a daily game of Russian roulette, every day a deadly game of chance, and their church family had been pivotal to their very survival these past three years.

So much of their time, which they now knew was precious and not to be taken for granted, had to be spent at doctor's appointments or in the hospital, and their church family had stepped up as Andrew's health crisis had become chronic. He had actually listed the congregation as part of his support system, right under Taylor's name, on the original transplant application paperwork. Having an effective support system is a vital part of the criteria reviewed when being considered for placement on The List. The church provided meals and offered help with transportation and yard work — all things that Taylor could have handled if he weren't balancing the responsibilities of career and caregiving. The constant stream of visits from church friends laden with food and flowers had lifted their spirits more than anything else during this dark and wearying time.

Their bags were packed, so just moments after Andrew had received the call, Taylor jumped into action. Pulling on a pair of jeans, Taylor grabbed their bags out of the closet and headed to the garage. Just like an expectant mother who must be prepared to deliver at any time, they had prepared as best they could. They too had been awaiting new life. Only their bags had been packed for nearly three years now.

"Yellow Alert!" Andrew posted on his CaringBridge site as Taylor pulled out of the driveway. "We were just called to the hospital for blood work. If everything clears, I'll be offered lungs! So take a deep breath for both of us, and PRAY OUT LOUD that everything is a GO! I'll update when I know more either way."

Andrew had been deathly ill the last several weeks. His body wasn't getting enough oxygen, and that left him mentally confused and completely devoid of energy. It was during this agonizing period of waiting that Taylor was able to convince Andrew to finally tell his family his truth. They deserved to feel the relief that their precious son was being loved and cared for by a committed partner, not just a good friend. And at long last, Andrew came to the realization that he needed them more than he needed his secret.

"Oh, my dear one. I have actually hoped that this was the case." His mother had sounded relieved. "That you weren't distanced from us because of some long ago hurt we'd caused you. I couldn't bear to bring it up myself, though, in case I was wrong. I was so afraid of making things even worse. Honey, more than anything else in this world your dad and I just want for you to be happy."

"Yes, we want you to be happy, son." His dad had been listening on the extension. "And to be well," he added.

"And the fact that you have Taylor to care for you and love you ... through all of this ..." She had been overcome with emotion, and none of them had been able to say much more.

Relieving himself of that burden had been so uplifting, so freeing. He felt as though he could breathe a little easier just knowing that his family loved him for who he really was. The gift his parents had given him that night on the phone had been every bit as precious as he imagined new lungs would be.

But he had continued to weaken, and he hadn't kept up his entries as usual. The last several posts had actually been entered by Taylor. After Andrew had been admitted to the hospital for another infection, he had asked Taylor to update their faithful following of friends, and now family, regarding his condition. Taylor had sat there, fingers on the keyboard for a long time, before finally starting to type: "March 17th — Where to begin? ... Our road continues to be a hard one. Andrew was placed on oxygen today, and we are still taking things one day at a time ...' Taylor paused. He had to find something to lighten this and still let everyone know how dire Andrew's situation was. 'Just looking for things to be thankful for and reasons to laugh out loud. Although Andrew's laugh isn't much more than a whisper these days, it is still heartfelt. He is excited to finally be carrying a purse — which houses his oxygen tanks, by the way.

He has lamented the fact that an empty tank is just as heavy as a full one! Poor boy just can't seem to catch a break! Thank you to the many angels who come our way — especially Beth Anne who brings us lunch several times a week, the entire Oak Lawn Boys softball team, and Jason Marks who helped us with our taxes. If only we could have filed a joint return ... he would have had half the work and only charged us half the fee, right? Looks like we get screwed by Uncle Sam AND our gay accountant. Damn! Please keep Andrew in your prayers. We've still got a very long walk through these dark woods. Miles to go and all that, but hopefully there are more behind us now than what we still have to face."

CaringBridge had become the best way for the couple to stay in touch with family and friends regarding Andrew's health. The sites were interactive, allowing visitors to leave comments or even message each other. Writing updates and reading the caring responses from loved ones was an enjoyable way to pass the long days and even longer nights they spent together at the hospital.

"March 20th — Well, the wheels have come off the lung wagon, yet again. I left Andrew after dinner to go home to wash clothes and to do a few things around the house tonight. I even considered sleeping in our own bed since he had been doing so well. Silly me. I called to check on him around 8:30, and he said he was lightheaded and felt really dizzy and that he had been throwing up. I told him I was headed back up to the hospital. I got the charge nurse on the phone but she wouldn't tell me anything. She apologized but said that it was hospital policy that since I wasn't a legal spouse or relative, she couldn't give me any information. But she knew me!! We had told her we were partners and had been together for thirteen years. She had seen the two of us together for the better part of a week, but she said that to be in compliance with HIPAA she had to have a copy of Andrew's medical power of attorney. So I had to turn around and go back to the house, not knowing whether Andrew was dead or alive! If we had been a heterosexual couple, all I would have had to do was say we were married. They don't ask them for a marriage license![36] When I finally arrived back at the hospital with the REQUIRED DOCUMENT in hand, I was finally told that his blood pressure had tanked, and the quick response team had been called in. They thought he had had a heart attack. AT NO TIME DID THEY EVER CALL ME! I promise you they would have if I had been his wife!!! I entered his room to find a room full of doctors and nurses and Andrew on a heart monitor. So now we are back on the 10th floor where he is both a lung patient AND a heart patient. It is a quarter to two in the morning and no end is in sight. So here is one more request for prayers for my boy and the miracle he so desperately needs. And say a quickie for me too, that I may remain calm and cool, and that I stay focused on Andrew's immediate health needs rather than attempting to "fix" a broken health system by decking all the doctors in sight. It is odd to be hoping that Andrew gets sicker (the sickest person the docs will ever HAVE seen actually) but still strong enough to survive the surgery. But that is exactly what Andrew has to do to receive priority placement on The List. It is a delicate balance and we have no control. Please pray for strength and patience as we walk this tightrope and as we wait together for the gift of new lungs for Andrew. Andrew just asked that you please also pray for the one who will give us this gift, and for his or her family as they share a final act of charity and love. One that gives us a new beginning."

It was still very dark as they made their way along the deserted streets to Baylor. Not too many people were out at 4 a.m., which was a good thing. Like an expectant father, Taylor was intent on getting to the hospital as quickly as possible, and the way his adrenalin was pumping, he was having to take care not to be too heavy-footed. That would not be a good thing on these wet streets. They were making good time when the light ahead of them turned red. He let out an exasperated, "Damn!" and punched the steering wheel with a fist as he screeched to a stop. There they were, stopped by a red light with no cars in sight in either direction and Andrew's new lungs awaiting them just a few miles away. He drummed his fingers on the steering wheel impatiently, tempted to go on through.

"Don't even … think about it." Andrew wheezed without looking up. "No point."

Taylor looked over at the frail, almost wizened, old/young man slumped over his iPad in the seat next to him, and he grinned. Of course, Andrew was right. He breathed deeply and tried to calm himself. If this night was like every other interaction they'd ever had with any medical facility, it was going to be another 'hurry up and wait' kind of night. The lungs probably weren't even there yet. *The whole process of harvesting an organ is amazing — and complicated*, he mused. *Emotional aspects notwithstanding.*

The light changed and he started off more slowly. Teams of doctors would have delicately removed the donated organs from the deceased by now and placed them into basic hand-held coolers. *Humble vessels for such precious gifts*, he thought. They could just as easily have been used to lug beverages to a tailgate party as to gingerly carry life-saving, vital organs to desperate patients miles away. *Like us.* He breathed in deeply. *Thank you. Thank you. Thank you*, he breathed out. He hoped the donor, whoever he or she was, could hear him and know just how much his or her gift meant to them.

The rain was picking up, and the windshield wipers slapped out a rhythmic beat as halos of light surrounded the street lamps lining the street. Taylor thought of the transport team who would deliver Andrew's new lungs, and he squeezed the steering wheel a little tighter and lifted a silent prayer for their safety. Most transport teams were volunteer pilots and medical personnel who were willing to take off to anywhere, at any time, to deliver the gift of life to another whom they would never meet. *What a selfless lot. True angels of mercy.*

They got to the hospital as quickly as they could, but as Andrew had predicted, it was only to wait. One hour turned into three, and Taylor was becoming quite agitated. It was past seven o'clock. There was still no news on the blood work, and now they had a whole new crew to work with due to the shift change.

With his arms folded, Taylor stood on the other side of the room. "I don't understand what is taking them so long." He barked his thoughts to the large plate-glass window that overlooked the tangle of covered walkways and close-set buildings below.

But Andrew remained subdued. He lay in bed, a medical Medusa with tubes running into and out of his body. "Come sit down." He patted the covers, careful not to set off the IV alarm again. "I ... do better ... when you're ... close to me."

Taylor turned and smiled broadly as he walked back over to the bed. "Ditto, my man." *That made two of them.*

Andrew had been drawn to that winning smile the first time they had met. Taylor's deep-set dimples suited his gregarious nature and were set off by his clean-shaven head, perfectly shaped and perpetually tanned. His happy, playful disposition put a bounce in his step, and his eyes danced with merriment, especially when he laughed. But not only then. They were animated by a lively and infectious spirit at all times, and that spirit had shone through even in the hardest of times. People gravitated to Taylor like those moths in that well-worn adage were mesmerized by a flame; Andrew certainly had. He had been smitten in the first few minutes of their acquaintance. Of course, it hadn't hurt that Taylor was so nice to look at too. He was elegantly formed — tall, with a broad chest and strong arms. Army proud.

As Taylor sat on the bed, he put his arm around Andrew and gave him an affectionate wink and began to massage Andrew's neck and shoulders. "I guess I won't get to do this for a while."

Andrew looked at him in a troubled sort of way, the same way he looked at some of their friends who dressed their dogs in sweaters and bows. "And ... I can't ... believe ... that I'm happy ... about that." Andrew grinned a crooked smile and then leaned against the rail on the bed, bending in half with spasms he could not control.

The years of waiting had taken a toll on both men. They had come very close to getting new lungs once before, but Andrew had had to undergo a bronchial artery embolization to stop him from coughing up blood. It had been just successful enough that another prospective transplant patient was determined in greater need and, therefore, the better match. And in a matter of minutes, they had gone from euphoria, to desolation, to guilt that they had resented another's life-saving treatment, finally settling back into their habitual routine of waiting, hoping, and worrying about what each new day would bring.

This was why they had agreed not to call Andrew's parents until they knew it would really happen this time. No need to wake them for something that might not even occur. They'd been down that road before, and Andrew didn't want their hopes to be dashed yet again.

Competing for lungs, or for any organ for that matter, was a difficult issue to wrestle with. Fortunately, this time the only other lung candidate with Andrew's blood type who had made the priority list was a young girl, aged twelve. Since the size of a recipient's chest cavity limits the pool of available donor lungs, they would never have to be in contention for the same set of lungs. Size matching is second only to one's blood type and overall health as a match indicator. It was a relief, therefore, for Andrew to know that he would not keep a little girl in middle school from receiving the lungs she desperately needed to survive.

And, as was his nature, he said a quick prayer for this little girl who still needed another family's tragedy in order for her own family to claim a miracle. This was such a tough business all the way around. His thoughts returned to the donor and to his or her family and, as is so often the case with organ recipients, he began to agonize over the issue of worthiness. Who was he to regain a chance at life because of someone else's death?

"I guess ... the biggest fear I have ... is a feeling ... of inadequacy ... Am I really worthy ... to accept such a gift? ... Such a sacrifice?"

"How can you say that?" Taylor took Andrew's face in his hands. "You are the most worthy person I know. And whoever it was that has given you this opportunity did so because it's what they wanted to do. A last loving gesture from someone who wanted someone like you to have a chance after he or she did not."

"I know ... It's not that I don't ... feel I deserve ... this chance ... You know ... how long I've dreamed ..." Andrew succumbed to a rasping cough that seemed to bring up his very toes. He wiped his mouth and Taylor dabbed at his forehead. "It's just that I struggle ... with the 'Why Me' ... and not someone else."

"Well, I've always had faith that you would get them when the time was right." Taylor rested his hand on Andrew's chest. "So, you've already got experience being one of the longest-living cystic fibrosis patients ever. Now it's time to get to work on becoming the longest-living post-transplant patient ever."

There was a knock at the door.

"We've got a match, and it's a 'Go.' The nurses will be in to prepare you for surgery shortly."

Both their eyes brimmed with tears. They had waited for those words, for this moment, for so long.

Everyone thinks of changing the world, but no one thinks of changing himself.
— *Leo Tolstoy*

Chapter 25

ED MEETS THE RECIPIENT

It had been four months. Four interminable and heart-wrenching months. There had been days when Ed couldn't concentrate. His appetite was poor and his sleep was interrupted by nightmares that wakefulness could not end. His attempts at keeping his own grief at bay were foiled each time he saw or spoke to Edith, Amber, or one of the little girls. The first few days following the accident had been a painful blur, their feelings dulled by the shock of it all. Then over the next several weeks, the business of death, which might actually be deemed a blessing in disguise, had kept their hearts distracted and their minds set on other things, rather than on the staggering loss which they all faced. Ed had done his best to be there for them, but it was taking a toll. Why had his family been chosen to suffer such loss? What more could he stand?

And the pall had extended into the office too. He found no respite in his work these days. Everyone in the building had known and loved Henry. He had been everybody's friend, and they sorely missed his cheerful, uplifting presence. They were each dealing with their own grief. Holly, Trey, Mary Anne, Dennis, Mac — all of them. They each had their own sense of loss. And Ed had been forced to face them all, armed with nothing but his own vulnerability.

Then, within a month, Holly was gone, too. Just up and moved in the middle of all this tragedy. Two big holes. Two people who had meant so much to him — just gone. The emptiness he faced simply going in to work these days was almost more than he could bear.

And then there was Tammy. He hadn't found much comfort at home these days either. As they made their way up I-35, he glanced over at the passenger seat where she was busily reading something on her iPad, and he felt the knife twist in his gut. He missed his old Tammy. She had always been so soft, so loving, so giving of herself. The perfect wife and mother. And their home had been a happy one. But now they hardly talked to each other, except when the kids were around — or when they were arguing. And worse yet, she was still insisting on sleeping separately. That really hurt. It wasn't like her to hold a grudge or to punish him. And doing it now when he needed her so badly … The knife turned again. They had always been so compatible sexually, and she had always been such a warm pillow on which to lay his head when he needed comfort. She had changed, and he didn't know why, and he wasn't exactly sure how. Of course, there was the obvious, her infatuation with the O'Dells and everything gay, but he was beginning to realize it went much deeper than that. He just couldn't put his finger on it.

Did she still love him? The question erupted in his thoughts before he could tamp it back down into the recesses of his mind. That was a thought he could not face. He calmed himself by remembering that she had agreed to do this today. She did care. In fact, if the truth be known, it had been more her idea than his. Amber had asked for help and Tammy hadn't hesitated, volunteering them both for this mission.

Amber had received a letter, an invitation really, from the Baylor Health Care System's Annette C. and Harold C. Simmons Transplant Institute in Dallas. They were hosting their annual Transplant Reunion.[37] It was a big barbecue party where hospital staff, patients, donors, and their families would gather together to celebrate life — life given and life received. She was even provided the name of the young man who had received Henry's lungs, Andrew Colson. She and Andrew had corresponded, even making plans to meet at the barbecue. And she had thought, at first, that she could do it. Amber had been amazingly strong, forced to be so for the girls' sakes, Ed guessed. But as the date had grown closer, Amber had realized that she just wasn't ready. That was when she had called Tammy.

"It's in Dallas. It's going to be a western-themed event at the hospital's Tom Landry Fitness Center. I'm just spending so much of my energy everywhere else. I don't think I can do this right now. I just don't have it in me. "

"We'll do it, sweetie. Don't you worry a bit. And we'll take the girls too if you'd like. You know, give you a little break."

Amber had been working with Edith on putting together a program that would be a coordinated effort between Gracie's school and Westmont High to create safe learning environments for all kids. They had thrown themselves into their project, spending precious time and hard-to-find energy on their efforts. Ed didn't know all the details, but they were preparing for a school board meeting to get approval for something they were calling Henry's Kids. Something to do with bullies and schools.

But Gracie had received a last-minute invitation to spend the weekend with one of her little school friends, so they had only Savannah with them for this day trip to Big D. Amber and Edith were taking advantage of the opportunity by making this the final push before their big presentation next week. They had said the project was proving to be their salvation, but today, little Savannah was proving to be Ed's. She was in the back, kicking her feet against the base of her car seat. "Free-Too, Free-Four." Gracie had been teaching her how to count.

She was so much like Henry. That wavy blonde hair, her glowing eyes and her twinkly smile infecting all those around her with happiness. Looking at her was like looking at Henry — her reflection in the rearview mirror as touching, yet untouchable, as looking back at the memories he had of the father she would not remember. Ed tried to count with her, but only succeeded in half-choking himself with grief instead. Savannah laughed, thinking he was playing a silly game, barking like a dog as she believed he had done. Her innocence gave Ed the ability to regroup, retreat for a moment, and then compartmentalize his churning emotions. What was he supposed to learn from such tragedy? From the horrific change that had rained down on all those involved? He wiped the corner of his eye.

Tammy placed a comforting hand on his arm and turned to sing with Savannah. "Down in the meadow in a itty bitty pool, fwam fwee little fishies and a momma fishy too…"

Ed remembered her singing those silly songs with their own kids when they were little. And he remembered how she had stepped in, just like this, when Henry was little and Edith was broken with grief. Although it had been a painful period, it was also a wonderful time. A time of great contentment. Then, their lives had been in front of them, just waiting for Ed and Tammy to blaze their trails together, trails toward fulfillment and happiness.

Tammy still loved him. See how she had read his need and reached out to him? But, then why the continued distance? Why had she detached herself from him — the one she still obviously loved?

"Boop, Boop, Dittum, Dattum, Wattum. Choo!"

Savannah attempted to sing along with Tammy, "Boopem. Choo!"

Ed steeled himself. He just couldn't formulate a sound answer to all the questions swirling in his mind, and he was unable to return her compassionate gestures with a word, or even a look. He didn't dare, lest another tear fall which would demonstrate just how unsure his footing really was these days.

So they drove on. The baby's head soon became heavy, her babbling interrupted only by eventual sleep. Tammy went back to her book, and Ed watched as the countryside rolled by. The grass was a deep green and the wildflowers were long gone, already mowed down by the road crews as soon the blossoms were spent. But they had sprouted up in blankets along the highways this spring. *Just after the accident*, he remembered. And then Ed was blindsided — once again by unwelcome thoughts of Henry. *He had been mowed down far too early.* Every Texan knew not to mow their local treasures down too soon — the bluebonnets, paintbrush and Indian blankets — thereby preventing their ability to re-seed and bloom again the following season. But that is exactly what had happened to Henry Keene. He had been mowed down too soon. In the prime of his life. *Would Henry's children still blossom in years to come?*

Ed was forced to welcome his anger in order to keep the increasingly familiar and ever encroaching sadness at arm's length. It plagued every aspect of his life now and made it impossible for him to stay on any train of thought, or follow any conversation, for any length of time. It was as if his brain was filled with cotton, or was perforated like a sieve so that all his thoughts just fell through the holes, and then, fell through his fingers as he tried desperately to grab onto them. He shook his head, full of frustration. He knew he wasn't functioning like he used to, and he worried that he wasn't functioning at all. And his greatest fear was that he would be found out. *Damn it all to hell!* This pervasive grief was shit on a stick. And it was everywhere. Grief over Henry. Grief over Holly. Grief over Tammy, dammit. Grief for what once was.

He was suddenly transported to the night Tammy had told him about the pregnancy that would culminate in giving him his little cupcake. They had tried for so long after the twins had been born. He choked back a sob, covering his lapse quickly with a cough. Alerted to Ed's momentary vulnerability, Tammy looked up at him, questioningly, compassionately, but once again he dared not return her look. If he did, he knew he would fall apart, and all the king's men would be of no use. And so, he stared stoically ahead at the road before him and drove on. Tammy, after searching for any little crevice in the rock wall he had erected, wrapped herself in her own little cocoon and went back to her book.

Ed tried to distract himself by watching the countryside roll by and then by counting the hawks he saw, either on the wing or resting on fence posts, but it was no use. His thoughts inevitably returned to Henry. He ached from loss; he ached with loneliness. And he longed for comfort of some kind. It was crazy, he knew, but he secretly hoped that comfort would come in meeting Andrew Colson. Maybe he could keep Henry alive through this new young man that would come into his life, somehow dulling the ache that he now carried in his soul. Losing Henry had been like losing his first-born son, a heartbreak so deep that it bordered on taking him down.

As they began entering the sprawl of the Dallas/Fort Worth metroplex, Ed imagined what Andrew would be like. He couldn't help but picture someone of similar build and coloring to Henry. Try as he might to see him differently, this recipient of Henry's lungs looked exactly like his nephew, and he too would have children and a beautiful wife. He would be intelligent, successful, charming — everything Henry had been. And everything Ed needed him to be. Ed's heart swelled. In Henry's selfless way, he was giving them all the gift of his eternal presence through his altruistic gesture of helping someone else live. All those whom Henry had loved could now experience the joy of his existence in the new opportunity for life which he had given to another human being.

They arrived on the grounds of the hospital right on time. There had been a contingency plan in case of rain, but it was summertime in Texas, and with the threat of precipitation non-existent, the great lawn surrounding the medical facility served as the perfect setting for the many individuals and families who were already gathering there.

Tammy carried Savannah, still groggy from her long nap in the car. Ed had a bag in each hand, one for the baby and another with a small leather attaché that Amber had prepared for Mr. Colson. She had written down a few things about Henry, his accomplishments, his values, his unrealized dreams. She had also included a family portrait that had been used for their Christmas cards just a few short months ago.

As Tammy filled out their name tags, Ed scoured the crowd. He couldn't help himself. He was still looking for someone who looked like Henry.

"Ed and Tammy Sloan ..." The elderly woman working registration carefully checked off their names. "I have you right here. You're at table eighteen. And Andrew and Taylor are already here." She smiled broadly. "Lauren, will you show them the way?"

Lauren was a teenaged hospital volunteer who escorted them to their table for eight, complete with a high chair for Savannah. Tammy busily got to work settling Savannah in her chair while Ed stood next to her, continuing to survey the crowd.

Many were already seated, with plates full of barbecue and potato salad. Many others stood in small groups, shaking hands, hugging, and sharing photographs and tears. Ed wondered if this was really a good idea after all. He didn't even want to share his deepest emotions with Tammy. How was he going to do this with a complete stranger? But then he remembered that Henry would have wanted it this way. And Ed had promised Amber.

"Ed Sloan? I'm Andrew Colson."

Ed hadn't seen him approach the table. He had been looking for someone else, and Andrew Colson could not have looked more different than Ed's imaginings. He stood there, extending his hand. His brown eyes and dark wavy hair looked much more like a Sloan than Henry ever had, and he could meet Ed's gaze square in the eye. He was easily over six feet tall. Henry had been several inches shorter.

"Andrew, I'm Tammy. It's so very nice to meet you."

"And I'm Ed Sloan." Ed leaned in and grasped Andrew's hand. "Henry Keene was my nephew." Ed cleared his throat and did his best to avoid the emotional difficulty embedded in this simple introduction by focusing on the details at hand instead. Andrew looked healthy enough. The transplant must have taken, at least as far as he could tell. And Andrew had a firm grip. Ed could tell so much from a handshake. He was direct, straightforward, and he seemed pretty self-assured too.

"Yes, I know. They told us that Amber was unable to come, but that his aunt and uncle were coming in her place. But there's someone else here that I don't know." And he knelt on one knee, bringing himself down to Savannah's level. "Who is this lovely little princess?"

Savannah opened her mouth wide, in mock surprise as toddlers frequently do.

Tammy answered. "This is our great-niece, Savannah. Henry's younger child."

"Well, hello there, Miss Savannah. My name is Andrew."

Ed watched as this stranger, who breathed the very breath of life through his nephew's lungs, interacted with little Savannah. It was touching. He was obviously good with children, just like Henry had been. Ed had seen Henry connect with his daughters just like this all the time. Andrew Colson was making this whole thing easier. He seemed to be a good guy.

"She doesn't know a stranger. She's just like her father in that." Tammy hesitated, then asked, "Do you and Taylor have any children, Andrew?"

"No, not yet. But we hope to. My health problems have made it next to impossible to even entertain that idea in the past. But now, thanks to your nephew's priceless gift, we may actually be able to realize our dreams of starting a family soon." As Andrew spoke, another young man approached the table, a plate of food in one hand and a cup in the other.

"Good for you. There's nothing like having a family." Ed possessively rested his hand on Tammy's shoulder. "So where is your wife, Andrew? Will we get to meet the little lady today too?" And Ed once again searched the crowd, hoping to pick out just the right lovely girl.

"Well, actually, Taylor is …"

But Andrew was interrupted by Savannah, who shrieked and clapped her hands in unadulterated joy as a clown wandered up to their table. She was clearly enamored of this silly, red-wigged comic dressed in polka dots.

"Boon! Boon!" She shouted over and over again while the clown expertly fashioned a balloon hat for her and then placed it on her head. She clapped her hands again, "Yay!" and then gently touched the bright blue monstrosity which now perched on top of her blonde curls.

"Can I have one too?" The man who had been standing next to Andrew put down his plate and waited as his chapeau was now twisted into shape. The polka-dotted jester playfully polished the man's shaved head before setting it into position.

"Yay!" Savannah cried again as she clapped her hands together. "Yay!"

The clown offered, in pantomime, to create more balloon art for everyone else, but Ed waved him off. "What were you saying, Andrew? About your wife? Are we going to get to meet Taylor today?"

The man with the yellow balloon hat looked over at Andrew and shrugged his shoulders before speaking. "It's awfully nice to meet you. I'm Taylor McCloud, Andrew's partner."

Tammy didn't hesitate. "I am so glad to meet you! Both of you!" And she jumped up and extended her arms in greeting.

What? Ed froze. Although Taylor's revelation felt like a freight train hitting him, he couldn't move or speak. He was completely immobilized. And with his grief and shattered dreams of comfort lying exposed before him, Ed watched, defenseless, as this train wreck that was his life became a pile-up. *How many more disasters could one life hold? How much more pain and humiliation could one soul endure?* Tied up like Gulliver, he was bound by shock and horror, which slowly gave way to revulsion. He watched as both men bent in half to embrace Tammy.

His beloved Henry now a part of THAT! And the three of them together appearing to float all around him as they laughed and talked and played with Henry's baby. It was too much. *Too much!* Ed stood there. Unmoving. Unresponsive. He was stranded, not in a strange land called Lilliput, but on the island of his own narrow-mindedness.

Contempt began to write itself in the lift of his chin and in the downward turn of the lines around his mouth. "I'm gonna go get a plate," Ed announced imperiously.

"Would you get me one too, dear? While I stay here with the baby?"

"Sure." It was all he could manage. He was still having trouble grasping all that had just happened.

"And I'd like to visit with Andrew and Taylor too."

That was something that Ed definitely did not want to do. Thankfully, the line was long. He needed some time. He hadn't seen this coming. Not at all. He looked back over his shoulder. *They didn't look queer.* At least he didn't think so. Ed could usually pick one of their kind out a mile away. It was usually so easy to spot pansies — all of them. But Andrew was wearing a Ralph Lauren polo, just like himself, and Taylor had on a black T-shirt that said Army Strong. Ed wouldn't have suspected a thing — except for their own admission.

"One chopped beef sandwich and one sliced brisket."

Ed looked back again. Tammy was chattering like a magpie, and the baby was the center of both men's attention. They were fawning over her like a couple of women. "Hmph." Ed was smug in his disregard. How could he have thought, even for one minute, that this Andrew Colson fellow was anything like his Henry. But he knew why. It was his emotions. *Dammit to Hell!* He had let his emotions get hold of him, and look where that had led. He had let down his guard, softened his stance, and then he was blindsided once again. When would he learn his lesson? This was becoming an uncomfortable pattern in his life — he would trust, maybe even hope, and then get bowled over by the unexpected.

Ed squared his shoulders and returned to the table with a plate in each hand.

"Ed, Taylor here is in the Army." Knowing Ed's high regard for servicemen and veterans, Tammy had proffered this information as a starting point, common ground so to speak, for the afternoon they were going to spend together.

"Really? What's your rank?" Ed sliced off a healthy portion of brisket and began to chew, careful not to meet Taylor's eye.

"I'm a Staff Sergeant, an E-6 actually. A warrant officer in Human Intelligence for the National Guard facility in Grand Prairie."

"Now you're being much too modest, Taylor." Tammy waved a hand at the young man seated across from her. "Ed, he's a supervisor of personnel and missions, and he's involved with interrogating and debriefing people. He can't even talk about a lot of what he does because of the security regulations."

Ed raised an eyebrow of seeming approval but countered with, "Hmm. You seem to know a lot about something that no one can talk about," and then he wiped his mouth with the corner of his napkin. "And what is it that *you* do, Andrew? Can you talk about that?"

Tammy flushed, a combination of anger and embarrassment at his obvious dismissal of both Taylor and her. She could only hope that Ed's insolence hadn't offended them. Here they were, hoping to give thanks to the family that had made their new lease on life possible, and instead, they were being subjected to such rude behavior. She was so mad she could spit.

Tammy shot Ed a look, but he didn't see it. His clenched fists were resting on either side of his plate and he was staring straight at Andrew, almost daring him to answer.

The partners exchanged glances before Andrew answered, meeting Ed's intent look with one of his own. "I'm an accountant for the Sammons Center for the Arts. It's a non-profit corporation that provides low-cost office, rehearsal, performance, and meeting space to emerging arts organizations and individual artists." Andrew paused, but seeing no resistance from Ed, he continued. "Sammons has gained national attention as a leader in increasing awareness of the numerous possibilities for the reuse of old buildings in urban settings. I'm proud to be affiliated with Sammons, even if all I do is deal with the debits and credits on their balance sheets."

Ed's bottom lip protruded and his head nodded, but he offered no response. Instead he once again focused his attentions on his barbecue.

"Oh, we're big supporters of the arts. Our daughter Kelly plays the clarinet in her school band. She's attended a fine arts camp the last two summers at the Dougherty Arts Center in Austin, and I really believe all that extra study over the summers helped her get into the top band for next year." Tammy was determined not to let Ed's sour countenance bring down their conversation.

"I bet you're right. One of our current tenants is the Greater Dallas Youth Orchestra ..."

Ed tuned them out. Instead, he watched Savannah pick up her pinto beans one at a time and fist them into her mouth. He wished he could be as oblivious to this whole situation as she was. He didn't want to learn any details of these men's lives. He hadn't asked to be a part of something like this. He just wanted to finish this lunch and get the hell out as quickly as he could.

"... It's really been a godsend to work for them. Everyone there has been so supportive and so understanding of my physical limitations, especially this past year. They've let me do most of my job from home."

"I guess it's all been very hard on you." Tammy reached out and placed her hand over Andrew's. "On *both* of you."

"You have no idea." Taylor swallowed hard and then answered Tammy. "Andrew hasn't left the Metroplex in over three years. He's had to stay within one hour of Baylor Hospital since he got on the transplant list."

"Which means you've done the same." Andrew smiled at his partner.

"But all that's gonna change here real soon. Now that the military is recognizing same-sex marriages, we're gonna get married."

As hard as Ed was trying not to hear what they were saying, those words broke through his sound barrier. He almost spit the mouthful of beans he was chewing back onto his plate.

"Oh, congratulations to you both!" Tammy slapped her open palms on the table top, both to cover Ed's gaffe and to express her sincere gladness for them.

"And since it's impossible for us to get married in Texas, the Army will allow me to take up to ten days of leave in order to travel to one of the states that will grant us a marriage license and perform our ceremony."

"Now we just have to decide where we'll go. And where we want to spend our honeymoon. And we couldn't be doing any of this if it weren't for my new lungs."

Good God! Ed set his elbows on the table, knife and fork held upright in his balled fists, head hung low. He now shook that head despairingly. Not only were Henry's lungs inside this homo, affording him a new lease on his immoral life, but they were also allowing him to travel to another state to get married. To another man! He dropped the knife and propped his forehead on his right forefinger and thumb to steady himself. *And didn't they say they were going to start a family? The poor little kids. What kind of family issues were those little ones going to have to overcome, just for their basic survival?* He locked eyes with Andrew and threw down his challenge.

"I don't approve of gay marriage." This was right in Ed's wheelhouse. He had been silent long enough. "It's wrong and that's all there is to it."

Tammy was seething and she spoke very quietly and very slowly. "Ed Sloan, I believe you owe these men an apology."

Ed ignored Tammy and stood his ground, holding both men now in his unnerving glare.

Andrew picked up the gauntlet Ed had thrown down, took Taylor's hand in his own, and looked straight at his opposition. "Ed, you can't stop me from loving Taylor any more than you can stop me from loving you. I will be eternally grateful to you and your family for the gift of Henry's lungs, just as I will be eternally grateful for the gift that God has given me in Taylor. You can 'not like it,' if you wish, but you can't stop our love from being what it is."

"All this talk about love. I don't believe any of it. Isn't this really all about perverted lust and liberal agendas designed to bring down our cultural and religious traditions — all in the name of tolerance — whatever the hell that is?"

"ED!" Tammy was horrified. She turned to Andrew and Taylor to apologize for her husband's boorish behavior, but Andrew waved her silent.

"I'm sorry you feel that way, Ed. But Taylor and I are people, not agendas, and Taylor and I love each other very much. We have been in a committed relationship for thirteen years now. And Taylor, for sure, has taken the 'till death do you part' part of committed love very, very seriously. Our sexual orientation may be different from yours, but our love is just as real and just as true as yours."

Probably truer, Tammy thought. If only Ed could understand the selfless love and intimacy these guys seemed to share and that she longed for with him. *Was Ed even capable of putting anyone else first? Did he have any true compassion, any real feelings at all? Or was marriage just a socially acceptable contract to him? Something that kept the status quo static?* She leaned back in her chair and submitted to these awful questions.

"Believe me, Ed, I didn't arrive at acceptance of myself overnight." Andrew offered in a conciliatory tone, "And I don't expect you to, either, but we need ..."

"Good. 'Cause it will be a cold day in hell before I do." Ed hissed. He stood up and barked at Tammy, "Get the baby and your things. We're leaving."

But Tammy remained seated. Savannah had picked up on the tension around the table and had begun to cry, and Taylor was attempting to distract her with his balloon headdress. Tammy wanted to crawl under the table. This was supposed to have been a good, healing time for all of them, and look at what Ed had brought them to.

It was Andrew who walked around the table and placed his hand upon Ed's shoulder.

He could feel Andrew's breath on his neck and hear his lungs filling with air that should have been Henry's. Henry's face sprang to his mind. *Dammit! That infectious smile and wonderful personality that everyone loved.* He wasn't sure he could control the rush of anger, and then the sadness, that overtook him. And he certainly wasn't about to love this man — if you could call him that — that now was living off Henry's generosity. He swiped at Andrew's hand with his own. "Don't touch me."

Ed's façade cracked, and his pinched face crumbled. He avoided looking at Andrew directly, but his face went slack, and Tammy saw it all then in a flash. Ed was weighing the choices facing him. To turn away from these two young men would be to reject a living part of Henry and to turn his back on a way to keep Henry close. But to accept them would mean even more. It would represent surrender.

As hot as the August sun was outside, their ride home from Dallas was frosty. Ed and Tammy had barely shared three words since they hit the interstate, and Savannah had fallen asleep. Ed stayed transfixed on the traffic, and Tammy absentmindedly looked out the passenger window, staring at nothing in particular.

This was supposed to be a day of new beginnings. Seeing the life that lived anew because of Henry's sacrifice. How would she tell Amber what had happened? She had almost forgotten to give Andrew the satchel she had prepared for him and had to go back to the table after Ed had stormed out. At least she had had the opportunity, then, to apologize to them properly. "I am so sorry for my husband's behavior. It's extremely important to me that you know that Ed and I don't see eye to eye on this. Well, on many things really. I am truly happy to have met you both, and I'm so happy for your good health and for your dreams of a future together. I would love to stay in touch." And they had exchanged contact information.

She had really enjoyed her visit with them while Ed was off getting their food. She had explained that Amber's absence was partially due to the freshness of her grief and partly due to the call she had experienced and was now answering with her mother-in-law's assistance, that call being "Henry's Kids," the anti-bullying program that she and Henry had actually planned together shortly before his death. It was her way of giving back. Of making a difference. Of making something positive come out of something — so many somethings actually — that were so senseless.

Tammy had then gone on to share with them her experiences as a volunteer at Trevor. It felt good to have received affirmation from someone who had actually lived some of the stories that she had been hearing. They had told her that what she was doing was "admirable" and "important," but she was a little embarrassed by all their praise. "I was Seth." Taylor had said with tears in his eyes. "And if it hadn't been for a couple of really good friends, a school counselor, and my new church, I might have made the very same decision. My father threw me out. My mother was afraid of my father. And that's why I joined the Army as soon as I turned eighteen. I had nowhere else to turn." Tammy hadn't realized until then that she was in need of that kind of encouragement: the support from someone who had been there and who had survived, the validation from someone who really understood what these kids were facing out there. If there had been any question in Tammy's mind before, she now knew the answer. *Yes, it was all worth it.*

But instead of the new beginnings she had hoped this day would bring, she sensed the tolling of a death knell. She had not wanted to see it — or face it. Tammy had known that her marriage was on fragile ground for some time, and yet she had continued to hold out hope. It was that hope she felt dying now. She had long since resolved herself to the fact that they would probably just have to agree to disagree on lots of things. But now she saw that even establishing such a simple accord as that might be well beyond Ed's capability. He had demonstrated that over and over and had done so, humiliatingly so, again today in his boorish demand that she evacuate the scene when he wanted to show his displeasure with Andrew and Taylor. It was this domineering insistence of Ed's that she always yield to his positions that was becoming more and more impossible for her to accept. And where was the hope in that?

She ventured a glance in Ed's direction. His knuckles were actually white from his intense grip on the steering wheel. *He was as tight as a rubber band, fully stretched and about to snap,* she thought. That called to mind a quote she had once read from a John Maxwell book on leadership: "A rubber band is useless until it is stretched."[38] He had gone on to say something along the lines of needing to stretch a little more in order to grow, of needing to get outside our comfort zones. Well, Ed certainly had been outside his comfort zone all morning long and especially during lunch, but once again, instead of letting his grief, or the opportunity with Andrew and Taylor teach him, he had become more defensive than ever. They were growing further and further apart. Something leaden settled in her stomach. Would either of them be able to cross the great divide in their marriage? Unfortunately, she felt she knew the answer.

It was almost dark when they finally got home, and all Tammy wanted to do was get in the bathtub with her book and relax. But Ed followed her into the bathroom as she was turning on the water.

"So what the hell was all that about this afternoon, Tammy?"

"What are you talking about?"

"What am I talking about? Are you kidding me? I'm talking about the way you teamed up against me. You and those two faggots."

Her mouth actually dropped open, she was so taken aback by his ludicrous interpretation of the day's events. And then, she began to boil.

"You know what, Ed? I'm done." And she nearly twisted the handle off the faucet of the tub as she turned around to face him. "I'm done with your ugly comments. I'm done with being blamed for what you think is such an evil change going on in the world. I'm done with being associated with your shallow way of looking at people — good people who don't deserve to be discounted simply because they don't resemble your way of living. And I'm done with not being able to share my thoughts, my hopes, my dreams, my feelings with you without being criticized. I'm done with not being able to live my *own* life according to my *own* values without your telling me I'm wrong or accusing me of being out to get you. I'm sorry, Ed. I truly am. But I'm done!"

Furious, she tried to push past him, intent on getting out of there, of getting away from him as quickly as possible. But he grabbed her by the arms, turning her to face him and, in the process, toppled her book into the tub. She shook loose to retrieve it and turned back glowering at him.

"Godammit, Tammy! You're putting words in my mouth again!"

"No, Ed, I'm not," she countered. "These words are *my* words and they just came out of *my* mouth, not yours. And they expressed *my* feelings quite accurately!"

Ed attempted a comeback, but before he could gather his startled thoughts, she talked over him.

"Come to think of it, I said some other things about my feelings a long time ago — in our marriage vows. And I meant what I said then as much as what I'm saying to you now. I meant every bit of it. But I understood a loving union to be one of mutual respect, honesty, and intimacy. And it's been a long time since I've felt any of that from you, Ed Sloan. A very long time. What we have now is not a marriage. It's a feudal system!"

"There you go again, turning all this around on me!"

All of a sudden, Tammy became very still. It was as though everything started to happen in slow motion. She felt like she was standing outside herself, observing herself deconstructing her life as she had known it for twenty-three years, the import of this moment marking itself indelibly on her consciousness. She looked up at the man that she had loved — and still probably did, if she were honest with herself. But she knew that a healthy marriage took more than love. She began very calmly.

"I guess you're right." The tears welled up in her eyes and it was hard for her to focus. "It *is* up to you, Ed. It's completely up to you. And you need to decide what's most important to you. Is it most important that you have a vassal for your wife who bows and scrapes and keeps her mouth shut when she disagrees with you, one who is content to wait on you and live *your* life vicariously rather than find and live her own? Or is it most important to stay married to *me*? The *real* me, Tammy, whose needs are every bit as real as yours and whose values are every bit as important as yours — just different? Tammy, who needs you to love her enough to respect and honor those differences?"

She paused to catch her breath. She had choked out those last words — an impassioned plea, a last-ditch effort, a final stand. And she had done so through soul-wrenching sobs. *Please, dear God*, she pleaded. But she realized she didn't know what to pray next. It really was all up to Ed now.

She wiped at the tears as they streamed down her face. "You know who I am, Ed, for better or for worse, and now you have to decide if that is the person you want to spend the rest of your life with, or not. I love you, Ed, and I guess I always will, but I cannot live another day like this."

Ed just stood there, arms limp at his side, as he watched her walk out of the room. He was still staring at the empty doorway when she stepped back into it.

"And for the record. The only thing I said this afternoon was that I believed you owed Andrew and Taylor an apology." She didn't say it, but in her heart of hearts, she prayed that Ed would realize that perhaps he owed her one as well.

Change will not come if we wait for some other person or some other time.
We are the ones we've been waiting for.
We are the change that we seek.
— *Barak Obama*

Chapter 26

OLD FRIENDS

It was late morning when Ed finally opened his eyes and was startled to see how well underway the day already was. He had a pounding headache and a stale taste of scotch lingered in his bone-dry mouth. He must have slept with his mouth open all night long, he thought. In his groggy state, it took him a second or two to get his bearings and to realize that he was in his study, not his bedroom, and in his recliner instead of his bed. It took only a second more before he remembered why he was there. And the second he did, his gut wrenched in a spasm of anxiety like he had never felt before. Tammy had left him. She had told the kids that she was going to stay with Edith last night, and they had assumed she was going over in order to help their aunt get through this next week. This coming Thursday would have been Henry's birthday.

But Ed knew the real reason. She wanted to get away from him. She'd said as much. Said she couldn't spend another day with him and gave him an ultimatum. He prickled at that memory, but then that disconcerting jab at his innards returned full force before he could pick up his trusty anger to defend against it. *Dammit! What the hell was she thinking?* She'd actually told him he'd have to choose between her or someone else who could agree with him and would wait on him. Well, what if he didn't want either option? He didn't like the shrew that Tammy had become and the constant bickering that created, but he didn't need to be coddled either. He couldn't believe how condescending she'd been and how it hadn't seemed to bother her at all to suggest he find someone else. *Jesus Christ! Was she that callous now?* But then he remembered her tears, and that memory softened him. *She did still care.*

He lingered a bit on memories of happier times, when they could laugh together, when she was sweet and affectionate, and when he could count on her support, not just in his career, but at home too. She had been his bedrock. With that admission, Ed felt a sudden burning at the back of his throat and the corners of his eyes. He swallowed hard, eyes clenched to dislodge the once foreign urge to cry which was becoming all too familiar now. *Dammit.* He hated that feeling! He swallowed again to regain control. He wanted *that* Tammy back. He wanted things back to the way things were before all this damn gay stuff started happening. But she had made it abundantly clear last night that that person wasn't coming back. So he was fresh out of acceptable options. And that was a position Ed Sloan found intolerable.

He got up, stretched his back and neck, which had been confined in an awkward position for far too long, and ran his fingers through his hair before he padded to the kitchen to make himself some coffee. He hoped that the caffeine would quicken his senses enough that he could make some sense out of this whole mess. Surely she wouldn't leave her own marriage and her three kids over a disagreement they'd had over two gay guys. If she did, then she was the one who needed to come to her senses.

Hannah was already dressed for church and was out in the den, eating her cereal in front of the TV, and Kelly was finishing hers at the table. The comics page was spread out in front of her, but she was currently absorbed in texting some friend or the other on her new iPhone. Since the twins had both received upgrades on their cell phones for their birthday, he hadn't seen either of them without their noses in those things, and it irritated him no end. It was like they had abdicated from the family altogether.

"Kel, get your nose out of that thing and finish your breakfast."

"Well, good morning to you too, Dad." Kelly spoke these words to her father's back as he rummaged loudly through the pantry, but she obediently shut off her cell phone.

"Where the hell does your mother keep the coffee?"

"I dunno, Dad. I don't drink coffee. But I would think it would be in the cabinet over the coffeemaker." Kelly got up to vacate the kitchen. When her dad got this way, it was best to give him as wide a berth as possible. "Oh, by the way, Mom called about meeting for church. Wanted you to call her back when you got up." And she exited before he could say anything else.

Well, she would just have to wait until he had his morning coffee, he thought. He had found it right where Kelly had suggested it might be, and now he was standing perplexed in front of the coffeemaker. *How difficult could this be?* He filled the reservoir with water and spooned a goodly amount of grounds into the basket. He found the button that said 'Brew' and pushed it, and was rewarded by the sounds and smells of coffee brewing. *Aah!* He sat down at the table to wait and gathered up the scattered pages of the Sunday paper. And then he saw the headline. *Good God Almighty! The Treasury Department had actually gone and done it.* They had reacted to the Supreme Court decision on DOMA by now allowing married gays to file their IRS returns jointly'.[39] He scanned the article quickly, becoming more and more incensed as he read their reasoning. Under the ruling, legally married same-sex couples would now be treated as married for all federal tax purposes, including income and gift and estate taxes. And the ruling applied regardless of whether the couple lived in a jurisdiction that recognized same-sex marriage or not.

They were all headed for hell in a hand basket now, thanks to all those gay-loving liberals pushing their agendas on virtuous people and common decency. The damn federal government was not just recognizing those immoral unions now; they were actually calling them marriages, and extending to those faggots — he remembered Tammy's words from last night about his needing to self-edit and mockingly complied — all those queers all the same rights and benefits that he and other God-fearing Christian couples were receiving. He shuddered to think what would be next. There were apparently no bastions of righteousness left in this world.

He got up to pour his coffee. He needed a good strong cup to calm his nerves. Shakily, he raised it to his lips and sipped. "Blatt!" He spat the offending liquid into the sink. It tasted like someone had washed a coffee pot out and put it in his cup, grounds and all. Irritated at his ineptness, appalled by the government, and furious with Tammy, he yelled out to the kids: "Kelly! Michael! Hannah! Get a move on. It's time to go."

Hannah was the first to arrive. She took in her father's rumpled clothing from the day before and his disheveled appearance and stopped abruptly. "Daddy, aren't you coming with us today?" It was part question, part challenge.

"Not today, honey. I have other things I have to do. Kelly! Michael! Come on now, or we'll be late." He needed to get to Starbucks and get there now.

Hannah had caught his choice of pronouns, though, and looked at him askance. "Where are *you* going, Daddy?" Caught, he prevaricated a bit. "I don't feel well, honey. I'm gonna pick up some coffee at Starbucks and come back here and lie down."

Hannah thought about that for a minute. "But I thought you said you had lots of things you have to do?"

"That's enough, Hannah." Ed's head was pounding now. "Michael! Kelly! This is your last call."

Kelly appeared at the door, "I'm ready, but Michael says he's not coming. Says he's not feeling well."

Ed started to object, but saw Hannah watching him and thought better of it. "Okay, go get in the car, and I'll be right there." He went to check on Michael, and sure enough, when he peeked through his son's open door, he could see him playing on his iPhone, not looking sick at all. *Hell!* he thought. He knew he should address the issue, but he just wasn't up for another confrontation this morning, so he quietly backed away before Michael could see him.

After dropping the girls off at church and telling them they would need to ride home with their mom, he headed for the Starbucks, picked up a tall black coffee and a couple of pastries and headed back to the car. It was a pretty day, even if it *was* already showing signs of becoming another scorcher later on. He had decided, while standing in the long line at the counter, that a ride in the country would clear his head better than sitting like a sardine in the shop's close quarters. He settled himself and his breakfast in his SUV and headed west out of town. He had no particular destination in mind. He just needed to get away, get out into Texas' wide open spaces to clear his mind and gain perspective. But after an hour or so of driving aimlessly, he found himself turning into Horseshoe Bay and headed to Henry's — NO — Amber's house. His heart lurched. He couldn't handle going there and risk them being at home.

Things were changing everywhere, and all of it was painful, but it was the hollow eyes of Amber and the girls and the downcast eyes in the Land Office that did more than sting. They pierced. They pierced him straight to his core. He changed course and headed instead for the little dock there on Lake LBJ where he had taught Henry how to fish for bass all those many years ago. He parked the car but didn't get out. Instead, he just stared ahead at the blue expanse before him, tree-lined and set with clusters of large, limestone boulders. He couldn't say how long he just sat there before he began to watch the guys on the shore who were happily pulling bass and crappie, and the occasional catfish, from the lake. But it was later, when he noticed a seven or eight-year-old kid running up to one of the men, a small bass on his line, that it hit him. And it hit him like a ton of bricks. Henry. His golden boy. *Oh, Henry!*

He saw a ten-year-old Henry holding his first fish, caught on a lure that he had tied himself. Ed had taught him how. He saw him on his wedding day, checking the soles of his shoes for price tags so they wouldn't show when he kneeled beside Amber. He saw Henry nearly explode with pride upon the births of his daughters, when he had promised to love and protect them for the rest of his life. But Henry's face morphed into Andrew Colson's. "Why?" Ed actually yelled aloud. "Why did all this have to happen?"

His grief refused to be bottled up any longer and exploded to the surface, accompanied by a heart-wrenching wail. Ed was caught in convulsive sobbing that he could not control, that he could not fight his way clear of. He had no choice now but to ride it out, trying to stay in the saddle until the wild thing within him ran itself into exhaustion, no longer heaving to and fro, but settling into a tameness that would allow bridle and bit. He had cried for Henry, the son he had been and the dear friend and colleague he had become. And he had cried for

Tammy and the uncertainty of their future together, a future they had once both seen as inviolate. And he had cried for himself and all the loss he had sustained.

Spent, he was resting his head on his forearms, which in turn rested on the steering wheel, when his cell phone buzzed. Blearily, he looked over at the caller ID. It was Tammy. There was no way he could talk to her now. He needed to get back in control and stop being such a blubbering idiot before he dared face her again. He couldn't afford to let her see him this way, to hear his vulnerability. So he didn't pick up.

But he felt so alone. The thought crossed his mind and then lodged there: Was he even relevant any longer? Did his opinions matter? There was such a groundswell building against his way of thinking, all across the country and in his own home. He needed someone to tell him he was still worth something. He needed a friend.

It was extremely difficult to do, but after summoning up his 'in control' persona, he called Bill Pritchett. He didn't know where else to turn. He had scared himself sufficiently with his outburst just now to know that he needed to talk to somebody, and Pritchett had always proven a good confidant and support.

"Pritchett," he had laughed, "my life's in the toilet. And, I dunno, I guess I need a friend to talk to. Mind if I come over for a while to bend your ear, old friend?" As he hung up, he sighed his relief for having gotten through that reasonably well.

Pritchett had encouraged him to come on, and now here he was, sitting on the couch in Bill and Ginny Pritchett's living room and feeling a fool. Asking for help, exposing himself this way, was so far out of his comfort zone that he was floundering. Maybe this was a bad idea. He shouldn't have come. But there he sat, no easy way out now, and Pritchett seemed content to wait him out.

But where to start? My career? My marriage? Losing Henry? Meeting that Colson? DOMA and the Supreme Court attacking my core beliefs? Shit! He felt his borrowed bravado slipping away and the feelings from this afternoon overtaking him again.

Bill watched his old friend struggling, but he knew enough not to try to help. Ed would find his own way eventually. For such a big and proud man, though, he seemed rather small sitting there. Usually

Ed stretched out, taking up enormous space and communicating his importance, but today he seemed almost sunken into the cushions, back curled, chest pulled in, arms slack at his sides. It was not the posture of command that Bill was used to. It was the posture of defeat, and Bill Pritchett raised an eyebrow at this departure from Ed's norm.

"I've never felt so uncertain about everything in my whole life," Ed finally began. "I don't know what to do any more." He dropped his head, unable to sustain eye contact with Pritchett. "I feel like I have nothing left."

This was new vocabulary coming from Ed — all this talk about feelings. Bill had never known him to be anything but a scoffer at all things emotional, and it took him a moment to formulate an appropriate response.

"Have you talked to Tammy about everything you're feeling?" Bill winced at how much he sounded like a counselor, but this was new territory they were forging together. For all their years together, and in all their conversations, they had never broached anything so personal, so emotionally laden. And he wasn't sure how to proceed.

Ed ran his tongue up over his teeth and swallowed hard. His eyes narrowed as if to squeeze the words out of his eyes, since his mouth didn't seem to be functioning. But finally he uttered, "We don't talk much these days." He picked at a piece of lint on his trousers. "She's been sleeping in her study for a little while now."

Oh shit! This could get a lot more personal than he had bargained for. Bill smiled weakly and shook his head in a way that he hoped showed compassion. "That's rough," was all that he could think to say. It put him off-balance to learn that the tall, strong, brash Ed Sloan was vulnerable after all.

As he watched, Ed seemed to sink deeper into the sofa, his despair pushing him further down into its soft leather seats. It swallowed him like quicksand. "Everything's upside down for me, Bill."

Pritchett reached over to give Ed a slug on the shoulder. "Then I'm glad you came by, old friend. I know you've been hurting — what with Henry and all — and I figured that things might be getting difficult for you and Tammy — what with her going off on her own so much lately — but I had no idea you were in this rough a shape." Again, he shook his head slowly. This time the gesture was purely one of commiseration. "Whatever the reason, it seems we're all hurting these days. I'm just sorry that I haven't been there for you lately."

Ed stared at the floor as Pritchett continued.

"Wish I could offer you some comfort, Ed, but I'm learning that it takes the strength of a superhero to be willing to see and then break free from all the ways we've shackled ourselves when it comes to relationships. I mean, look in the mirror at the men we've become."

"What are you talking about?" This wasn't at all what Ed had come for. If he had wanted someone to point the finger at him, he would have just called Tammy.

"We've become set in our ways, Ed. Comfortable in our ruts. And certain sure that we have truth on our side."

"So what's wrong with that? Seems a good way to live, if you ask me."

"Yeah, it makes for a pretty comfy life — easy really — until you're hit over the head with some new reality and you don't know how to deal with it. And that's what I'm talking about, Ed. It's time for us to step into the booth of reality and be willing to change. Change the way we look at the world and our role in it. And that, my friend, takes gargantuan effort."

Ed cringed. Pritchett had just described his situation exactly. He'd been bombarded by too much "reality" lately that he didn't know what to do with. He just sat there with his arms crossed and studied his friend. He hadn't expected Pritchett to be so wise — and so direct in sharing his wisdom.

"I've been turned on my head lately too, Ed."

Pritchett lifted his eyes to meet those of his good friend, and Ed noticed for the first time that he was unshaven and carried heavy bags under his eyes. He had been so preoccupied with his own misery that he hadn't observed these changes before, and now he wondered if Bill and Ginny were having problems too.

"Greg just told us he's gay."

"What?" Ed spluttered his surprise, and the shock of the news sent him reeling forward, almost causing him to fall off the sofa.

Greg was Pritchett's son. He had just finished his junior year at Texas A&M and was a highly ranked officer in the Corps. Bill and

Ginny had gone down to College Station when he received his saber and his senior boots, the distinctive brown leather boots worn only by Zips, as they called themselves. Only commanding officers and staff were entitled to carry sabers.

"But he just got his boots. I mean, how has he survived the Corps all this time?" Ed was astounded. "Do they all know?" He couldn't imagine any other organization that was more macho than the Texas Aggie Corps of Cadets. It was filled with both long-standing tradition and testosterone. No fairy could survive the Corps.

"No. He's kept all this a secret from the guys there. Actually, he'd never told anyone until he told Ginny and me last week."

Greg Pritchett was twenty-one, but he had known about his sexuality since he was very young. He had confessed to his parents that his feelings had scared him, so he pushed them way down, refusing even to acknowledge them. As he had grown into a teenager, suppressing his desires had become more difficult, but he had managed to sublimate them by keeping himself busy with leadership positions in school, in church, and in scouts. And he had actually been very popular. He was handsome and a big man on campus, so all the girls had wanted to go out with him, but they had known going in that he was too busy for a real boyfriend-girlfriend type of relationship. He had always made sure of that. And because he was popular with the girls, he had become popular with the boys. He was a gifted athlete. He knew how to dance. And he made good grades. He appeared to be perfect in every way, except for the way he felt inside. And, as high school had drawn to an end and plans for college were being made, he realized that he longed for the intimacy he had previously denied himself. So he had joined the Corps of Cadets at Texas A & M University.

"It's hard to believe, but he told us he chose A&M and joined the Corps so that he could learn to be around other young men in a safe place. Said he yearned for the brotherhood, the intimacy, that he couldn't get anywhere else. And he could get all of that in the Corp without having to come out — to himself or anyone else."

Ed was still reeling. Was everyone in this godforsaken world gay except for him? How on earth could Pritchett just sit there and calmly tell him all of this?

"He explained to us that going through the Corps was a condensed lesson on how to develop healthy relationships with other young men, which we now know he'd been very wary of doing before. He told us he'd been thrown in with a bunch of guys he didn't know and that through suffering together, they'd built close relationships. He said he'd learned to trust himself as well as the other guys as they'd learned to work and lead as a team, and that even though the competition had driven wedges between some of those friendships, that in the end he'd realized that his friendships were more important than his rank, and that the Corps was not the be-all-end-all after all. I couldn't be more proud of him.

"But it was so hard, Ed. Ginny and I sat right there where you are now with our hearts breaking, breaking for us that there would be no grandchildren, and breaking for him that he'd had to live such a lonely journey for such a long time and that we hadn't even known it. We felt guilty for not knowing and for not being there for him in the way he needed us most. We sat there looking at the young officer sitting at attention in the chair opposite us. With two shiny diamond-shaped discs on his collar. A handsome and impressive specimen of dedication and discipline if ever there was one. And all we could see was our six-year-old son, confused, and scared, and all alone."

Ed let the silence hang between them as Pritchett wiped a tear and blew his nose.

"But it was perfect for him, Ed." Bill leaned forward, elbows on his knees hands clasped together, and smiled tearfully. "All this time Ginny and I had just thought he'd gone there to be an engineer." He laughed wanly.

Wow. And he'd thought *he'd* been dealt a bad hand. Ed sat looking at his longtime friend and shook his head in disbelief. He had known Greg since he was in Little League. He was six or seven years older than Michael, and Ed had fantasized many times about Michael's achieving the level of success in school and in the community that Greg Pritchett had accomplished. *What was the world coming to? Were there any real heroes anymore?*

"Getting back to your question, Ed, I asked him how on earth he'd been able to keep his sexuality a secret in such a close-knit group.

After all, he had entered the Corps as a freshman when the strongest bonding opportunities occur. He told me that that was why he had pursued all the leadership positions he had. He knew how hard it would be to keep his secret in the intimate camaraderie of the outfits, so he did what we learned he had done throughout high school. He created a reason to explain the distance he still had to keep. You know, in a way you could say that it was his gayness that spurred him on to his stellar accomplishments." There were only two officers in the entire Corps who outranked this Ross Volunteer, Lieutenant Colonel Greg Pritchett.

Oh my God! Ed thought. *What has happened to you, Pritchett?* He seemed to be an apologist for the other side now. "So … you're okay with all this?"

"I have to be, Ed. For Greg's sake. He's my son."

Both men were quiet for a while, each grappling with what that admission meant. It was Bill who broke the silence.

"How many times have we said it, Ed? If I'd only known then what I know now. Ginny and I have been tormented thinking about how lonely Greg was all this time and how much energy it must have taken him to hide his true identity from every person he had ever known, including us. And himself, even. I've always been a fence-sitter on gay issues, Ed. I've never taken a stand. Oh sure, last year I suggested you calm down your vitriol regarding gays, but not because I really cared about the issue or about them. I just knew it would hurt you and your career. Remember? When all this first came about, we sat in your study that afternoon, and I told you that I wasn't on either side."

Ed remembered that day, and many others, all too well. It was about that same time that he and Tammy had begun experiencing their troubles.

"I've always been able to duck the question or change the subject. Happy to just side-step the whole damn time bomb. Honestly, the only conversations I've ever had about homosexuality have been with you this past year. Isn't that a kicker? The two men in this world who could care less about same-sex issues sure have spent a lot of time and energy on that very thing."

Ed snorted his agreement. "I'll say. Way too much time and energy, if you ask me."

"It has taken my own flesh-and-blood bravely standing up and telling his mom and dad who he really is for me to be willing to actually think about the whole issue of same-sex relationships and re-think some of my suppositions. And it hasn't been easy. Not at all. It had to hit me where I live, Ed." Bill thumped himself on the chest, just above his heart. "Nothing else — not protests, nor documentaries, nor letters to the editor — could sway me to really look at this before. Not even you. Not even all the trouble you've been in this past year was enough to get through my thick head. But I'm taking a stand now, and I stand behind my son."

Ed's first thought was "another boomerang." And, unbidden, contempt rose up within him. He had always disparaged those who vacillated on moral issues, but he couldn't fault Pritchett for wanting to support his son. Ed was torn. Would he, or even could he, do the same thing for Michael? It was a question he hoped he'd never have to answer.

"It took a while, but after some real soul searching on the issue, I came to realize that my only uncertainty was rooted in my religious beliefs. I wanted to embrace my son fully and completely, but I struggled with how to do that and still stay true to God. But then I remembered that preacher guy who came to speak at the Rotary right after Seth Graham killed himself. It didn't mean too much to me then." He looked down at his shoes, searching for the words he needed to continue. "But I've thought about his words a lot lately, and surprisingly, I remember a lot of them."

Ed noticed a difference in Pritchett's expression. He was softer somehow. Maybe just not as intense? Ed couldn't really put his finger on it, but he noticed a visible change in his long-time friend.

"And Ed, I've been doing some reading. I ran across something by an author named Anne Lamott that really turned me around. Just listen to this." And he recited from memory: "'You can safely assume that you've created God in your own image when it turns out that God hates all the same people you do.' Isn't that great? It's so simple, but I had to hear it from someone else before I could see that's what I've been doing."

Ed smiled at the author's joke, but Pritchett didn't return it.

"No, really. I think I made a wrong turn somewhere between kindergarten and here. Back then, if someone had asked me about God,

I would have answered, 'God is Love.' Right? Isn't that what we were taught?"

Ed nodded his acquiescence. *Where was Pritchett going with this?*

"And everyone knows, love is a relationship, right? Something that happens *between* two beings ... And that got me thinking. Maybe the Bible isn't finished? Maybe God is still speaking to, in, and through people today."

Ed's mouth turned down and his smile gradually converted to a frown. This was beginning to sound perilously close to blasphemy.

"I've come to realize that the Bible is a living document, Ed. Only the Ten Commandments were cast in stone, and even then, when Moses broke the first set, God created a new one."

"Now hold on, I ..."

"Just let me finish, Ed. I'm going somewhere important with this. If God is truly in us and between us, then that makes His word a *living* word that is still being written today — written by people like you and like me — and like Greg, and Holly and the O'Dell kid too — as long as we all have love in our hearts."

"What the hell are you saying, Pritchett?"

"I'm saying that if God pronounced all of His creation good, like it says He did in Genesis, and if He's created every last one of us who's ever walked the earth, as we believe that He has, who am I to say that He only loves us — and not them. Or to even imagine that there *is* a *them.*

"I think we stand to lose a lot in our relationships — with others and with God — when we hold resolutely to a static picture of God as people conceived of Him thousands of years ago, instead of honoring the living, loving, dynamic presence that He is today."

Ed opened his mouth, but then closed it again. He had heard what his old friend was saying. And for the first time, it almost made sense.

"It's just like your marriage, Ed."

Ed's head shot up to meet Bill's soft eyes. "What?"

"You said you and Tammy have grown apart. Why? Could it be you're looking at different portraits of your marriage these days? Is one a still picture of your past, sepia tones and all, while the other is more dynamic, like a video that takes into account the shifts and changes that happen with the passage of time?"

Ed remained stone-faced. He didn't like that Pritchett seemed to be taking Tammy's side. Nor did he like the implied message that he was the one at fault.

"Are our values not shaped in part by our life experiences? Think about it. Do you view every issue of social consequence the same way today that you did thirty years ago?"

Ed sighed loudly, but didn't answer. His face was flushed, and he just sat there, motionless.

"Let me put it this way, Ed. Do parents who lose a child to handgun violence sometimes become advocates of new gun laws? Don't children who lose a parent because of a drunk driver sometimes dedicate themselves to getting drunks off the street? Does my overwhelming love for my son, who has now told me he is gay, make me open my eyes and my heart in ways I haven't been able to before?"

Ed blinked hard several times, and Pritchett, seeing this as evidence that he had hit his mark, risked pressing on even more directly.

"Change is part of living, Ed. It can't be avoided, but it doesn't have to be all bad. Every individual, and every marriage, goes through natural stages of life which require change. Just think how your lives changed when you had kids. You and Tammy have changed over the years, and change always creates tension. Hell, Ginny and I have certainly had our ups and downs, but we've gotten stronger because of them. Because we changed together as we let life teach us."

"But what about my principles? I can't just turn my back on all that I believe."

"No, but we're entitled to change our minds without sacrificing our principles. Our views regarding relationships and social issues aren't determined at birth, Ed. We acquire them based upon our life experiences. And my life experience has recently changed, Ed. So has yours." He paused to give his thoughts time to resonate. "Changing as we grow and learn is being true to our conscience, my friend, and I now believe it brings us closer to God."

"Come on, now. Closer to God?" Pritchett had gone too far in Ed's estimation, and he didn't mind letting him know it.

"Okay." Bill rose to the challenge he had heard in Ed's voice. "Show me someone who continually points out God's judgment in the Bible and I'll show you someone who likes to judge. Then show me someone who points out the commandments to love in the Bible and I'll show you someone who knows how to treat his brother. Who do you think is closer to God?"

Pritchett was sounding a lot like Tammy now, Ed thought. He cleared his throat. "I've never heard you talk like this before, Pritchett."

"That's because I've never really felt compelled to think about any of this, much less talk about it before. And you know what else? I've learned things. And I'm incensed at the injustices I'm now really seeing for the first time."

"What injustices?"

"Well, for starters, when you walked in here a little bit ago, one of the things you brought up was DOMA. Do you really understand what that's all about, Ed?"

"Of course I do. It's been the federal government's way of protecting the sanctity of marriage between a man and a woman. Well, up until recently, anyway," Ed smirked.

"No, my friend, actually the Defense of Marriage Act was written with the sole purpose of denying rights to gay people who wanted to be married."

Ed frowned.

"Be honest now — what did DOMA do for you and Tammy?"

"The whole thing's brought me nothing but misery."

"Do you see? It didn't help anyone at all. All it did was deny a large group of people their civil rights because of a personal dislike. And I think that having gay marriage labeled as 'bad' has even enabled some of us to ignore the areas within our own lives and marriages that need improvement."

Ed looked Pritchett in the eye. *Was he leveling an oblique criticism at him again? Or just making a general statement?*

"I think it's kind of like that Bible saying about eagerly addressing the speck in your neighbor's eye while totally ignoring the log in your own. Doesn't it make sense that we can make our own relationships more fulfilling if we choose to put our energy into them instead of using it to criticize others?"

If the foo shits ... No question about it, Ed thought. Pritchett was talking about him and he was getting pretty preachy about it to boot.

"I personally believe that we'll all win with DOMA out of the way now. But even with all the rights that gay couples can now receive, there's still so much to do. ENDA needs to be next."

Whoa, who was this stranger he was talking to? And where did all these liberal attitudes come from? Ed sat staring at his friend. *He had to be talking about Greg's situation now, right?* This wasn't even close to what was going on with him and Tammy. *Or was it?* His head was spinning now even more than when he first entered Pritchett's house. *Was Pritchett's new way of thinking really based on love, as he had claimed? Or was he just guilty of giving in when his principles were challenged? Threatened, even?* He started to ask, but Pritchett turned to reach for a notebook on the coffee table.

"Ginny and I went to a counselor the other day. This is what she gave us." Bill placed a flier in front of Ed, but he waved a dismissive hand at it.

"Okay, I'll read it to you instead:

1. Give up your need to always be right.
2. Give up your need for control.
3. Give up on blame.
4. Give up your limiting beliefs.
5. Give up the luxury of criticism.
6. Give up your resistance to change.
7. Give up on labels.
8. Give up your fears.
9. Give up your excuses.
10. Give up the past."

"Ed, I'm gonna have to learn how to let go of the emotional connections that I've tied all those behaviors to. And it isn't gonna be easy, 'cause I've been damn good at most of the things on that list. Hell, you know me about as good as anybody. You know how hard some of those changes are gonna be for me. But what choice do I have? I have to change. I realize that now, and I'm gonna go for it. Give it all I've got. I mean, I can stay the same and be left behind by all those I love, or I can get to work and try to keep up. And all this is as much about me and Ginny as it is about me and Greg."

The two friends sat in silence, facing each other, but looking down at their shoes until Pritchett finally broke the uncomfortable quiet.

"You came here for help, Ed? Well, I'm sorry to say the only help I can give you is to tell you what I'm doing to help myself and hope that something I've said will make a difference for you. As for me, I know I can no longer be part of the divisiveness that is splitting our country and our families. Whether it's with Greg, or Ginny, or you … or hell, with anyone any more. It doesn't matter who. I just know I can't be that kind of judgmental person any longer. And Ed, I know our situations are different, but I think the solutions to what we're both facing are pretty similar."

Ed looked up from his shoes to meet his old friend's eyes. They looked tired. Pritchett looked tired — kind of used up. Ed wanted to say something, but what could he say? This was all so unsettling to him. Overwhelming even. He had come here so he could feel better about things, not worse.

"We're leaving for College Station in a little while. After going through all this with the counselor the other day, Ginny and I realized that neither of us had hugged Greg goodbye when he left. We had been so stunned by his news that we just sat there. My head was so far up my ass at that point that I didn't think of anything except myself. But we're going down there this afternoon and we're gonna each give him a big hug. We don't want him to think, not even for one minute, that we don't love him anymore just because he's gay."

And that is when it hit Ed. He might not have a gay son, but he did have plenty of other issues and relationships in his life that he knew he had *to hug* or risk losing altogether. He wanted to, but he just didn't know if he could step into that booth of change, or not.

In a novel, people experience heartbreak, sickness, births and deaths, and that is the end of it. But in real life, we must continue to eat, drink, sleep, talk, work, love, pray, accept — all of those things we do in the name of living we must continue to do when all that is light has left our world, when the blackness of unendurable pain seems all too unbearable and attempts to overtake us.
— *Harriet Beecher Stowe*

Chapter 27

LENSES OF COMFORT OR CHANGE

Ed stumbled out into the glare of the Texas summer sun, temporarily blinded until his eyes, which had been accustomed to the dim lighting of Pritchett's living room, could adjust to the new baking brilliance. The sunlight stung his surprised eyes, catching them off guard and causing them to water profusely, which complicated his efforts to navigate his way across the lawn to the safety of his car and exacerbated the feeling of disorientation that had been growing all day long.

It had begun as he'd awakened in his study and remembered the argument of the night before and Tammy's unprecedented action that may have altered his life forever. It had continued as he felt a fish out of water in his own home and with his own children. And then it had grown as he succumbed to the grief he had been carrying since last April. He had let it take him and have its way with him, and he had felt violated, forced to feel those things he had resolutely refused to feel for all these months. The experience had been an out-of-body one.

And now, he had come here seeking a friend, looking for comfort, looking for sympathy, but he had found instead one more revelation of how out of kilter his world really was. *A lieutenant colonel in the Aggie*

Corp, a fairy? And his father, Ed's longstanding compatriot, turned liberal because of it. He felt more alone now than he had been before talking with Pritchett.

He drew a hand to his forehead in order to shade his eyes from the fiery blaze above only to have them pierced by the reflected flame glinting off his rear windshield. He staggered forward, eyes to the ground.

Would this ever end? This constant bombardment? He brought his hands to his temples and squeezed hard. He wanted to force all distressing thoughts from his mind. The hurt. The loss. The fear. But they came anyway. He was flooded with thoughts of Tammy. Tammy, holding the twins for the first time, her face glowing with love and pride for him and the new babies. Tammy, standing by his side as he took his first oath of office, bursting with pride at his accomplishments. Tammy, warm and comforting, her soft body always welcoming at the end of a long day. Oh, how he missed her and missed their life together. But remembering how it was, was just too painful these days. Even if she came back, it wouldn't be *his* Tammy returning. He felt a sob welling up deep inside him but stomped it down. He'd learned what emotions can do. Yet, he still grieved the death of their past, and he suddenly realized he was already grieving the possible loss of their future together. *How do people survive this kind of pain?*

He reached the car door and fumbled in his pockets for his keys. Where had he put them? He kicked himself for not looking for them on the walk over. He had to get out of this hell fire of a sun. How was he supposed to get along without Tammy by his side? And Holly too. She had bushwhacked and then betrayed him. What would both of them leaving mean for his career?

He turned the ignition key and punched the air conditioning to its highest setting. He was losing it. And it scared him to death. The world as he knew it no longer existed. Even Pritchett had said he needed to change or fear being left behind by everything and everyone who was important to him. But why should he be the one to change when he was one of the last voices standing up for what is right? "Dammit!"

Perspiring profusely, Ed leaned his head against the steering wheel and shut his eyes, attempting to close out the overwhelming brightness outside — and the overwhelming anger welling up inside. "It just isn't right!" He sat up and struck the steering wheel with his fist. "I need to stay strong and not bend."

He must somehow convince Tammy that he was just being faithful, and *not* rigid like she'd accused him of being. One of the things she had always loved about him was his loyalty and integrity. *He* hadn't changed, but *she* sure had. Holding up what she used to love as something she couldn't stand now. And then all of this stuff about sharing feelings ... *Hell. "Feeling emotions" wasn't all it was cracked up to be. I wonder if she would've liked it if she'd been there and seen my little crack-up at the lake this afternoon, all snot-nosed and wailing like a little girl.*

It's not that he wasn't capable of changing; he just didn't see the need. Why should he put on rose-colored glasses like all the rest of those namby-pambys? He didn't want to see the world through a softened lens. He preferred to see reality straight on and not the bullshit they were all trying to get him see. He expected the world to behave in the rational, moral, and predictable way it always had for him. How could Tammy and all the others — even Pritchett now — expect him to purposely choose not to see the glaring immorality in a world that he couldn't tolerate?

His phone buzzed and he looked up. It was a voicemail from Tammy. He had three missed calls. How had he missed her? Guess he'd left the phone in the car when he'd gone into Pritchett's.

Her message was short. "Ed, I can't stay married to someone who doesn't allow me to be myself. Or to someone who so carelessly and callously dismisses the feelings of those he loves and of those he chooses not ever to know." The tears welled up in Ed's eyes as he listened. "I've made a counseling appointment for tomorrow at 2 o'clock and if you'd like to work on the issues in our marriage that we need to address, I'd like for you to be there ... I do still love you."

Ed continued to hold the phone against his ear although Tammy's voice had already trailed off in choked sobs. He still loved her too. But counseling? He thought back to that list that Pritchett had just read to him. *Give up being right? Give up my beliefs? May as well tell me to give up being me. And give up control of my own life? Might as well shoot me! Either way, I'm already dead. If I change to please Tammy or if I stay true to who I am and lose her forever. Either way, I'm fucked!*

He put the car in gear and drove off to — he didn't know where. That's exactly where he was — nowhere. After driving a short distance, he found a neighborhood park and pulled over. It was just a green space with a walking trail, but at least he wasn't in Pritchett's front yard any more. He pulled out his phone and listened to her message again. *Dammit!* He knew he needed to call her. Wanted to call her, even. But what the hell was he going to say? He needed someone to tell him what to do.

He looked to the sky. "God, please help me. Make everything be okay." He turned the phone over in his hands several times before punching in Tammy's number. But he hesitated to hit the call button. He still didn't know what to tell her. He'd never been so unsure in his life. Agitated, he flung open the car door and stepped out onto the pavement. He marched down the path releasing pent-up frustration with each kick at the rocks he encountered along the way. Hot and sweaty after three circuits around the park, he needed to rest, so at the next bench he dropped down and propped his head in his hands, breathing heavily.

Once he had caught his breath, he looked up again, and there was Henry's smiling face, lit as brightly as a beacon, despite the brilliance of the day. Ed blinked hard in disbelief. *What was going on?* His eyes were open. This wasn't a dream or a memory.

He blinked again trying to avoid the pain of seeing Henry so alive, when he knew — he *knew* — that he was dead. This was more than a dream or a vision. It was some sort of mysterious reality. Goose bumps tingled his scalp and spread across his body, and everything around him faded into a hazy background. He had lost his bearings, had been set adrift from all that he considered 'normal.' He could only stare at Henry, whose visage shone brighter now than even before.

And Henry just continued to smile, his blue eyes shining with warmth and affection. Ed heard no words of guidance or reassurance, but he felt the hushed comfort of Henry's presence, and as he gazed on his beloved nephew's radiant countenance, he sank into the gentle peace of knowing that he was loved.

Henry was telling him something. *What?* Without his familiar self-assuredness, his relationship with himself and with everyone else had no traction. What was he to do?

"Henry?"

Even as Ed spoke, Henry was gone. And Ed was shattered, more desolate now than he had been before. He had not been able to discern Henry's meaning. And he knew that Henry had come for a purpose.

Think! He knew, of course, what Henry would do. But he wasn't Henry. And he knew what Henry would want. But what did *he* want? *He* wanted what he apparently couldn't have. *So how do you choose between the two things that matter the most to you when you can only have one?*

Maybe Henry had come just to give him the strength to make a decision — any decision. Regardless of the consequences.

He reached into his pocket for his phone and discovered a pair of sunglasses there.

"Hmph. Whose glasses are these?"

He hadn't realized they were there. He pulled them out, wiped the fingerprints off the dark glass, and put them on. They weren't a perfect fit, but that didn't deter their effectiveness.

Blinking away tears, he smiled. "Ah, what a relief."

He dialed Tammy's number again and this time he did punch the call button. He had to wait through several rings, his tension mounting.

"Hello?"

"Hi, Tam. It's Ed ..."

Epilogue

Current as of February 26, 2014 — publication date
of this volume

Since I began work on this book in February 2013, much has happened to further the rights of the LGBT community, but in the words of Bill Pritchett, there is still much to be done. The following are highlights of the advances made within this time frame, and the steps backward that have also been taken.

Marriage Equality:
When the writing of this book began (mid February, 2013) same-sex marriage was only legal in nine states: Massachusetts (5/17/2004); Connecticut (11/12/2008); Iowa (4/24/2009); Vermont (9/1/2009); New York (7/24/2011); Washington (12/9/2012); Maine (12/29/2012); Maryland (1/1/2013)

As of the publication date of this book (February 2014) eight additional states have added marriage equality laws and five other states' bans have been ruled unconstitutional by federal judges: California (6/28/13); Delaware (7/1/2013); Minnesota (8/1/2013); Rhode Island (8/1/2013); New Jersey (9/27/2013); Hawaii (11/13/2013); Illinois (11/20/2013); New Mexico (12/19/2013); Utah★ (12/20/2013); Oklahoma★★ (1/14/2014); Kentucky★★★ (2/12/2014); Virginia★★★★ (2/13/2014); Texas ★★★★★ (02/26/2014)

★Utah – after a brief period (12/20/2013 – 01/06/2014) in which same-sex couples were allowed the right to marry, the state appealed Judge Robert Shelby's ruling and this right was stayed 'pending final disposition' by the United States Supreme Court.

**Oklahoma – U.S. Senior District Judge Terence Kern made the ruling stating that Oklahoma's ban on gay marriage was unconstitutional, which is stayed pending appeal. Marriages will not immediately occur in Oklahoma.

***Kentucky – U.S. District Judge John G. Heyburn II made the ruling that Kentucky must recognize all same-sex marriages performed in other states. However, Kentucky will not issue marriage licenses to same-sex couples. Judge Heyburn's ruling coincided with similar legal challenges in Texas, Louisiana and Missouri. According to the advocacy group Freedom to Marry, there are currently 45 pending marriage-equality cases in 24 of the 29 states that do not allow same-sex marriages.

****Virginia – U.S. District Judge Arenda Wright Allen made the ruling stating that Virginia's ban on same-sex marriage is unconstitutional. She issued a stay of her order while it is appealed, meaning that gay couples will not be able to marry until the case is ultimately resolved.

*****Texas – U.S. District Judge Orlando Garcia issued a ruling striking down Texas' ban on same-sex marriage stating that he was complying with the U.S. Constitution and not trying to defy the people of Texas. Garcia stated that Texas' prohibition conflicts with the United States Constitution's guarantees of equal protection and due process but he immediately stayed his ruling pending appeal by the state.

Marriage equality is still banned in thirty-three states (including those with stayed rulings) by either Constitutional Amendment, State Law or both.

www.gaymarriage.procon.org
http://gaymarriage.procon.org/view.timeline.
    php?timelineID=000030#2012-present
http://thinkprogress.org/lgbt/2014/01/10/3147931/
    federal-government-recognize-utahs-sex-marriages-utah-wont/
http://www.huffingtonpost.com/2014/01/14/oklahoma-gay-
    marriage_n_4598228.html

Religious Liberty or Discrimination?

On February 20, 2014, the Arizona Legislature gave final approval to legislation that allows business owners asserting their religious beliefs to refuse service to gays and others. Similar religious protection legislation has been introduced in Ohio, Mississippi, Idaho, South Dakota,

Tennessee and Oklahoma, but Arizona's plan is the only one that has passed and awaits signature by it's governor, Republican Jan Brewer.

Republicans stress that the bill is about protecting religious freedom and not discrimination, stating that Arizona "needs a law to protect its people from heavy-handed action by courts and law enforcement." Republican Sen. Steve Yarbrough called the proposal a First Amendment issue: "This bill is about preventing discrimination against people who are clearly living out their faith."

Democrats have called the proposal "state sanctioned discrimination", pointing out that gays could be denied service at a restaurant or refused medical treatment if a business owner thought homosexuality was not in accordance with his religion.

The Associated Press, February 21, 2014:

> *http://hosted.ap.org/dynamic/stories/U/US_ARIZONA_GAY_RIGHTS?SITE=AP&SECTION=HOME&TEMPLATE=DEFAULT*

Defense of Marriage Act (DOMA)

This far-reaching Act, passed by both houses of congress and signed by President Bill Clinton in 1996, aided in the discrimination of gay Americans, effectively barring them from all federal benefits typically afforded *legal spouses*. Clinton later aided in repeal efforts by offering his public apology and stating that he had made a mistake.

On June 26, 2013, the Federal Supreme Court declared DOMA unconstitutional, thus paving the way for equal protection under the law for all legally married gay couples regarding taxation and immigration.

However, despite great positive movement since the repeal, **Social Security** remains a proverbial dinosaur. The Department of Justice is tethered to individual state laws when it comes to distributing retirement and survivor benefits. Currently, if a gay couple resides in a state recognizing marriage equality they will qualify for spousal benefits; but if a couple resides in one of the thirty-three states that do not recognize same-same marriages as legal unions, spousal Social Security benefits are still being denied.

http://en.wikipedia.org/wiki/Defense_of_Marriage_Act
http://www.hrc.org/files/assets/resources/
    Post-DOMA_FSS_Social-Security_v3.pdf
www.ssa.gov and *http://ssa-custhelp.ssa.gov/app/answers/*
    detail/a_id/2503

Employment Non-Discrimination Act (ENDA)

This 2013 Senate bill would make it illegal for employers to make hiring, promotion, or firing decisions based upon an individual's sexual orientation or gender identity.

Similar bills have been introduced in every Congress, save one, since 1994. Three actually came to a vote in either the Senate or the House in 1996, 2001, and 2007, but were defeated each time.

Currently, only 21 states protect sexual orientation and only 17 of those protect gender identity. Consequently, in Texas, and 28 other states, men and women can still lose their job simply for being gay or transgender. Simply moving to another state could bring with it the loss of equal protection under the law.

"This great country, The United States of America, should not continue to allow certain states the authority to withhold rights, benefits, or protections to a subset of society, for whatever the reason. This is not justice. This is not equal protection. This is, instead, an obstruction of citizens' liberties." - *Washington Post*

http://m.washingtonpost.com/opinions/workplace-discrimination-against-
    gays-at-turning-point-in-the-senate/2013/11/03/c74c36c8-432e-
    11e3-a624-41d661b0bb78_story.html

Boy Scouts of America / Trail Life

On May 23, 2013 the BSA's National Council approved a resolution to remove the restriction denying membership to youth on the basis of their sexual orientation. The resolution took effect January 1, 2014. However, the policy for adult leaders remains in place: the BSA does not "grant membership to adults who are open or avowed homosexuals." Although this is a huge step toward equality for gay youth, this resolution continues to allow discrimination based upon sexuality, implying that a gay adult would in some way be less moral or even dangerous to young boys.

The policies of the BSA had been more restrictive than any other Scouting organization throughout the world or within the United States — until the formation of its new alternative: Trail Life.

Trail Life USA is a new Christian scouting organization for boys. The organization was founded in July of 2013 in reaction to changes in the membership policy of the Boys Scouts of America. Trail Life USA membership is not open to gay youth who are open about their sexuality. The program officially launched in January, 2014.

"Trail Life is very much what families want. They just don't know it yet."
- *Rob Green, former BSA executive and new CEO of Trail Life*

http://en.wikipedia.org/wiki/Boy_Scouts_of_America_membership_controversies
http://www.dallasnews.com/news/metro/20131215-after-boy-scouts-vote-to-admit-gay-youths-rival-group-takes-root.ece
http://en.wikipedia.org/wiki/Trail_Life_USA

Pope Francis

Pope Francis has said the church has the right to express its opinions but not to "interfere spiritually" in the lives of gays and lesbians, expanding on his explosive comment made in July, 2013 about not judging homosexuals, "if a homosexual person is of good will and is in search of God, I am no one to judge."

"The church sometimes has locked itself up in small things, in small-minded rules. The most important thing is the first proclamation: Jesus Christ has saved you. And the ministers of the church must be ministers of mercy above all."

— *Pope Francis, September 19, 2013*

The pope's comments don't break with Catholic doctrine or policy, but instead show a shift in approach, moving from censure to engagement. The Pope has emphasized the need for compassion over condemnation when discussing divisive issues such as gay marriage, abortion and contraception.

http://religion.blogs.cnn.com/2013/09/19/pope-francis-church-cant-interfere-with-gays/

Edie Windsor

Edith Windsor, the elegant and unassuming 84-year-old force behind the Supreme Court case that resulted in the Defense of Marriage Act being declared unconstitutional, was a runner-up for the 2013 Time Magazine Person of the Year. "Now she's the matriarch of the gay-rights movement," the magazine correctly declared. Windsor's case set off a legal chain reaction that is putting committed same-sex couples on equal footing with their straight counterparts.

Windsor lost out only to Pope Francis for this *Time Magazine* recognition.

http://www.washingtonpost.com/blogs/post-partisan/wp/2013/12/16/
not-so-gay-in-russia-india-and-australia/

United States Military:

Despite the repeal of DOMA on June 26, 2013, several states initially refused to offer benefits to same-sex spouses of National Guard members at state military institutions, despite the Pentagon directive. Oklahoma, Texas, Louisiana, Mississippi, Georgia and West Virginia each cited conflicts with state laws that do not recognize same-sex marriages.

Defense Secretary Chuck Hagel said these states were violating federal law by not complying with his order to all branches of the military that gay spouses be given the same federal marriage benefits as heterosexual spouses.

Not until December 14, 2013 were all 50 states in compliance with the Pentagon's order. These holdout states finally resolved the issue by requiring federal employees, not state employees, to issue the ID cards necessary to receive benefits. In many instances, the National Guard Bureau agreed to switch service members to federal status so they could process benefits without violating state laws.

http://www.nytimes.com/2013/11/11/us/texas-and-5-other-states-
resist-processing-benefits-for-gay-couples.html?_r=0
http://thinkprogress.org/lgbt/2013/11/19/2970531/
oklahoma-national-guard/#
dallasnews.com, 12/14/2013, Issue of benefits for gays resolved, Josh
Hicks, The Washington Post

World Travel

Throughout most of the world LGBT visitors are welcome, but there are some African, Caribbean and Middle Eastern and Eastern European countries where it would be a bad idea, and in some cases even dangerous, to be completely open. Although some countries may have laws in place to protect gays, that doesn't necessarily mean the country and its citizens are tolerant. Even in the United States and Western Europe where, for the most part, views on homosexuality are changing, gay-bashing and the denial of legal protection is still common.

Most support is only on paper in many areas. LGBT people still face discrimination and denial of basic rights around the world.

Countries leading in issues regarding Equality:
Canada, Denmark, Norway, Sweden, South Africa, Belgium, The Netherlands, Argentina, Iceland, England, Wales

Countries least tolerant of Equality:
Russia, Ukraine, Uganda, Nigeria, Georgia, Armenia, Cypress, Azerbaijan, Macedonia, Monaco, Turkey, India, Australia

http://wikitravel.org/en/Gay_and_lesbian_travel
http://www.takepart.com/photos/10-gay-friendly-countries/
    usa-close-but-not-quite-there
http://www.businessinsider.com/
    these-are-the-13-least-gay-friendly-countries-in-europe-2012-2
http://www.dallasnews.com 12/12/2013
http://www.washingtonpost.com/blogs/post-partisan/wp/2013/12/16/
    not-so-gay-in-russia-india-and-australia/

END NOTES

1 Texas General Land Office, http://www.glo.texas.gov/GLO/the-commissioner/
2 Andrew Clements Yoshi, *Big Al* (Picture Book Studio), 1988
3 Douglas Wood, *Old Turtle* (Scholastic, Inc.), 1992
4 At the time that this chapter was written, February 2013, there were only nine states where same-sex marriages were performed and recognized. When *The Door of the Heart* was sent to the publisher — February 26, 2014 — seventeen states issued marriage licenses to same-sex couples. Five more states have had their marriage bans ruled unconstitutional, but these rulings are currently under appeal.
5 Alfred Kinsey, *Kinsey's Sexual Continuum* of 1948, http://www.examiner.com/article/sexual-fluidity-the-kinsey-sexuality-continuum
   Curve Magazine, http://www.curvemag-digital.com/curvemagazine/20130102/m3/Page.action?Im=1358872546000&pg=53
6 PFLAG, http://community.pflag.org/Page.aspx?pid=194&srcid=-2
7 PFLAG, http://community.pflag.org/Page.aspx?pid=194&srcid=-2
8 Gay population statistics, http://community.pflag.org/page.aspx?pid=539, http://gaylife.about.com/od/comingout/a/population.htm
9 Journey: A Coming Out Workshop, http://events.r20.constantcontact.com/register/event?oeidk=a07e5ih0ncrd45fe1a3&llr=ffaqd8cab
10 Jack Rogers, *Jesus, the Bible, and Homosexuality,* (Westminster Knox Press), 2009
11 The Trevor Project, http://www.thetrevorproject.org/section/get-help
12 Morality Clause Ruling, http://thinkprogress.org/justice/2013/05/17/2029361/texas-judge-forbids-lesbian-woman-from-living-with-her-partner/
    http://www.huffingtonpost.com/2013/05/21/lesbian-texas-morality-clause_n_3308136.html

13 Common Law Marriage definition, http://en.wikipedia.org/wiki/
    Common-law marriage in the United States
    National Conference of State Legislatures – Common Law Marriage,
    http://www.ncsl.org/research/human-services/common-law-marriage.
    aspx
14 DOMA, Defense of Marriage Act, http://en.wikipedia.org/wiki/
    Defense of Marriage Act
15 SCOTUS hearings on March 2013 – United States vs. Windsor, http://
    thelede.blogs.nytimes.com/2013/03/27/latest-updates-on-supreme-
    court-hearings-on-same-sex-marriage/ and http://en.wikipedia.org/
    wiki/United States v. Windsor
16 Elizabeth Rose, *Lessons from a Gay Couple*, an article published in the
    Dallas Morning News. Ms. Rose granted written permission to the author
    to use her words and characters in the writing of this book.
17 Joyce Hollyday, *Then Shall Your Light Rise*, (Upper Room Books), 1997
18 Conversion Therapy definition, http://en.wikipedia.org/wiki/
    Conversion therapy
19 Boy Scouts controversy regarding homosexuality, http://en.wikipedia.
    org/wiki/Boy Scouts of America membership controversies
20 Family acceptance/rejection and suicide, http://en.wikipedia.org/wiki/
    Suicide among LGBT youth
    Caitlyn Ryan's Family Acceptance Project, http://familyproject.sfsu.edu/
    files/FAP Family%20Acceptance JCAPN.pdf
21 Conversion Therapy definition, http://en.wikipedia.org/wiki/
    Conversion therapy
22 Aversion Therapy definition, http://en.wikipedia.org/wiki/Aversion
    therapy
23 Cassandra was based upon a compilation of several young people's stories
    from the documentary *Bully*, http://www.youtube.com/watch?v=
    W1g9RV9OKhg, http://www.imdb.com/title/tt1682181/
24 ENDA, Employment Non-Discrimination Act, http://en.wikipedia.org/
    wiki/Employment Non-Discrimination Act
25 Trail Life, http://en.wikipedia.org/wiki/Trail Life USA
26 Douglas Wood, *Old Turtle and the Broken Truth*,(Scholastic Press), 2003
27 Human Rights Campaign, http://www.hrc.org/the-hrc-story/about-us
28 PFLAG, http://community.pflag.org/Page.aspx?pid=194&srcid=-2
29 GLAAD, http://www.glaad.org/about
30 Stonewall Democrats, http://en.wikipedia.org/wiki/National
    Stonewall Democrats

406

31 Log Cabin Republicans, http://en.wikipedia.org/wiki/Log_Cabin_Republicans

32 Scott Valley High School's anti-bullying campaign, http://scottsvalley.patch.com/groups/schools/p/elementary-students-get-lessons-in-anti-bullying

33 Rick Brentlinger, *Gay Christian 101,* (Salient Press), 2007
Rick Brentlinger, www.gaychristian101.com

34 Huffington Post: Gay Teen Suicides More Common in Politically Conservative Areas, http://www.huffingtonpost.com/2011/04/18/gay-teen-suicides-and-str_n_850345.html

35 Metropolitan Community Church, http://mccchurch.org, http://en.wikipedia.org/wiki/Metropolitan_Community_Church

36 Health Discrimination, http://www.google.com/search?q=discrimination+same+sex+health+care&ie=UTF-8&oe=UTF-8&hl=en&client=safari

37 Annette C. and Harold C. Simmons Transplant Institution annual reunion, http://www.dallasnews.com/news/community-news/dallas/headlines/20120415-organ-transplant-recipients-reunite-at-baylor-center-in-dallas.ece

38 John Maxwell, *15 Invaluable Laws of Growth*, (Center Street Book Group), 2012

39 Treasury Department and IRS announce that all legally married same-sex couples will be recognized for federal tax purposes, http://www.irs.gov/uac/Newsroom/Treasury-and-IRS-Announce-That-All-Legal-Same-Sex-Marriages-Will-Be-Recognized-For-Federal-Tax-Purposes;-Ruling-Provides-Certainty,-Benefits-and-Protections-Under-Federal-Tax-Law-for-Same-Sex-Married-Couples